MAKHORKA

THE GREEN CIGARETTE

Matilda Yenowich Dumbrill

November 2014

To Shango —
Who carries Mema's
dreams forward

Matilda Yenowich Dumbrill

ISBN-13: 978-1502383396
ISBN-10: 150238339X

To my parents,
who once knew joy
and heard the earth sing

Author's Note

My parents were Russian immigrants. They came to the United States in the first quarter of the 20th century along with millions of others, through the portals of Ellis Island. Though they were promised to each other before they left Russia, it was 11 years before my mother could join her betrothed in a small town in rural Connecticut. And therein starts our family saga.

As my parents aged I knew I had to tell their story. I sewed up some dashing travel clothes, packed plenty of notebooks and pencils, bought several months of Eurail passes, crossed the Atlantic on the Dutch ship Amsterdam and went off to Europe to write.

This book is fiction, based on some events that were told to me and some events that I can remember from my childhood. It is my parents' life expanded through imagined and real events. As youthful lovers they were separated through familial deceit. As partners they faced crushing disappointments. As parents their family was torn apart and nearly destroyed by mendacious acts and accusations of a single pious person. I present their world as it was controlled and influenced by characters I created, loosely drawn from persons good or evil who became part of our family lore.

In the fourteen months that I traveled throughout Europe I met people who had lost family or lands during World War II. I heard within their words the same hatreds and heartaches of my parents' experiences. When I lived for nine months in a small

Spanish village I met French families who had lost lands in Algeria. There were retired English who had served in the old Empire countries who had nowhere to go. There were Germans who had lost everything and vowed never to return to their country.

It was the nostalgia and the longings of these people that helped me to understand my parents, the yearnings of immigrants to own a piece of land, to find some roots. And from those people came tales of intolerance, subjugation, deceit and survival. Some had tales of their own "Bulldog." Some could let go of disappointments; others held on to their hatreds. It seemed to me that so many of them were in a limbo of life, enjoying the casual life of sunny Spain. Waiting? For what? I asked, but there were no answers. I remembered my father's years of waiting. He had an answer.

So I wrote.

The town of Stanton is a fictitious town, bearing some elements of the town I grew up in. The "Bulldog" of this story was a real person, long gone to his maker (or worse). Aside from his actions, which are well recorded, I took the liberties of fiction writing to give him some intolerable afflictions. I enjoyed his angst.

The minister who was the force behind our family's rescue is a character based on a true person, and I have taken creative liberties with his persona as well. He remained a family friend throughout his life, visiting us on many Sunday afternoons.

My parents' story folds into the era of the "new immigration" which, at the end of the 19th century and beginning of the 20th comprised millions of Italians, Russians, Poles and Jews, unlike the earlier "old immigration" of the 19th century which brought mostly the English, Irish, German and Scandinavians who had integrated more smoothly. Many of the new immigrants were peasants or farm workers. They saw opportunities to have their own land, their own small farms. Established owners of very large parcels of land were happy to sell off plots to the foreigners. Some farms, left idle by heirs who moved for employment in large cities, were bought at bargain rates by these immigrants. My father bought one of those old farms.

Before the upheaval of the First World War and the depression, industrialization impacted many of the towns in Connecticut. Small farm villages along Connecticut rivers were booming with factories that turned out products ranging from hats to lace to celluloid shaving mugs, to knitting needles to auger bits. Now the immigrants were welcomed because they were needed to keep the factories working and expanding. My father, along with so many of the men who had farmed their own lands, were easily lured into the noisy machine environment with the promise of paychecks that did not depend on weather and sweat. They bought land, they built houses, their families multiplied.

But to some old Yankee families these newcomers and their large families presented a threat against an established way of life in which everyone spoke English and where town governments and schools were run by the pillars of the Protestant churches. The children of immigrant families who spoke or heard a foreign language at home had no choice but to quickly learn English as they started school. There was no ESL. The goal was to make them good Americans. And it worked out that way in our family.

There were a few among the old timers, and my "Bulldog" was one, whose resentments were hidden behind the façade of do-gooding. The growth of bureaucratic entities during the depression of the 30's gave him, and others, unchallenged powers to harness good deeds for a galloping ride to the feeding trough of government largesse. My mother's unwise challenge to this man's integrity brought about our family tragedy.

As children we were taught not to hate and I could never understand the vitriolic condemnations that my mother reserved for her Bulldog. She gave us a foundation of belief in goodness through her bible stories. She sang old love songs to us. She smoothed our conflicts. She encouraged our individuality. She taught us tolerance of both the less fortunate and the rich. But as we heard her tell someone about her travail with words and emotion so unfamiliar, she seemed to us not the same mother.

Verbal communication with our father was sparse because of his deafness. But he was there, watching as we grew, his amazing blue eyes sparkling at our antics. His trip to the cellar to bring up a glass of wine was the welcome whenever we visited home as grownups. We found his writings after he died which opened to us his secret thoughts of his immigrant youth.

I began to understand these scars of memory when I traveled and heard so many other world immigrants recount their own. The Displaced Persons whom my mother helped had the scars of misery. It was only when I married and became a mother that I fully understood how hatred towards one who had harmed one's children could be harbored behind every-day joys of life.

Because in their beginning, there was joy. And I dedicate this book to my parents who once knew joy and heard the earth sing.

MAKHORKA
THE GREEN CIGARETTE

CONNECTICUT 1918

Mikolai sat with his head hung forward, staring down at the great square stones that formed the path from the farmhouse to the barn. The sun was gone, somewhere behind the barn, and the dusk was now darkness. He felt the coolness and the sharp edges of the step as he leaned back, not relaxed, for he had nearly killed a man today and the dread of the near tragedy rounded his shoulders like a weighted yoke.

Ordinarily he would have lit his pipe now that the day's work was done. But now his arms were limp by his side, his pipe unfilled beside him, as he anguished over the day's event.

This was the day when spring took over the land. Every growing thing was coming to life. Glistening dew had touched the grass and early blossoming trees. A green-scented sunlight has risen clear and sharp, its light covering the last brown twigs, moving gently over the trees. Mikolai had felt it. He'd heard the difference in the morning calls of the birds, so cocky they were now that plenty would replace the winter's scarcity.

He had stood for a while that Saturday morning after the barn chores were done, enjoying the day, then he'd walked to summon two neighbors who had promised to help with planting when the earth was ready.

Under this perfect day the men walked back to his fields with Mikolai. They worked steadily, Mikolai and Riznewsky turning the earth with sharp forks, Tuttle pulling the crumbled earth with a hoe to make hills for planting the potatoes. Each knew by the sun when it was time to stop for lunch.

In jest Riznewsky had called to Mikolai, "What, your woman doesn't bring our meal to the fields?"

Tuttle, working next to Mikolai had looked up, smiled and added, "Or does your woman exist only as a joke on us?"

Only that.

Inside Mikolai the response to that small jest became an urgent violence that took control of his senses. "Go to hell," he yelled in Russian to Tuttle, his blue eyes flashing with quick anger.

He pulled his turning fork from the ground and lunged at Tuttle with the full force of his young farmer's body as he raised the sharp prongs for a blow.

Startled by the curse, Tuttle barely moved in time. The fork caught the sleeve of his denim shirt as he pulled his arm in front of his face against the blow.

"For God's sake, Vorodinov," he bellowed as he fell unhurt into the rumpled brown earth.

"Mikolai, stop, stop!" yelled Riznewsky as he ran, stumbling into the soft ground. "Stop! What the hell's with you?" His boots hindered his running. "Go back...back!" He reached Mikolai as the dazed Tuttle was picking himself up from the ground.

Mikolai stood there, petrified, still holding the lethal fork in mid air as though for another blow. He slowly lowered the fork and pushed it into the ground. Riznewsky slapped against Mikolai's arm with the back of his hand. "Mikolai, what the hell are you doing?"

"My golly, what for, what for," mumbled Mikolai Vorodinov in his thickly accented English. He threw up his hands in a gesture of puzzlement. He shook his head like a man coming out of deep water. The blaze in his eyes was covered with the more familiar soft blue shyness. He looked at the squat older man standing next to him, then at Tuttle who stood some paces behind. Allen Tuttle's ruddy complexion was still drained of its color. He frowned and shook his head.

Mikolai put his hand to his face, covering his eyes and his forehead. "Oh my God, oh my God," he moaned in Russian.

"What's the matter, what was that for, Mikolai" asked Tuttle as he walked toward the other two.

Mikolai could say no word in answer. He looked to the side, to the sky, to the men's faces. He shook his head and drew in several sharp breaths. He raised his palms to the sky in a quick flinging motion.

"What kind of day is it," he blurted to the men. He shook his head, eyes toward the ground. "Look," he pointed to the sky, "the whole world has sunshine today. What for do I take it away?"

He looked at Tuttle. "My golly, I must be crazy from the sun, Tuttle. I mean no harm to you. For such a small joke I should not make something big. When I call neighbors to help me, should I beat them too? Maybe it is the sun. Come, come to the house for some wine. I ask forgiveness with my wine. Come, take a drink with me." He pulled the fork from the ground and walked toward the farmhouse.

"No harm done, Mikolai," said the American Tuttle.   He shrugged his perplexity to Riznewsky. They took up their turning forks and the water jugs and walked behind the silent Mikolai.

Timidly, a bird silenced by the men's shouting resumed its song, chirping quick notes as if it must give an all clear signal now the men had moved afar. Before the farmers were out of sight, other birds descended into the furrowed earth to sample whatever had been scattered out for them.

I nearly killed him, Mikolai was thinking to himself as he walked. If Tuttle had not moved quickly he, Mikolai, would have killed his neighbor with a great stabbing blow from the fork. And why, why? For what reason? Was he mad? Was he losing his mind and his senses that he could do such a thing over a small joke?

Only a small joke. It was true, his woman could exist only as a joke, so far as anyone here knew. Sometimes even he could not be sure anymore. Was it a joke on him? Was it possible that she would never come to America as she had promised? If he still believed she was waiting should he be so angry when Tuttle teased him? Shouldn't he know it was only a joke and not fly out in anger?

Supposing he had killed Allen Tuttle? What would they have done to him? It was not like the other one. Oh my God, why should I think of it now? That other one, killed with no sound except the gasping for breath, his last earthly breath. Was he, Mikolai, safely now in America, to pay for a deed done in the past. Was he a madman, a murderer? Never, never could he kill, would he kill. He groaned in his silence. But he had killed, and now he had nearly killed again.   And this time not to save himself, but for no reason. No reason.

What would they think now, that he was crazy? That they must watch out for his madness? The same look was in Tuttle's eyes as he had seen in the other man's. That same awful flash of fear. But Tuttle had moved. He had been saved. The other one was dead. He had killed him. Would he spend his life remembering? Or would he do it again and have to pay for both deeds? But who would ever know about the other one? He must put it out of his mind. He must forget it. No, he was not a murderer. He had killed to save his life. Only that. He had not thought about it for years, not until this moment. Now it all came back so clearly, too real. He must say something to ruddy-faced Tuttle. They should not think him a madman to be feared. He should say something; he should try to return a joke to him so that he would know he was no madman.

"Did you ask us to take some wine?" Tuttle called the question from behind. They were at the garden gate where the paths separated, one to the house, the other past the barn to the road.

Mikolai stopped and turned to the two men. He pulled a red printed handkerchief from his overalls pocket and wiped his brow. He must somehow cover the anger he had shown. They must know it was a mistake.

"Ah, of course," he said, still embarrassed. "Come in, come." Then, in an effort to heal he referred to their joke. "You know I have no woman in my house, but that is why I have plenty of wine. Come in, there is still much left from the winter. I think enough to feed me until the summer is ended."

As the men waited in the kitchen Mikolai went into the cellar and drew from the last barrel a gallon of wine. Three glasses he took from the small pantry off the kitchen and poured them full, offering the wine to his neighbors with a mild apology, lest they should find the taste not as good as last year's, which he reminded them was the best he had yet had from his spreading grape arbor.

They disagreed. Riznewsky laughed, "No, this is the best, even better than last year's wine. You must have had a good harvest to keep such a supply so late into the spring."

Tuttle offered to give Mikolai clippings for planting of a variety of grape some new Italians had brought from the old country. "I took some in payment for the plowing and the loan of my horse. I don't use as much for grape juice as you do for wine. I'll bring some plants next time I come up the hill. Then Mikolai, you can treat us again."

Riznewsky added, "In five years more your grape vines will cover your farm, Mikolai. You won't have space for anything else and you'll have to beg for food from my farm or drown in your wine."

"No, I'll keep my garden and the potatoes, don't worry my friend. But look out, there to the barn. See how far the vines have spread already. I think I have the best soil of all the farms."

"Yes, yes, for grapes. But remember my potatoes last year? No one could match them. This year my Hazel will put them in the town fair competition. And the squash, too. There is no crop finer or bigger in the state."

"You both brag on your lands," said Tuttle with a farmer's cynicism, "but what about your cows? Are they so bad you can't speak of them?"

Riznewsky chortled, ready to catch the American with a joke. "Yes, they are bad because they are all serviced by your fine bull. What kind of heifers do we get? Nothing but weaklings who cannot walk to the fairgrounds to stand in the competition."

He clapped Tuttle on the back as he got up to leave.

In his reticent manner Mikolai thanked them for coming to the farm to help. They would come again, they said, only ask when you need us.

The three walked to the road without further words. Mikolai said thanks again. The two men raised their hands in a short wave and walked down the hill. Mikolai watched for a few minutes with a tightness of the heart, wondering how he could have made such a crazy action toward such good neighbors. He sighed with disgust at himself, then slowly walked the hundred fifty feet to the mailbox alongside the road.

Nothing there but his newspaper. Again no word. Why did he even hope any longer? More than six years since he had left Russia and in all that time not one single word had come. Why do I believe, I don't know why I believe, why I hope, he mused.

And now the Revolution there. What was happening? How could he know? He went inside to read. The newspaper told stories of big battles and small battles. The Tsar's family was killed or had disappeared. There was a new government, confusion all over, maybe another government. "What should I believe, what should I believe" he muttered aloud. No one there to hear him.

He shivered slightly as he read of the revolution. It could be true, all the things he was reading in his Russian language newspaper. Sometimes they were wrong in the newspaper, Tuttle had told him. Or sometimes the papers told stories bigger than they actually were. Maybe it was as bad as he read in his paper, maybe not. He remembered from his childhood stories of the wars. But then it was the Turks who slaughtered the women and children in their houses and on the streets. He didn't believe the Russians would kill their own people. The stories could not be true, he decided, at least not all of them.

Supposing Danya and his family had been killed? And everyone else in the village who might know where he was. Who would send him the news? How would he ever know what happened to them? He wouldn't believe it. It couldn't have happened. But there was fighting near their place, he'd read that in his paper and he had asked Tuttle if he thought he should believe that part. Tuttle had said yes, the battle was reported in the American paper also. And no word, no card or letter from anyone all those years.

Not from Danya, not from his mother, not from his brother Vladimir. What should he think, here alone, without any way to find the truth? What should he think?

He could not pull himself back to reading his newspaper as he tried to shake off the discomforting tremors of unknowledge. He chewed on his unlit pipe, then went inside. When in his loneliness and feelings of confusion he would write in his journal. His own language was his refuge. He reasoned that he must keep his language strong even as he learned English. And he must keep his hand-writing as clear and pure as the priests in the seminary had taught and complimented him.

This day he wrote:

> *The soul is crying, full of sadness and melancholy, and tears, as diamond stars are falling down.*
> *Falling and pouring down. They sing a sad song, a song full of a strange torture*
> *A song of sad thoughts.*
> *The soul is crying, as a wounded swan bleeding out with purple blood.*
> *The soul is crying in thirst for different shores, different world and different songs.*
> *The heart is dimmed with sadness*
> *Life used to shine, pleasures used to tempt*
> *The beauty used to call so powerfully.*
> *And everything that used to be so dear, laid down to the cross pedestal.*
> *The dreams, aspirations and brave thoughts fell asleep for an everlasting sleep.*
> *White wings of a deadly wounded soul came down*

He closed his journal, sat for a few moments to dream, then opened again his paper and read the realities of the day. Besides war news there were stories of other governments, of people moving around the world. Each day there were small items of someone else's troubles. A widow in New York left with five children. He sent her a dollar. A carpenter in New Jersey who lost his hand at the saw. He sent him a dollar. It diminished his own concerns when he did this. Somewhere, he thought, Danya or his mother might be asking for help. He should do what he could here, and he would pray that good deeds would be returned to his own family should they be in need.

After his paper, well read, he pulled out the colored funny papers Tuttle gave him each week from the Sunday American paper. He could read most of the words now and began to see that Americans had some humor after all. They were not all so stern and straight as the Yankees he knew in this town.

Like the Westham girls with their skinny legs and narrow backs. No wonder no man wanted them. How they embarrassed him with their tight smiles when they came to offer freshly made ginger cookies or jams. He could see them as they walked down the hill. Usually they came just before noon on Saturday. If he saw them soon enough he would go to the barn to work so he wouldn't have to talk to them. They always left their basket there on the kitchen steps. True, they made good cookies and jellies. He knew from John that they were looking for husbands. But he couldn't marry a skinny Yankee. He must have a woman who could bear children and help on the farm. Whenever the Westham girls invited him to a Grange supper he would decline. "Too much work on the farm," he'd say. "You need someone to help in the house," one would reply. He smiled, embarrassed. He knew what that meant.

But he would wait for Danya. She was meant for him, and in God's eyes and God's plan they should be together. Perhaps only a little while longer before she would write and then she would come to America. He would wait for her. He would hope. He would pray.

He was touched by the constant quiet loneliness that returned so often in the days. He sighed.

There was plenty of work. Spring brought plenty of work to keep him busy.

He tried to move his mind away from loneliness. With no one to talk with, now he would write.

Who is going to say that I forgot the charm of spring?
Who is going to say that I forgot my first love?
No, even the older people, whose blood has cooled down
Won't say this looking at a shining day.
But isn't it always that we see in front of us
Our darling images with the eyes of our soul?
Didn't we keep in our hearts
Our first kisses and our first dreams?
When the radiance of the purple dawn fades out,
Burning down to a newborn darkness
A little star will come out
Which we have welcomed some time ago.
Full of delightful excitement
And I, left alone and tired of vanity and noise,
Remember again
With joyful excitement and sad affection
My love which has never died in my soul.

In his journal he could write words that came silently from his heart. He did not know how to speak these thoughts, could never share the sense of beauty that formed the words. Not even to Danya, not even to her. Sometimes when he was with her he had the words in his head but his tongue would not make the sounds. He could say to her " I love you, your hair is beautiful." Plain talk. Yet here in the silence of his loneliness, in a perfect Cyrillic hand, carefully and thoughtfully, he spoke from his inner mind and aching heart.

He moved outdoors and stood before his grape arbor, pleased with the results of his late winter pruning. He marveled at the red-tipped maple trees, and the elderberry bushes by the barn, all alive, all obedient to nature's plan.

Six years he had been in this haven. So long that he could barely recall the sights of his youth, his years of schooling at the seminary and his return to the farm when his father died. True, the events of his short army days lingered. But when those times came back they would not leave his mind so easily. Today was one of the worse days because of his crazy action against Tuttle. The memory of the hard ugly days had rushed like muddy floodwater into his brain. He couldn't understand why he should do such a thing. Even as he worked he couldn't keep the troubling memories completely in check.

He had been among the thousands of young Russian men who were pulled out of ordinary lives to form the Tsar's army. There were many, and he was one, Tsarist soldiers who deserted the army and eased the way for the revolution that was boiling inside Russia, erupting, spilling and spreading parts of old Mother Russia into the modern century.

Mikolai's small part in the upheaval was uncalled by himself. He had come from the isolation of rural farm life and cloistered seminary to take an impersonal part in events he could not understand or even care about. He was pushed by luck, and Danya, yes, by Danya, and had come to America before he was forced to confront the actualities of any battles.

Sometimes now, even as he worked, the loneliness brought back the ache and frights of his tedious escape. Or at times events would bring fears back too clearly, as today. Muttering to himself, "for no reason, for no reason, why, why?"

The next day he pushed his physical being into work. He clipped some of the grape vines, took down the storm windows, pruned off dead sticks on the pear tree, cut potatoes for tomorrow's planting. When he came back to the house he looked to see if the Westham girls had come by. He was hungry now. He would have liked to find some of the sharp tasting ginger cookies to take with milk or tea. There was nothing.

He took the milk pail and walked to the barn as the day was fading. The last memories of daylight were overtaken by dusk as it stole through the half-naked maple trees and the twisted network of leafing grape vines, erasing the square outline of the old barn. The unlit house disappeared into darkness minutes before he finished milking the two cows. He looked out of the barn to nothing. Only a reminder of his loneliness, the quiet that comes with the spring night just before the early insects begin their conversations.

The house, unseen from the creaking barn door was empty. Empty of woman, children, songs, light. His house, his barn, his animals, his land. His, alone.

A big gray tabby cat still thick with the late winter fur, steps lightly through the square hole at the bottom of the barn door as Mikolai closes and latches it. She follows at his heels along the stone path that goes straight from the barn to the kitchen door. Mikolai kicks from his path some of the grape prunings he had clipped during the afternoon, giving the cat unexpected pleasure as she followed him, stopping to pounce on the prunings as though they might hold a surprise victim beneath. Mikolai's heart lightened as he watched. He could smile.

He sat on the bench beneath the grape arbor, absorbed in quieter thoughts. Let the milk wait to be strained. He had started the grape arbor the first year he'd bought the old farm. From six strong stems the vines climbed and spread over the path, guided by old wire latticed to seven-foot cedar poles he had cut out of the woods next to his farm. As he cut each year's dead branches away he would imagine the first shoots coming in the early spring. He would imagine Danya sitting there on the bench with him. There would be children, boys, blonde like himself, healthy and laughing, singing as Danya sang, songs of fun and beauty.

He rose, he sighed. He walked to the mailbox. No word, no word. He sighed under the burden of his growing doubts, took the milk pail into the house, poured a little milk over some pieces of dried bread for the cat.

No information in all these years. Nothing from his family. Nothing from Danya who had promised she would come to be his wife. "I will come to you when it is time," he remembered her words. He wrote to her once a month, always to the same address, his home, as they had agreed. That was where Danya was to wait until he sent enough money for her passage.

Every month he sent a few dollars, sometimes a five-dollar bill. He heard nothing in return. Once he asked his friend Riznewsky what he should do. John's wife wrote in English to the immigration authorities. There was no answer. She wrote again to the address on Mikolai's papers. No answer. Always hoping, Mikolai sent his letters and the money as they agreed, expecting somehow to hear from Danya even after these six years. But often the doubts came and were beginning to stay longer each time.

He lit the kerosene lamp and picked up his old book of Poushkin's writings, leafing through to find his favorite lines from Ruslan and Ludmila. Now in his melancholy he understood the meaning of the words he'd studied when he was young.

> *In vain I long for fascination*
> *They faded, my poetic dreams*
> *The days of love and golden beams,*
> *The days of happy meditation.*
> *Ye fleeted, moments of delight*
> *And thou hast vanished out of sight*
> *Oh, Muse of cadenced inspiration*

He read his Poushkin and dreamed, though the doubts would not be pushed out of his mind for long.

There came the poignant sounds from across the pond, the Italian neighbors singing their country songs after the evening rosary. Another sign of spring when the fourteen Albertis, children, parents, aunts, uncles and cousins, came outside after their dinner to recite the evening rosary and to sing. Mikolai knew when they recited the rosary. It was like a soft hum moving across the pond. Then they sang, peaceful longing sounds that carried over the pond and sifted through the trees, hanging in the air, swallowed into the darkness. He himself made no sound. He was alone. He surrenders to the quieting of the music. He is soothed. The day's disturbances flow far out of reach. He is refreshed, ready for the night and the coming day.

There he lingered, listening, thinking. He knows that nature has a pattern, seeking and finding it in every sound and form. Mikolai, like any farmer, learned this without being schooled to see. It is all reasonable. The seasons come and every year they come again, returning with the same beauty and the same grimness, and always with the same promise, that they would return again. Nothing is lost. Nothing can end. One day's work is necessary for the next day's rest. One day's sadness for the next day's peace. One day's knowledge for the next day's contentment. Everything waits for its time, knowing that nature's patience is never tried. All things happen in due time.

"I pray, I pray" Mikolai says to himself. And from those prayers and his cloak of nature he keeps the same patience that would seem incredible viewed in the future but which now is the very rhythm of his life. The sure, safe, puzzling rhythm of patience, of waiting. The slow dull quiet rhythm of waiting. Because he must. "I will wait." Patience to see and to feel the pattern that was God's gift to him whose existence and labor was justified by that knowledge.

But yet the doubts. In his solace he must keep writing.

> *I want to laugh again*
> *I am tired of a gloomy thought.*
> *I want to devote myself to dreams*
> *Let a playful flow carry*
> *A merry run of a noisy life.*
> *And I, careless and happy,*
> *Will forget the heavy pressure.*

Let the dreams replace
This heavy pressure of an eternal thought
Of this annoying dirty prose and
A gloomy look of this annoying life.

He re-read his words but did not change them. He ached to laugh again, to laugh again with Danya who always had a story to tell, sometimes silly and girlish, and sometimes wishful and romantic, always with a brilliant light in her dark eyes. Where is she now, where is she?

RUSSIA 1911

It was Danya who had put together the plot that sent Mikolai to America. She had heard men talking on the street one morning, telling about the young village men who were conscripted into the Tsar's army and were never heard from again. She stopped to listen. She knew one of the older men who had seen two sons go to war. She saw him wink as he said to the others, "They lose their way, so they take the road that goes west."

Strange? She followed the man when he walked away from the others and stopped him by calling quietly to his back, "Neighbor, neighbor, what do you hear from your son Andrei?"

The old man turned and his face, unfriendly, showed the suspicion common to the surprised peasant.

"You tease me behind my back, little dressmaker," he said gruffly when he recognized her. His expression did not change. "The village knows I am a sad man. I have lost my two sons to the Tsar, and in my old age my wife and I must work our pitiful land alone."

Danya smiled and spoke a bit shrewdly, "Yes, neighbor, but you know where they are, your two sons, isn't that right?" She hesitated. "I heard you talking on the street."

"Don't bother an old man with sad questions. My sons are gone."

As he spoke they watched each other's eyes, trying each other's game. She smiled. He scowled and tried to turn from her.

She touched his coat, pulled at the sleeve. Her intense dark eyes squinted; she smiled again.

"You must tell me," she said, "my man is pulled from the seminary and is taken to the army. He is too gentle to be a solder, too kind to harm and kill in war." She hesitated, then leaned toward the man's ear, "Where is the road that goes west? You know something. Where is the road that goes west?" Her voice hardened with the repeated question. Something in the dark glare of her eyes disturbed the old man, almost frightened him.

He grunted and gave a curse against the Tsar and Tsarini who spilled the blood of Russia's youth for their own follies. With his eyes he motioned to Danya to come aside. They both faced the street so they could see anyone approaching and he felt forced to tell her all. In short breathy sentences he told her how he had saved his sons.

"There is a man of God in Riga, not a priest, but a good man, like a priest. He is a Doukhobor from a strange group, but they believe in God, in peace for all men. They do not like war and fighting, and they care for the young men who are forced to fight for no reason. They help us find ways for our sons to be free of the army. Oh yes, he cares too for money. Can you get money, young Danya? I cannot tell you these things if you cannot get money."

"How much money?"

"If you make a contact with this Doukhobor he will send word. But you must first be sure you can get money. The price changes with the risk. If your young man is not an officer the risk will not be so great for him. And sometimes the money is returned."

"Why do you say returned? Why? You mean if they do not make the escape? Is it so dangerous?"

"No, no," the old man, becoming impatient, shook he head. He wanted to be done with this talk before anyone came along and overheard.

"No," he said again, "the Doukhobor keeps only what is needed for the passage and the supplies and for closing certain persons' eyes. The rest comes back to the family, sometimes as food or wood, not always as the money that was given. No one suspects."

"How do I talk to this man, this Doukhobor?"

"Go to the synagogue and ask for the Rabbi Schenky. Tell him you want to join his new flock. Use these exact words, nothing more, just that. That is all."

"But then what?"

"That is all I can tell you. He will understand why you came. He will send your message to our Doukhobor friends in Riga and through him you make all the plans."

"Do they work together, the Jews with the Christians?"

"Yes, the young Jewish men are taken to the army like our own sons, but kidnapped right off the streets sometimes. I know a few who have gone the western road this way."

"Where do they go?"

"We cannot ask. We cannot know until later when it is safe. Then the message will come back to us the same way as our sons left. That is all I can tell you. The rest you must learn from the Rabbi."

"To America?" The excited question from Danya.

In anger the old man said again, looking around carefully first, "We cannot ask. You hear much later from them. Say your prayers and go to the Rabbi. I can tell you no more."

He whispered the last quickly and walked away before Danya could say another word.

She stood for a while, the fullness of her young body trembling inside the caracul coat. Her face, half hidden by the great collar was lighted with excitement at what she had heard. Her hands came together, the right clasped over the fist of the other, in prayer, in determination.

Now in the dull heavy September air there was the sense of eagerness. She had created an adventure. To America! It must be that. Mikolai would go to America. He would send for her and as soon as he made money there she would go to him. New York, that is where he must go. To New York. She knew something about New York. She had seen pictures in an American dress book that Marmolsky the tailor in New York had sent to his daughter. Mikolai must go to him in New York. He could apprentice there as a tailor and she would come later to help him. They would work together and they would have a business. A New York business!

In the feminine capacity to see adventure in terms of beginning and end results, Danya's mind contemplated none of the hardships that such an adventure might in reality include. Those difficulties are matters for men, she knew. A woman must work with the idea, must soften the fear that a man might have by making the adventure's end so logical and unquestionably right for them both.

She wanted to run to the synagogue. Or should she tell Mikol first? No. He would not agree. But if she already made the plans then he would not try to change her mind. She knew that.

In the dimness of a lamp turned as low as possible to conserve fuel, Danya that night pondered how she would tell Mikolai of the plans she had made for them.

He came every third night to her people's house on the edge of the village. It was a long ride for him, sometimes by horse drawn cart, sometimes on warmer days by foot. Usually he brought a book with him. He was a dreamer and a romantic and liked to read aloud from the Russian poets and writers while Danya did her knitting or hand sewing that brought small sums of money that she hid away. Sometimes Danya would say, "Yes, you have read that before," and she would repeat as he read:

> *Not for earthy agitation*
> *Not for gain or battle grounds*
> *We are born for inspiration*
> *Rev'rend prayers and sweet sounds*

She would put down her work for a few minutes as they laughed together. He always watched her eyes when she laughed. More than laughter was there in those eyes. Deep, brown, direct or indirect? For fleeting seconds it always puzzled him. No matter, it was still Danya.

This night Mikolai sat on a wooden bench facing Danya. His hands were spread before him, holding a skein of yarn from which she was winding the wool into a ball for knitting. He was telling her a story, his bright blue eyes dancing as he laughed with the words. He was so absorbed with his tale that he nearly let the skein of yarn fall. In thought, not joining his humor, Danya pushed his arm to remind him that he must hold the yard out taut.

He realized now that his story was unappreciated, and he was hurt into silence.

"Mikol," Danya said quietly after a moment of thought, "I want to tell you something I have done for us."

"Mnnnn...yes?" The eyes, no longer bright, for Mikolai could withdraw easily when slighted.

"I am going to save you from the army. I have found a good way."

He was angry, no, more troubled than angry. Danya had so many ideas and plans and schemes. But she should not interfere with serious things like the law and the army. That was authority and you must not look for trouble with the law. He shifted uncomfortably; hoping none of the household was awake to hear what she had dreamed up now. For whatever it was he knew before she spoke that he would give in and agree, even if at first he ridiculed the idea. He knew already that it was her strength that he leaned on, much as it annoyed him. He felt always safest and sure with her ideas. But they came strangely sometimes and she always persisted when he tried to disagree. Finally he would see the things her way.

"Listen, Mikol, there is a man, a kind of priest, a Doukhobor, who arranges everything. When you go to the Army you stay three months and when the army sends you to a new place, along the way you disappear on the road that goes west."

He was taken aback and asked curtly, "Which road goes west? What do you say about disappearing? How can someone disappear?"

"I think it is to America that the road goes."

"There is no road. It is across the ocean, a wide ocean." He scowled but now he was intrigued. For him, too, America was a dream. He knew people from nearby villages had gone to America and he'd heard men speak about it. But never had he believed that he...

"They call it a road, only in joking, so no one can understand. But I am sure it is to America, I am sure, I am sure!"

Already Danya took for granted that the plan was accepted by Mikolai. It had grown so fast in her mind that it was now reality. She could go on with the plan now, ignoring any opposition he might have. He must accept the plan.

"No, it is dangerous and I will be caught. You know there are spies looking for army deserters. Remember they found Petri last spring? Maybe he was trying to go west?"

"They found Petri, yes, they found Petri. He came home to hide in his own barn, the fool. But this is for braver and smarter people, Mikol. You go to another country. I know it is America. There is no war there and no conscription. The authorities of our country will have no claim on you there. You will be free of them. Free of the Tsar's army. Listen, while I tell you. But first we talk about the money."

"Where do we find money, eh?" Mikolai shook his head.

"Look what I have," She put down the yarn and pulled from her sewing basket an old leather pouch generally used for carrying food on short journeys. "Look." Inside, hidden in crumbled paper was money earned from sewing and knitting over the six years since her mother had died.

"I have all this saved. I give only a little to my stepmother, just enough for bread and food. My father tells me to keep the rest so I can take more schooling. And now I have a good amount. I think enough for the journey, enough to save you from the army, Mikol, enough to send you on the western road. Look!"

So, it was real he thought to himself. She had made the plan. Then he knew. He was certain. He saw the money and knew he would not resist this scheme. Here was his safety and his help, in this woman with her imagination and her sure quick mind. He pretended to withdraw his interest, knowing his silence would enthuse her so in the end he would seem forced into surrender to the arrangements.

"I have talked to a Rabbi who makes the plans and sends the money on to the people who help you on your way, all along the way, even making the ticket for the ocean journey. After the first training, when you go by train to the fighting, that is when you leave your army. In the late winter, in March I think it will be."

"So you know the plans for the Tsar's soldiers?"

"No, but I am told it is always the same for the new soldiers from this place. That is why the plans can be made. Three months in the training camp and then they move you closer to the fighting. In Minsk you leave, while the trains wait for soldiers from the different small camps to come together."

"How can a soldier leave so freely? They watch, I am sure."

She leaned toward him and spoke in a near whisper. "This is the way. You leave your overcoat in the train car. Try to be near the last one to leave the wagon. Go about twenty meters with all the others, then act as foolish and go back for your coat. Wait in the wagon. The charwoman will come. She will be angry. She will take your coat from you and look for your number under the collar. Then she will ask if you are named Mikolai. Say yes, of course. From her rags and pails she will put out clothes. You must change very fast. She will take all your clothes, everything. She will bundle them to take them away and you will walk from the wagon together. You go with her where she tells you."

"And where does she take me? How can I trust her?" He spoke back in the same whispered tones.

"Have no fear and do as she tells you. She is paid well, not just for you but others to come, so she can be trusted. She takes you to a man who will tell you the rest. He will give you food and a heavy coat. Then you will know where you go next. Even I do not know more."

"To America, can that be true?"

"I am sure. But Mikol, be wise. Make no close friends in the army days. Say nothing. Nothing. Never one word, for it can mean trouble for many, perhaps death, yes, death." She sharpened her voice, looked hard into his eyes.

He nodded, frowning with thought. He was still holding the yarn, which he then placed slowly over the edge of the bench. He took his pipe, held it in his mouth, chewing the stem without lighting, wondering if all these things could happen so, wondering if they could really make it so.

Danya moved her eyes to her work, not ready to question his reaction. She would not look at him, not wanting to see doubt. She would hold the belief in her heart for both of them.

***

When Mikolai left for the army with two others from the same village, Danya cautioned him again to stay by himself. "Even if they call you names for your unfriendliness, do not spend your hours with them, these men who know you. Otherwise they will cling too closely and they will watch your moves. They will notice you if you are missing at the changing of the trains. Be alone. Do not be a friend to anyone. Make no friendships and speak very little. Speak nothing of home, of family, or of me. And speak not a word of the future, of any plans. Remember there can be spies in the same uniform."

Yes, he understood, he answered, then said in a soothing voice, "I am not a child to be told again and again. You have told me and I know what I must do. I will be all right. Do not worry."

She nodded, "Yes and we must pray every day for your safety."

Christmas came. The new soldiers were surprised that they were given three days' leave from the nearby camp. This was the last Christmas Mikolai would know in Russia. Their world seemed heavy this year, despite the beauty that unexpected sunshine gave to the snow bound countryside.

They had the Christmas feast in Mikolai's house. As his betrothed, Danya tended to the cooking. Mikolai had come early to fetch her and they drove soberly over the snow packed sleigh path, not hearing the tinkling joy which the Christmas bell tied around the horse's neck tried to ring out to them. His mother welcomed the younger woman, happy to know her son would someday soon bring a wife and female companion into the house.

Danya gave Mikolai a small prayer book bound with black leather. She wanted to write a message, a private prayer, inside the cover, but she told him she could not because he must keep the bible with him and it should not tell tales to others who might look into it.

With the little money he had, he gave her a white blouse bought in a small shop near the camp. The pleated ruffles on sleeves and collar were set on starched bands. It pleased her very much for she has never had clothes from the shops and had never seen this mode before.

When his few days were gone they said good-bye. Her dark eyes were bright with held back tears. Her round face with the full pouting mouth was flushed, from outer cold or inner warmth. In the manner of one who is too shy to show emotion that he too might feel, Mikolai was almost casual, holding her hand in front of him, touching his cheek to hers to whisper good-bye. She whispered back, "Good-bye my sweetheart, I will come to you when it is time."

After he left, Danya went to a photographer, an extravagance she would not regret. She wore her new blouse with the starched ruffles pushing against her chin. She stared full-eyed at the camera. The picture was circled by a heart shaped mat and mounted on a postcard which she sent to Mikolai at the army camp.

"Good-bye my sweetheart, I will come to you when it is time." She wrote the words on the card.

He would treasure it; he would always remember her this way.

The next time he would see this face the bloom would be faded by eleven years endured through war, disease, famine and doubt.

Even as she turned from him there at the train, Danya's thoughts fell into a passivity that would mark her deeply as she waited and prayed for the fulfillment of the adventure that was now so real and frightening. Will it be the same adventure she had planned and contemplated with such clear high excitement a short time ago? She watched the train leave. She prayed. She walked away, singing to herself, "We are born for inspiration, rev'rend prayers and sweet sounds," adding "I will come to you when it is time, when it is time."

POLTAVA 1912

Back to the camp on the edge of the historic city of Poltava came the new soldiers from their short leave.

"You can't make a soldier from a farmer's son." That was the way the army officers resigned their problems with most of the recruits. There was no sense of urgency in the attitudes of these young men who came from scattered nearby regions to train for a short period before being sent on to battle. Most were conscripted, some snatched off the streets as the Tsar's horsemen rode through the Jewish sections, very few were there willingly.

They were, first of all, clumsy. They had no flair for working in the stiffness of uniforms. No matter how new, the shirt always looked farmed in. The great coats, worn belted, looked worse. The thick-shouldered peasants were not inclined toward such confinement in cloth. The belts were always askew, loosened and pulled out of place by the constant flexing of arm and throwing of shoulder in search of comfort.

But they were obedient. Sullen and so quiet that to some officers unused to this sort of fellow it would not have been a surprise if any had just put down his gun and walked away, sullenly, quietly, never igniting the awful energy that surely fueled their strong young bodies.

Rumor of numerous deserters had spread through the officers' quarters. They were warned to watch for anything suspicious. They were to isolate any troublesome recruits. That was the mystery. There was never anything suspicious. No grumbling or cloistering that might be regarded as dissidence. No change in the hard set faces. No hint of a secret from those pale sunlit eyes under the military caps, nothing but a smoldering of hate from the Jewish recruits. But nothing that would stir a problem for the officers.

When he came back to the army from Christmas leave Mikolai grew a mustache, as light as his fine blonde hair. With several others he went to the town and had a picture made for Danya, posing with two other soldiers, each individualized by the careless way they belted their tunics over trousers that tucked into high, unpolished boots.

In a mildly defiant manner Mikolai held a cigarette out toward the camera. Like many of the peasant youth he had been introduced to the common soldier's vice of cigarette smoking. This, too, contributed to the raunchiness of the uniform. In one pocket the soldiers carried a wad of newspaper folded into small squares. In another trouser pocket was the loose-chopped green tobacco called makhorka from which the rough bitter cigarettes were made.

Any new recruit must accomplish with one hand the feat of tearing the small square of paper from the wad, folding the chopped makhorka into the paper and sealing the cigarette by rolling it down the side of his trouser leg. The timid would practice beyond the scrutiny of the others. The daring, self-confident would brashly make their mistakes under the amused perusal of superiors.

Now Mikolai could roll a makhorka with one hand while he held the gun in the other. The pride in his accomplishment was caught in his careless pose. When she received the picture Danya noticed it with some disappointment, but she was sure that her

Mikol would never actually take the foul habit to smoke cigarettes after he left the army. A man should have his pipe in the evening, she would tell him, but there was no need to smoke the crazy makhorkas.

The weeks ran quickly. Mikolai was no longer timid of the gun that he now used with some style. He alone knew he could not kill with it. Not a creature of the field or the woods. On the farm it was his brother Vladimir who killed the chickens or the pigs, who shot the wolves when they came close to the barn at the end of a long hard winter. Oh no, never could he, Mikolai Vorodinov, kill a man, not even in war. Oh yes, Vladimir could kill like a soldier should. But he was the eldest son and he was on the farm with the widowed mother, not here training to fight. He would not have to kill.

By early March the recruits were trained to be soldiers. They marched to the train station, not always in formation, some hunched over, some with heads held high, ready for adventure. They were going to war.

DESERTION

Mikolai was afraid. The idea for his escape from the army was like a fanciful story that would never be written. In three months the plot he and Danya planned was routed by the regimentation of army discipline which now seemed to control him.

Even so, he surprised himself when he went automatically to the corner of the freight car that transported the soldiers to Minsk. He took off his coat and put it in the corner as he had been told. He went to sit with six others at the open door of the car, feet dangling, arms folded along the wooden bar that crossed in front of them to hold the sliding door open.

The train was slow, stopping at intervals for no obvious reason. At these times more recruits crowded near the door, eager to get a glimpse of their future. All they saw were the remnants of winter, patches of snow blending into beige fields that barely sloped toward the horizon.

Here the Russian winter was on the wane. Those last wads of snow burrowed into the embankment where the train curved away from the vast land, a few scattered clusters of fir trees still held the white memories of winter. Then some murky swamps as the train slid away from the trees, leaving thin wisps of snow like giant lace weeds, punctured and patterned by the snow melting from the branches above.

The men stared without feeling. Most of them had seen these beauties under much harsher conditions many years over to catch any joy now from the sights. But to Mikolai there was beauty in the lands, beauty that brought words into his head, never to his tongue.

> *Farewell forever, my dear distant land,*
> *A heavy sigh of my soul is sinking into an abyss.*
> *A distant edge of the sky darkens and soon the night will cover*
> *The azure and light world of magic.*
> *The soul will sing with new strength…*

When they knew they were near Minsk, Mikolai began to panic, wondering if he should really go through with the plan, wondering if he could. Wouldn't it be easier to go as he was ordered? To go with the soldiers? He swallowed fear, close to vomit. Or supposing no charwoman came as he waited there in the empty train wagon? They would find him. What would they do to him? They would guess why he was hiding, know that he was trying to desert.

He turned his head away from their destination, looking at the sky, mumbling to no one, "I see it might rain." Inside he was burning with the agony of his timidity. Did it show in his face, or his voice? Evidently not. No one gave him any attention. The man sitting next to him mumbled something about rain, not even looking at Mikolai. He spoke in the same flat gray sounds of his own voice.

When the single track multiplied to two, then four, the men all knew they had come to their station. There were some curses, light groans, rummaging for gear. Two boys, probably from a small village, made their way shyly and hastily to the hay in the corner, knowing that this toilet was only a bit more private than what they would have in the future.

Mikolai imagined that his hands were frozen to the pole across the door. His feet hung still and leaden. His eyes blinked in time with the heart beating inside him.

Someone kicked the bar away from the door, surprising the men who were holding on to it. Mikolai came back to the realization of his plight. The train groaned and clanged to a halt. Two men jumped out, then laughed, motioning that the platform was some distance ahead. The train lurched, throwing the cursing or laughing men off balance as it moved on, stopping behind another troop train at the end of the platform.

Now.

I should pray, Mikolai thought. But how, how here in the midst of the pushing and the cursing? He wanted to make the sign of the cross, to call on God, to ask for help. But not here, not where someone might notice or wonder at his weakness.

He held the sliding door back for the others, his gear beside him. As the car emptied he preceded the last three men, jumped down, pulled his baggage and his gun slowly from the car floor.

He began to walk away from the wagon, knees bending like rusted pipes. No one watched. He said aloud, "My coat." Did anyone hear?

He turned, walked with a racing heart back to the train car. Inside, in the dark corner near the noxious fumes of the day's eliminations he waited.

Now he looked up toward the unseen sky. He crossed himself, asking the Lord to calm his fear. How long, how long, trembled his heart.

Two heavy buckets clumped into the wagon.

A squat wide shadow followed, puffing with the exertion of lifting itself from the ground.

A woman? The charwoman? Gray and black, wrapped with rope and shod in clumsy gray felt boots held together with rope. The head was obscured by a strange hat with flaps nearly to the shoulder.

A man? Had the plan been forgotten, had something gone wrong?

No, a woman's voice whined an angry question as the form picked up the wooden pails and walked toward him. He couldn't see her eyes in the darkness of the wagon, just the form of a face.

She grabbed the coat which he'd held tightly as he prayed. She looked under the collar.

Oh Lord, it was she, the charwoman, it must be.

"You are Mikolai?"

"Yes, old woman."

No more words. With surprising quickness she slapped his chest and motioned him to undress. She pulled from her pail some rags and ropes that would transform him into her image. From him she took each piece of clothing as it was removed, almost pulling him over when she hurriedly helped him with removal of the high boots.

No one, not even his mother, had seen him so naked as a grown man, white skinned, like a plucked chicken. In minutes he was covered by loose, dirty trousers and a blue tunic, so quickly, helped by the unclumsy hands of the charwoman used to dressing others. The embarrassment of his naked state was no more than a thought before its cause was concealed.

His liberator handed him a short pitchfork of wood as she tied the ropes around his cloth boots.

"Work," she ordered as she packed his uniform in the pail and covered it with the stinking hay. In time Mikolai reached into the trouser pocket to retrieve his small black bible.

The woman grunted when she noticed, and motioned him to keep work. "Break your back," she growled. "Get the other bucket from outside. Don't look around. Work."

They left the train carrying four pails of refuse, walking behind the train, twenty meters to a building, past the building. Mikolai looked as old and used as the woman, shuffling along in the makeshift felt boots, hunched over the heavy pails, his hat pulled down over his forehead.

In measured tread they carried the still warm stuff to a dung heap far behind the station house.

What had Danya told him, what had she said? That someone would come. Would someone come now? He dared not look about. He dumped out the pails. Oh, to be home on the farm away from such crazy puzzling.

The charwoman scooped up some of the old dung and covered deeper the uniform, boots and all record of his brief soldier's life.

"So now we go." she smiled.

"Where?"

"Follow."

Back to the station house? Was she deceiving him? Was he to be turned back to the army?

With the empty pails they made their steps back. There was a train on the first track, emptying more soldiers.

"In the last car," she ordered, "clean up. One more trip to the dung pile and you will go."

She walked to another car and left him alone. He waited, head down, feeling as dreadful as he must look. The soldiers gave no notice. Then, as he had seen her do, he threw the pails in ahead of himself, climbed into the car and pitched the refuse into the pails.

He carried the buckets back to the dung heap. There he saw a farmer shoveling the dung into his low bed wagon. Mikolai stopped, frightened. When the old woman came alongside him he nudged her to stop, pointing to the farmer who was digging into the place where she had buried his uniform.

"You go with the manure, you and your uniform, dig. Don't cry, young man, we are paid and you will be safe." She chuckled, amused at the confusion in his face. Then she was gone, disappearing past the dung heap with an empty pail on each arm.

Mikolai helped fill the farmer's wagon. No words were spoken until the farmer motioned Mikolai to get into the wagon and take the horse's reins.

"The horse knows," the farmer said to his questioning look when Mikolai lifted the unfamiliar reins.

Mikolai shuddered as they drove through dirty streets in the first large city he had ever seen. He had heard many stories, but this was the first city ugliness he had ever witnessed. He was, and would always remain, a child of the open land, the open field where nature overtook any ugliness with the sweet smell of drying hay, with blossoming trees, with fresh green sprouts working their way out of tilled soil.

He had seen tragedies, oh yes, truly. He had seen a man's hand severed by another's scythe, a child lamed by a horse's kick. But these were consequences of broken rules that he understood from that kind of life. The farmer's scythe is sharp, so beware; the horse's hooves are strong, so stay clear. There on the farm he knew for what she should have care. Tragedies and ugliness came from actions that were reasonable mistakes.

But what he saw on those streets in the putrid dusk had no reason. They passed maimed children in rags, their strange faces warped with the grimness of hunger or idiocy, hardly aware enough to move from the wheels of the farmer's cart, the old beggar, half naked in the creeping chill of the night's beginning. And the smells, the awful odors that he had never known before, so foul they made the manure of known origin seem perfumed in contrast. The sounds. Was it moans or screams or the labored breathing of too many souls panting at the door of death for release? Was he going toward hell? Had he done a great wrong, and was he now to pay with the knowledge of a lingering hell like this?

His mother's warnings of Purgatory's tortures were illuminated on that ride through the edge of the rotting city. It took an actual hour by horse cart but stayed for years in Mikolai's private fears, pricking at times the conscience that wanted no part of remembering.

To his questioning look the farmer shrugged. He held his hand over his mouth and pulled his coat around him, sitting calmly and looking straight ahead as Mikolai held the reins.

They rode in silence for some time when the farmer indicated a dull light well beyond the city's edge. At the same moment the horses quickened their pace without a signal from the reins and stopped when they came to a small house and barn.

From the hay mound where he was told to sleep Mikolai could hear the voices of two women and the farmer. Their living quarters and the barn shared a common roof and the sounds came clearly through the board walls. He heard the farmer explain he had picked up a stinking old beggar and wanted to feed him. No, the women shouldn't carry the food. He might be diseased or wild. He would take the food himself.

He brought Mikolai a supper of milk and bread. "Listen carefully, soldier. You set out in the morning before light. You will go by foot, go straight west. At the first road, perhaps two hours away, stop and wait. Stay behind some bushes. When you hear a cart, start walking. It will be the old priest from the next village making his morning trip. He will pick you up and take you with him. Don't talk too much, and don't give your name. Use Petrov if you are questioned. Say you look for work in the village. He will take you to the railroad station. He is a jolly sort. He will beg the stationmaster there to give you a job. Be stupid. Say nothing. Trust the priest, no matter what he says of you. He will get you the same job you learned yesterday. Yes, you will shovel manure, like a charwoman. But this time you travel with the train. All the way to the port city of Riga."

Mikolai felt the sweat inside his rags as he visualized another scene like the one they had driven through, but he continued to chew the fresh bread between gulps of warm milk as he listened carefully.

"Here is the address for you. Keep the paper in a good place. Don't lose it...so, you can read?" noted the farmer when Mikolai pulled the small bible from inside his ragged shirt. "Can you write also?"

"Yes, I am schooled," answered Mikolai.

"Then you must write it in the bible. That is the proper place for a priest's address. I will destroy the paper. That is better. Keep the address in your head also. The priest has the great church by the sea, not far from the railway station. Here, eat plenty. I will return with pencil for you when the women have gone to bed.

They are relatives, they know nothing, but they should not be made curious."

The fresh milk was a treat for him, the first he'd tasted since leaving the farm, it seemed to him. He hummed with every mouthful as it rolled into his throat. How strange, he thought, to enjoy so deeply such a common thing, fresh milk. Ordinary milk, as he had drunk hundreds of times without a thought that he might ever be forced to go without a drop. He drained the last bit, relaxed now and tired from the strangeness of the sights he'd seen. The barn cat found him and tarried to sleep near this new barn friend who offered the tiny last drop from the tipped milk pail as a sign of welcome.

The shuffling sounds made by the cows ceased. The nervous stamping of the two horses at the far end of the barn stopped at the same time. The cat gave a long snuggling sign in the midst of its marvelous purring, and the silence closed over them all. Mikolai slept.

***

The flash of light and clanking sound awakened him. In terror he beheld a white-robed priest at the portal, swinging the incense cask before him. Oh God, I am found out. He crossed himself in anguish and his quick movements caught the cat, still asleep under his arm. The cat growled to be free, scratching at Mikolai's well-covered arm. At that instant Mikolai saw it was the farmer in nightdress coming through the door. Not the priest, thank God. That vision was the end of an agonizing dream where Mikolai, sleeping in the hayfield, was discovered by his old village priest who was no friend to the young, and who had many times thwarted Mikolai and his young friends in their pranks. Only a dream, thankfully, only a dream left over from the past.

The farmer brought another container of milk, cheese and bread wrapped in cloth. He brought a scratchy pen and ink. His somber aura was undisturbed by the surprised Mikolai. He smiled, or Mikolai thought he did, he wasn't sure. The face was so unchanging.

"Write the address quickly. I must close the house and go to bed. Here. Remember, wake before dawn. The chickens and cows will call you. Here is food. Eat sparingly on the way. You will find nothing in the fields yet, not even seeds. Hide these few rubles, you may need them for bread. Buy behind the stations, ask for the old bread. Do not steal. If you are caught stealing, everything is lost. No one can help you then. No one will know you. Beg if you must, but go hungry rather than steal. Remember all this."

Standing over him as he wrote, the farmer put his hand on the young man's shoulder.

"Goodbye, my son. You take with you the blessing of the old who must stay behind, mourning for the sons who will not return. I bless you twice with the bitterness of my heart toward those who killed my own sons. I bless you for some must stay alive to claim our lands when we are gone. Remember my name, Kharkov, but keep it silent in your head to protect others who will come to me afterwards. And pray for my sons' souls."

Mikolai could hear the tears in Kharkov's voice. He knew without looking that real tears were falling. Kharkov turned without another word, going through the door into the house. He took with him the lighted candle he had placed near the doorway. All was dark.

Sleep would not return so easily. How many minutes passed while he tried to recall his dream. Was it an omen? Would he be found out? Should he start out now, in the middle of the night? How could he go such a long way? But he must trust them all. Each one along the way. Everything would be done according to plans, as Danya had told him. He must trust. She had told him it was safe. Everyone could be trusted. None of the others were found, none who had come this way west. They had all made their escapes safely. He must believe that. They were all well paid; they would all be there to help him, just as Danya had been told.

Strange, strange, the dream was not good; it would not leave his mind. Some parts he could not remember. Only the end, where he was found in the hay by the priest. That was clear as if it had happened and it stuck in his memory. Found by the ugly old priest whom he had always hated.

That one, that ungodly priest. His rotten breath reeked of wine and old age. He never had kind words for the young, only for those who gave plenty of rubles. You could smell him from the choir loft when he came past clad in his white robe, swinging the incense past the choir loft where Mikolai felt the safest in the small church. Swinging the incense past the dark haired girl who had just lighted a candle to Saint Olga. He had never seen her before. He remembered it so clearly now. The dark-haired girl with strange deep brown eyes. As she turned to leave, her hands still clasped in prayer, she looked at the choir, she looked at him. Unquiet eyes, direct, unblinking. He lowered his eyes as he continued the low, slow chant. He raised his head and watched her leave. That was Danya who would be his betrothed. There was such peace then. There, long ago.

The utter quiet that precedes morning was an attack on Mikolai's fitful sleep as the rooster's alarm wounded and wakened his senses to the reality of the day. He would have preferred to tarry there in this safe barn, just a short time longer, rather than face the unknown beyond the heavy door.

He finished the milk and took a small piece of bread, then tied up the sack and slung it over his shoulder. Outside there was no promise of light, only trust that light must soon come. He plodded his way west, guided by the sinking moon, past the gates and skinny trees that marked the path to the house.

The damp fields sent a cold reminder that Kharkov was to have given him a coat. Without it Mikolai warmed himself in the habit of his youth, crossing and slapping his arms across his chest as he stepped faster along the way.

How many steps make an hour? How fast does the light come after the cock crows? How many waken before the dawn? Having never been this unoccupied in the early morning, Mikolai's intellect busied itself while his physical body moved with a mechanical awareness that it could do more than match steps with the earth at this light time.

Then morning filled the skies. From horizon clouds there sprayed out glittering edges of light that had been held captive throughout the darkness, held back by the night.

When his shadow was clear in front of him Mikolai could see the trees and small bushes, which marked the old roadway to the next village. In a kind of numbness he waited behind the bushes, evergreens and bared shrubberies intermingled. All would be done. He felt like a pawn. The plans were made; his moves were staked out. He had only to wait.

He heard the hoof beats in the distance, took up his pack and began to walk. Too late he realized the fast steps belonged to horse and rider and not the old priest who was supposed to come with his cart.

The horse came closer. He dared not look around behind him. The rider passed some paces, shouted and reeled his animal around, walking it direct to Mikolai, ordering him to halt.

An army officer. Mikolai was caught. He would be killed. No, by God, not now. He would kill the man first. Let him get down from the horse and he would kill him, the weakling, harnessed in the uniform of authority.

"Where do you go, ugly one?" asked the soldier.

Mikolai kept his head down, mumbling like a fool. "Forgive me, forgive me, to the village for work I go."

"What do you carry in your pack, eh? Food, I think. Open it, idiot, do you hear?"

Mikolai stepped back, pretending not to understand, shrugging his shoulders.

"Have you food, fool? Answer me, idiot!" The officer's voice was harsh and angry. "Do you understand, I need food. Give me your pack."

Mikolai shook his head again, mumbling incoherently.

The office drew his saber.

Mikolai ran to the clump of bushes, propelled by terror, sure that this was his end.

The officer jumped from his horse. With saber ready, he came after Mikolai.

Where are the saints to whom I have prayed? Where is my God who will spare my days? His insides cried out in anguish. Then by the mighty power of fear, Mikolai's arms moved. He pulled the pack from his shoulder and brought it ripping across the soldier's saber, pulling the weapon from his hand.

As fast as a chicken is caught and strangled, Mikolai killed that man. With his quick young hands he took another young man's life, giving no reprieve. He was threatened. He was the stronger.

The horror and the tears after the deed, tears hot, and a beating heart heating his insides as he hastily tore the saddle and trapping from the horse and slapped in on an unknown path. The soldier carried no money. He had no papers. A deserter! He, too, like himself. Oh God, why didn't the man speak? Why hadn't he, Mikolai cried out the truth? He shook the soldier, once, twice. He was dead. Mikolai laid the head gently to the ground, not believing he could have done such a foul action. He stood above the corpse in the morning cold, chilled and shivering. Oh, he would like to have his coat, the heavy warm coat worn by the officer. The gun? No, he must not. There was only danger in the taking, no comfort.

He pulled the man and his saddle away from the roadway into a thicket. He uprooted some of the bushes which were still half frozen in the ground and threw them on top of the man. He could not look again at the face. The saddle and saber he dragged farther off and covered in the same manner. Let him be found, later. He would be gone, well on his way to another country.

He retied the torn knapsack and with a calm that suffocated his fear he began again to walk along the roadway.

After some miles a more welcome tread of horse and cart came behind, passed him and stopped.

"Come take a ride, beggar," shouted a merry voice, the priest who was bundled in the cart. If you are not diseased sit here beside me." Gratefully Mikolai pulled himself up onto the cart. The priest took an old coat from the cart floor and smiled as he gave it to Mikolai.

Oh father, father, I have sins to confess. I have just taken the life from a man too young to go to his hell unconfessed. Mikolai's heart cried the words silently. No message, no confession went out to the priest. He dared not speak aloud. The jovial man hummed and chanted holy tunes unconcerned with his passenger's silence.

As they rode along the priest pulled out from a basket a loaf of bread that he shared with Mikolai, then gave him the leftover for his pack. He had some wine that was welcome, too, and some soft white cheese freshly taken from the press boards. Ah, to Mikolai, manna from heaven.

As they came closer to the next village the priest told Mikolai to get into the back of the wagon. The holy man asked no questions. He spoke of the sun and coming spring, repeating over and over, "The sun brings a fine day. When the sun shines, the day is good. No bad news, no bad news comes on the sunny days. Nothing but good comes with the sunshine."

Behind a small railroad station they stopped. The priest seemed a little nervous now Mikolai thought, and it made him also uneasy. But just for a moment.

"Hello inside," rang out the holy happy voice, "who sits in authority here?"

A large bland looking man opened the door to the shout. He made the sign of the cross when he saw the speaker. He asked what he could do for the priest.

"This beggar needs work. He stinks and is diseased. Can you put him on the train and get him out of here, away from people? Maybe on a train to the port? Put him to cleaning the wagons, anything to keep him away from people. He won't mind the smells, for he stinks more than that. Mind you, don't let his breath reach you, for he is could surely send out a disease."

Mikolai, scrutinized at a distance by the stationmaster, kept his eyes down to hide his disgust. Or was it to hide his fear?

"Yes, father, it can be done. We lose all our old men who clean the wagons." He chuckles unkindly. "I think they prefer the war. Come along beggar, the train comes along soon and won't wait for the likes of you."

The stationmaster bowed his head to the priest's thank you and blessing then led Mikolai around the station house, waving a hand out to the train as it was pulling in.

"Take the buckets and shovels from the first wagon and clean out the piles of hay in each wagon. Dump them behind the station house. You will see where. Work quickly, for another load of soldiers come through in an hour. Travel in the last car, and keep away from the soldiers. They should not catch your disease. At each stop do the same, clean out the cars. You will have to work fast, old one, if you want to finish and continue on your way. Do you understand?"

Mikolai nodded. How easily it was all moving along.

"It is three days or more to the port city. Clean out the wagons there also. But don't come back if you are diseased. We can find others for such work. You will have to stay there to beg. It will be easier for you in a city with plenty of people." With a touch of kindness he added, "You will find food at every station, near the manure piles. Our wives are soft you know, and they send the old bread for the likes of you. You will not have to pay. The bread waits there for you if the dogs have not taken it first."

The three days, like so many times of disagreeable consequence disappeared quickly. His work became habit and habit carried him through the necessary motions, through the dullness and the disgust of those days.

He worked as he was ordered, he ate what he found, he slept. He neither spoke nor looked into the eyes of those humans who slept and ate within his sight.

RIGA

The Port announced itself to Mikolai early the fourth morning with its curious new smells mingling with the awful city smells he now recognized. There was so much activity. The hoots of foghorns, the groggy shouts of men mingling with those horns in the semi darkness. With whistles shrieking and metal wheels clanging the train moved slowly to find its way to the station.

The wind coming from the water was icy cold, biting through Mikolai's rags as he walked away from the train. He made his way toward the smell of the sea. He had never seen the ocean before. He wondered if he could see America from there. It wasn't far to the water.

Should he have waited and finished his job, cleaned the wagon here as the station master had told him to do? No, he must hurry to the next stop on his journey, to the priest whose address he had in his bible. He must find the church. The big church by the water, near the station, as he was told.

There it was, several paces from the quay, rising above the dark buildings, so graceful with its onion domes in perfect silhouette as the morning cracked the skies behind it. Mikolai bent his knees in thanksgiving. Now, seeing the cross at the highest point he felt as at no other time the power of the promise of help that the cross represented.

There was light in the church, flickering light from candles and some chanting, which meant the early morning service had begun. He could not enter in these rags, but he would wait behind the steps, like a beggar, until the priest came from the church. He could hear, he could feel. All was well. He had come safely beyond the edge of Russia. Soon he would be on his way.

People came from the church, more than three dozen as he counted. Mostly old ones, penitent, with hands still folded and heads bent, mumbling their prayers as they walked into the wind. There were a few uniformed sailors, young dark men who came to life as they walked through the church door, swinging their arms and making their way quickly toward the ships.

"Father, wait," Mikolai called when he saw the priest go past the steps. "Father, help me."

Steel blue eyes turned on Mikolai who was still huddled behind the steps in his beggar's attire. The priest stood for a moment, his long white hair and beard caught by the wind.

"Who are you, beggar?"

"I am Mikolai Vorodinov. I am sent to this address from the Rabbi Schenky."

"Follow behind me. I know of you. I am Father Ousatoff. The Doukhobor is gone on the last ship with his family, gone over the ocean to a place called Canada. I now do his work. Do not fear."

Within a short distance the priest motioned him into the house, then into the kitchen.

"Sit by the fire. My wife will bring you food. You have had a hard journey?"

Mikolai nodded. Should he tell about the soldier he had killed? Perhaps it was only a dream, no, only a wish that it was a dream. He would wait, he would confess later.

"You are blessed. The ice has broken early this year and the port has been open for two weeks. Another man like yourself waits to go also. The ship leaves in three days. You will sleep here in the woodshed until then. We will feed you, but you cannot leave the house, you must not be seen. And you must keep your beggar's clothes, I am sorry to say, because if anyone comes near to question you they will see you are only a beggar. I am sorry, my son. But in God's eyes you are the same as before, and you will be the same afterwards in your new country."

Mikolai's heart skipped. He dared to ask "America?"

"Yes, but not by this ship. This Swedish ship will take you to Stockholm, the big city. Do you know of it?"

"No," he answered, "no, I do not know of it." He shook his head, he was disappointed. Not to America right away, but when?

"The Swedish people have helped men like you, young soldiers. It is a wide country. After you land at the Swedish port you will work your way across the country toward the west. It will take many days, maybe weeks until you get to the port of Gothenberg, and there you will find the ship that will take you to America."

The priest's wife came into the kitchen, nodded to them and took food from the stove for this beggar. She made tea for the priest, which he drank from a tall glass, sucking it through a piece of hard sugar. After she left the room the priest continued.

"You will travel across Sweden, across the farmlands and make your way sharpening tools and knives. Others have gone before you in the same manner. It is safe. You must learn in their language how to ask for knives and tools to be sharpened. Don't take money, ask only for food and lodging. It is a poor country but the people are kind. Your travels are mostly on flat lands I am told, but it is still cold there. You must aim for certain cities, asking as you go to be sure of your direction. I will write the cities for you. Can you read?"

"Yes, I carry my bible. You can write the towns here."

"Good. I will write it in the bible. So, after you come off the ship go southwest for a town called Jonkoping. You should see signs. It may take several days. I cannot say. Perhaps you will get a ride, but be wary of talking. Then go straight west to the great port city of Gothenberg. Ask by words, do not show the writing. You must remember the names of the towns and cities as you go. Practice as I tell you now. From there, from Gothenberg, the ship sails to America, to New York. Here, I draw a bad map for your directions. Only for your eyes."

"How will I know where I am?"

"There you can ask anyone. Do not be afraid. You will no longer need to fear, because you are far from Russia. Here, I will write the name of the ship, the Liepaja. Pronounce it carefully. It leaves the fourth day of each month. If you miss one sailing you wait for the next. The agent knows who sends you. Your passage is paid."

"How much time to America?"

"Two weeks or less, I am told."

"Is it so far?"

"Very far. You will never return."

"How do I get to New York, after the ship?"

"New York is the port city. That is the end of your journey." The priest looked long at the shy young man's face. "You must have someone there. Do you know someone there?"

"Yes, Marmolsky, the tailor's son from our village. It is to him I go in New York. I go to apprentice."

"Good, good. You have his address?"

"Yes, written somewhere inside the bible, I can find it."

"He expects you?"

"Yes, they cannot let him know until I have left the country well behind, but he will not turn me away. His sister is friend to my Danya."

"Your wife?"

"I am betrothed. I will wait there for her. I will send money to her as I work, then she will join me."

"So that is arranged?"

"All arranged, all promised."

"How old are you my son?

"Twenty-one years."

"Keep your trust into your old age. Then it will not be so simple to believe in tomorrow. Have you parents?"

"Yes, my mother still lives."

"She is well?"

"Yes, but old. I am the child of her old age."

"She would allow you to leave?"

"We did not tell her. She thinks I am with the army still. Danya will tell her afterwards and then will go to stay there with her to wait for my message. She will tell her when my first message arrives."

"Good, good. But remember, your first message must come through me. It would be dangerous to send a letter right away, or to send it directly. Wait until fall or winter. Meanwhile, send word to me when you arrive and I will send the message back to your people. Send word in Marmolsky's name. It will be understood and forwarded to your home. Do you understand?"

"Yes, I will wait."

"Good, God will take care of you. Have you no warmer coat? Just your rags?"

"Only these."

"Hmmm. My wife will find a warmer old coat for you. Our son is gone. He ran off to be an officer in the Tsar's army. We are waiting to hear from him. See his picture there in his fine uniform?"

Mikolai barely heard a word after he looked at the picture of the priest's son. Could it be, could it be? Was it this priest's son racing home astride his horse? He had wanted only food and now would never come home. And he, Mikolai, was here eating the bread in the dead man's home, from his mother's hand, in his father's kitchen.

"I think his old coat will be big enough. I am sorry. I must send you outside to the woodshed. My daughter comes soon with the children and they will be too curious when they see you."

Mikolai could hardly move as the priest motioned him to go through the kitchen along a dark hall that led to the woodshed. Oh God, how can I confess, how can I tell my deed? I cannot. I dare not.

A form stirred in the corner of the woodshed, a man dressed much like himself. The priest explained that they were to travel together. They should exercise by chopping wood. Both should not be out of the woodshed at the same time. One at a time, just to get a little air. They would be fed by his wife. He would teach them tomorrow the Swedish words they must know for their journey.

Mikolai bowed his head under the priest's evening blessing. The other man, he noticed, did not. The two sat in silence after the priest left. The man spoke in a dialect Mikolai did not recognize.

"You came far?"

"Yes, many days."

"From where?"

"I cannot say."

"Yes, that is best for me too. Later, after the ship sails we can talk freely, but not yet here."

"Yes, it is better to wait. For now call me Petrov."

"I am Fydor, until later."

Mikolai was tired and settled himself into the hay in the corner of the shed hoping for some sleep. It must have been hours later that he was awakened by the sounds of Fydor chopping wood. He peered out through some cracks in the shed to see more clearly what his companion looked like. Taller and more slight than he, with dark hair and unfamiliar kind of nose. The narrow eyes had a slant that Mikolai knew belonged to the Russians beyond the farms, in strange places. From the awkward way he swung the axe and from his concern with his hands Mikolai could see that Fydor was no farmer. What then, a gentleman's son from one of the northern cities? He sank again into sleep, beyond the place where dreams disturb the half-wakened conscience.

Fydor was quicker than he to learn the Swedish words that the priest taught them. "Knives and tools. We sharpen knives and tools. Give us bread and lodging for our work." Over and over they practiced.

When they boarded the ship they carried on their backs the grindstone and water box they would use for sharpening tools. They were immediately put to work in the kitchen hold, sharpening knives that belonged to the ship's crew. They slept with the kitchen crew, deep in the darkness with no window and no sign of daylight when the ship took off from the moorings for the new land beyond.

Mikolai never knew how long the trip took. He and Fydor were fed twice. They slept much, spoke little. The Swedish crew spoke words neither man could understand. Aside from feeding them the crew ignored the two old Russian peasants parked in the hold.

SWEDEN

In the late day they arrived in Sweden. As they left the ship they presented the papers the priest had prepared for them. The customs officer looked them over briefly, shrugged and stamped the papers. He motioned them on their way, down the gangplank into a frigid city of strange looking buildings quite unlike any Mikolai had seen in Russia. The smells of the city were there too, held frozen in the air. But you could still smell them and he knew when the warmer weather came the city would smell as bad as the others he had traveled through.

With no word the two trudged through the city, across a wide canal, through narrow cleaner streets and finally toward the open flat fields that surrounded the city.

The sun was hanging low in sky edge, a gray ball covered by the darker gray wisps of clouds, which moved slowly across the sky. The day was cut short by the low arc of the sun's path. Mikolai had read that in the north there was sometimes no daylight. Fydor said, "Yes, it is so, but in summer there is no darkness so it all evens up."

Three times they asked for work before they were needed. It had grown darker and the cold was bitter and damp. These quiet people seemed not friendly but hostile, cold as the gray air surrounding them and their neat white wooden houses.

They ate salted fish, some hard flat bread and some warm milk and potatoes after their first work. They were grateful to sleep in a well-built barn protected from the crackling cold outside.

In the morning Mikolai offered to help with the milking, trying to make himself understood with motions of his hands. He hoped in this way they would get more warm milk before their journey was resumed. He laughed to himself when he prayed, "Big-eyed cow, give up more milk." Fydor watched but did not work. So, he is no farmer, Mikolai thought. He couldn't even milk a cow.

As they walked on their way their pace was steady and easy. Fydor called more frequently for rest. They encountered few travelers and only once did they get a lift from a farmer. That was the third day. Or was it the fourth? Mikolai had meant to keep the days marked in his bible but he had forgotten, and now it meant nothing.

The next day and for several days they found work and were fed by the grim silent people who looked them over with pity in their eyes. Mikolai, sorry for Fydor who was so thin, gave him a portion of his food. He, Mikolai was accustomed to light eating. Fydor, he could see, was not used to such scant food.

The same gray sun followed their days, never changing into the bright sphere Mikolai longed for. The flat lands became shallow rolling hills topped with bare birch trees that would be white if the sun allowed, but which reflected only the dull and gray of the skies. Sometimes the birches showed the deep green of moss which clung to the trunks through summer and winter, always reaching, but never feeling enough light of the sun.

The hills became sharper and the birches mingled with evergreens. They were muffled by gigantic forests of pines after some miles more, and after that the tall graceful birches stood in feeble respect at the outer ring of the dark pine forests, thin stalks waiting and waiting for the spring and summer sun.

The dampness clung to the men. It soaked through the felt boots they wore which had to be retied at intervals as walking wore through the makeshift soles. Often now they found rides with passing farmers who took pity on them, but also needed their sharpening work. They would ask to dry out their boots by the fireplaces or stoves in the houses, but they always slept in the barn, in the hay, wrapping their bare feet in new rags they were given.

They walked on. Coming down from the evergreen slopes they came to an open valley. Spread before them was a great body of water which Mikolai was sure must be the ocean. But Fydor, who had greater wisdom of foreign lands, said it must be the great lake that would tell them they were two-thirds across the country. They had been in this cold, quiet land for more than two weeks. And only two-thirds of the way gone.

They saw the tall smoking chimneys of a city at the base of another hill. Fydor thought they should go around the city and find a farm.

"We are not welcome in cities where there are already too many beggars," he said.

They walked the ridge, following it into the spreading countryside where the tall evergreens grew sparsely, then a few more trees, then farther on, no trees at all.

Sometimes their requests for work were refused and hunger stalked them. They had to wait until the night came so they could find a shed or barn for their sleep.

One day as they walked fatigued and hungry a wagon stopped beside them. A young man called out in his strange language. Fydor answered with the words the priest had taught them.

"Yes, get in, come with me. Get in, get in." the man spoke but motioned with his hands when he realized they were mute in his language. He brought them to his farm.

They were fed in the big kitchen by a young woman, so tall she looked down even at Fydor who was four inches taller than Mikolai. Two other younger girls looked with curiosity at the two men, but the older girl ignored them and they obeyed the wave of her hand, an unspoken order to stay away from these strangers.

It must be a big farm, Mikolai thought. There were beds of iron with hay mattresses in the barn, which were separated by doors from a stable of several horses. Here they slept on the first real beds they had seen for many weeks. The rough blankets seemed like silk sheets to the exhausted men who looked like used old gnomes inside their worn ragged clothes. They were tired and discouraged under the burden they carried on their backs, and worn in the mind from the times of hunger.

They slept undisturbed far into the next gray morning.

Mikolai remembered only that he dreamed again of being found by the old village priest. When he tried to waken he was wet with sweat, groaning in fright. But the morning stayed so dark. There was no light. Morning would not come. Helplessly he fell back into a hot sleep dreaming again and again the same dreadful moment of his discovery, sometimes by the priest, sometimes by strange women who stood above him, watching while the priest came toward him.

"What...help...oh God...he tries to choke me." No, it is not the priest. The soldier from the roadside. Was he not dead, had he not covered the dead body? "Oh no, God, help me. Help me now, I pray. He takes my breath, my life. My arms do not move. He is too strong. He is the stronger this time...The women, they have taken my strength. They have taken my hair and my beard...Oh my God...Forgive me, forgive me. I was afraid...Forgive me as I die..."

A great fever had locked Mikolai in this intolerable dream world for three days while he was tortured by all the distorted dreams of abrasive memories, which could not, for their awful textures, be pushed away until they were dreamed again and again and smothered by exhaustion.

The fourth morning he awakened in the early dimness, thinking he had spent one dreadful night. But when he felt his face, clean-shaven, without beard he believed his dreams were reality. But the same bed, and next to him, sleeping soundly, the same Fydor. But wait...he too, even by vague light, looked clean and shaven.

"Fydor, waken. Some things are happening, something has happened in the night. Waken."

He leaned over and shook Fydor who woke as Mikolai's voice rose in a hoarse whisper.

"Fydor, look, do you see. Someone has come in the night and found us. They have taken our beards and they will know who we are. They have found us out. We are caught."

"Ah, Petrov, good. You are awake."

"Yes, I am awake. But what has happened in the night?"

Fydor smiled and shook his head to waken himself. "Petrov, you have visited the world of dark shadows. But you are lucky; you have made a return. We thought perhaps you would not."

"What do you say?"

"You have been held by a fever since the night we came to this place. This is the fourth day. Do you remember nothing?"

"Yes, I remember that we came, but it cannot be four days. I remember only ugly happenings, so real they could not be dreams."

"Yes, you dreamed. We could tell you had disturbing dreams. We could hear your shouts and your prayers."

"I spoke aloud in dreams?"

"Nothing for history," Fydor chuckled, relieved that the ordeal was over. "But you were in high fever, coming and going with such wild motions. A doctor came, but you struck at him. Finally when you slept more quietly the women of this house washed you and cut your beard. They found lice, so you see they have taken my beard and hair too. Now we are like Roman monks. But oh, we are finally clean again."

Sitting on the edge of the iron bed Mikolai shivered and then crawled back under the rough blanket, pensive and still distressed. He tried to shake out the dream, moving his head back and forth. He sighed.

"A good thing it is that I am sick here and not in the middle of the forests. God must have found this place for us."

"God or chance, take your pick. We are fortunate that when you were sick they didn't throw us out into the snow."

"It has snowed?"

"Since we came, for nearly three days."

"But we must continue. Maybe another week will pass before we reach the ship to America."

"There will be time. Today is the first of the month, so we will miss this sailing. Next month we get the ship and will be on our way."

"You know the days? You have kept a record?"

"Yes, I have been marking the days."

"It is…?"

"April, the first day of April."

"I did not think so much time had run past. I though we would be there already by April, there in America."

"And I also. But we must wait, we must wait." Fydor shrugged. "We can stay here, perhaps for a week or ten days so you can bring back your strength. There is work we can do. No need to run for the ship when we would have to wait at the port, perhaps without work or food. And for your health, too, it is good that we can wait here."

"How do you know this?"

"The doctor who came speaks in German and he talked for us. They will feed us if we work. It is a big farm. There is plenty of work we can do to earn out bed and food."

"Yes, and what work do we find here, sharpening the knives?"

"You milk," then, as if to make a private joke of their bad times Fydor added lightly, "and I shovel, my special job."

They rose from their warm beds and pulled on their ragged felt boots, waiting awkwardly there, wondering what would be next.

As if nothing unusual had occurred the tall woman who had fed them opened the door and motioned them to come into the kitchen. She inquired of Mikolai's health by raised eyebrows, touching her forehead with the palm of her hand. He understood and nodded with a faint smile. He could say only "thanks, thanks" in Swedish. But if Fydor were not there he would kneel to her, for had she not saved his life with her care and her feeding?

They were sitting on the wooden benches drinking hot milk with the dark bread when Mikolai noticed the picture. He stared at it. It hung in the next room but he could see it clearly from where he sat in the kitchen. It was the Christ, praying at Gethsemane just before his capture. He knew it because Danya had shown him the same picture taken from a magazine someone sent from America to Marmolsky's daughter. The familiar dark bearded man, lifting his holy eyes to a dark sky, his elbows resting on a rock, his hands folded in prayer. He remembered it clearly. It pulled at his homesick heart and threatened his eyes with tears.

Across from him Fydor caught him staring and looked also at the picture. He seemed uninterested, smiled a bit and went back to his eating. He said nothing.

A man younger than either Mikolai or Fydor came to the door and spoke to the woman who was busy at the stove. He called her Ada. Mikolai would remember it for a long time. They must have been speaking of them, of the two sitting there eating a leisurely breakfast. Ada nodded and he left. She waited until they finished their food and then directed them through their sleeping area, through the horse stables to the adjoining dairy barn. Mikolai was put to work milking as Fydor had predicted and Fydor was given the pitchfork, which was by now to him, a familiar tool.

This was much to Mikolai's liking, the days on the farm. It had the cozy familiarity of hard, endless necessary work. Although he tired more quickly after his illness he worked steadily and quietly, two welcome hands added to the five young people who worked this great farm for the first winter after their parents' death.

Fydor shoveled manure and shoveled snow, walked and curried the horses, and that too was welcomed help.

Ada was the woman of the house, they could see that clearly. The older brother who had given them the ride was Linus. He was a big quiet man, and was the one who was the boss of the farm work. He never spoke directly to the two beggars, but a few times almost smiled with them over some farmer's joke. Mikolai would remember their names years afterwards, but the others he forgot, for they stayed far from these two odd strangers, never overcoming the fear that isolated country youngsters have for the unknown traveler.

Ten days of hard work. Then time to go. They were given cleaner clothes and some makeshift stronger boots, were fed well and sent on their way on to the next part of their journey.

As they walked away from the house in the sharp early morning they turned to see Ada standing at the doorway. She raised her hand in a gentle wave.

She had been kind to them, the two agreed, kinder than anyone else along their way. She had no fear of them. She had fed them well and she had happily given them plenty of bread and cheese for the long journey to the big port. Their packs felt lighter now as they began the walking. They trekked over flat lands that were still frozen. Now the sun had lost its grayness and came back each day shrouded in a strange yellow sky. A great yellow sun it was, deep in color like a winter moon which had forgotten its time and place in the sky. A quiet unwarm sun, waiting and anxious also for summer to come. Along the way they found work and shelter, just enough to keep them moving on.

Mikolai was astonished when they came near the harbor. He had never expected to see so many ships, such great white hulks. After weeks in the country lands the bustle of the quays was a bit disquieting. Yet there was something welcome in the snappy seas that crashed against the piers. It meant to them that their journey was near its final days.

Yes, it was the ocean this time, Fydor told him. They had arrived in Gothenberg, ready to board the ship to America. Mikolai stood against a pier railing staring hard beyond the edge of what he could see clearly. Still a long way, he knew, but finally they would be on the ocean, with no more walking until they came to America.

They moved about like country boys, sniffing the sea, watching the dockworkers, moving apologetically out of the way of the workers. Fydor showed the paper with the name of their ship. Four more days until it would come, four more days and it would dock at this place they were told by sign language. They must wait four more days.

They discovered an old warehouse where they slept, going about the docks during the days asking for work and food. Someone directed them to the ship company's office where they showed their papers to an officer who looked through his passenger list. He nodded, he understood. They stayed another two nights in a waiting room filled with men, women and children, mostly Swedes, and a few others who spoke assorted Slavic dialects, which both Mikolai and Fydor could understand.

But they kept to themselves, having formed the habit of secrecy. They were apprehensive that even in this safe country that if they showed less caution now something could undo all for which they had suffered. When they heard the other Slavic voices they both wanted to speak to those others, but after a whispered short conference they decided they should not take any risk.

With all the others, Fydor and Mikolai shuffled onto the ship as they were directed, pushed and jostled by an impatient crowd. After the strangeness and discomfort of the past weeks being on the ship seemed less strange to Mikolai than the thought of it had been when the plan was proposed. He submitted to a growing detachment from things and people around him.

He and Fydor had not become iron friends, but remained companions of necessity. Fydor spoke of ideas and in terms that meant nothing to Mikoali, and Mikolai's simple ways and his shy attempts to speak of the earth and the wonders of it as he had been able to write, were not of interest to the more sophisticated Fydor.

From the voyage Mikolai would take few good memories. It wasn't comfortable, but there was a kind of haven for him who had known every human discomfort before these that he now endured and saw around him. At least this was really the last part of his trip. Soon they would land in New York. Of course all the passengers knew where they were going, all filled with anticipation. He heard the words: New York, New York. It jumped out in the conversations in every language. It was the dream that would come true, the place that would welcome them. There, Mikolai too knew, he would be safe and cared for.

NEW YORK 1912

The excitement that swept through the ship's passengers at the docking made only a small stab at Mikolai's feelings. Relief, a weakness of the stomach, the softened knees. That he remembered for a short time afterwards, not much more. Except the noise. Every kind of sound thrown together in one place as the ship slid into its berth.

Should he feel the grand welcome of a free land? Of course, America was called the land of the free. Yet coming down the gangplank onto the dock he felt more afraid than free. Perhaps a man actually released from physical chains recognizes freedom and calls out his salute, registers his joy for that gift. But to Mikolai, a young man homesick and now hungry for a familiar face or garden path, the impact of arriving on freedom's soil rang quite another tone.

In his other life, in his youth on the farm, he had never thought he would one day look for freedom. He had never felt in bondage, only that short time in the Tsar's army. Even as he dreamed of America it was not for freedom, but for the great lands that were held out in promise. He could not visualize the immense acres that supposedly belonged to one man, which could belong to any man willing to work hard. There was so much open land that the government came asking the farmers to take it, to farm it, to raise their animals. All they must do is live on the land and make it useful. He'd heard all this on the ship as he was able to understand some of the Slavic accents.

He had accepted the facts of his conscriptions without complaint until Danya had brought forward this plan. Yes, he had to admit to himself, he'd felt in some kind of bondage, but he never felt that he would make this great effort for freedom. But he had done it, pushed by Danya. Against his will? No, not now, he didn't feel that way now. Because here he was in the free land, a free man, safe. In a country where there were millions of people who spoke a language he could not understand.

For hours there was confusion as the immigrants milled about the docks. They were herded through various gates on Ellis Island, past authorities, past doctors who looked carefully at eyes, throats, gave injections. He lost and found Fydor several times and saw him for the last time when they were sent through the final gate as certified visitors to the new land.

"Where do you go now, Petrov?"

"I have the address here in my book. I will stay in the city to work with a tailor. And you?"

"I wait here for relatives who take me with them to another province. Ah, but we are here, finally, eh?"

"Yes, finally. It is a blessing."

Standing there, relieved of the burdensome equipment and their common fright, they both felt the thinness of their relationship, the awkwardness of a not unwelcome separation.

Fydor clapped his hand on Mikolai's shoulder. "Petrov, we have kept our secret, we never spoke of our families or…listen, they call my name!"

From the loudspeaker came a name, repeated several times with instructions in Russian to "go to gate D, gate D. Georgi Primorvitsky…to Gate D… Georgi Primorvitsky."

He took Mikolai's hand, shook it firmly, very excited. He gathered him into a man's hard hug and was gone before the good wishes were finished.

Here alone now, standing, unknown to the world moving about him. Was this he, a grown man, crying at his good fortune? For had he not made the journey safely? Why should he grumble now with his fate, why should he cry, here among strangers, a grown man, a free man?

People bumped against him and never gave him a look. The knapsack he still carried caught at a man's arm and was pulled from his back, falling open when it hit the concrete. He kneeled to retrieve the few contents. The worn old mittens from the kind Swedish Ada, the soft warm rags their bread and cheese had been wrapped in when they left the big farm. And when…this…a piece of paper rolled and tied with a ribbon, a woman's ribbon. He looked around to see if someone could have dropped it. No, no one had stopped. It must have come from his own knapsack.

He pulled at the ribbon and unrolled the paper. The face showed first. Like a gentle understanding blessing the eyes turned up at him from the paper. The Christ at Gethsemane. She had seen him then, the woman Ada. She had noticed him each day as he stared at the picture, as he made the sign of the cross, sadly, homesick for the safety it represented. She had understood. Oh, how he cried now, this desolate man, kneeling, holding the picture to his chest.

Someone spoke to him, roughly at first, then, sensing his despair, the man laid a hand on Mikolai's bent back.

"Do you speak Polish?"

"Yes, I understand. I am Russian," he answered in a voice thick and slow, turning his head up to the speaker.

"What is the trouble, why do you kneel here weeping?"

He could not answer. He stood up before the man who spoke again, more slowly, as to a child.

"What is your trouble? Do you understand my words? Why do you weep? Have you lost someone?"

Mikolai shook his head.

"Do you need help?"

"Yes, yes, I need help in this place."

"Are you sick?"

"No, no, I am well. I need only to find my way and I will be safe. Here," he pulled out the bible, "I go to this place. Can you tell me where I go to find the tailor Marmolsky. They did not meet me here."

"Yes, the address is a street near here. I can see by the number, not far, not far at all, just across the city. That way, straight across. Just show the address when you pass the wide street. Someone will help you further along. Ask any policeman. They will help."

He smiled as he handed the bible back to Mikolai.

"I will walk a few minutes with you, it is on my way also, to the train."

Mikolai gathered the knapsack under his arm and they walked together.

"So, you are a tailor, eh?"

"No, I go to apprentice."

"And from where do you come?"

"Noradnovo, in Russia."

"You are a farmer?"

"Yes, I am schooled in the seminary but I am born to be a farmer."

"Why then do you go to a tailor?"

"It is arranged."

"Mmm." The stranger was quiet, thinking. They walked, the man in thought, Mikolai terribly aware of the city smells and sounds crashing into the street from all around, even from the windows and the stores as they passed. The clanging of iron trolleys, the horses, the shouts, the people, the smells, the smells, oh, the noise.

"You say it is arranged? Are you not too old to learn such a trade?"

Mikolai stopped. "I must."

The stranger's eyes twinkled. "But you are a farmer, isn't that true? You were born a farmer, eh?"

"Yes, that is so."

"And would you choose to farm if you could, here in this country, rather than go to be a tailor in this huge city?"

"Yes, yes of course." He hesitated. "But it is arranged otherwise."

"Have you money?"

"Yes, only a little, given by the people where we last stayed and worked."

"Do you need work, do you want good honest work?"

"Yes, I came for that, to work, to apprentice to the tailor. That will be my work."

"Aha, tell me," he slapped Mikolai's shoulder jovially, "no, I will tell you. No Russian farmer makes a good tailor." He lowered his voice. "In New York the best tailors are the Jews. Let them tailor, they cannot farm. Now, look at me. I came ten years ago from Poland to farm. In Poland I was a farmer, that's what I was and that's what I am here in America. A farmer should stay with the land. Isn't that true?"

"Yes, perhaps you are right. Yes. That is true."

"Good, then I offer you a choice. Stay here in this stinking city and become a tailor or come with me to farm. What do you say?"

Mikolai shrugged. Did this man taunt him? He was quiet. He walked some paces with his head down, in thought.

"Is it such a hard choice for you?"

Hesitating, Mikolai spoke. "No, but do you speak the truth or try to make a joke of me?"

Now the man spoke earnestly and gently, sensing he may have offended Mikolai. "I speak the truth. I am here to look for my brother who should have come on this ship, but he is not here this time. I need help on my farm. It is far from this city, almost two hours by train, and one more by cart. Look," he stretched his arm towards the building walls on each side of the street, "do you prefer this kind of place, you, a farmer, or a good farm in fresh country air?"

"Can it be the truth as you tell me?"

"Believe me, I could swear it on your bible. I ask you in truth. Come with me. There is much land. I need help, you or someone else who comes new to this country. I give you a choice, but you must decide because I will look for another."

"I can make my choice. I will come then, to your farm."

"Good, you made the right decision. You will be glad all your life for this moment. What are you called?"

"My name is Mikolai Vorodinov, from Krutoy Bereg. I have traveled with another name until I came off the ship. I am glad to say my name again."

"I am John Riznewsky. Step fast, then, keep up with me. We catch a train to the country."

"First I must send a message, a card to my priest, as I was told to do. It is necessary to let him know I am here safely."

"Of course. From the railroad station. You can send it from there, but we must hurry."

Riznewsky was amused by the young man's amazement when he saw the tremendous echoing caverns of the railroad station. He smiled as to a child when Mikolai took a card from the counter at a newsstand, then stood there wondering how to pay.

"It is one penny, Vorodinov, have you a penny?"

"No, I do not know about a penny. I have only this paper for money."

"Here, I will pay. It will cost more to go so far. You will have to work for it later. Now write."

They went to a postal window where Mikolai painstakingly wrote the priest's address, then in his careful Cyrillic he penned the simple message, 'The spring has come. I am well. Good wishes. Abe Marmolsky.'

Then he closed his eyes and imagined how Danya's eyes would light up, how she would smile when the message came to her.

STANTON, CONNECTICUT

They came to the farm after passing through small villages made up of white wooden houses, some huddled together on little hills under the moonlight, like chickens on a roost.

The tall thin spires of New England churches stood out from the hills, watching silently as the two men drove through the streets, the clack of the horses hooves and an occasional creak from the wagon wheels the only sounds echoing against the night. Nothing else moved around them.

Mikolai would have slept, but something had caught hold of his mind and forced his whole being to stand vigil, watching for signs as though he had traveled this way before. What did he expect at each turn of the road, or beyond each hill? Had he come home to his own village at this hour he would not have felt so familiar or so safe as he did in this place. It was the absence of fear that possessed him, wrapped around him, warmed him. So great that it touched all the nerve edges exposed in the past ordeal of survival. The knowledge of safety now settled over him like the dew cloaks the grass, weighing lightly until it was absorbed with the same natural gratitude with which the grass absorbs the dew.

He would have liked to express what he felt and what he thought, but by nature he could not articulate his heart's messages. Only in his journal could he speak his heart. But his comment when they stopped before the farmhouse was understood by the Riznewsky.

"It is good to come to the farm."

"Yes, it is a good farm. A good land. In the morning you will see."

After just a short sleep Mikolai arose to the welcome sounds of the barnyard. He pulled on his shabby clothes and joined John who was already in the yard pumping water for the animals.

Mikolai honestly thought he felt the earth humming beneath his feet, as if a whole chorus was waiting to rise out from the ground with the grand message that spring had come. It was all around, anywhere he looked, from the far fields tinted by the pink blossoms atop gnarled apple trees to the flat leafed bushes beside the kitchen door that concealed the lilac buds but could not conceal the scent. It might have been the first time he saw spring, so great was its glory this day to Mikolai. It might have just happened this very morning, all those colors and odors of spring because he hadn't been there to watch their gradual birthing.

With some pride Riznewsky showed him the chickens, the cows, pointed out the fields outlined by stone walls, and the marsh behind the apple orchard. The animals were breeds Mikolai had never seen and John explained their good features, their differences from the animals they had both known in their native lands.

How they worked. In solemn unison, milking, carrying hay, turning the earth for the garden beside the house. No greater gift could the sun give Mikolai than the sweat that ran down his brow under the noontime heat. How long since he had seen such a sun and wished for a chance to work the land under its joyful watch.

The sameness of their days like the pattern of all farm life, changed only with the kind of work, never with the number of hours that must be consumed to keep a farm functioning. Nature moved faster when the sun stayed clear, and this particular spring and summer the ideal weather gave the farmers an early hay crop and a generous cutting to stuff the barns for the winter. The potatoes and apples were untouched by any blights that at times could diminish the marketable quantity of a small farm's crop. The berries ripened early and stayed long into the summer. For the farmers there was no bad news.

At first the woods beyond and around the farm brought back some memories of the dangers that Mikolai remembered from his youth. But when he spoke of his fears, Riznewsky laughed.

"Who would be a robber in the woods when all we have is in our lands? You are safe here in the woods. When the summer berries ripen even an old country thief would be too busy picking to stop and bother you."

John Riznewsky, established in the American ways, became teacher to the shy younger man he had picked up at the wharf. In payment for his work he bought Mikolai a suit, shirt and new shoes, which transformed the meek blonde man to a dapper example of the young immigrant in prosperous America. In appearance, that is, for Mikolai could not yet feel happy in this place, not until Danya was here and the plan was completed.

He had some slight guilt that he could enjoy the social activities of the town. Every Saturday they drove to a nearby town, tied the wagon before the Grange Hall and paid a nickel to hear the American ladies play the piano and sing songs. The words he did not yet understand, but the music lifted him out of pity for himself. Afterwards they went to the local movie house where the short silent films thrilled the naïve foreigner more than it did the children whooping around them.

Riznewsky gravely tried to teach Mikolai some of the American language he had learned so easily himself. But whenever they went to the town for trading or for pleasure, Mikolai made no attempt to speak to the Americans and only slowly absorbed the names he must know for things on the farm. Together they spoke in Polish and John reminded Mikolai often that he must make friends when they went into the town so he could learn to become an American.

John's brother was expected in September this time. By then Mikolai decided it was safe for him to send his first message directly to Danya who should be living in his mother's house. In the letter he put a five-dollar American bill, writing that he would send more money each month until she had enough to pay for her passage. He made no explanation for his Connecticut address, just told her that he was now working on a farm. Nor did he explain how he had come to this life instead of staying in New York. He wrote that he was well and happy here. That he was learning English and was waiting with a beating heart for her to come soon to America so they could have a farm of their own. As far as he was now concerned, Marmolsky the tailor had never existed.

The letter was sent. The weeks went to months, and he waited.

KRUTOY BEREG - 1912

Old Anna, wrapped in the embroidered shawl she had taken out of the trunk for Easter service, rocked back and forth in her chair, looking at Danya with disbelief in her faded blue eyes.

"No," she whined, "you lie." She moaned. "My son would not leave his old mother, never."

"Yes, to save his life, Anna Vorodinov. It is true as I tell you. He has gone, gone to America."

"D you not lie to me, Danya? Perhaps he is already killed in the war, eh? Why is he not home for Easter as he promised? Why should he leave his mother? He is killed, is that what you mean to tell me by this lie?"

"No, no, he is safe, believe me. Today the first message came, the secret message, signed as Marmolsky, to say he arrived safely in America. He has made his way safely. Soon it will be safe for him to write in his own name and then we can go to him there."

"How can I, an old woman, go to him? Explain that. I don't trust you, Danya, you with the black strange eyes. You think I am so old that I do not know a lie? You think to trick me, eh, like an old fool? But I know you lie. I know."

"Please, please, you must stay quiet. No one should know or we will be in danger. Believe me, on the bible I swear to you, it is as I tell you. Mikolai is saved from the fighting and soon we too can go to him. Just as I tell you, exactly that."

"How could he go, how could he leave his mother in her old age?"

Danya tried to console the weeping old woman who kept rocking in her chair, wringing her hands in anguish, now moaning her disbelief.

"Please Anna Vorodinov, please understand. We should be glad that Mikolai has found his way to another country. If not, surely he would be killed in the fighting. Many are killed, you know that. Only this week came news that Rayme Federanko was killed. With every mail every family waits in fear. Believe me, we are lucky, you and I. We are lucky to be waiting for good news in the mail, not bad news."

"Lucky? Lucky to lose a son?"

"Understand," Oh please God make this old one understand Danya said to herself. "Mikolai is alive and safe. You have your son still alive and safe. He has left Russia for another country and is alive and saved from the war. Soon you can go to him. You will have your son." She repeated, "Your son is saved."

A harsh man's voice interrupted.

"How much noise you two woman make. You rock the house."

It was Vladimir, Mikolai's elder brother, coming in from the fields. He stood in the doorway, his face unsmiling, eyes squinting with annoyance when he saw Danya.

"Alive and safe, eh, who is alive and safe? Of whom do you speak? My young brother who sends no letter for three months?

Oh what a fine time the young have in the army. They forget their mothers and brothers. No letter and no money do they send. All for fun, for themselves."

Before his mother could speak, Danya broke in to tell Vladimir of the news. She would have preferred to keep the knowledge between old Anna and herself, but this commotion must be explained and she must hope he could be trusted. But why should she think he could be trusted, she thought for a second before she told him. He, the drinking braggart. Still, she must say what was necessary and have him swear to stay quiet.

"I see, I see," said Vladimir when she finished the story. "And who arranges such a fancy escape from the Tsar's army, eh? And how much money do they take from us to make such an escape?"

"I cannot say who, but the message will come when Mikolai is safe in America, when he can write in his own name."

"America? You tell the truth? So far?"

"Yes, all the way, across the oceans. When he is settled it will be safe for his to write to us. He will send money here to me, American money, and we will go to him in America."

"Who, you and our old mother? And what happens to me if you go, eh? I stay in this farm, alone, with no one to help or to cook for me?"

"Yes, Vladimir, you should stay with the farm. It is yours now. Mikolai is gone; you can have the farm as your own. Find yourself a wife to cook and you will have help on the farm."

Danya sensed that Vladimir might make trouble. She should have known he would be angry, and that he could not be trusted. She should have made up some other story.

"Don't worry little sister, I will be happy to have the farm. For a while. But maybe you will send money for me later, eh? It is hard here in Russia. In America I know everything is better, isn't it so? Aha, you think I know nothing of America? I have heard stories. Marmolsky's son, the tailor, is in America. Marmolsky says his house is full of money. They have no place to sit because there is so much money in the house. They even have to take some to the bank, that is how much they have."

Danya was startled.

"What do you know of Marmolsky?"

"The old man comes to the tavern. He comes with money, the old braggart. You should see him show his American money. He has such a rich son in America. Everyone knows."

"Please, Vladimir, tell no one what I have told you, I beg you. We could be arrested and even killed for what we have done, for what we say, all of us, you too. You must keep this all to yourself. Speak of it to no person. You must promise."

"Trust me, on my brother's memory. I swear you can trust me to be quiet."

"Before the next message comes, Vladimir, I will come to stay in this house, as Mikolai and I agreed, to wait for the letters from America. They will all come to this place with American money until we have enough for traveling."

"So, you will run my farm, and you are not yet my brother's wife. But you want to come to take our farm, eh?"

"No, it is arranged. Mikolai will write to me here at this house. All letters will come to this address every time so my own people cannot know, so on one will know except us. It will be easier for you, you will see that also because I will be here and I can help care for your mother and help in the house and some things on the farm. You will see."

Vladimir smirked as Danya spoke so earnestly. He shrugged. "Yes, it makes some sense, I agree. It will be fine. Come when you are able. But watch your way that you don't think you are the woman of this house. I am the master here. Walk carefully in my house."

Often in the weeks that followed Danya stopped at the synagogue to inquire of the Rabbi whether another message had come, if any word had been received after the priest's lone message that Mikolai had safely boarded the ship at Riga.

One day in sadness and great consternation the Rabbi told her a tale, which saddened her so that she slept under the weight of it for weeks afterwards.

"The road to the west has closed," he told her. "The old priest at the port city is dead. Some farmers found his young son, an officer in the Tsar's army, strangled and half buried under some bushes beside a road far from his military unit. They said he was trying to make an escape from the army. The priest, informed of the news, fell into a faint and never recovered from the shock. He died soon afterwards. It was his only son and he had begged the boy to run away to America before he went into the army. But his son wanted to be a gentleman soldier, an officer to the Tsar, and as such he died. Now their road is closed, the road west is no more. This was the last news that would come, no more can we expect. We can learn nothing more of those who had gone through these plans. My heart is aching, young Danya, for you and for others. After the Doukhobor left, this priest was the last one we could trust."

Danya waited before she spoke. "Will I never know if Mikol arrived safely in America? How would I know, for he was told not to write directly to his home for many months, that the first message must come through this priest." Her voice became strident. "Will I hear nothing? Will the message never come to me?"

Rabbi Schenky wanted to console her, but felt he must be truthful. "Probably not. Perhaps the priest's wife...but that would be dangerous for her, to try to contact her might put her in danger. She might be found out. Besides, she may not know of her husband's good deeds for the young men. It is not good."

Danya did not tell Vladimir or his mother what she had learned. She still went to the Rabbi seeking comfort, just to talk, to see if he had heard anything. Sometimes she went three times a week, asking, hoping. Inside she was pressed by doubts that began to grow, but she lingered to speak with him, holding hope, wishing, wondering.

But in August, somehow a small packet came to the Rabbi. It contained some pictures, a Hebrew prayer book and two post cards. One card was from Abe Marmolsky. Spring had come. He was well. The next time Danya came to visit he showed her the card. The message was understood.

STANTON 1915

The local Stanton Grange Association held its annual Labor Day picnic at the town lake. So many men were gone to service that this year they invited non-members who could contribute twenty-five cents and eat as much as they pleased of the New England baked beans, corn on the cob, coleslaw and hot dogs that the Grange ladies prepared for the pot luck lunch.

That was where John Riznewsky met Hazel Phillips, an American girl who, he decided, should be his wife. She worked in the town clerk's office. She was educated, she could type and keep figures. She even spoke German, just from learning it in school. She was blonde and husky, good natured and honest in her eyes, he told Mikolai. A kind and good woman who understood people and could help a man in his life.

John decided it was time to bring a woman on to the farm. It was time for him to take a wife and raise a family, he told Mikolai, talking it over aloud in thought-length syllables. She was just like an old country woman, only smarter. She looked strong enough to work on the farm and raise plenty of children. Now was the time for him to take a wife.

He talked it over and over with Mikolai who always agreed with the questions he asked. Yes, it was a good idea. Yes, truly he remembered her, yes she looked honest and good, and she was a good catch for a farmer.

Nor was John a bad catch for the girl. Most of the single men near her age were away in the army, and even if all of them came back there wasn't one smart enough that she would care to marry. Oh, maybe Angus Bent. He had a good future. He had finished college before the war and he was clever. He could be a good catch, perhaps. But she really didn't like him that much. He was tall and skinny, really too skinny, she thought. And his white skin and long skinny fingers...something about him...no. John Riznewsky, even if he was foreign, was a good catch for Hazel Phillips.

John was bright, Hazel knew, because she saw the town records. She knew how much land he owned and she knew he got the best prices for his crops. She would marry him. He was courting her in earnest now, calling every Saturday evening. She knew he liked her a lot and she admired his kindness and his honesty. She knew he would ask her soon, and she decided before he asked that she would certainly say yes. Here, in this small town, a life with John Riznewsky would be a good life for her. She did not want to leave her hometown and to find someone like John was what she had always hoped. They would stay here and raise a family. It would be the life she wanted.

For the two years he stayed on at the farm after John and Hazel were married, Mikolai lived in the same house and ate his meals with them as a brother.

Hazel tried to teach him more English, and although John pushed him, Mikolai stayed shy even with her. He learned fast enough, or seemed to, but when it came to speaking English to others he acted as if he understood little of the American language. Hazel understood him. She felt kindly toward him for his shyness, and she told John they mustn't criticize him. He would pick up the words when he heard them or when he needed them. And they must always speak English together in front of him. That way he would understand more. He would learn, she was sure.

Another year passed and there was still no word from Russia from Danya. Hazel told John they should find a wife for Mikolai. Probably his Danya was by now married to another.
Why else would she not answer his letters? But why wouldn't his family write and tell him the news? Then he could find someone here. He would be free from his promise to his Russian sweetheart. He would be free from waiting and hoping for letters that did not come.

"He is too shy to look for his own woman," Hazel reasoned to John "but he is good looking enough, especially when he laughs. He should find someone here. There are lots of unmarried girls in Stanton and in nearby towns. Right nearby, how about the Westham girls? The older one is too sophisticated and educated, maybe too old, but the younger one keeps the house and she might be a good one for Mikolai."

She urged John to tell him, that he ought to somehow encourage Mikolai to look for someone else. John could convince Mikolai that he was foolish to wait so many years to hear from someone in the old country. She would not be waiting for him so long…so why should he be waiting in vain?

"He thinks the letters can't come because of the war," John told her. "He says when the war is over the letters will come. They are held up somewhere. He knows how it is during wartime with the mail. You never know when the mail will come through. With the trains and the ships, it all takes time. That's how he's reasoning. I can't make him lose hope."

"But it is more than three years since he left!"

John shrugged. "He says the letter will come. He really believes that. He sends a letter every month with money, and when she has enough for her passage he thinks Danya will send a letter.

He says sometimes the postman can lose a letter also. But he always expects to see a letter in the mail from his Danya. He really believes that."

"But after more than three years?"

"Well, I talked to him, as you asked me."

"I give up. Well, he's not a woman. At least the waiting won't take away his good looks."

No, he could wait longer without that harm, they agreed.

***

Hazel was sure she would have twins. "It runs in my family, John."

"But mine, always boys."

"Two boys at one time. That's pretty good for your farm. I hope we both win."

***

"Next week I should stop working," Hazel told John one day. "It isn't smart to sit in an office when I'm in such a condition."

"That's fine. We should keep the boys here on the farm."

"But do you know what I heard in the office? The small farm on Ledge Hill, the one near the White's house, you know it?"

"Yes, of course I know it. What do you hear?"

"It's being sold for taxes. The family won't pay the taxes."

"Do they live there?"

"No, when the father died the mother moved to her daughter's in New Haven, to an apartment I think. They don't want the farm and they can't sell it. They've been trying for some time. Now they've stopped paying the taxes. I think it's because they are buying the apartment house with the old man's money and they are in a tight situation."

"Are you hinting that you want us to buy it? It's too small for us, and too far for me to go from our farm here, just for planting."

"No, I don't tell you about it for us. For Mikolai. He has money enough saved if he can get the farm for the unpaid taxes."

"Where did he get so much money?"

"I pay him from the farm income."

"Who told you to pay him? He gets his room and board for his work."

"He works as hard as you do, John. I pay him his share, like any hired man."

Yes, she was a good catch, John admitted silently to himself, puffing at his pipe. Not only a smart woman, but a kind and good person.

Hazel made sure before she left her job that Mikolai had his farm, the five pretty acres on the hill. An old house and a well-built barn. Just right for a man like him. Quiet and small, room for a few animals and a large garden. Later they would find him a wife.

KRUTOY BEREG 1916-1918

Danya came to the Vorodinov household with only her little sewing machine, some pieces of cloth and those of her clothes she could stuff into the bundle she carried over her arm. She was full of hope since the secret message, had come, "I am well. Abe Marmolsky." At least now Mikolai was in America. Soon she, too, would make the journey and finally join him.

Very soon they should have a letter directly from him. He was safe. No matter that the road to the west was closed. He could now write directly to her, to his own address as they had planned.

Vladimir had promised to help her move, to fetch her with her bundles at her father's house. But in the tavern his promise was erased with drink, so she had to beg a ride from another farmer who passed in the same direction. She carried her things the last two miles, stopping often to rest, thankful that it was the sun and not rain that hindered her walking.

Slowly, slowly, the days went by, watched on the calendar hung over old Anna's bed with the dry palm fronds from last Easter still hanging from a nail.

But no word came from America. Day after day and no word came. Week after week, and month after month. No letter. Nothing. Could she still hope?

When Vladimir taunted her, Danya reminded him that it would be dangerous for Mikolai to send any letter before it was surely safe, not just for him but for his family here. It might take many months more before it came across the ocean. But she knew, she told him bravely, she knew a letter would come. She held the hope in her heart that Mikolai would be impatient as she was and that he would send a letter very soon. But to Vladimir she pretended that she would not be surprised if they heard nothing until later in the year.

Her heart kept saying, perhaps, sooner, sooner. It probably wasn't so dangerous now. They had been waiting long enough to hear. The danger must be gone. Just to know, to have one card, even a few words.

It had been so long since they parted. Maybe she could have arranged to go with him somehow. No one would have noticed them among all the people who moved from place to place. She saw strangers all the time, people moving from bad farms or from diseased households. No one paid attention. They could have gone together.

She wrote a letter and gave it to Vladimir so he could mail it in the village. It was addressed to Marmolsky in New York. They would know for whom the letter was meant, and would tell him it was safe to write. She dared not use Mikolai's name on the envelope.

Every month after that she sent another letter, hoping, hoping for just one card, any information that her Mikol was safe, that he was there waiting for her.

But now, all around them even in the village, people were on the move. It was the beginning of a madness that would grow worse. There were already opposing forces at work pressing against every soft place in a tottering monarchy to see where a break would come. Rumors ran as boldly as loosened dogs through the village streets. The more isolated and superstitious the village, the worse were the rumors.

To the old ones who remembered, the Turks were on the move again. To the young in the taverns, the Germans were eating Russian children as they closed in around Moscow's walls. To the religious the angels of death had sowed a pestilence that consumed crops before they could spring from the earth. To the half worldly a dark monk had taken the throne from the Tsar and held him captive in St. Petersburg while he planned with the Tsarina how Russia should be delivered to its enemies.

The preparations for chaos were in every Russian's mind.

So also it had become with Danya. She could not, as the months ground slowly past, maintain the high hopes with which her plan had been launched. Not one letter had come. Not a single word after the first simple message.

Every family had a tale of woe to add to the last one, and each time she heard of another's misfortune Danya's heart was inclined to believe that she, too, would join the village flock who carried their woes so heavily.

Vladimir's unkindness depressed her all the more now. He would taunt her when he came home late from the tavern. He could she be sure Mikolai would wait for her? Wouldn't he find a fine American lady and spend his money on her instead of sending for Danya? Shouldn't she look for another man instead of taking over his household as though she were the mistress of the place? Wasn't she afraid she would grow old here, waiting for someone who had long ago forgotten her? What man would want her then?

Once he tried to come to her bed. She was asleep and hadn't heard him come home. His heavy hand against her head awakened her. She pushed at him with the back of her hand as she sat up in fright. She could smell the stale wine odor he carried about him.

"What do you think you are doing, you mad man?"

"Aha, Danya, don't be so proud. You must pay for your lodging here in my house in some way."

"Keep away from me, Vladimir." Her voice was harsh, unafraid. "I warn you I am not so soft as I look!" As she spoke she reached under her pillow for her matches. She took three and held them together against the striking box.

"Ah yes, you are soft. You should be used by a man, you are so soft."

"You are no man, you are a fool!" She hissed the words toward his face.

"I'll show you I am a man," he growled as he moved closer.

She struck the matches as his head came hear her. As quickly as his surprise came she held the matches to his hair. The flame caught his hair immediately and made a small flash, followed by the distinct smell of burning hair. He stared in panic at her and for a second seemed not to comprehend the source of the light or the smell.

She glared at him without moving from her bed.

In his drunken slowness he then felt the heat and the pain. With a blanket grabbed from her bed he smothered the singed burning hair, yelping like a kicked dog.

Danya struck another match and lit the candle beside her bed. With a set smile she watched as he pounded his head through the blanket, hard with the palms of his hands, snuffing out the burning.

When he stopped he pulled the blanket so it fell from his shoulders. His maddened eyes sparked the dim light. Danya spoke first in a low angry tone, hoping that old Anna would not be awakened.

"Do not think you can treat me this way, you dog. I can protect myself against you. I am not afraid of you, not one small bit. And I warn you that worse than burning hair will happen if you ever try to touch me or come near me again, you ugly hearted person."

"What kind of crazy woman are you?" He threw the anger back at her. "Why should you come to my house to burn me up in the night?" His emotions in the candlelight contorted his face into gross and jumbled features.

She said nothing, just stared back at him and then held the candle close to her, should he attempt to come near her again.

He backed off. "Why do you stare so? You are mad, I can see that, you haggled female. Don't you know when a man is only joking? No, I see you do not. You are crazy, waiting and going crazy thinking of your Mikolai. You are a mad woman, lying in wait in my house, trying to burn me to ashes."

Danya said nothing.

Vladimir squinted and looked back for a few seconds. He was now somewhat sobered. He sighed, threw up his hands in disgust and turned away.

"Hah, what a lunatic my brother chose. Lucky for him the ocean is between you, to save him the suffering."

When he went to his own room and she was sure he was asleep, when his snores sounded deep and real, Danya snuffed the candle and lay back on her bed. Her heart was still pounding with fear and anger. She clearly saw that she must find her own safety in this world. Even in the house of her Mikolai's family she must protect herself against such an animal. She prayed in her heart that when she and Mikol had their children none would take the heart or the habits of this terrible man who was so opposite her beloved in looks and actions that they could be strangers and not brothers born of the same flesh.

She quieted her thoughts and tried to pray. The time was lengthening and the hope she held was not as strong now. She could find no excuses or reasons for Mikolai's quiet. But still she believed she would somehow hear from him.

Again and again, always in the safety of daylight, she was chided by Vladimir. She tried still to defend her hopes. As he teased and berated her she stood fast against showing her doubts to him.

"Mikolai has found an American woman, someone rich and pretty and younger than you. See how long the time has passed and you have no word from your fine soldier. And we, his family have no word. He has deserted his country, his family and you. He has his own family by now in America. I know this."

She stared at Vladimir with disgust, saying nothing. No, no, he would not find another she thought to herself. She knew that. She knew she belonged to him and in God's eyes he belonged to her too. He must believe the same, there, far away. He must be waiting also. The mail delivery is so bad with the war and the troubles. Those were the causes. At such times it could take months for a letter to reach their place. And mail can be lost, going either way. There were wars all over. She would shut out Vladimir's noise.

"Be still Vladimir, you do not shake me. I will hear from Mikolai, I will hear. I know that, and I will hear soon."

"You will grow old waiting, Danya, year after year. More than three years have you been waiting in this house and no word. You grow old in front of our eyes with your waiting."

"I will have a letter soon. I know I will. Is there not a great war, with half the world fighting? How can a letter come at such times, you stupid man? I will wait until the wars are finished. I will hear. Do not try to shake me with your crazy words, Vladimir."

"Hah, you grow old waiting for a man who has already forgotten your name. See, there in the corner, you will be an old one like the mother before long, before your time."

"Be still, Vladimir, do not raise your drunken voice to me."

"You will grow old, alone, alone. Old and ugly."

"Be still or I will kill you in your bed as you sleep you drunken fool."

"You are mad, you dark eyed gypsy. You do not belong to us. Leave our house. Leave my house. Find another man. Go run to your Rabbi. Is he maybe your lover, eh, while you pretend to wait for my brother?"

"You are mad, not I. You know I cannot leave old Anna now."

"Go to hell, then, you with the black witch's eyes. Take her with you."

Many times the same words raged back and forth.

Then finally there was no more need for such scenes. After years of slowly fading into infirmity Old Anna died in her seventieth year on a cold brittle late afternoon when the new snow was piling up in the fields.

In a rage of loneliness, her heart filled with anger and hatred for the man in whose house she had stayed, waiting and praying, Danya walked with her possessions into the snow of winter, leaving the old woman's corpse to greet Vladimir when he returned that night from the tavern. She set out to go back to her own family.

***

Darkness fell before she could go far with her burden. She continued toward the village, stopping to listen for sounds that might be Vladimir returning to his house. Too early, she thought. I must stay on the wayside or be lost in the snow. Her back ached with the effort of carrying her bundles.

She had to take the sewing machine with her. She could not leave it and she could not replace it. She had bought it years ago with her own money. A new design that sat on a table and worked by hand turning a small wheel. She had seen pictures of machines called treadles and vowed that some day she would have one. To survive alone she must be able to sew. She could always make a few rubles or take food in exchange for some sewing. If she left the machine there at the farmhouse she was sure she would never see it again. Certainly Vladimir would never bring it to her. She must endure these aches and pains in order to live.

Hours may have gone, and still there were no lights from the direction of the village. There were barking dogs, but no lights. Or was it the winter wolves Mikolai had told tales of? They weren't far away now, and from the louder sounds she could tell they were coming closer.

She left the roadside, thinking if they were wolves they might stay on the road to follow scents of horses and not bother with her.

The sounds became more shrill. Closer. She realized now they surely were wolves. She had never heard dogs make such eerie cries. Closer. Great panic replaced the anger she had walked with. She could not run. She knew it would do no good.

She remembered a story Mikolai had told her. She put down her bundles and burrowed into the deepening snow, her heart beating so wildly it pushed at the ground as she lay there. Her head throbbed madly. Fear so warmed her that she didn't feel the cold of the snow against her face.

Yes, it was wolves. Would they smell her under the snow? She dared not move. If she was not covered by snow they would get her. The howling stopped. They must be nearby. They must have found her bundles. They would have her scent. Then the howling began again. Were they coming closer? The sounds seemed muffled, but louder now, coming closer.

In her fear, close as it had been to the heat of anger, she had forgotten to pray. She thought something was nudging her foot. She wanted to move, to pull her leg deeper into the snow. She dared not.

My God is near me. My God is near me.

There were other muffled sounds, then a shout, a human shout, loud and careless. Then some other sounds, more shouts, the quickened hoof beats of a horse and the continuing shouts of the driver. A horse and sleigh flew past on the road very close to where she lay beneath the snow.

She waited until all was quiet. She was sweating, nearly suffocated under the mound of snow. Now she felt the cold.

Slowly she pulled herself from the ground, head first, her back still covered with the snow. It must have been drunken Vladimir who had saved her. She recognized the shouts. He had saved her, not knowing. He went on, unknowing, home in the dark, home to what she had left there to greet him, the corpse of his mother.

What had she done, why had she done such a cruel and inhuman action, even to a fool like Vladimir? Oh my God, help Vladimir whom I have wronged. Help him who has saved me through Your help. Give back my hope, oh God, give back my hope and help me on my way.

She stood weakly, brushing the snow from her clothes. She made her way toward her bundles, guiding her steps by the path she had made. She hesitated for a moment before she picked up her burden. She held her hands over her face, head bent down and began to cry. The deep sobs hung about her as though they had no place to go. They echoed around her.

No! She straightened upright. No, she would not be that kind. She must go on. She would find her way. She wiped her eyes, pulled her coat collar around her freezing face and walked on.

***

Danya arrived at her father's house hours after all had gone to bed. With her aching arms and frozen fingers she pounded the wooden door, calling, "Open, open up. It is I, Danya. Is no one home? Open up, I am freezing here in the dark."

Finally the stepmother came to the door and let her in reluctantly.

She was not welcomed back by her family. News of the revolution was all about and the great fear of the village people was the long winter and scarcity of food. No new mouths were welcome anywhere.

Her stepmother had three young ones and an old aunt to feed, and just yesterday had come a sister whose husband was killed in the fighting. With her came two more children who must be fed.

There was no place there for Danya who had left them when times were better to go to her betrothed family. There was no way they could feed her, no place for her to sleep. Even her promise that she could earn money for them had no worth. There was no need now for a dressmaker. There were no parties or christenings, no thoughts for clothes. It was only for firewood and food that the people were concerned, and sometimes for their very lives.

The next day she walked about the frozen village with her bundle of fabrics, asking for work, looking for someone who might take her into their home or their shop. She could cook and sew, and help with the old people, she begged.

Everywhere it was the same. No one could take on another mouth to feed. The uncertainty of political rumors coupled with the certainty that there would be little food had stagnated the activity in the shops. No one dared use money for pleasures when that money would be needed as the winter wore on to save their lives.

The ovens in the village bakeries were cold. Such bread as was baked by one remaining shop went to those who stood before the bakery door, willing to pay what was asked for a loaf of bread, no matter the size, never knowing if there would be another loaf the next day, never knowing when the bakery door would be closed before them.

Danya begged her father to keep her in the house. The stepmother gave her a small space for her belongings, a space hardly big enough to lie down and sleep. The days and nights passed away.

Her father lay sick with an old man's disease and would die before another winter was spent.

You could buy no meat anywhere except on some Saturdays when a few farmers brought their skinny winter chickens into the village.

The wiser women went to meet the dairy farmers on the road, waiting in the cold so they could have even one egg or a little milk for their children, paying high prices or begging a trade with a treasured fancy shawl, embroidered belt or shiny holiday shoes. A soldier's heavy overcoat and boots paid for the food his fatherless children ate that winter.

Her despair brought Danya to the synagogue from where the last good news had come years ago. She hadn't visited the Rabbi for more than a year, having given up hope that any further message would come that way.

He had aged more than the years. He was so old now and so thin from the deprivations of the times. A great many Jews had left the village, he told her, in response to rumors that revolutionaries were killing Jews in the towns and burning their houses to the ground. The streets were strangely quiet near the synagogue, the houses dark throughout the nights. He too was afraid for his family. He must decide whether he should stay with the few who were left or go to a safer place.

"So, you have not heard any more from your man?"

"Never, not since the message which came through you."

"And have you written, my child, have you not written to America?"

"Every month, the same place, to the tailor Marmolsky's son in New York. Yes, I have written so often, the same words to the same place, and not one answer in return. I weep over the words, 'How are you, my Mikol, why do I not hear from you?' But never an answer, not one word all these years."

"Do you ask old Marmolsky if he has letters from him family in America?"

"He hears nothing any more, he doesn't understand why, he says. I asked him many months ago. He has not heard for three or four years, maybe more, he says. It is the war, is it not? The wars and the revolution keep our letters away. What else can it be, if he does not hear either?"

"Ah, my poor girl. What cruelty the world holds, for the young and the old alike. I cry out to God in my prayers, but even as my voice echoes in the synagogue I do not believe help will come for our people or for yours, for the sick or the well. We all pay now for the sins of others before and after us."

"I will not pay for the sins of others. I will not suffer for things I have not done."

"You say so, Danya, but look how you pay for sins you could not know or describe, a girl growing old from the burden of hope, oppressed by time, by waiting. That is how the young pay, with their youth and their trust. And when it is paid you have nothing, not even the memories of your own sins. You are marked forever by the debts you have paid for others. Yes, you pay, you pay."

His word disturbed her. "Rabbi, tell me, is it a sin to be cruel to another who has wronged you greatly?"

"Cruelty is the just desert for one who has been cruel. It is as a law. It goes round and round. The first cruel act begets another, and from that comes all the cruelty we know."

"But cannot the cruel be forgiven their sinning?"

"Yes, perhaps, after the law is fulfilled, the cruel are forgiven, even as they hold the memories forever. When the eye is taken for the eye, the tooth for the tooth. Then the law says all is justified. But now it is easy to talk of cruelty. It is all around us. That is why we know it so well. Goodness is a stranger hiding from us even in the brightest sunlight. We no longer know where to look for her, for goodness. Perhaps if we saw her we could not call the name of kindness. I fear we would not recognize goodness if she came to our face."

Seeing that she was looking even more downhearted, he managed a reassuring smile.

"But you did not come for such a lesson. You see, we have talked and done no good. I would offer you tea, but..."

"I know, Rabbi, I know how it is," Danya said soothingly to his embarrassed offer. "And I am sorry. I must go. To old Marmolsky. It is so sad. Can you forgive me if I leave you?"

"You say to Marmolsky? Why do you say so sad?"

"Yes, sad. The old man had a stroke last month and he is alone in his house. I take him some soup and bread."

"Where are his daughters?"

"Both gone. They went in fear for their lives, leaving their old father speechless and crippled."

"Who then takes his business, his tailoring shop?" He shrugged. "Who wants a tailoring shop now?"

Danya, after a second's thought blurted out, "I do, Rabbi, I do!"

Her vehement reply startled him and he smiled in relief after the somber time they had spent talking.

"Well, come then with me. Perhaps it is a good thing. It will bring some cheer to see you."

"I could care for the old man."

"Yes, perhaps yes. It would be a big help."

"You see, Rabbi, I need a place. I have no place. In my father's house I have a corner, just like a dog. I need a place to live, and I must work."

"There is no work in this village for you, I must tell you in truth, Danya."

"Children are born and they grow. Clothes wear out. I will find work."

"There is no money, even if you find little bits of work."

"I will take bread, then, or wood. Anything. I will find work."

He nodded, impressed by her enthusiasm but a little amused. "It is possible. It could be that way. I will go with you to Marmolsky and you can decide when you see him and I will explain for you."

She had made up her mind before they came to Marmolsky's door. She knew it was a good omen. It was a place for her, and she knew she could do all that is necessary in caring for the sick man.

The treasures she found in that dismal dusty tailor's shop were just payment for the ordeal of tending to the helpless crippled old man. The half-finished overcoat, the trousers, the few bolts of woolens, the threads. They all became barter for food and fuel for the two of them. She grasped each thing as a handful of gold. She dreamed of the things she could make from the stuff, the fabrics, that were there in the shop. Just waiting for me, she thought with a little smile and a lighter heart.

A crafty old supplier from the next village brought some fabric with an order for military shirts. When would he pay? "Well...the money comes late now..."

"But I know how you go, old man. Bring me money when you come back for the shirts. You are paid well, I know it. I will make the shirts and you will bring the money or you will not have the shirts. I can sell them elsewhere."

Soon there was work enough to use all her energies and all the day light hours. At night she bent close to the glow of the stove and worked buttonholes by hand, not daring to lose one hour more than necessary to sleep or rest.

All the living, the cooking and working, was carried on in the one big room, heated by the wood stove in the middle of the floor.

The old man in his corner watched dumbly, barely able to comprehend the circumstances about him. He ate and slept fitfully, at times mumbling, generally quiet. Except when she fed him Danya could have been alone in that house.

The winter passed. No word, no word. When she visited the church she learned that the priest had died and the doors of the church were closed by the new government. All her prayers were said in haste as she knelt holding the small cross she had found abandoned on the floor of the church. She kept it hidden so as not to disturb old Marmolsky.

Whenever she could spare money for stamps she sent a letter to America, to Marmolsky's son's address. If she heard steps on the empty street her heart could still hope it was the postman with a reply, but the hope was a habit now, without the full strength of belief there once had been.

She went sometimes to the Rabbi for company. He was anxious for her to give up her hopes and find a local man who could take care of her. She was strong still and would make a good caring wife, he said. There were men in the village who had come back from the war to empty houses. She should take a husband now and forget her blonde farmer. He could make some arrangements for her if she would give him the permission.

How could she explain? Even to herself she could not say why she waited and believed. It is only that I know, I cannot say more. I know in my heart and I do not know why. I cannot say more. How could he understand if she told him these words, the kind Rabbi, when she did not have any reason behind the words?

When the first warm days came the Rabbi gathered his family and walked away. Such were the terrors of rumor that no one any longer knew from whom they should flee. As the weather warmed some who had left the previous year returned to their cold empty houses, empty save for the rats who prowled in search of food or other vermin.

Marmolsky's elder daughter Serina returned too. She told Danya she had been all the way to Moscow. Everywhere people were starving and dying, she said. They looked for nothing but food. All the shops with fancy goods were locked tight, the dust gathering as they were passed by. Some shops were destroyed by the revolutionaries and the goods were sold wherever there was money. She, Serina, had been lucky. She had some fancy brocade and some woolen stuff from England.

"How did you come by such goods, Serina?"

"Oh, I had money."

"From where did the money come?"

"Do you think I left this place with no money? Fool, Danya. I could not have gone one day without money."

"But the Rabbi said Marmolsky was broken and without any money at all."

"We knew he would be cared for by someone."

"You took his money and left him sick and alone?"

"Yes! You would so the same, would you not? Are not the young entitled to something in these times? Look what they are doing to us, killing brothers and husbands and chasing us all over the world like rabbits running for our lives. Yes. I took the money, and he never knew. And I have lived through hard times and hard winters, too, because of that money."

"Why do you return now?"

"For more money, that's why."

"There is no money here, Serina. You will find no money, not one ruble in this house now. I work only for food and firewood. No one has money."

"Oh, you must not worry, dressmaker, I do not come to take from you. I will leave you with the old man."

"Where then will you find the money?"

"Aha, that I cannot tell you, Danya. That you cannot know."

"But if you get some money, could you not leave some for us, for wood, for your father's health? Some days we have no heat."

"Oh, well, maybe a few dollars."

"Dollars, why do you say dollars?"

"Oh...Danya, I only joke. I am joking with you. Of course not dollars. That is a city joke. I will try to find extra for you and the old father. I will come later with something for you, I promise."

Serina stayed only half the day. Danya thought she might return at night but she never came.

How strange. Weeks later they found her frozen body at the swamp's edge. Too bad, they said. She was a little crazy, that one. Why else would she walk alone near the swamp during a thaw? Poor Marmolsky. A fine thing he has the dressmaker to care for him.

It was Holy Friday before Easter while Danya was saying her prayers that Marmolsky took a fit. She had seen other illnesses, but she had never seen such as this. If he could die, if he could only die in his misery. What should she do for him now?

She ran from the house into the dark deserted street, thinking she could find the local doctor. She herself could do nothing. The fits came and went and the old man suffered so.

The doctor? He is not home. No more work today, she is told. No, he is at the tavern. That way, down the street, turn where you see the light.

She ran.

Even before she reached the open tavern door she recognized the thick halting laugh.

No one noticed her standing at the open doorway. They all were watching the dark man who sat on one of the wooden tables, his legs crossed under him. He was laughing drunkenly as he performed.

What Danya saw there emptied her heart and her guts like a great thundering empties the air of all other sounds. In rushed all the hatred she had ever felt, thickened and blackened by astonishment when she realized what this man had done to her.

Vladimir sat cross-legged
Like a thick ugly frog.
His eyes puffed with drink,
Telling the tale

Of his green cigarette.
"In America," he slurs,
"The streets are made of gold.
Every farmer
Owns his land
And keeps two women.
One for the house and one for the barn.
You laugh when I tell you?
But I speak what's true.
These dollars are nothing.
They fall from the trees.
I swear by my brother's name.
Look for yourself.
This time he sends me three for a smoke.
An American makhorka.
You make one like this
And keep two by your ears..."

It may have been a growl or a scream from her own mouth that turned every man's eyes to the doorway where Danya stood. And such a silence when Vladimir saw he was found out.

"You dog in a manger,
You devil's vomit.
I will scratch your fat eyes
From your thick wine-filled skull
For what you have done
To me and my man."

She advanced on the stunned Vladimir who still held the lighted green cigarette in his teeth. It was the sight of the scissors she pulled from her apron pocket that brought him to action. No one else moved.

Danya pounced on him when he jumped from the table, attacking like a cat when he corners his prey.

Vladimir fell and yelled with pain when the scissors slashed his arm. He threw her from him.

Someone bent quickly to pull Danya up from the floor. The scissors had flown under the table.

Vladimir jumped up, his eyes filled with rage and the terror of a trapped animal, inflamed by the alcohol he had consumed.

One man moved to keep Vladimir from Danya, but it wasn't necessary. Clinging to his bleeding arm he cursed her and ran through the door, pushing aside whoever stood in his way.

Once, when she was still a girl, she would have cried. A long time ago when she was young. Now, standing there watched in silence by the puzzled men she had shocked out of relaxed inebriations, she vindicated her performance in a voice so full of bitterness that what she said chilled every man there.

"You see these dollars," she leaned to pick up the two unburned dollars Vladimir had rolled into cigarettes. "These dollars belong to me!"

"For six years I have been waiting. Yes, six years it has been since my Mikolai left this country for America. And not one word has come to me. But how to Vladimir, that despicable one, oh yes, how to him? How could he get these dollars? He has been stealing from under my nose. He has stolen the letters and the money from under my nose. I tell you, I see it now, I know it."

Her voice rose with anger.

"You have all seen him show his money, his American dollars. You saw him burn up a dollar now. And not one of you would come to tell me anything. Did I not come to some of you asking if you had any news from America? Not one of you would talk. Would you let me become an old woman while my husband's brother burns the money that is mine? The money that should send me to American to be with Mikolai?"

One of the younger men, nudged by another, interrupted her.

"But Danya Protovnaya, how should we know? Vladimir told us only that Mikolai sends money to him. That you should not know because Mikolai has found another woman in America. You must know then that the money was not sent for you after all."

He looked around for corroboration. Several men nodded in agreement.

Danya tossed her head.

"Oh, you men are fools! You drown your brains in vodka and you think you can see straight. If it were as you say, why should Vladimir not tell me? So I could cry, eh, and go on my way to another man. And you, postman, to whom to these letters with the money come? Do they come addressed to Vladimir? Say the truth."

"No, to you, but the address is to Vladimir's house. He takes them from me here in the village to save me a trip. How could I know he keeps them from you?"

"How could you know? Did I not ask you, month after month, year after year...'is there any word from my Mikol, any word from America?' I asked so many times. How could you look on my face as the years went by and say no to my face?" She scowled and gave him a suspicious look.

"Perhaps he gave you some of the dollars to tell me nothing? Is that how your daughters could afford new blouses while the rest of the known needs money for food just to stay alive?"

The charge brought raised eyebrows from the men whose jealous wives had seen the girls in their new blouses at Christmas. There were grumblings direct at Narvich the postman. The emotions ignited by the drama turned dangerously toward the round-faced man.

He tried to laugh. "Now, my brothers, could I be such a man? You all know me. I won the money in fairness, I swear to you. You have all seen me, here in this very tavern. You have seen me matching dice with Vladimir. How should I know from where the money came when a man pays his debts? And Marmolsky, too, you remember, he used to play the dice, too, the three of us. But I, I had the luck."

Danya gasped. "Marmolsky! Oh, the pitiful old man. For him did I run here. Please, please, doctor, come with me to Marmolsky. I am afraid we are too late. Run with me to Marmolsky. He suffers there alone."

The doctor grumbled over his unfinished drink, but because of the row he could not refuse Danya's request. The postman urged him to go, calling on his pity for this poor woman who must bear so much of the care. Go, go, urged the others. He could not refuse.

Danya stood staring at them, hating them all in these few moments. Hating them for their unconcern, for their stupidity, for their cowardice, for their lying.

"Come doctor, run quickly. I think he will die. But he suffers so. Come, help him to die easily."

STANTON 1918

Mikolai stared in disbelief at the envelope when the letter came. Could it be? Was it in truth Danya's handwriting? His hand trembled as he studied the markings. At last, could it be true?

Riznewsky was there at his farm helping to roof the barn and he had brought the letter and newspaper from the mailbox by the side of the road. Knowing the significance of a long awaited message from Russia he fairly stumbled into the barn where Mikolai was standing at a workbench straightening nails in a vise.

He stood awkwardly, between politeness and curiosity while Mikolai, with flushed face, read the two pages.

"Oh, to hell, to hell," he mumbled as he read. "All goes to hell there. It cannot be. No, it cannot be so." He read the pages again.

"Six years, six years, and now comes this letter. What kind of story is this?"

He put the letter on the workbench, laid some nails on top of it and stood there shaking his head.

"It is that Danya. How she can spin up a tale from nothing. My brother, my own brother, she says, has been stealing every letter I sent, every letter for six years. Can you believe such a thing? My own brother. Up to this time, she says, she has been writing to Marmolsky's place in New York...you remember the tailor where I was going?...for six years she sends letters and hears nothing. No one knows anything, not old Marmolsky, nor the Rabbi who cooked the plan, nor the postman who takes the mail. Only Vladimir, my own brother who steals the letters Danya sends and steals the letter and the money I send. It can't be so."

"But how does the letter come to you after all this time? How did she find where you are, how did she find all this out?"

"Vladimir ran away, she writes. He made of my money a makhorka. She found him smoking these green cigarettes at the tavern, drunk and crazy he was, she says. She almost killed him with her own hands, and he is two heads higher than she, and she almost killed him with her own hands..."

"And...?" Riznewsky leaned toward Mikolai who stood bent over, shaking his head.

"After that, when my next letter came with the ten dollars, the postman remembered her name and ran to her with the letter. Then she could see why her letters never came to me, and why she never heard one word from me, not one letter had come to her. So now she writes and says send more money. It will be safe. You see, she runs my life from across the oceans."

Not since he had found Mikolai kneeling at the wharf had Riznewsky seen this tranquil man so moved in sadness.

"By gosh," Mikolai repeated several times in English. "By gosh, what is this story? How can such a thing be?"

The tears came. Then his hands, reaching for the letter trembled so that he had to still them by holding at the edge of the workbench. Then his knees became weak. "What an old woman I am. I weep like an old woman."

Riznewsky quickly pushed a nearby milk stool to Mikolai and helped him sit down. He stood over him puzzling what he would do if Mikolai fell into a faint. He had seen it before, but he couldn't remember what he should do.

Mikolai started to laugh, then they laughed together like two boys who had discovered a secret. Mikolai threw up his hands.

"Well, what can I do? You see, my friend, you hound me and hound me and finally I will take a wife."

John said he must run to tell Hazel. She would never forgive him if he didn't tell her right away.

"Yes, yes, run and tell her the good news. No more work today, no more roofing. I shake like an old man. I cannot hammer the nails. Run to tell Hazel. I will send some wine with you. Drink some wine for me and my Danya. Tell Hazel she should not hunt for a wife for me any longer. I have found my wife. Hazel can rest now, I take a wife of my own."

John came back the next day. He said Hazel thought Mikolai should borrow money from the bank and send it all at one time. They will give money for your farm, Hazel said. She understood it all, and you pay back little by little.

But when they talked to the banker the plan was not so simple. Russia was now in a turmoil, maybe going into a civil war. They would be lucky if mail got there from America at this time. But no money could be sent now. After things settled, but not now. There was no order to the life and law there now. Everything had to be settled first. No money could be sent. Later. Wait a while, maybe later.

Even so the letters between Mikolai and Danya crossed the ocean and found their destination unhindered at either end, though it took many weeks before answers came back.

***

There was little cause for joy in Danya's village during these bad times, but since the exposure of how she had been wronged, the arrival of each of Mikolai's letters became a link to hope, the evidence that somewhere life and times would be better.

She must read the letter to them, the men gathered at the tavern must hear what Mikolai said of America. The men gathered to grumble, for there was little drink now. They coaxed her to bring the letters to the tavern, to read them aloud.

What a country it must be, America. Is it true, he talks to the banker, a common farmer? And they will give him money? Not now? Oh too bad, Danya, but things will be settled soon he says? For us, too, here in this country he says?

Oh look, what a fine house he has, all of wood, painted white like a Tsar's palace. And five rooms you say, all his? With a stove to heat every room? How can it be? No snow yet, he says, and we have two months of snow before he sends the letter. Think how the grain must grow. And he rides in a car, an American car? He must live like a king in America. He, he is a smart fellow, that Mikolai. He in his dandy American suit with the fine necktie. And yes, he is handsome, Danya. What a fancy mustache. Your life will be blessed now with good fortune, we can see that.

But nothing was settled. When the great famine swept through the villages even the letters ceased to distract from the immediacy of hunger and death surrounding them all. Vacant eyes listened, no voice had strength any longer to comment.

Old Marmolsky lived another winter, but even such a shrunken body needed more than a crust of bread and boiled water to function. On such a diet did Danya subsist, the crust so hard she could hold it for minutes in her mouth before it was fit to chew and swallow.

Months went by between her letters before she could find money to buy stamps. She would explain to Mikolai that the winter was hard and there was little food. Even when Mikolai sent five dollars or ten in another letter the money was of no use. There were no goods to buy.

When and how times got better no one could remember for sure. They had lived so long in a daze that their hopes could find no expression. Perhaps the farmers' wives, groveling in the spring ground for last year's overlooked potatoes were the first who saw the hope, who could remember what hope was, and could call it by name. Was it possible that the grass could come so early. They should plant right away. Plant what? Every potato was devoured, every seed of grain long baked and eaten.

They ate the early grass roots, the buds of trees that offered themselves to unbelieving eyes and hands weeks earlier than any could remember seeing them before.

Some said the rail lines were mended and the trains would come with seed, with food. The new leaders would send food and help for all the people, for all who were left alive.

AMERICA 1923

Eleven years after she had sent Mikolai off to America, Danya came to that country to join him. She came in the confusion of anonymous masses streaming out of Europe toward the promise of something that might mend or erase the suffering, the horrors they had endured as insignificant entities in a struggle few of them understood.

Riznewsky went with the nervous Mikolai to meet the great ship that was bringing Danya to America. Mikolai was self-conscious yet carried himself proudly in his new glen plaid suit with the high starched shirt collar. He'd borrowed a hat from John that he held with new gloves in one hand. He'd driven his own wagon to the railway station from where they took the slow train to New York City. He hadn't been to this city since he'd arrived as a destitute fugitive years ago. Now he had money in his pocket, understood the language around him. Now there was no awe or fear of the city.

During those good years he had spent in America, the memories of his past came in occasional dreams, the worse of which was the awful discovery by the old priest. Other than that he was not, in his own mind, the same man who inhabited the dreams.

Good fortune had served his appearance well, too. The blonde hair was still thick, bleached lighter by long days under the sun.

The nose, straight and proud, the brilliant blue eyes no longer so timid, frequently reflected the enjoyment of a good life. Early fears had left no scars there.

If some shyness remained as he was forced into the outside world it was balanced by a private conviction that he had earned his way and good fortune by the grace of God, and nothing could be taken from him now. He was still a stranger in a strange country, but on the farm, on his own land, he was surrounded by the comfort of knowing he was all that he might have been. His job on earth was matched to him. He was fulfilled.

Had time or troubles aged him he might have been prepared for the woman who came finally to be his wife. Ravaged more by deprivations and terrors of the times than by a gentler wearing of time, she stood before him such an unfamiliar creature that he could not believe it was the strong bright-faced girl who had sent him away that long ago Christmas.

Goodbye my sweetheart. I will come to you when it is time.

It was her eyes that held his attention. They had changed the most. The quick dark eyes, at once young and shrewd and bright were hers no longer. They were glazed by suffering, suspicion and knowledge of hate. Strange endless depths came fleeting through the glaze. The fine straight brows had dropped into a small scowl, and the lips, still full, turned down in thin cheeks as though they had never been moved by a smile. Her skin was still white and unmarked, but had the pallor of the old who cannot walk into the light. The once glossy deep brown hair was dulled by the same absence of light.

"My golly, Danya, my golly!" he said in English, then in Russian. "What trouble, what trouble have you seen!" He caught her in the self-conscious embrace of a man who cannot find words to speak.

"What a miracle, Mikol, that I am here. It is a miracle." She could not even cry.

"My golly, my golly, what was our Russia like?"

"Like hell, I tell you. Like hell. It is a miracle I came to you through that hell."

"How long, how long I have waited and prayed and worried for you. How many hours have I prayed for your health and your safety."

"Oh, to thank God, I am here. Finally I am here."

The time consuming, tiring formalities must be attended to. Like so many who came in those years, Danya had no record of her birth, and no exact knowledge of her age. When the clerk asked for her age or her birth certificate she turned to Mikolai for help. He consulted with John who explained the difference between the Russian and American calendars and asked the clerk if they could have some time to figure it out.

"It's not important, just guess," the clerk snapped in an impatient tone.

Danya was confused. Mikolai asked if she was younger than he. Yes, maybe three years, she guessed. He wrote the numbers for the clerk, Age: 32.

John said they should be married there in the city because there was no Russian Orthodox church near their town. He made inquiries and though it was late in the day they went to the city hall where they stood in line with others like themselves to be officially married in the eyes of the American law. In a language she could not yet understand, Danya heard, "What God has joined together let no man put asunder."

The three made the long slow journey back to Mikolai's farm. They spoke few words. John pointed out the house and farm as they came toward it.

"Mikolai has found such a fine place for you. Alone he has kept this small farm, waiting for his wife. See, up the hill, the house on the hill over the pond. He will not say, but I will tell you he is proud like a king of his farm."

"Oh, it looks fine, so fine. Yes, it is as in the picture he sent, but now it is real." Danya could not keep the tears back. She bent her head into the palm of her hands. "Forgive me, my husband, I cry like a child. I cry for my happiness. I had nearly lost my hope and now I am here in our own place, together with you."

Riznewsky did not tarry. It would be late when he got to his farm and Hazel might worry that they had not found Danya. He must hurry home.

***

Hazel had found a big bed and matching bureau at an auction. She and John had convinced Mikolai that it was worth ten dollars, that he must have something better for a wife than the white iron bed he then had. The new bed was of wood. The high head board and foot board were painted black and traced with a delicate border of yellow daisies connected by a thin gold vine hung with green leaves. The bureau was the biggest one Mikolai had ever seen, and much bigger than two people would ever use, he was sure. But he gave in because they knew about such things, and they installed the furniture with some difficulty into the room, now made very small, next to the kitchen where his married life would begin.

Hazel and her sister had come days before Danya's arrival and scrubbed away some of the evidence that no woman had touched this house for many years. The windows and doors, the oak floor of the kitchen and the linoleum under the big cook stove must be rid of splatters that accumulate under a man's unseeing eyes. The wooden slat bench next to the sink was so soiled with grease and old milk stains that Hazel wanted John to make a new one. But how could he, in just two days? Just scrub, he said, it will get clean.

And those sheets and the quilt, fit for a farm hand, not for a wife. Part with some of your money, Mikolai and we will find some fine cotton sheets for your woman, they told him.

The least of all they did to prepare for her arrival would have been a gift for Danya to whom the very existence of such a house was miracle enough. With its great kitchen and three other rooms it was the biggest house she had seen for just two people. And to have a special room for sleeping when for these past years she had shared the dreams and snores of others in the big rooms that combine eating, sleeping and living. They need not have worried that she would be offended by a dusty floor, not in a house like this.

In that new bed with the border of daisies and gold vines, their marriage was consummated with the naturalness of people to whom the propagation of their own holds no more mystery and needs no more explanation that does the freshening of the farm herd.

Mikolai had never been with a woman. Of these things he had spoken to no man. Of the subtle pleasures and expectations of the modern marriage bed he had no knowledge. In their togetherness Danya found the safety her body had yearned for without knowing for what it ached. She had come to be wife and mother, and if there were realm of emotions beyond what they had together, she too had no expectations of them. In the pain of pleasure they belonged to each other.

***

Mindful that she was not the strong young woman he had left behind, Mikolai worked the farm alone, never asking or expecting Danya to help. John also was aware of this and on occasions would stop by to offer help.

Gradually strength and some of her youth returned to Danya, thanks to a short winter and long days of sunshine when she could walk with her husband to the pasture beyond the swamp or go with him into the woods to pick the blueberries that ripened so fast they could return the next day to fill the same buckets with yesterday's green fruit.

When she was no longer so tender Mikolai dared ask again for more news of his family and brother.

"Your mother, gone, as I told you in a letter, gone long ago without suffering or tears. Gone from old age."

"And the brother?"

"That stinking snake, gone too, no one knows where. They took all the farms, the new government, and Vladimir had no place. He just went away. No one cared. No one could say where."

"And the old priest, the ugly drunken one?"

"Gone too, early in the first famine, behind the closed church door."

"And the family Katrovskya, the farm next to mine?"

"All gone."

"And their children too?"

"All gone."

"And Marmolsky, the old man, he too?"

"Yes, died in his sleep of hunger or old age, who can tell which."

"And Narvich, the postman who brought you my mail?"

"Oh, what a viper, a poison viper. God spared him too long. He died with his wife by his very own hand."

"A viper? Why do you say a viper?"

"He stole from Marmolsky as Vladimir stole from me."

"What? Stole his money?"

"Yes, his hot hand in the mailbag, stealing the money sent by the son from America, and helped in his crime by the Marmolsky daughter Serina who wrote back send more."

"Serina, the young one who sat in the shop? The laughing one, the pretty one, you say so for sure? How can I believe such a thing?"

"For sure, I tell you. That greedy one, who stole from her father to dress herself in fine clothes. But she could not keep her own life...she was thrown to the swamp for fear she would talk."

"How do you mean thrown to the swamp?"

"Found frozen in the swamp, pushed by the postman, I'm sure, for fear she would talk."

"It was so bad?" Mikolai did not want to believe.

"Worse than the telling. Much worse, Things I cannot say for fear they will come back into my mind too often."

Later into the fall Danya was strong enough to help in the fields with the second haying. She cut off her thick dark hair so it fell just past her ears. It was too hot on her neck, she said, and took all her strength.

She walked lightly now over the paths. She measured the fields with her eyes. Her place, her land. Finally they had their place together. Mikolai had made the wise choice, even if it had meant the confusion and sadness of waiting, all that time, not knowing where he was. God had guided him to this place, she reasoned, where they had come together. Every tree, every bush, every flower in the swamp, every blade of grass belongs to them.

One day when she carried water to the men in the fields she came close to Mikolai and in a quiet voice she told him they would have a child in the spring.

PROSPERITY

The madness of good times in those years before the great depression had the same relentless force of any madness that must end in tragedy. As in the chaos that she had lived through, Danya watched again the same unconcern for the future. This time instead of the agony of hunger, the search for food and warmth that had taken hold of people in her Russian village, the madness was the frantic need to find ways to spend the money, which indeed seemed to drop from the trees.

John came with the news that a new factory in the town needed workers. They paid so much it was better to sell your livestock and your farm and go to work in the factory. In two months a man could make a farmer's yearly wage. He would go tomorrow and Mikolai, he advised, should go with him to find factory work.

No, Miklolai said he would not go. His farm was good and the money was plenty for them. He had six cows now and the chickens gave up the biggest eggs in the market. He had leased an acre for more potatoes and every plant was growing. He would not leave all his hard work to sit in a dark factory.

Danya felt otherwise. Perhaps it was because she had gone through another diseased time that she was an easier victim for the fever to find. She sat in her rocking chair, rounded by the months of her pregnancy, listened and said nothing so long as John was there.

After he left she put her knitting in the basket and decided she must speak to change Mikolai's mind. After all, they would have a house full of children pretty soon, and he should think of that, too. A farmer's wage might be enough for two of them, and maybe one or two more. But they would have a big family and would need more money, more food. Even a bigger house.

"Mikol, maybe you should go to the factory for work."

"Why should I work in a factory? You see I have a good farm and plenty of food. Riznewsky makes a joke. He will not go either, for his farm is good and he could never make so much in a factory as he does from his fields. He has the best crops in all the towns near here."

"Go only for the winter, then. You could go now and through the wintertime when there is not so much work on the farm. When spring comes the farm will be waiting for you. Think of the money we could save, enough for a bigger house, Mikol. We could buy more land, the lots next to our swamp, the one with the spring and the great patches of berries."

"We have enough land now for one man to work."

"But soon we will have sons. And they grow fast and can work. They will need land of their own. Now we should make the money and buy the land for their future."

"Who milks the cows while I work in the factory, eh? And who throws the hay and feeds the chickens every cold day when you have all the children? You say there is no work in the winter, but you cannot see from your rocking chair. There is plenty of work, plenty of work here for one man, all winter long, all the year round."

"My husband, you see I am strong now. I can work now. I can work like a man, like I did in the old country. There did I not milk the cows and chase the chickens? And sew and tend old Marmolsky, and in harder winters than you see in this place, I tell you!'

"You are strong because you sit and rock with the child. When the child comes you will be too busy and then what? Do you think to hire someone else to do my work then?"

"No, no. I can work now. I have all the day. I will go slow. Have I not worked in the fields and at the plow helping you these months? Did I complain? Did I not do my share almost like a man?"

"All right. We will see, when the child comes. We will see if you can do so much on the farm."

"That is too late. John says now they want the workers, now, Mikolai. You should go tomorrow with him and find a job."

"It is too soon."

"No, go when they need you. Go before they have too many."

Mikolai thought for an out. "Maybe they have enough hired already."

"No, I know they do not. John said in today's paper they ask for more workers. Go tomorrow, Mikol, and see if they will take you. Go with John. I saw he was serious, he was not making a joke. Go early. Don't worry about the farm."

They hired John and Mikolai and twenty other men who came from the vicinity, farm laborers who would leave their small farms to take a richer paying job turning out the products demanded by the growing numbers of the prosperous: fancy bone button hooks, cosmetic cases, bone buttons and combs, celluloid shaving cups. Every week another product, velvet lined cases for manicure tools, pink lined celluloid handkerchief boxes, things Mikolai never knew existed until he saw them come to form on the work tables under his hands.

With few misgivings Mikolai became accustomed to the new schedule. He woke early each day, milked the cows, then walked the two miles to work inside the factory. The noise of the machines annoyed him, but the pay envelopes compensated for the discomfort. Business was booming, the men now worked Saturdays as well and families welcomed the monetary fruits of their husbands' labor.

Danya lost the baby in the seventh month. She was in the barn pitching hay for the cow beds when she realized it was happening. She'd shouted as loudly as she'd ever known she could and the neighbor across the road came to help.

She told Mikolai he must accept it because of her age and because it was the first one. Her own mother, she reminded him, had lost her first one. It was common and nothing to cry over. Others would come, too fast maybe. He shouldn't be so dark about it. She would have more. Soon enough she would have more, she knew.

"In a way it is good, my husband, because we have time to make the house bigger."

"Do you think I have made so much money to build a bigger house?"

"Hazel tells me that they build a new house, not with their own money, but borrowed money from the bank. A building loan bank, a special bank just for building houses.

"Is this house not big enough?

"Yes, for now, but this is the best time to make it bigger, when the building company loans money and when I can help with the work."

"I know only a little about borrowing money from buying this house before you came. If John and Hazel want a new house they can find more money than I can. Borrowing is not for me again."

"We will ask Hazel. She showed me, she has a book. Every month she goes to the bank and they mark it in the book when she pays. Not much money each month, Mikol, and now you make plenty of money."

He shrugged. He gave in. She probably was right. Women know more about such tings, about keeping a family comfortable. He would agree. He sat down by the kitchen stove and read his paper while Danya, thinking of tomorrow, worked happily at her sewing.

***

The next baby came and the next. But they both died at their birth. Hazel said Danya must go to the hospital next time. She should not wait to have the baby in the house, but must go to the hospital to be safe. She should go to New Haven, to the hospital where she, Hazel, had gone for delivering her children. She must go early, before the time came, and they would keep her baby alive.

John, with Hazel, drove Danya to the hospital in his new car weeks before the next baby was due. It was a Sunday afternoon. Mikolai couldn't go with them. He had to stay on the farm to take care of the animals.

In the hospital they punched her with needles and gave her medicine and food she couldn't put in her mouth. No one there spoke her language, no one came when she called in the night.

She heard babies crying somewhere nearby. New babies crying out to the world. Her own would cry out soon, she was sure of it, her own son.

"How much money to stay here, Mikolai, in this hospital?" she asked when he came to visit.

"We have enough. John says we have plenty. Pretty soon the times will come and you will come home with the child."

"Bring me my own bread, Mikol. They try to feed me bread made of paste. Bring my own bread to me so I can eat."

"Next time, yes Danya, next time I come."

But this baby, too, was stillborn despite all the hospital care.

"Four sons have I lost, four sons," she wept to the night. No one understood her and she slept in her tears. "Four sons I have lost" and she cried far into the night.

In the deepest time of her troubled sleep He came to her, while her cheeks were still wet with tears and her head throbbed from the pain of it all.

When she turned on her pillow she saw Him, dressed in a soft white robe that barely covered the scars on his hands and feet. He stepped down, floated down from the cross, moving more like an angel than a man. His dark hair moved as though a faint breeze went before Him, and His eyes looked out at her with a greater compassion and understanding than could come through any human heart. He spoke to her with words that had no sound, yet the music of them came to her ears and she understood all He said.

"Have I not been with you all the days of your life?
Have I not saved you from the cold and the wolves?
Found you shelter and food?

Swept you out of the devil's hand when he thought to make his claim?
Guided your feet from the edge of the cliff to the place you belong?
Kept your breath in your body,
Given the gifts to your hands?
Have I not bent toward you to lift the weight from your heart?
Stay with me, trust me, only believe.
Be comforted. Wait and believe.
Wait, for the time will come.
Wait and believe."

His hand touched her forehead and she pulled the edge of the robe to her lips, felt the softness of the white cloth before it moved like a cloud away from her hands.

All the gentleness the world could know looked out from those eyes when He went from her, and she understood. The light of the cross was behind Him, around Him. The sky above His cross and the ground under His feet gave back the incredible light, at once cool and warm, dark and bright. She breathed in the blessing and passed into the happy sleep of a beloved child.

The nurse who wakened Danya in the morning noticed nothing unusual. She was relieved that the woman was calmer. She had been so upset last night, the chart noted. Danya smiled at the nurse who remembered she had not seen her smile at all before, poor woman. Well, it was hard on her, to lose this child at such an age. But she seemed much calmer this morning.
'Patient calmer' she wrote on the chart.

The disappointment for Mikolai this time was as great as to Danya. They had nearly had a living son. Is it possible there would be no children for them? For this, for nothing, did he sweat on the farm and run every morning to the factory, for a house with no children?

Danya understood his mood and would not join it. "Never mind. Never mind. There will be more. I know there will be more. Do not be so deep and troubled this time, my husband."

"How can you say, how can you be sure? Already I am an old man, soon old enough to be a grandfather to the children I do not have, maybe will never have."

"Don't keep your worry, my husband. The time will come."

She could not tell him of her visitor in the night. He would not believe. But she would not let the calm slip from her. She would believe for both of them. She wouldn't listen to his worrying. She would not listen even to her own doubts which tried every day to work their way into her new peacefulness. She would wait. She would believe. She knew the time would come.

That winter Mikolai was taken with a bad cold, which kept him a week home from work. Danya went to the doctor in the town, Dr. Cobb, whose office was next to the grocery store where she shopped.

It was pneumonia, worse than a cold, the doctor said. He must stay home, stay in bed or he could be worse. It was a dangerous cold. It was a great danger to him. He must stay in the house, in bed. He must be very careful. Did she understand?

"Yes. My husband says his head hurts."

"It is the fever. He has pneumonia and with it comes a bad fever."

"Not just his head, in his ears, he says, there it is painful."

"Maybe there is some damage there. Was he sick before like this?"

"No, he says he doesn't remember that he was sick before."

"An infection in the ear, perhaps, from another cold?"

"He says the noise pounds in his head."

The doctor examined Mikolai again. "A bad infection, I can see. There must have been damage before. He doesn't remember anything from before, another sickness like this, are you sure?" Days later he came again to see how Mikolai was coming along.

"No, I am telling you, doctor, he can't remember any time that he was sick like this."

"Nothing to worry about too much, perhaps just an ear infection. It will go away."

"But he says the noise is bad, it is always there."

"That's because the was some damage before. He won't hear so well from now on, especially in one ear. There will be some deafness in that ear, but the pneumonia is gone. The real danger is over."

"The noise bothers him all the time, even now when he should be better."

"From the deafness, the damage, some catarrh left from the pneumonia, that might make the noises in his head. But there is nothing else we can do."

Danya tried to understand everything the doctor said. He repeated and repeated so she could get the words. She tried to explain it all to Mikolai. He blamed in on the factory. The noisy damp factory where he sat nine hours every day. What kind of life for a man, to sit in one place all day, in the middle of so much noise. No wonder his head goes around all the time.

Danya wouldn't listen.

Mikolai grumbled behind his newspaper.

John said he should go to another doctor, to an ear specialist. He should have an operation and he would hear all right after that.

"It will cost some money, Mikolai, it is a big doctor you know, in Hartford. But he is a good one, he is a specialist in head noises from deafness."

Mikolai listened, he was somewhat relieved. "We have plenty. I will go to him."

The operation couldn't help. The damage was from a time long past, long gone from his memory. There would be some good days and some bad days with the head noises. Nothing more could be done, the specialist told him.

Mikolai's detachment grew. Danya's voice, half heard through the head noises irked him. She should speak louder, not in such a small quiet voice like a girl.

He made the wrong answers to questions and was annoyed, then embarrassed when the men at the factory thought he joked and he meant to be serious. He should have stayed on the farm, he kept thinking. The factory was no place for a farmer. No sun all day long, only noise from every side. That was the place for city people, not for a man who belonged out on his land.

Danya kept her silence in the midst of his unhappiness and his grumbling. Oh, he begins to be like an old man, she thought. We must not go into our old age without children. Everything will be good again if children come to us, as I was promised. I must believe. Nothing will shake my belief now. And she prayed. Her answer came.

Doctor Cobb delivered the child, the girl child who arrived the next year. He drove up the winding dirt road in his car with the nervous Mikolai who had run all the way to town to call him when Danya said it was time.

There in his house, in the bed trimmed with daisies, his first living child was born.

He looked up from his newspaper when the doctor brought her little form into the kitchen.

"Her eyes look big as a cow's," he said. That's all he could speak. He had no more words. He couldn't really see much more, his own eyes were so full of thankful tears. He went back to his newspaper, but then remembered he should feed the chickens. He walked outside, down the stone steps, wiping his tears. Well, one girl, if she's strong, can work like a man on the farm, he reasoned.

He was standing in the middle of the cackling chickens when he realized he had forgotten to bring their feed.

DANGER

Years before, in this little town, Angus Bent had come into the world with the somewhat musty distinction of extending the direct lineage of a man hung on the gallows as a Salem witch in the early days of the New England colonies.

Whatever credence the story lost for grownups in the retelling, it never failed to thrill and frighten the young people in the family when it was held generation after generation as a warning that the wages of disobedience and sin were certainly suffering and death.

As it was told, Jarvis Bent had preferred the company of tinkers and wastrels to the proper company of the young people with whom he was raised in the new town of Salem. Instead of attending church on Sunday mornings he would sit in the tinker's wagon laughing and singing the most unholy songs.

Without the blessings of his parents and against the laws of the church and the land, he took for a woman the tinker's daughter, a dark skinned girl who sang under the moon and ran through the woods with her uncombed black hair streaming in the wind.

When Jarvis came to his senses and tried to leave the girl to return to his home, she fell into a strange fit, cursed him and died right there, curled into an anguished form at his feet.

A few years later, after he married a proper young lady and fathered a son, he was struck by the hallucination that someone else possessed his body. He began to sing and run about in the wind, and when the townspeople saw him they too believed he was possessed, inhabited by the dark witch he had taken in sin.

They came upon him one day, sitting in the woods, singing with a woman's voice and combing his long uncut hair with the twigs of a tree, staring out from strangely glossed eyes that shone deep and brown without blinking.

At least that's what they said, his wife and his brother, and why should a wife holding her young son in her arms tell anything but the truth before the judge and the people? And the woe-filled brother, wringing his hand after he swore to the truth of the terrible scene.

They hung Jarvis Bent by the neck until he died, taking with him the witch who had lured him from his family in the unwise days of his youth.

The children could learn later, if they cared to, that Jarvis's widow soon married his kind brother. There were no children to add to that tree, and the one son Jarvis had left behind carried Jarvis's name and fateful lesson through to ongoing generations.

Of course, after they were grown and understood these things, none believed such a tale.

Except for Angus Bent.

He couldn't remember when he first heard the story, but he never doubted the truth of it.

She came often to him in the night, too, dancing and singing when he tried to say his prayers. And she tried to possess him, tried to steal his body in the night when he slept. But he woke just in time. There he would be, floating high toward the ceiling, looking down at his own body asleep on the bed. And there she was, a dark-eyed witch, looking up at him, laughing and singing, sinking into his body, disappearing into his body asleep on the bed.

Most often he got back to his body in time. He would waken, greatly frightened, but he would feel his arms and his stomach, his head and his legs, until he was sure he had gotten back to his body before she could do it harm. It was still his. She was gone. Until the next time.

As he grew up she became more brazen. She would come to him in the church while the minister gave the sermon, or while the choir sang a hymn. He never saw her then, but he could hear her laugh and feel her creeping into his body. Sometimes he was afraid to sing the hymn, stung with a fear that her voice, a woman's voice, might come out of his mouth, that perhaps this time she would take her claim, take his body for her own.

He was sent to college and it was during the fourth year there that he knew she was gone forever, gone perhaps to haunt another Bent until she was vanquished by another woman in real flesh.

Angus Bent was a respectable man. He fought for his country in the war and returned to his grateful small town where he courted the handsome new schoolteacher and married her in the prim white Congregational Church that rose like a white spike out of the giant elm trees at the end of the village green.

When his wife's father died Angus left his banking job to take over the prosperous insurance business left behind.

There was such prosperity about. Because he was such a respectable man and educated in business and banking, he was elected president of the building and loan society that was formed to accommodate the needs of the population moving into the valley towns. The men worked in the small factories, which were more evidence that America, indeed the land of opportunity, could supply all that was needed by those who came looking.

He really didn't like dealing with those foreigners. They had no education and besides not knowing the language, they couldn't understand the terms of the loans, the building restrictions that must be followed to validate the loan.

The women were the most difficult for him. He would spend a half hour explaining that one must cash the paycheck at the bank before taking anything out in payment. No, he wasn't a real bank, only a business to loan money for building and improving homes, he tried to explain.

The misunderstandings and squabbles between the contractors and his borrowers were all brought to his office, annoying him but were somehow resolved. There were times that Bent couldn't follow what was spoken in front of him. They should make them learn the language before they could buy property in this country, he thought. It was a shame really, they probably couldn't read or write or count, either. Well, it was business for him.

He couldn't explain even to himself why he was so discomforted in their presence, as more of these foreigners moved into the village. Their multitudes of children, their clothes, the cooking smells that clung to them when they came to his office to apply for mortgages. He began to know before they spoke from which country they came. He could separate the Italians and the Poles by their clothes and usually by their coloring. And the German Jews, well he had no use for them either, but at least they could count and understand numbers.

There were the unusual ones. The tall reserved German who spoke refined English. The Irish girl with her bastard son trying to buy a house, showing the money with which her lover's family had sent her to this obscure little town far from where they lived.

And there was Hazel Phillips. Her name was Riznewsky now. They had gone to high school together. She was pretty shrewd, smart as a businessman. In fact, he knew it was because of her that John Riznewsky owned what he did, one of the best farm pieces in the entire valley. Too bad she had married a foreigner. She should have waited until after the war when the local men came back. It was a relief from the other annoyances to have her stop by the office with the payment for their new house. A relief to be able to understand the words spoken to him.

This time she brought a woman with her. Italian, Bent thought at first, but no, by the clothes he guessed she must be Polish, maybe Russian. What was it that made him stare at her? She seemed familiar in an unsettling way. He couldn't place the name, though he checked the files later to see if she had been in the office before. Her English was barely passable...probably arrived a short time ago...but something about her, the voice? No, the eyes, the way they stared back, the way those eyes listened, staring at him as he spoke, as she leaned toward him. Too familiar.

Happily Hazel had learned enough Polish from her husband to translate what this woman wanted, Bent thought. Sometimes when she couldn't explain Hazel would speak in German to her as well. She would take the forms to be filled out, Hazel said. She wanted to take the papers home to her husband.

Curious, the way she looked at him. Half humble, half defiant, Bent thought after they left. And still so familiar. He was sure he'd seen her somewhere before. He couldn't place her at all. He went through the form Hazel had started to fill out. Born in Russia, he read. No, he was sure he hadn't seen her in his office before. He didn't remember that they'd had any Russians before. It bothered him, made him uneasy, that something about her should be so familiar, yet he couldn't recall a reason why. So irksome. He fumbled with the paper trying to recall.

That night the dream, that long absent dream, returned to Angus Bent. The dark-eyed witch pushing, pushing at his unconscious form. He was there, light headed and vacant eyed, floating away from his own body below on the bed beside his sleeping wife. Farther away, higher he went. Oh God, are these ceilings so high? Stop me, stop me. Help me, stop! Came the soundless cries.

She was down there again, the dark haired witch, trying to claim his body. But her appearance had changed. Her hair was cut short and her body was slower, less graceful than the witch of his youth. Her body was fuller, rounder, softer. She had aged with the times, and her voice, her wild singing voice, came more slowly, more calmly, more sure, with a song much less teasing. This time the song was sharper, more sure. And the black eyes, not laughing, but defiant and sure. She had waited and waited, and now Bent realized she wasn't teasing, she was sure.

He was helpless to stop her, helplessly suspended far from his body, watching her take his body. She sank into his body as she'd tried to do before. This time he watched her, helpless, too late to stop her. He couldn't waken himself to stop her. Her unblinking deep dark eyes, now half laughing, defiant and sure. She became one with his body. He watched while she possessed his body, his unconscious body, there below him on the bed.

Too late. Then by an effort that left him rolling in sweat Angus got back into his body. Too late. He knew in the morning he no longer had sole ownership of his body. He was possessed by another. Possessed by the witch of the old stories and his dreams.

He walked with that knowledge. He sat with that knowledge. He opened his mouth to speak not knowing whose voice would come forth. He wanted to race out of the office, afraid to be found out, afraid he might sing out as he'd heard her sing. But he must work. Every day there was another mortgage to attend to. The town was growing.

The houses sprang up on every hilltop, a sorry sight to some of the native New Englanders whose fastidious pride in their heritage had preserved the sleepy little town of Stanton and its old houses in quite the same fashion their generations had done before them.

Prior to this great influx of new factories and foreign workers, most of the houses could boast, on a neat plaque, the early date of their structure. 1742, or 1786, and one even earlier, 1689. Some of course were built in the latter 1890s, but in dignified good taste, not like some of the houses built by these foreigners. Well, they knew they had to resign themselves to this with the changing times, but it really was all too common, too crude and unsettling, too foreign for the staid set folks proud of their American heritage.

In the late years of the 1920's the pace of everything quickened. With their children together in classrooms and graduation services, and the tempting strawberry festival that the Catholic ladies had every summer, many of the differences were resolved, even forgotten, and these foreign families became an accepted part of the town.

Times were too good to hold a grudge about what had happened to the pretty little town. You could understand most of the foreigners now, they had picked up some English. And with the strict New England schooling their children were hardly discernible from the rest. Maybe by their clothes now and then, but at least they had proper manners and could speak English as though they were true Americans.

And of course, men like Angus Bent had to admit, without all these new people the town businesses would not be having such a tremendous boom as they did. These people were not lazy. They worked hard as any Americans. They saved money and were always ready to buy better goods, wiser insurance, bigger houses. He must admit, he said to a business friend, they had made a big difference in the town.

And to me, he said to himself with a slight shudder.

One afternoon Hazel Phillips came again to his office and waited for the little Russian woman to come with her papers. When Danya Vorodinov walked in and sat on the edge of her chair opposite his desk, Angus Bent looked into her familiar face. He drew back with a sharp grunt. He knew now where he had seen those eyes before.

STANTON 1929

When the silence came, most of the new houses stood finished on solid ground. Some may not have been completed on the inside, but families were able to move in and their mortgages were active.

The shops closed. The men rose to the morning with no hope of work. The money was spent. The fields were unplanted. The children kept growing. The mortgages would not disappear. Yesterday's source of pride, the stone and wood houses, the salute to prosperous times, were today's ogres on their owners' backs. The bewildered waited. There was no good news.

Mikolai was among the bewildered. Part of him was always an onlooker, seeing without knowing what part he himself played in the world about him. With the good times he had erased the other reality through which he had suffered so long ago. He could not now feel a part of what fell down around him. He could not sense the magnitude of what had happened. He listened to the wails of doom, not believing these things could be happening also to him.

Danya was not bewildered. It was too close to the past for her not to recognize the savage textures of a population tainted with fear. She had seen it, smelled it, tasted it and lived through it, and she was not bewildered. She knew what this was all about. What was happening was as real as the child she carried on her arm against the swelling presence of the next one.

She had seen babies shrink and die when the mother's milk dried in her breasts for want of a glass of water. She had seen men, old and young, sitting like this, dazed, not part of the world around them. They sat through the days in the light they never knew when they went to their jobs. Stolen from them was their reason to live, their very manhood. The vacant eyes, the thrice-told joke that could no longer bring a smile. She had seen it all before.

She had seen bare shop windows, shopkeepers sitting at the door because they had no other place to go, nothing to do. The stores emptied of bread, grown men waiting in line for soup so thin and tasteless they might in other days have beat their own wives for serving them such. She had seen neighbors' doors close to a child's knock for fear the hand would be held out for food.

All this returned vividly from memories that had begun to fade away. This catastrophe destroyed the last fragments of the youth that had somehow clung to her through the ordeals of losing her children. Fading was the defiant toss of her head, the teasing eyes, the light-hearted songs. Old memories began to register the pain in the places they had once occupied. They stole into the light of her eyes and grabbed at her hopes.

She said her prayers at night with grim deliberation while her mind was divided by the doubts she felt. Into her eyes crept the discomforts of her soul. She gathered her senses in the fear ridden days and tried to squeeze from them some promise of hope. She found little.

This time it was not she alone who must survive. There were the babies and her husband. His eyes could still dance and laugh in the sun. But he had not suffered, and how could he know what was to come? He had not seen what could happen to human animals when the food disappears before it reaches their mouths. She must keep him strong and well, somehow, for if she should die he must be able to care for the children. There was no one else here. Everyone had the same miseries. She must keep him busy. A man should not sit through the day, only to think. He must stay busy.

The house. What of the house, not yet finished? What is to happen when the time comes and there is no money to mark in the book? What did they tell her in the office when she took the papers? If they took the house from them, what then? Where would they go in the winter? There was no brother, no mother, no Marmolsky this time. The barn? But the land and the barn, they would be taken too. They would take it all from her.

NO! By God no! She would not move. Let them come to her and try to march through her door. She would not let them step one inch into her house. Not one inch! They could wait for their money. What should they cry about? They could wait for a while for their money. Everyone was in trouble together, so they should not chase her out from her own house. Somehow later she would find the money. Then she would pay what was owed.

There must be wood for the stove. They must keep wood for the cooking and heating. The children must be warm in the winter. Mikolai must work and pile the wood for the stove. If the baby comes early there must be a warm house.

Peel the potatoes thinner. Store up the cheese. Drink milk mixed with water. Chew on the seed of the apples and pears. Pick the pumpkin seeds from the chicken feed, the last bag of chicken feed.

Mikolai should have his tobacco. A man should have his tobacco when he chops wood in the cold with no meat in his house. Somewhere, the snuff, the tobacco, hidden for him in a good place. But in her worries she couldn't remember the place.

The winter passed, each day going away heavily, leaving the place for another uncertain day.

The second girl was born in the same bed trimmed with the pretty daisies. It was May and there was some hope that this summer would bring good crops. The pears could be canned. The grass looked good, better than last year. Maybe the cow, their last cow, would calf and they would have milk and cheese into the next winter.

By a miracle the baby was born on time and healthy. She would need cow's milk because she could not find enough nursing from Danya. All winter she had deprived herself, eating only after Mikolai and the other child were fed. Now her body was unable to give the new child enough milk.

The fears came again like an overwhelming black wave. She had brought the child safely to the world, and now should she watch while it starved? Could they find enough food? Who could help them?

Mikolai worked hard in the fields, but there was no money for seed. He could plant only what was left from last year, the potatoes and onions stored in the cellar. The last potatoes.

"Mikolai, what do you plant in the yard?" she called to him from the open kitchen window.
She was up from her bed, holding the two-day old baby in one arm, feeding the older child in her chair.

"A new tree."

"A new tree? You think we need a new tree?"

"For a new child."

"A tree for a baby? What kind of tree?"

"A maple tree, like the other. She how fast it has grown."

"A maple tree! Are you crazy? Do we need maple trees? What can we eat from a maple tree?"

"It takes nothing from us, it only grows here in the yard."

"You plant a maple tree when we should have food. Plant an apple tree, or a pear tree. Or go look for peach seeds under the old peach tree. What good are maple trees?"

"What do they take from us? And look how the big one gives shade to the house. And in the fall, how nice to look at, and leaves for the cow's bed when the winter comes."

"What a fool you are, what a foolish man. You worry more for the cow's bed than for your children's food."

He didn't hear her. He'd turned from the window and finished planting the sapling along the stone wall just fifteen feet from one he had planted for the first child.

The third girl he favored. She had the same round face as the others, but when the hair finally grew in it was blonde like his family's. Her eyes, unlike the others, were light, a pale green with lights like her hair. She laughed more, unlike the dark-haired little girls, and she stayed fat and round like an old country baby. She came like sunshine and brought some hope again. He planted a tree for her next to the others. Danya watched him, but she said nothing this time. A man should do something for his family, even if only to plant a useless tree.

Four years they lived on the edge of hunger, kept alive by whatever their garden would give, the chickens and eggs, and from some sewing. Danya discovered that like the other time in Russia, people would pay in food for new dresses or shirts.

The pieces of gingham and percale she had hoarded away in the good days were pulled from the boxes in the unfinished upstairs room. Hunched over the treadle machine she worked to turn out the little dresses that would bring a pound of potatoes, a jar of tomatoes, a box of snuff.

She made a coat and snow leggings for one family's young boy and for that came a half-pound of bacon, the first Mikolai had in three months. Four shirts paid a dollar to keep his Russian language newspaper coming in the mail for another year. She knew he must have his newspaper.

The fourth child, another girl, added another mouth that they could not feed. Danya had decided before she was born what must be done if it was a girl.

She must go for adoption. Hazel and John had come all the way from Hartford where they now lived with Hazel's people. Hazel talked about a Russian couple who had no children, people who were educated and had money, even now. They lived in a good house near her own family and had spoken many times to her mother about their wish for children. They were not so young, but they would take a young child. They were so anxious to have a child in their fine house and she was sure they would take Danya's latest child for adoption.

Mikolai reacted with a pained expression when Danya told him what was in her mind to do. When she explained to him she told him they would keep the child only until times were better. He could see that the baby would not live if they had to find food for her as she grew.

"Only if it is a girl, Mikol. We will keep the child if it is a son. We could send one of the other girls to them if this one is a son."

It was a girl. When she was three months old Danya went with Hazel and John in their car, all the way to Hartford to give up the child for adoption.

The couple to whom the child would be given lived in a truly fine house, three stories tall. They looked healthy and fat, nothing like the people she had seen around her these past four years. The man, George Primor, spoke good Russian to her. She couldn't place the dialect, but she thought it must be from the north. He was educated, she could tell that. Hazel said he was a lawyer. It would be a good place to leave the girl, a better life than they could give her on the farm.

Mrs. Primor already held the baby as if it were hers. The other three girls clung close to Danya, timid and afraid in the big strange house with the soft stuff on the floor. The blonde girl, just learning to walk, fell to the floor and discovering the joy of soft carpeting she laughed and pushed her face and fists into the plush.

Mrs. Primor jumped from her chair.

"No, no, get up," she cried out angrily to the child. "Take her up, pick her up! Look, she's drooling on my good carpet. She'll stain it. Take her up, get her away from there."

Danya was shocked. Was it to a woman like this her child would go? To such a nasty voice? She scowled in embarrassment when her other three began to cry, then the fourth, the smallest baby, still being held in Mrs. Primor's arms.

Wait and believe.

"Wait!" Danya cried out. "I change my mind. Give her to me. Give back my child. I take her back, give her back to me!"

"Now Danya, what is the matter?" soothed Hazel.

"Why, what do you mean?" asked Mrs. Primor, quite annoyed.

"My mind is changed, that is all. Give back my baby." Danya's voice cracked and she feared she would cry. She pulled the child from Mrs. Primor's arms, gathered the others and ran from the house to the car where John waited.

Hazel made a puzzled apology and followed, but she could explain nothing to John. There was too much noise, anyway. The four children crying and Danya's creaky voice singing an old Russian lullaby that did absolutely no good. She'd tell John later.

They came to the farmhouse after dark, three tired grownups and four sleeping children. By the lights of the car Danya saw the fourth maple sapling that Mikolai had planted while they were gone. It was drooping a bit from the night coolness, but tomorrow, with the sunshine and more water it would be upright and ready to grow, she knew.

Her husband was reading his paper when she came into the house with all four children.

"It wasn't such a good place," Danya told him when he wanted to know what had happened. "It's better to wait a little longer I think, perhaps there will be a better family who needs a child."

GOOD NEWS 1933

Sometimes, if you are listening, good news travels as fast as the bad.

It was like a bonus attached to the jar of strawberry preserve that Angie Krakowski gave for the blouse Danya delivered. Jim, her husband, heard it that very day when he was in the town hall paying his taxes. He tried to learn more about it from the radio, from the news program, and he was listening when Danya knocked on their door.

"Stay a minute, Mrs. Vorodinov," said Angie. Jim heard something good on the radio. Wait until his news program is over and he will tell you about it."

It was a speech by the new president, Jim said. The president would help all the people. He would make work for the men, put food in the children's mouths and bring back the good times for everyone.

"How can one man do all this?" asked Danya.

"He has made new laws," Jim explained. "He has passed laws to take the money from the rich and divide it among all the people, the poor and all the rest."

Danya looked at him with a suspicious expression. "Does he take the land, too, does he take our land away to divide among all the people as in Russia?"

"No, just the money. He has passed new laws for the banks and makes new laws for the rich Wall Street people who brought the depression."

"Will the factories open again?"

"Maybe not right away. But he has made jobs for all the men all over the country."

"You mean here, too, in our town?"

"Yes, it will be in every town. The selectmen in each town will give out the work. The men will go to the town hall and sign, that is all your husband needs to do. Tell him to go right away and sign and the selectman will give him work."

That selectman was Angus Bent. Because he was a respectable man, well educated, knew about business and because he had been so kind to the people when they couldn't make their building and loan payments the town voters had elected him to the office of first selectman. He understood about their troubles and their money problems. He always had time to listen when they complained. They had chosen him because they believed he would know how to help them. They voted for him because he vowed to represent the president who had found new laws to help them out of their hunger and suffering.

After the new laws were passed Selectman Bent carried out the wishes of the president who had saved these people's lives and homes. He administered the new welfare program and the work program. He carefully read all the instructions that came from the nation's capitol and he put together the local WPA program that gave work and wages to those men who had been idled for so many years.

He administered the welfare food program himself. He made the deliveries of food to the homes each month. He understood. It was an effort for these families to walk with their children to the town center. He came one day each month to every family on welfare. Many of the men had worked in the factories and had been left jobless. More than half the town's families were on welfare. They depended on him for the canned beef and rice, and other canned foods. Every month there was the corned beef in the can with the silver paper wrapper.

When he brought shoes for the Vorodinov children he came with a state administrator, Miss Drake. She came to measure the children to see if they had clothing for school. As she gathered the children together, Bent gave the papers to Danya to sign.

"Sign please, here at the bottom of the paper."

"For what do I sign?"

"To say that you receive the food. And the shoes. That's all. For the state records, that's what you sign for, and to be sure you will get the next delivery."

She made him uneasy. That dark-haired little woman with all those children hanging around her. He tried not to look at her, afraid of those eyes. He tried to convince himself he'd been mistaken, the eyes couldn't be the ones in his dreams. He realized his palms were sweating as he held the paper out for Danya to sign. That antagonizing woman. She was staring at him as she signed the paper. Why did she bother him so? The eyes were only a dream.

He shouldn't work so hard. His dreams and his days were running into each other. That was the last time, the time he was so tired. He was working too long with his business and the selectman's office. It would be better now; he would slow down a little. His imagination would recover. It was just those dreams, after all. He couldn't shake out of his thoughts as Danya kept staring at him, waiting for him to say something. The dream, those eyes. They really weren't the same now when he looked closely. Or...no, he shouldn't look so closely.

But weren't they? Weren't they the same eyes that looked out of his dreams? No why should it be; how could it be?

Each time he made the delivery to the Vorodinov household he had to steel himself against showing his discomfort. But each time he was more affected by her eyes. He hated to look at her because he became fearful that she would haunt him that night in his dreams. He would look away when she talked to him. She began to change in her way toward him. She was becoming more aggressive, less humble, less thankful than at first. Tossing her head a little like the witch of his dreams, trying to catch his eyes, trying to hold him in her gaze as he spoke to her.

She began walking out to the car with the children each time he drove to the house to make his deliveries. Before he stopped the car she would be walking across the yard with the children trailing behind her. When the wind caught her dark hair and the sun splashed into her dark eyes it was almost as bewildering as his dreams.

He noted with disgust one day that Danya was pregnant again. He couldn't understand those people, unable to feed the children they had and still breeding others before their smallest one could walk. She asked him to increase their food allotment. He looked away from her, mumbling.

Danya sensed that Angus Bent was uncomfortable in her presence. She noted his disdain when he looked at her body. Poor man, so important, with no children and going into old age. She could feel sorry for him and couldn't understand why she made him so nervous.

Could it be that he was reading her mind? Could he know that she was thinking he looked just like the neighbor's old bulldog with his loose shaking chin and low puffy cheeks? "Jowls," Hazel had told her when she asked what Mr. Bents's face was called. "Jowls, that's the English word for that." Danya would stare at him while he talked and think "jowly bulldog, jolly bulldog, jowly, jolly bulldog." Oh, maybe he knows what I'm thinking.

But she gave him little thought as she began to blossom into her middle months. Secretly she thought this one would be a boy. She said nothing to Mikolai. Why would he believe her, after four girls?

In her heart she felt it was true. Everything was better now. The world was turned around and going in the right direction. Shouldn't she have some more good luck? This time a son? She would wait. Mikolai would get disgusted if she told him what she believed. Just making up stories, he'd say, making stories for nothing. She would say nothing, but she knew. She would wait.

Mikolai was working now. He could hear a little better, too. He said the factory destroyed his hearing. He liked the WPA roadwork. It was not so different from farm work. He was outside all day. It was better for him than working in a factory.

He worked just half days, but later, said Mr. Bent, they would have work for full days. Later when the program was under way, when all the plans were put together.

Mikolai's newspaper came every day, the only mail in the box. Danya would watch every day for the postman. He drove in an old car, so old it blew water when it got to the top of their hill. She would watch for him with the children so they could see this funny sight. He came just to deliver the paper in his weak old car. A horse would be better she told him while he waited for the car to cool off.

She began to worry that the children wouldn't learn to read. She didn't want them to know only Russian before they went to school. They couldn't get along in this country with only that language and her broken English. She should find them some books or some American newspapers. She would ask Mr. Bent. He could bring extra papers, maybe, or old books. She would learn to read, too.

He understood.

Yes, he would find something. A catalog, a Sears Roebuck catalog was the best thing for that. He would bring one next time and they could learn by the pictures. Yes, sign here please. Next time, yes, he'd remember the catalog.

Danya was amazed when she looked into the catalog. Why did no one show her before this? So many things, so many things. Everything had names and numbers. The oldest girl was quick to learn her numbers and letters. She should learn the names of everything, thought Danya, and know how to read every word. They would all learn to read from the catalog.

"Is it possible to have another catalog, Mr. Bent?"

"The catalog? What happened, did you lose it?"

"No, the two girls fight for it. One wants to read and the other wants to cut out pictures. Can you bring me another catalog, please, for the children?"

"Yes, next time. Sign here please. Yes, I'll remember, next time. Sign here please."

Why does she look at me like that, why stare at me with those strange eyes? I must be going mad, I must be imagining. Was she singing when he left? Or was it the voice from his dreams? No, of course not, not that. He was wrong. It couldn't be that. He was tired from all the work.

A DIFFERENT FISH FROM THE POND

At first Doctor Cobb didn't bother to look carefully. He assumed, as always, that it would be another girl.

"Aha, something different this time, Mrs. Vorodinov."

"What do you mean?"

"A different fish from the pond."

"I have a son, my doctor?"

"A boy this time."

"A son? Let me see if you tease me. Yes, a son. Finally, I have my son. Finally Mikolai has his son."

"What will you call him? I should fill out the papers."

"Joseph, Joseph I'll call him," she said after a short thought.

"Not Mikolai?"

"No, Joseph will be his name. He doesn't need a Russian name."

"And not after the president? I've had two this week named after the president."

She laughed. "No, Joseph is his name."

"I must fill out the rest of the paper. Where were you born?"

"The same place as last."

"What is the father's name?"

"The same as before."

"What is his occupation?"

"Farmer, the same as the last."

"How long?"

"Always."

"His age?"

"Forty-eight."

"Mother's age?"

"Forty."

"What, the same as the last time and the time before that?"

"Yes, my doctor, the same as the last time and the time before that. God has put a new song in my mouth. I am younger now with a son."

Dr. Cobb told the oldest girl to find her father who was somewhere out in the fields.

It was a hot sticky July day and Mikolai could smell the threat of rain. He was sure it would rain the next day. He was hurrying to gather the hay before the rain. He mused that he should call a neighbor for help. Maybe Tuttle? No, he could do it himself. By the time he walked to get Tuttle he would be able to do it himself.

He was standing out there under the sun, wiping his head with the red cotton handkerchief when she his daughter called to him.

"Pempa, Pempa, the man is here!" She called loud and breathlessly.

"What man?...move, move from the hay while I work." He spoke impatiently.

"With the black bag. The man who comes with the black bag."

"Mmm? OK. Look out, move from my way, I need to rake the hay."

"He told Mama she has a different fish from the pond. He told me to call you."

"A fish from the pond?"

"I saw it, Pempa, I saw it!"

"A different fish from the pond? What?"

"I saw it Pempa, it was like this." She lifted her skirt and showed him with her finger. Then he knew.

"My golly...move from my feet," he said as he raced to the house.

The children all knew something wonderful had happened; something different had come into their lives. Pempa was laughing with the man, the doctor who came with the black bag. They drank glasses of wine together. Mikolai walked back and forth from the bedroom to the kitchen, laughing and talking so loud, wiping the sweat from his forehead, wiping his eyes. He picked up the youngest girl and held her when she cried, rocked her on his foot until she stopped crying. He laughed and drank more of wine with the man who came with the black bag.

When he left, the oldest girl gathered the two next ones to her. "I know," she said, rolling her great brown eyes, "I know what the man brings in his black bag." Then, to their waiting, believing ears she whispered, "Fishes! He said so. He brings new fishes from the pond!"

Mikolai never forgot that day. A perfect full moon rose above the big hickory trees, lifted by a golden halo sent before it, like a promise to be fulfilled. It lighted his way so he could finish the haying before tomorrow's rain. And tomorrow he must find a maple sapling and plant a tree for his son, no matter if it rains.

He could see every acre of his land under the moonlit sky. The earth gave up a fragrance he had smelled a multitude of times, but this day the freshly cut and drying hay became a gift and an offering. Now he gathered the hay from fields that would be his gift to his son. Time and again he would offer it back with his simple deep thanks to the Maker who had blessed his family.

Of course Danya told the children they now had a brother. The oldest girl figured it out. It wasn't fishes that came in the bag after all, but babies. She told her mother she knew all about the black bag, but she wouldn't tell the others. They were too young to know, she said. They thought the man brought fishes in the black bag. How young and silly they were.

The comfortable days continued. Mr. Bent came with the cans of food. Mikolai worked every day. The children were all healthy. They ran in the fields with their father, they followed him to the pasture with the cow and the new calf. They fought and they cried, but they had food to eat. They were all saved from a famine as she had seen in Russia, and Danya thanked her God in prayers.

Saved, she realized, by the man who was president of the country. Helped by Mr. Bent. They both understood how it was to see children without bread, men without work. She heard the president say that on the radio once, on her neighbor Jim Krakowski's radio.

She took twenty-five cents from Mikolai's pay envelope and sent for a picture, to Washington D.C. Krakowski had told her about it. He copied the address for her on an envelope and she put it in the mailbox. When the picture came she a found wooden frame in the cellar and hung the picture in the kitchen over her sewing machine table, next to the picture of the Christ, which Mikolai had brought with him from the old country.

It made practical sense to her that both men had the power over people's lives. She saw it was nearly the same. The Christ came in a dream and said believe, and did not everything get better for her after that? Did not everything become better when he said fear not, believe? And didn't the president say to trust him and not to fear, but to believe? And didn't everything get better after that?

Danya couldn't vote, but she would some day, and she would vote for this president Roosevelt. She had heard a song as she waited in the grocery store. She herself taught the children the song, for future times. "Roosevelt, Roosevelt, rah, rah, rah; Landen, Landen, blah, blah, blah." They must remember who it was that helped to save them in their troubled years.

Everything was comfortable now. They would stay in the warm four rooms through the winter and then in the spring maybe there would be enough money to finish the rest of the rooms and the children could have better beds.

It was worth so much trouble to have such a family, she thought. They are quick-minded and bright. They learn to read even before they go to school. And she can teach them herself, an old woman like her who only learns to read the English words one day before they ask her the meaning. They are all healthy and good. She and Mikolai have been blessed.

With better times returning, the neighbors are not so afraid anymore. The Westham ladies, the two old maids, stop on their way to church. They ask if the children would like to go to Sunday school some day. They will take them in their car, to the Congregational church, the big white church in the middle of the town.

"But our church is the Russian church."

"But you don't take the children to church do you?"

"Our church is too far and we have no car."

"The children should go to Sunday school and after to church. They can't be good Americans without going to church. It is only a Sunday school. They learn the stories of Jesus and his disciples. It won't harm them. It isn't so different from your beliefs. They should have some religious education. They are growing very fast, and they should have some religious schooling to be good Americans."

"Well, if you can take them, the two oldest, I will let them go for their education."

"It will be good for them. We will take them next week at nine. Have them ready just before nine o'clock and we will take them to Sunday school."

"They have no fine clothes, though, like I see you ladies' wear. Only little cotton dresses that I make by myself."

"It doesn't matter at all, Mrs. Vorodinov. They should come to church in whatever they have, so long as they are clean."

"We have plenty of water, so they will be clean. Yes, they should know all about Jesus. You are right, they are old enough to learn about Jesus, no matter from which church, it is the same Jesus."

WELFARE

The two oldest girls were in school now and even if they had no extra money, at least the family had food. The families in Stanton who had depended on factory wages were thankful for the help that came through the welfare programs administered by Angus Bent.

"Please Mr. Bent, is it possible to have more canned meat? My son is growing and another baby comes in the summer. Can you make the allowance bigger for my family?"

"Yes, next time Mrs. Vorodinov. Sign here please. Next time."

"Is it possible Mr. Bent you make a mistake? I sign for six cans and you only leave four."

"No, you are mistaken, you sign only for four. You are mistaken, the paper says four."

"But it looks to me like a six."

"You are mistaken, the number says four. Sign here please, and next time I will bring a bigger allowance for you."

I ought to be more careful, he thought, next time.

***

"Is it possible you make a mistake again, Mr. Bent? The paper says five and I have here only three?"

"No, you are wrong. The number is three. You should learn your numbers better. See here, see how the three can look like a five. You are mistaken, you sign only for three. You must learn your numbers before you try to read."

"You said you would allow me more this time. My family is growing and they need more meat."

Yes, I remember. I will come back with more. When I come with the shoes I will bring more food. In two weeks I'll return and bring you more. Sign here please, Mrs. Vorodinov for the three cans of corned beef."

***

"Is it possible, Mikolai, that Mr. Bent lies? He cheats me I think when he brings the canned food and the shoes."

"What kind of story do you make now of Mr. Bent?" Mikolai was annoyed.

"I tell you, I think he cheats me. He asks me to sign the paper and he takes it so fast I cannot read what I sign. He gives me three cans of beef and the paper says five. I can read the numbers even as he pulls the paper away from me."

"You imagine. I'm reading my newspaper. Don't bother me now with such stories. Mr. Bent is a good man. Why would he cheat you? Isn't he the one who has given me my job?"

"But somehow I think he cheats me."

"And if he cheats you, what does it matter? We have enough. He brings you plenty, the canned meat and the shoes. Before, without him we had nothing."

***

"Angie, I think old Mr. Bent is cheating me with the welfare food. He asks me to sign and he won't let me see what I sign. The paper says one number and not the same as the number of cans and shoes that he brings."

"Now, Mrs. Vorodinov, Angus Bent is a respectable, kind and good man. He has no reason to cheat you. You should be grateful for the things that he brings to you and not accuse him of cheating you."

"I can tell by his face he does something wrong. I tell you again, he cheats me with his papers. He cannot look into my eyes. I know he cheats me."

***

"Miss Carrie, can you help me? I can't read English so well. Can you look at the papers I sign for old Bent? He brings me the papers and I sign where he says to sign. But he pulls the paper away so fast from me I can't look again to see what I sign. I know he cheats me, he makes me sign so fast. Can you look at the papers in his office and see how he cheats me?"

"But Mr. Bent is the selectman. I just work in the town hall. Why should he cheat you? You must have made a mistake when you tried to read the papers, that's all. He wouldn't cheat you. He's a respectable, kind man."

"But I am sure he cheats me. I can tell when I look on his face."

"Why of course he wouldn't cheat you. He is respected by everyone. Are the children dressed and ready? We'll be late for Sunday school."

***

"Yes, can I help you? Who would you like to see Mrs. Vorodinov?"

"I'll talk to Miss Robbins, the town clerk, please. I want to talk to Miss Robbins so I can complain."

"Complain about what? What is the trouble?"

"I want to talk to Miss Robbins, please, of some serious things."

"She's busy right now. What is the trouble, can I help you?"

"I have come to the town hall to tell you all that Mr. Bent is cheating me with the welfare, and I want to complain about his dishonesty."

"How can that be?"

"He cheats me with the papers. He makes me sign for more goods than he brings. I watch on his face and I know he cheats me. Look on the papers you have in the town hall and you will see. I can tell you how much he gives me and how much he writes on the paper."

"Oh, that's too bad, Mrs. Vorodinov, but we can't do anything. Angus Bent is the selectman and very respectable. He has charge of the welfare. Why would he cheat you? He's such a kind man. You know how hard he works administering the welfare program. He uses his own car to deliver the food, going to every house like yours. He wouldn't cheat anyone, I'm certain."

"I tell you, I know it, I can tell by his face!"

***

"Doctor Cobb, old Bulldog Bent is cheating me, for years now, I bet, making me sign papers for thing I don't get."

"Now, Mrs. Vorodinov, you should rest and stay still. This girl took more strength than the others. You need to rest, to stay quiet. Don't do yourself harm."

"You think I need rest, but I know what it is. The old Bulldog comes every month to cheat me. I hold tight on the papers when I sign and I look carefully, and I know what he does.
He can't fool me anymore. I know he cheats me."

"Now, now, you should rest. You are getting too old to jump up after every child. Stay in bed this time and rest. Stay quiet and rest. Your husband can help care for the children."

"I tell you, he will be found out. I will prove he cheats me, and he cheats the government, too. I will get the papers and show how he has been cheating for a long time."

"Now, now, Angus is a respectable business man, Mrs. Vorodinov. After you rest you'll feel better. Don't be excited, it's bad for you. Stay in bed a little long, stay quiet and rest."

1937 ALONE

The big musty cellar had an earth floor. It was deep and the corner bins where the wood and preserves and wine barrels were stored were dark and strange places to a child. The six small windows in the concrete foundation let in only enough light to make the cellar more mysterious to the four children sitting on the steep wooden steps leading down from the hallway. They couldn't make a sound. Their mother had rushed them to the stairs and told them to sit there without one sound. They must not make one noise or the devil would come and steal them from the cellar and take them away.

The four little girls sat there, hands over their mouths, the oldest laughing to herself behind her hands because she knew it was a game. There was no such thing as a devil, but she wouldn't tell. The others were too little and they believed in devils. How scary it was to them, how scared they looked, she thought as she suppressed her giggles.

The older girls could see the two black cars stopped on the road by their yard. They saw the two men in black suits and shiny boots and wide funny hats. They saw the third car with the nice man who came with the big cans of corned beef and new shoes. They could see their mother walk to the cars. She was waving a stick, the stick she carried when she chased the cow to pasture.

One of the girls giggled out loud. It looked like Mama was going to whip the men with the stick, like she whipped the cow when it stopped to eat grass. The oldest girl poked her, reminding her to be quiet, don't make a sound!

Boy, Mama looks mad, like the time they were playing and tipped baby Joey out of the crib and she chased them out of the house with the switch and wouldn't let them in until suppertime. Boy, did she look mad now.

She was yelling, too, but they couldn't hear the words clearly, just the sounds because the windows were all closed to keep the warm air out, to keep the cellar cool. The oldest girl tried to stand on a barrel so she could open the window to hear what Mama was yelling. The barrel rolled over and made a terrible noise.

Oh, were they all scared. They ran down the stairs to the farthest bin, the one that held wood in the winter, and they huddled together there, crossing their fingers to keep the devils away, as the oldest had showed them.

Soon the door opened at the top of the stairs.

"Here he comes, here he comes," whispered the oldest girl. The smallest child started to cry.

"Girls, girls, where are you? Where are you down there? Who's crying, what's the matter? I told you to stay quiet down there, to stay on the stairs. Who's crying? What happened, where are you? Speak up!" There was more fright than anger in Danya's voice.

The oldest ran out of the bin to the bottom of the stairs and called up to her mother, "It's the baby, the big baby, she always wants to cry."

"The devil," the child whimpered from the dark bin. "The devil was coming."

"Come out, my children, come up the stairs. Come eat some peaches. Your father brought peaches today from Krakowski's lot. There is no devil when I am here."

"Was it the devil who came in the black car?"

"No, just a bulldog. Never mind, come eat some peaches. You will feel better."

***

The next time they were playing in the barn. Papa always let them jump in the hayloft, in the new mown hay after it had been in the barn a few days. He said their jumping helped pack down the hay so the barn could hold more for the winter.

He had put two ladders up to the hayloft for them, tied the top of the ladders to the beam so it wouldn't slip. He showed the little ones how to close their eyes so the hay wouldn't stick in their eyes. Jump one at a time, don't jump on each other. Watch on the ladder so you don't make a fall. Keep out of the way of each other.

The oldest girl climbed to the higher beam. "Look, I'm up so high, I'm not afraid. Come up if you are." Only one dared. The others' legs were too short for the climb.

Jump, turn a summersault, look, you can fly. It's not far to land there, get out of the way. Come on, move out of the way. It's my turn, my turn, you've got to wait.

They were laughing and jumping, then heard someone calling. A woman's voice calling, "Children, children, where are you? Where are you children?"

It wasn't Mama. They stopped their fun to listen.

"Come here children, we have candy. We've brought candy for you. Where are you children? Would you like some candy? We have chocolate candy for you."

They came out of the barn and were running toward the lady who was standing beside a big black car when their mother came yelling out of the house.

"Go back, girls, go back, run back to the barn!"

But the lady had candy, a whole bag of candy that she held out to them. She showed them the candy: chocolate bars, squirrel nut twins, green mint-leaf candies.

Mama was really mad, too, and she was crying and screaming at them, so loud like she said you should never talk to people.

There were three men in the black suits. And the nice man who brought the cans with the silver paper wrappers.

The men in the black suits told Mama to be quiet. It would be all right they told her in loud voices. They went toward the house but she ran ahead of them screaming at them, " Stay out of my house, stay out of my house, get away you devils!"

She got the cow switch but they took it away from her. Boy, was she mad now.

The nice lady with the candy said they could get in the black car, the one with another man waiting at the driving wheel. She said he would give them a ride. She gave them the whole bag of candy. Boy, what a big car. Why was Mama screaming so? The four girls got into the car and the men closed the doors.

Then the nice lady went into the house and came out with the baby girl. One of the men was carrying their baby brother. The other man was holding on to Mama. Wow, was she madder and madder, screaming so loud it hurt your ears, even in the car, and she was saying nasty words she had told them they should never say.

"Sons of bitches, sons of bitches, leave me alone, leave my children alone. Get off from my land, sons of bitches, leave my children alone. Mikolai, my husband, where are you? Help me, help me, where are you?"

Mr. Bent said quietly to the girls, "Would you like to go for a ride?"

"Oh yes, goody, how exciting. All right."

"Fine," he said, then told the driver, "Go on, they can go for a ride."

The men put Danya in another car. She was screaming, in a frenzy.

"My children, my children, give back my children!"

One of the policemen in the black uniform pushed her into another car.

The lady put the two babies in a third car, got in beside them and Mr. Bent drove them away.

The three cars drove down the winding unpaved hill, past the red house. Professor Bennet waved from his window when he saw the children in the car. He couldn't hear Danya's cries from the next car, "Help me, Mr. Bennet, help me, they are kidnapping my children!"

Past the Wheeler's where a sad-hearted mother looked out to the sound of the cars as she spoon-fed her grown impaired child. Down the hill, past Senator Hefford's stone house with the glass balls sparkling in the manicured gardens.

The cars stopped in front of Mr. Bent's house across from the Maynor's. Mama jumped out of the car and ran toward the children. Oh heck, she would make them get out and spoil their ride.

"My children, my children! Kidnappers, sons of bitches!" Danya was yelling so loudly her voice cracked. "They kidnap my children, help me somebody. Bulldogs, devils, sons of bitches!" she screamed as she ran along the street. No one heard her. The two policemen ran after her. They pulled her back to the other car.

"Help me, help me! They kidnap my children. Where is my husband, call my husband. Somebody help me!" But her screams banged against silent houses. Where were the people? "Somebody, please help me! They kidnap me! They kidnap my children!" But no one answered.

The blonde girl, finished with her candy got out of the car. She would go home and jump in the hay. She didn't like the men in the cars anyway. And her sister had taken the chocolate bar right out of her hand.

Mr. Bent, coming out of his house with papers under his arm, saw her walking away and went after her.

"Come back to the car."

"No!" She started to run.

"Now, now, come back for a ride."

He picked her up when he caught up to her. She started to cry; she kicked him, kicked her bare feet against him with all her might, crying. He began to run as she twisted in his arms. Her crying frightened the other children. Something was wrong. The ride was not fun. They wanted to go home.

"Mama, Mama, let us go home."

"Kidnappers, leave my children alone. Run away, children, Call somebody to help me." Danya yelled from inside the car. But the children could not hear. They could see her banging against the car window.

"We want to go home. Mama, Mama!" They all shouted. The oldest girl knew the words.

"Sons of bitches, kidnappers, devils, take us home. We want to go home!"

And inside the car, silent to her children, Danya kept shouting. "Give back my children, somebody help me…who is out there? Help me, somebody please!"

Bent tried to calm the girls., but he could not. "Quiet, children, or we'll take your candy away."

"I want my mother, let us go home, leave us alone."

And another girl, "You son bitches, leave us alone, I want my mother!'

And still Danya persisted in her shouting to nobody, "Kidnappers, bitches, give back my children. Help me! Help me! Who is out there to help me?"

The cars drove past the pretty white church at the center of the town green.

***

Doctor Cobb put down the glass at the sound of the doorbell. The office was closed. Who would bother him now? No babies this week. Oh yes, the state police and Angus Bent. He remembered. Poor Mrs. Vorodinov. Well, she should have kept quiet about Angus Bent. She should have rested. Too many children so late in life.

Yes, he'd sign the papers he told the policeman at the door. Yes, a shame, he agreed, as he looked out at the black car. She was sitting there, hunched over and weeping. Then she saw him.

"Doctor, my doctor," she cried out. "Won't you help me? My children, the children you brought to me, they kidnap my children." She choked on her words, soundless to him against the closed car windows. He couldn't hear her.

Poor woman. She should have stayed in bed, stayed quiet and rested. He went back to his bottle when they left. Poor Mrs. Vorodinov, she never should have said those things about Angus Bent.

Everyone agreed later, she should have rested. She worked too hard, had too many children. And she was so wild.

"You should have seen her, what a fuss she made when they stopped in front of Bent's. I saw from my window…and there at the doctor's, you could see her in the car yelling, I'm sure, pounding the windows like a crazy person."

"Imagine a crazy woman bringing up six children. She really looked dangerous. I walked past the car. Her eyes looked so wild, really crazy the way she was carrying on in the car. Frightening."

"She would frighten me. You never know what a crazy person will do, you know."

"Yes, it's a shame, but it's a good thing for the children. You see how wild she was, not normal. That's bad around children. It's best for the children that they were taken away."

Nobody helped.

With tears choking her grief and her body aching with the milk that swelled her breasts Danya was torn from her nursing baby, her children, her husband, her home.

She was delivered to the regional mental institution, the Middletown asylum on the hill. The papers were signed. Things were in order. Yes, she would be more comfortable tomorrow. It wasn't unusual, such hysterics. They knew what to do. No, no more papers needed. The state hospital needs these, the rest go to the state records with Miss Drake. Yes, it's a difficult thing, we understand, Mr. Bent. Thank you, yes, everything is in order, Mr. Bent. Oh, the husband's signature? Will you bring it tomorrow, just for the records. Thank you Mr. Bent.

***

Mikolai was working slowly. There was no need to rush. No rain was coming, and the day was hot. Best to take it easy. He would take a nap in the shade, against this pile of hay. The children could play longer in the barn. Let them play while he napped. Plenty of time.

Not with fear but in annoyance the old dream came to him. He was discovered asleep in the hay, discovered by the old priest, long dead, though he knew while he dreamed and cried out that he really was here on his own farm, safe, asleep on his own farm on a summer day. He knew he was safe, but still, the sweat came, the awful feeling of tragedy…but he was safe, he knew he was safe.

Was it the breeze that awakened him or the voice? The priest, standing above him, his white hair whipped by the breeze…Mikolai was startled. He sat up, then laughed with relief. Only Mr. Bent. Not the priest after all. He was embarrassed. What had he cried out?

Bent pushed his hair from his face as it was caught by the wind. He'd forgotten the man was deaf. He'd have to speak louder so he'd understand.

"Excuse me, Mikolai, can you hear me?"

"Yes, what is it? What do you want?" Mr. Bent had never come into the fields before. Did he come to give him more work?

"Bad news in your house. Can you understand, bad news in your house."

"What bad news, what do you say?"

"Can you hear me, do you understand me?"

"Yes, I hear you. What bad news in my house, what do you say?"

"Your wife is sick, very sick. We had to take her away."

"What, what do you say? Danya is sick?"

"Yes, do you understand, very sick, much sick. We took her away to a hospital."

"What do you mean sick? She worked here earlier today with me in the fields. How can she be sick?"

"She is sick, a nervous breakdown, broken down, do you understand? She needs rest."

"No, how can she be sick?"

"From too much work, too many children. Do you understand? A nervous breakdown from too much work."

"Why take her away for a breakdown?"

"Because she needs rest."

"She can stay in her own house and rest. Why take her away to a hospital?"

"This is a bad breakdown. Like a crazy person, a nervous breakdown. She could not rest if she stayed home."

"Crazy person?"

"Yes, a bad nervous breakdown." Bent was getting annoyed.

"How can it be? Too much work? It isn't true. Danya always works. There is never too much work."

"Too many children. It brings a nervous breakdown some times."

Mikolai rubbed his chin and frowned. It could be true. He didn't know about such things, but Bent was a smart man.

"Where did you take her?"

"To a good hospital, not far, to a good hospital so she can be cured."

"I cannot pay for a hospital. She should come home and rest in her own bed."

"Don't worry, Mikolai, the state will pay for the hospital. The state will take care of her. But you must sign for her here, so the state can pay for her."

"You are sure they will pay? But she can rest here, in her house."

"No, we are glad to take care of her and the children."

"The children? Do they need rest, too?"

"No, but the disease is contagious, you know."

"No, what do you mean contagious? I don't know."

Now Angus Bent's anger stirred. Mikolai's accent annoyed him, his questions annoyed him, it annoyed him that he had to shout and repeat himself.

"The children can catch the disease, too, so they must go to another hospital for a while. Then they will be cured. They will get better, don't worry. Do you understand?"

Mikolai shrugged. How can children catch the disease? But Mr. Bent must know. He was a good man. He had given him work and he had brought them food when they had no money. Of course he knew more about it, and maybe he didn't hear the right words. He would trust Bent.

"Now, if you'll just sign this paper so the state can pay, and this one, sign this one please for the three cans of beef. I'll leave them in the kitchen for you when I get them from the car."

Mikolai signed the first paper and looked carefully at the second one. Three, it was written, not five like Danya had said. Of course Bent wouldn't cheat her. She always made things bigger than they were. She always thought he was cheating her, that he wanted to harm her when he really was a kind man; had been good to them.

He finished the haying at a leisurely pace since there was no supper waiting on the table. He would finish the back lot, then he would eat. Maybe some of the canned beef Mr. Bent had left.

In the late sun he stood marveling at the thickness of the trees beyond the stone wall that outlined the hay lot. He could remember back, how many, twenty years, twenty-two years, when he first came to this place. You could see through the trees then, maybe a mile into the woods, as far as the first blueberry patch anyway. And the sumac trees by the corner fence; they were just sticks, little bushes when he came. He couldn't see them over the stone wall then they were so small.

Maybe he should have cut down the sumacs before they grew so tall. In the fall, though, whenever he thought to do it they were so pretty with their red brushes standing out against golden leaves. They were good for nothing, he knew, but he couldn't cut them down when they were the most beautiful. Of course, in the spring you couldn't cut them because the poison sap would go all over and the cows might spoil their milk if they took in any of the grass with sap on it. And after all, they weren't even good for burning either because their smoke was poison. He would leave them another year and let them grow.

He pulled the last load of hay to the barn, going slowly, pulling the two stout poles on which the hay was piled, stopping to be sure the pile didn't slip sideways. It would have been easier if Danya was helping.

The cow and her calf came toward him when he got to the gate in the middle lot, thinking it was time for them to come in from the fields. He had to stop and chase them both away from the gate so he could get through without letting them out.

The giant hickory trees threw long shadows across the front field. He squinted, wondering how thick the hickory nuts would be this fall. You couldn't tell yet, they were still the same green as the leaves. But there were lots of squirrels around and they must know by nature that there would be plenty to eat from the hickory trees. By September he could tell, when the shuckings turned darker. An early fall this year, he could tell already, just from instinct.

The barn. How quiet in the dusk. Maybe his hearing was all gone. No, he would hear if the children were playing in the barn.

But the children weren't there. He could hear them if they were still there.

One of the hay poles caught the ladder when he went past it, and he landed a light kick, cursed it, looked up to be sure it was still tied safely for the children.

He pitched the hay into the loft. It was getting too high. The next load would have to come on the truck. He would send Danya to ask Tuttle to help with the truck. No, he would have to go himself, tomorrow, Sunday. He would have to go in the morning. Maybe Tuttle would come the same day if he worked on Sunday. Funny thing, some Yankees, they think it's a sin to work on Sundays.

The cow was brought in and milked. The day settled into the thickness of night, hiding the unlit farmhouse from view. Mikolai shuffled along the stone path that led to the house, guarding the full pail of milk. They should get electricity soon, maybe next year. He saw them clearing the side of the road for electricity poles at the top of the hill, so they must be bringing electricity soon. That would be good. He could see better at night. Damn cat, get away from my feet, you make me spill the milk, foolish cat. Here, here is your share, here is your supper.

No woman waited to take the milk pail from him. No food steamed on the blue enamel cook stove. No children under his feet, no songs, no light in the house.

He lit the kerosene lamp on the kitchen table, strained the milk, ate some of the cold canned meat, then settled into his chair to read his newspaper.

The quiet imposed by the loss of hearing had brought Mikolai the gift of a private world, an abiding place for a sensitive intellect that had not accomplished the task of oral expression.

Here, unshared, his fears ran the test of endurance, smothered in degrees by a simple faith whose greatest lesson had been learned: that he must accept the world as it surrounded him, for to do less was to keep afire the very fears and hurts he tried to extinguish. Thus had the plagues of his past gradually diminished their hold over him and his dreams.

Automatically that night he turned the pages of the worn black bible as he whispered his memorized prayers in the dark. He thanked God for the help of good man Bent who had taken care of his wife and looked after his children. He asked for Danya's health and his own, for the health and long life of his children. He made the sign of the cross two times, put the bible into the dresser drawer and went to bed.

He slept, alone in a suddenly too large bed, unjostled by young ones who for eight years had made tiptoed excursions to the warmth and comfort of their mother's body as she had slept beside him.

The house breathed with the melancholy of emptiness. The sounds that had lain unheard, squelched by the constant presence of living souls, came writhing their way out of walls and ceiling to explore the vacant spaces of the night.

When he awakened in the morning Mikolai tried to disentangle himself from the shackles of aloneness which still laid on his heart. He dressed and the morning sun rose to promise another beautiful day.

THE ASYLUM

From a foggy half-consciousness induced by sedatives Danya awakened in a small iron bed in the women's ward of the state mental asylum. The daylight was gone, leaving behind dull pockets of light that slowly drowned in the darkness of the damp unlit room.

She could see dimly the other beds, occupied by quiet creatures dressed as she was in white shapeless gowns. They peered at her with disappointment, for the scarce light had hidden from their curiosity what they wanted most to see, the inmate's realization of her predicament.

Into the hanging silence Danya's voice cried out to know her whereabouts. The others reacted to the sound of her hoarse voice as chickens to the call of the farmer come to feed them. Every voice cackled at once. Short chuckling pleased sounds of the mildly demented who no longer have knowledge of kindness.

"You are here, you are here," laughed one with utter logic.

"Shut up, don't cry, they'll take you away," warned another high tense voice.

Danya sat on the edge of her bed looking into the dark. Tears ran down her sunken cheeks. She begged, "Please, please, tell me where I am. Where am I, I ask you. Where are my children, where have they taken my children?"

The others all rallied again against her weakness, taunting her with incredible answers, imitating her accent, pretending to weep with her, laughing as they did so. Danya had known this before. It was no different from the animals on the farm. The hurt and weakened one, attacked by the others whose attacks increase with the agony of the afflicted.

Her heart churned inside her with anger. With an animal knowledge of a person not willing to be hurt, her voice, now stronger and angrier, broke into the fumbling cruelties of the others.

"Animals! Ugly bitches! I tell you to shut your sounds away from me if you are so wild. Go to hell back to your beds. Leave me alone from your stupid sounds!"

From her weakness she had turned on them so suddenly it had the effect of a smacking whip. Their noising stopped. They were quiet. The moment she felt her strength against them Danya asked again of the subdued phantoms, "Now, somebody with brains, tell me where I am. Tell me the truth and tell me right away."

After a moment's silence a little voice answered, tired and low, "You are here, with us, here in the asylum, the state asylum. We are all here together."

"In what place, what town?"

"Middletown."

"When did I come here?"

"When it was still daylight."

"This same day?"

"Yes, today while the sun was shining. It was very hot here."

"Who brought me here?"

"The nurse. The nurse in her blue uniform."

"Where are my children? Did they bring my children? Did you see my children anywhere?"

"We don't know more, not even your name. But look on your bed, at the bottom of your bed and you can find your name."

"I know my name. I know who I am."

"Some new ones don't know. You should look at the card on the bed to be sure."

"I am sure who I am. And I am sure who put me here."

"It was the nurse, the one in the blue uniform. We all saw her."

"What is her name? I will call to her."

"Her name is on the uniform, on a card. But you cannot call her. They will take you away. She comes to turn on the lights. Then you can talk to her."

"When does she come? It is dark already."

"Soon, when it is time to eat. Then she puts on the lights. If there is too much noise she won't put on the lights. Then we can't go to eat." The voice whined like a child's. "Be quiet now."

They hushed like good children waiting in the dark for a surprise. You might expect giggling, or some childish prank to cut the dark silence. It was the clack of flat heels coming down the corridor that made some of them gasp in anticipation. "Shhhh, stay still," someone hissed. Before the nurse entered the ward she switched on the lights, three large globes that hung from the high ceiling.

The women sitting up in their beds with hands folded obediently reminded Danya of her own children who would sit and wait this same way when she brought them candy or oranges from the store after her late shopping. This was grotesque, these frizzled-haired white-faced women behaving like small children. She wanted to protest to the nurse that she didn't belong here. She called to her when she came through the door.

"Nurse, will you talk to me?"

The large-boned nurse turned without a smile. She raised annoyed eyes to the new patient. Then she walked to the foot of the bed, picked up the chart and read slowly without looking up:

"You are Danya Vorodinov," she intoned with a professional cool voice. "You were admitted today to this ward, number two. Tomorrow you will be examined by the doctors. For now you will remain in the ward with the others." She turned to one of the women. "Mrs. Jones, you will show Mrs. Vorodinov where the toilet is. Then you will go with her to the dining room. Walk with her carefully." Then to Danya she said, "Don't create any disturbance as you did when you came or you will be separated immediately from the others."

"But may I not ask what you have done with my children? My six children. Where are they, cannot you tell me that?"

"I do not know where they are. Of course they are safe. You must not be concerned. They are being cared for, I am certain."

"But my baby, my youngest one, who can care for her? She still takes milk from my body. Who else can feed her?" Danya's voice threatened toward a wail, but she checked herself, afraid to weaken again.

The weight of growing helplessness settled on her heart. She felt thick and heavy with anguish. She stared back at the nurse, her dark eyes wet, lit with sadness and memory of how easily hate can be called up. She would wait. Tomorrow when she talked to the doctors she would tell them. Then she would tell them about Bent. She knew why she was in this place. She would tell them all about Bulldog Bent and his dishonesty. She would stand back now and wait to tell her story to the doctors tomorrow.

The nurse watched, anticipating some disturbance. When there was none she wrinkled her forehead and blinked with finality. That was done with. She told them they could now go to the dining room for their supper.

Each of the women behaved like a good child, wrapped herself in a striped robe and walked slowly toward the door. Danya did the same and followed them to the dining room.

***

She was taken in the morning to the doctors for a routine physical examination. When she tried to question them, to learn from them what had happened to her children, the younger of the two doctors confessed, most kindly, that they knew nothing and had no authority to discuss or help her with the matter. They would make her as comfortable as they could; they understood about the pain in her breasts. They could help her with that.

She begged them to realize she didn't belong in such a place. She belonged with her children, with her baby who must be crying for the milk that dried in her breasts. She tried to tell them her story, tried to make them listen to her, asked them to help her get back to her children.

The older doctor told her she would talk to a psychiatrist tomorrow. It was to him she should tell her story. They could do nothing about it. They could not help her in any way with that matter, but the psychiatrist had authority.

She left them, accompanied by another nurse in blue, and went despondently back the same way she had come to see the doctors, through the dim long hallways to the ward.

No day in her life had she felt so captured and stifled. She had nothing to do. In her room, only a bed to lie on, and she did not need rest. Her hands should be busy. She could not stay like this, like an old withering woman, useless and forgotten like the ones around her. Her energies, given no outlet, concentrated to make her mental discomfort greater.

For minutes she would stare to the ceiling, brooding over her misery, feeding her hate for the man who had done this to her. When she thought of Mikolai that too filled her with anger. How was it that he did not come to find her? What did he do there in the empty house? Shouldn't he wonder where she was? Shouldn't he come to help her?

But no, he would listen to anyone, believe any story told to him. Bent had probably told him a fine story, and he would do what Bent told him to do. He would believe the old Bulldog. He would sit and wait, like a puppet.

She knew she was alone against Bent and the welfare people who had tricked her and put her here, had taken her children from their house like kidnappers. She could stand against them. She had stood against others and she would show them again. Bent would suffer and pay for his tricks, the white-skinned Yankee bulldog.

To the psychiatrist who listened without interrupting, she told all she knew. All about Angus Bent's dishonesty, his cheating on the welfare papers and his reasons for putting her in the asylum. "He is a thief. He steals from under all our noses. He is cheating others besides me, I know. And he cheats the government. He makes us sign for more than we get and keeps the welfare money for himself. I know how he works."

She had made her plan. She would not be upset but would tell them in plain words what she knew. They would listen better that way, when she was quiet, she could see...even the other doctor who came in while she was talking.

The psychiatrist made a few notes on a card and waited with patience until Danya had finished her story. Then he asked, "Don't you believe, Mrs. Vorodinov that Mr. Bent is interested in helping you? Don't you believe that he could see you were troubled and needed a rest?"

"Why should I need a rest?"

"You are not a young woman. Shouldn't you be glad to be given a rest from your husband and your children? There was too much strain on you and you needed a rest from your family for a while."

"I tell you, doctor, that I do not want a rest. I do not need a rest. I can do all necessary for my husband and the children. I can work all day and God sends me the strength for each following day. My sleep is my rest. To stay in this place with nothing to do is not a rest for me!"

"But aren't you an old woman to have so many children to care for? Don't you think you are old, I should say, too old to handle the work of raising such a large family?"

"Maybe you see that by my years and my face I am old, but not by my hands and my feet and my eyes, and not by my heart." She constrained her anger.

"Aren't you thankful to be away from your husband's bed for a while?"

"Why should I be thankful? It is my bed too."

"Aren't you concerned, worried, that you will have more children at your age?"

"I take gladly all who are sent to me by God, even in my old age. In my young years I had not one child."

"But you can't feed them and clothe them."

"Help always comes in time."

"From Mr. Bent?"

"No, not from stinking, lying Bulldog Bent. The help comes from the welfare, from the president of the country."

"But isn't Mr. Bent actually helping you? If you need help and take it from him why do you say he cheats you?"

"If he helps me he should not be helping himself also at the same time."

"How does it harm you if he gives you enough? Why do you say he cheats you?"

"When I sign a paper it should be true."

"But still you do receive enough food and other things from the welfare, and it comes through Mr. Bent?"

"Yes, but not so much as he says he gives us."

"Why does that concern you if you get enough?"

"Because by my signing he makes me a liar and he cheats other people and the government too. He cheats me the same as if he steals from my pantry. And he takes money that the government says should go to the poor, not to him. When I see this I should report it. I know he makes others suffer who cannot read the numbers, and he makes a bad name for the government, for the president who pays him to do his welfare."

"Perhaps you did not read the numbers correctly?"

"I read them more carefully each time. I hold the paper tight in my hand even as he tries to pull it away. I know numbers. I learned how to read printed numbers from the catalogs that the Bulldog gave us."

"What catalog did he give you?"

"The Sears book, the big one. From that I have learned printed number and also how to read; from his own catalog I learned to catch the Bulldog in his tricks."

"He has been kind to you but you don't seem to appreciate it. Why do you call him Bulldog?"

"Because he is ugly inside and out."

"Can it be you don't like him because you are forced to accept help from him?"

"Help comes from God. It makes no difference who delivers the help. I should not hate someone for bringing me help. If he is the one God chooses to deliver the help he should be grateful and honest. If he was invisible I would take the help and I would thank only God. Is it not right for me to hate him because he has cheated me, because he has taken me from my house, kidnapped my children and put me in this black asylum? For any of these reasons I could hate him with all my might. But not because he delivers food like a grocery man. I am not so stupid. I think maybe you are stupid to ask me such a question. If you were a mother would you call him a kind man after he steals your children from your house and brings you to a place like this?"

She was becoming argumentative. The psychiatrist shook his head, smiling slightly. He saw no reason to continue. There were others to see and he had already spent more than the necessary time with her.

"You don't think you belong here? You don't need a rest?"

"No, I belong to my family. I will rest in my old age."

"You want to go back to your husband? You know that he signed to have you committed here."

"Like heck he signed to put me in here! Maybe he doesn't even know where I am or he would come to find me. If he signed to put me in here he could not look on my face ever again. He signs nothing by himself. I sign all the papers in our house. Yes, I want to go back to my husband and to my children, what do you think?"

She leaned toward the man. "Yesterday the doctors said only you can help me. I must go back to my family. Can you not help me?"

"Yes, I can help. We can arrange for a hearing and I am sure it will come out all right for you."

"Today?"

"No, it takes longer. There are rules, papers. It is the only way and it takes time."

"There were no rules to take my children from me!" She was agitated.

"I'm sorry. If you can try to understand it will be easier for you. I will make my report and the hearing committee will have a meeting with you."

He rose from his desk to ring the bell for an attendant. It wasn't his nature to be compassionate. He would like to say more comforting words to this woman sitting so grimly on the edge of the wooden chair opposite him. He would like to give her some comfort for the emptiness she must feel. He wished, though briefly, that he could give some word to her that would soothe her worrying.

As he left the room he repeated, "Try to understand. It will be easier for you if you are patient."

Two months passed before the hearing was arranged. During the wait Danya at times thought she would truly go crazy and join the world inhabited by the strange women around her.

Day after day she begged the nurse attendant to find work for her, to find something she could do with her hands. She said she could sew and asked if there was some work for her in the hospital, even hemming sheets or towels.

The nurse consulted with the doctor who agreed that she should be allowed to join a few others in the therapy room. There she maintained herself at an old treadle sewing machine. She was put to work making the starched hats and cuffs for the nurses' uniforms as well as the shapeless nightgowns both men and women inmates wore.

She spent those days at her sewing machine humming to herself, waiting for the hearing which she believed would release her from the hospital and return her children to their home from whatever place they had been taken. Sometimes the songs would bring back too painfully the thoughts of her children and she would have to stop sewing to wipe her eyes. Then she would think of a prettier song that would keep her mind easier. Often the other patients interrupted their therapy activities to listen as she sang. Some cried. Some laughed. Some tried to sing with her but knew not the words or the tunes that she sang in her Russian tongue.

Finally, the day. The court hearing was short. There were two doctors, the psychiatrist and a nurse. Each spoke briefly to the judge while Danya sat quietly in a chair placed against the wall. The judge turned to her after some minutes' deliberation.

"Mrs. Vorodinov, on advice of the medical staff of the hospital the court finds you mentally fit to return to your home. You will be under probation to your town health officer for the next six months. You are free now to leave the hospital." He smiled an impersonal judicial smile and rose to leave the room.

"Wait, what means probation?" Danya called to him, scowling suspiciously.

"It means that your behavior will be watched by the health officer to be sure you can adjust yourself properly when you go back to your home."

"Why should I be watched if you agree I am not crazy?"

"It is a matter of law, Mrs. Vorodinov," he answered with some impatience. "We want to be sure you stay well, that you do not have difficulties with those around you. It is for your own good."

"And do you send my children home, too, from where ever the Bulldog has put them?"

"The children's case is different. It is under another department of the welfare. You can talk to your welfare agent, Mr. Bent, and he will explain everything to you."

She stood up, angry. "What do you mean he will explain? He could not tell the truth before. How could he explain anything now?"

The judge was now visibly annoyed. "Mrs. Vorodinov, you must abide by the rules of the courts. Your children have been placed in foster homes. According to your local probate judge they will be returned to their home when you and your husband can provide for them. Your welfare agent understands everything and he will explain all to you. This court has jurisdiction over you, but the juvenile court and probate court in your area will decide about the children."

"But judge, if I am free to go home why are not my children free also?"

"Because you cannot provide for them. It is for their welfare that they are placed in foster homes. You must understand that when your husband can provide a proper home, food and clothing for his children they can go back to their home. While it is necessary for you to accept help from the state welfare department you must also accept their rules. They think it is better to have the children in good homes until you can support them and make the right kind of home for them."

"Good homes? What kind of home is better than their own?" Her voice shook. Again she forced herself under control, but her eyes filled with tears and the hurt of emptiness pulled at the anger inside her.

"Please, Doctor, did I not tell you I could care for my own children? What home is better than the one they were born to?"

"I'm sorry," said the judge. "It is best that you accept the circumstances. You are free to leave the hospital. When you talk to your welfare agent he will explain what is being done for your children."

"And where are they now? Can you not even tell me that?"

"No, I'm sorry. We have no records of that kind. Mr. Bent will have all the records. He will be glad to help you all he can. You must believe that he wants to help you all, you and your children."

The judge left the room. The attendant took Danya back to the hospital, told her to gather whatever things she had and to report immediately to the main desk where she would be given her release papers and her freedom.

During the months of her incarceration summer had turned into early winter. The attendant found a coat left by another patient. They gave her a dollar for bus fare. She left.

HOME

Danya walked away from the asylum in a low mood of disappointment, hurt and confusion. She had been alone in this city only a few times but as she passed out of the hospital gates and looked around she saw no familiar streets or buildings, nothing that she had seen before. The asylum was situated at the top of a rolling green hill, far beyond the center of the city, isolated from traffic and other buildings. She could see trees and beyond them what must be the city buildings.

Too proud to turn back and ask for help, she followed the black strip of road down the hill, not knowing how far she must walk or just where the road would take her. They had let her out of the asylum and she vowed she would show them she could take care of herself, of her husband and her children. If they watched they would see her. They would see she could find her way home. She needed nothing from them. She would walk until she found her way.

The hospital road joined the city street. She walked along the sidewalk until she saw someone of whom she could ask directions. Which way to Stanton? He didn't know. To the city? To the big stores? That way.

She recognized the wide main street when a half hour later she walked across an intersection to the Sears Roebuck store on the corner. It was like a friendly place, she thought as she read the name on the building. Her memory was pricked by pleasant jabs from past associations with that name. These were the first words she and her children could write. They had traced the letters from the front of the catalog and written the name over and over again until they could say each letter.

Through the glass door, into a world of surprises inside that matched the expectations aroused when she had first looked through the catalog. The store really had all the things she had seen in the pages of the catalog. It was to her like a confirmation of reality. The things were there, neatly arranged on shelves and counters. She stopped and carefully read the little cards and the prices. She walked down every aisle, oblivious to the clerks who stood watching from behind their counters. She had not one cent to spend, but she could see and touch all these things. She could remember with pleasure how her children had learned the words, the numbers, the names of colors as they studied pictures of things. Now she saw those things really existed.

Someone here in the store might help her, she thought. She asked the door man at the entrance who stood silently watching the people come through the wide glass door. Yes, he would help her, he could tell her what she wanted to know. The bus to Stanton? It stops one block from the store. No, he didn't know what time it stopped. She should ask there for the schedule. She had no time, she said, to wait and wait. She had only one dollar. Was that enough? He didn't know. He shrugged.

She was anxious now to get to the bus, impatient to be on her way home. She walked away from the store, lightened somewhat by her stop there. The bus had gone she was told. Another would leave for Stanton in two hours.

She wouldn't wait. She felt free and strong. She would walk. She would save the dollar and not take the bus. She knew she could walk.

As soon as she was away from the sounds of the city, when the silence of the countryside enveloped her, the sadness and realization of her plight returned. The road was before her, so was her empty house eighteen miles over the stretched green hills that were cut by the smooth endless black road.

Steadily and slowly she walked, turning when she heard a car coming from behind. She held out her hand to ask for a ride. Twice she had luck. The last ride left her five miles from Stanton. She knew now where she was. Everything looked as her heart remembered it. She gathered new strength over her fatigue and walked the remaining distance to her home.

Danya came to her empty house in the late afternoon when Mikolai was gone to pasture to call in the cows. Behind her the road she had walked was wet with her tears, wept in weariness, frustration, sadness, as she had approached her home.

She made some tea and sat at the kitchen window waiting for her husband to come home.

Few things in the house had been moved or changed since she had left those long months ago. The children's shoes, the toys, the books, were as they had been, so much the same she might expect to see her children running from the barnyard where they played. Oh God, that it might be. That they might be there now waiting for their father to bring in the cows so they could watch the milking. Why, why, could it not be that? Why this empty house instead? This house was made to be filled with life, not emptiness, not silence.

She sat in the saddening twilight looking toward the barn until she saw Mikolai coming from the fields with the cows. Only then did she light the kitchen lamp.

As though no days had lapsed she went along with the same motions that years had made habit. Despite the hurt and squelched anger she felt against him for his inactivity in helping her while she was in the asylum, she moved about the kitchen readying the pans and milk strainer, clearing the wooden slat bench next to the sink so her husband could easily set the milk pails down when he brought them in from the barn.

Again she sat at the window, looking about the big kitchen with its jumble of articles scattered around the blue cook stove.

Hearing nothing, no familiar sounds of children in the house, she wondered if this was what Mikolai's deafness was like. That so great quiet, as it might be for him even when the children were there. Could it be only that, please God? She would give up her ears for the gift of having the unheard children come running from the other rooms.

When she heard his step on the stone path she turned the lamp up and opened the door for him. He showed no surprise when he saw her, or so it seemed to her. He had seen the light and knew it must be that she had returned.

She took one of the pails from him and set it on the bench. He nodded toward the other pail and told her again, as he had so often, how good the old cow was, how unmanageable the younger one was during the milking. As usual she half listened and nodded acknowledgment as she strained the rich thick milk into enamel pans. He, as usual, carried each pan into the pantry, lined them up along the top shelf near the small north window. She washed out the two milk pails and the straining cloth. Then he carried them outside where he hung them over the forked pole near the doorway so they would dry and be ready for the morning's milking.

There was an awkwardness of unsaid words between them. It had wavered somewhat behind the familiarity of their evening chores. She harbored her bitterness. She had thought she would accuse him when he came in, but there was no way she knew to attack the silent, passive man. He also kept his feelings at bay. He could call up no spoken gentleness and his own loneliness had burdened his waiting with self-pity, which he dared not express, but which was now uppermost in his emotions.

Mikolai sat down to read his paper. It was then that Danya began a vituperative attack against Angus Bent. She railed, though she knew Mikolai could hear very little of what she said. She accused Bent of dishonesty, assessing him as the cause of her confinement in the mental hospital and denouncing him as a kidnapper of her children.

Mikolai grumbled that she should be thankful Mr. Bent had helped her when she needed rest. She angrily tried to explain that she had been put in a crazy house, not a rest place. He turned back to his paper, trying to keep from her the mortification and humility taking hold of him. He realized that he should not have believed all he was told. Perhaps he should have made some move toward helping to find the children. He should have tried to find her, too. He should not have believed Bent. He should not have just waited for her to return.

Extremes of anger stood between them while their past bonds begged silently for some understanding and compassion. The disappointments heaped up behind each of them with growing weight. With the gathering strength of bitterness husband and wife were in those moments separated from the common direction their lives had taken. The unknown force that had pulled and held them together had now lost its reason. Where small truths had been held under silence they now worked their way into the full realization of disappointment.

Danya knew she could never lean on Mikolai again. In this terrible thing he had believed not her, but the snake, the Bulldog Bent. How could he have believed his wife needed rest, that she was crazy from too much work? He had been fooled. He had made no effort to find her. He had stayed here on the farm, going about his work, eating and sleeping peacefully while she was a prisoner twenty miles away. She was struck with the anguish of knowledge that she had given her life to a weak man from whom she could never again expect the help she might need. At this time, when she needed his help so desperately, he had made no move. His shyness, his quiet, his trusting way which had been the traits that bound her to him were the parts of his personality that now turned her away from him.

There was no one now to whom she could turn for help. Her own husband was on another side, against her. She must look to herself now. The responsibility to her children was on her shoulders. She must do all. Her husband was more a cohort of the enemy than the man for whom she would once have laid down her life, for whom she had waited through the years of her youth.

She would have to tolerate him, because he was her husband, the father of her children. That could not be changed. She would have to pity him even that, because he could not protect his house and his family as a man should. But he was the father of her children. He had given her six children. For that shouldn't she be grateful? From their union had come those children, for that she was grateful. If she had it to do over again, knowing these children would come to her she would go through the same troubles. She would take for her husband the same man, even if she could see ahead to these times, to his weakness. Because she had the children. Now she knew she could even give them her life. In her thinking her anger lessened.

For his part, Mikolai had misgivings. But what could he do now? How could he distrust every man? How could he suspect Bent of lies when he brought work, food, shoes? He could not see how he had been harmed. Danya made matters more confusing for him sometimes. He couldn't look everywhere for troublemakers. If he saw harm coming his way he knew he could move from it, but when it was unseen he had no ability to dig it out. But even with all these things that had happened he knew in his heart that Danya would find a way to get help and to get the children back. She would know what to do, even if they were in deep trouble and sadness. He knew that she would find the way.

FOSTER HOMES

When the children were taken from their home neither Mikolai nor Danya were told where they were. All six children were delivered into the hands of a foreign speaking Bohemian family in a nearby town. With two sons and three daughters the family ran a large peach and apple farm. The arrangements were made earlier by Angus Bent whose savings bank held the mortgage on the farm. No one was to be told of the children's presence and no one was to see or visit them. They were to be placed in foster homes as soon as possible and they must be looked after and kept away from everyone until that time.

To the children old enough to understand the explanation for the events was reasonable and adequate: that their mother was sick and that they were on a vacation so she could rest. The days were spent exploring the fields, larger and more intriguing than their own. Each discovery of a cave, watering hole or hidden berry patch sufficed to keep them interested, excited and occupied. It all helped to dim their short memories of the parting scenes between them and their mother.

They were given small chores. They carried milk stools or held the burlap bags open for the apple pickers. They washed dishes, stacked them in the big pantry. The two oldest were allowed to iron pillowcases and dishtowels. The newness of everything spared them from questioning their situation.

Mrs. Neiderbild spoke little English. Necessary communication was carried through the older daughter. Even this bothered the children very little since they were accustomed to another language in their own home, which they also could not understand.

A week before the schools opened the three older girls were officially entered as wards of the state in the Cullham County Home for Children. The eight-month old baby and two-year old boy were given as wards of the state to a young couple who had a child of their own. They could have no more children and wanted companions for their two-year old daughter. The fourth girl stayed on the farm, a temporary arrangement until a foster home could be found for her.

Cullham was one of those small New England towns that grew in between other small New England towns with its white church, manicured town green and small one-room schoolhouse. Besides the County Home along the main road going through the town was the county jail, an old gray stone building that rarely had an occupant.

The Home was run by a registered nurse, Martha Bellows. Generally she cared for five children while they waited to be sent to foster homes. With the arrival of the Vorodinov girls she now had eight children to look after along with two of her own pre-school children.

The procedure was to find foster homes quickly as possible for the children placed in the Home. Money was allotted by the government for each child's care and was sent in a yearly check. There were no provisions for a recoup of the funds if a child should leave the institution within the year's time. Therefore it behooved Mrs. Bellows to cooperate in finding foster homes very quickly for new arrivals.

Mrs. Bellows was a respectable woman, a nurse, a sometimes substitute teacher, a faithful wife, mother of two children who shared the table but not the bedrooms or bathroom of the state welfare children. She was practical, and because of these depression times she viewed the extra funds left after a child's early departure as a proper bonus from the government. They gave the money in the first place, she reasoned, therefore had no other use for it, and it would cost as much in paperwork and personnel to keep track of the records in exchange of the money, anyway.

There was an understanding between her and Angus Bent. Half of the left over funds were returned to him and he in turn applied his influence in negotiating for a larger children's home to be built next to the current one. It was to be on a ten-acre plot that belonged to Mrs. Bellows and her husband. Both Mrs. Bellows and Bent understood the complexities of the new federal and state governments attempts at welfare. They perceived it would be more efficient to keep the state home in its present peaceful location. The monetary extras, they agreed, paid for their time and the worry they saved other government agencies.

For three months the Vorodinov girls attended a one-room school within walking distance of the Home. They were intrigued by the discipline both at the home and at the school where one teacher held thirty-nine children at bay with a yardstick, snapping blue eyes, ears that heard every misdemeanor while she turned her back to write on the blackboard.

For all those weeks, Angus Bent had searched carefully for a foster home in which to permanently place the three girls. He selected the home with great thought and care. He convinced himself it was not a matter of conscience that they should be given special concern. He believed rather that these uninhibited children from an unruly home should be exposed to the highest available degree of refinement available. It would enforce their assimilation into the American Way.

This was his pet project. He had discussed it at welfare organizational meetings. So many of the problems of ignorance, bad health, filth, crime could, he told his audience, be conquered with educational projects aimed at the young children of the foreigners who themselves could not be changed. If the children were taken from age two to six and placed in standardized homes, operated by the state, they would, by the time they returned to their original homes, be as Americanized as the children of native Americans.

With this proposed plan he hoped to receive funds to build the model county home, incidentally on Mrs. Bellow's property. It would be furnished as a typical home, run like a home, with units of six children living supervised by competent social workers. The children's speech, studies, play and housekeeping chores would approximate an average American home. It would solve one of the most challenging problems the teachers faced at the time: trying to teach a room full of first grade children, of whom more than half spoke various foreign tongues and very little English.

The swelling concern of the government for its underprivileged citizens was felt by all the members of the welfare board when they granted a portion of child care funds for the model home. Now, with the Vorodinov children, Angus Bent had launched an experiment to be watched carefully for favorable results so his plan could be advanced to a larger scale when the building was completed.

In his heart Angus Bent hoped the project, after a successful showing, might become a part of the national welfare program. As selectman in a town of fourteen hundred people there was no likelihood that he would be considered for higher governmental jobs. This particular idea came to him when he decided something must be done with Danya Vorodinov and her children. It was a double solution. He would be rid of the trouble she could cause him and with her children he could put into trial his effort at assimilation of foreign children into the American culture.

As it was outlined by him to the state welfare board, he knew he had prepared the correct method for recognition. He had received a letter from the governor afterwards that confirmed this. The idea was being considered by the state. Recommendations would go to the federal board after Mr. Bent had made a report on early results.

When Bent read the applications for foster children sent by Reverend and Mrs. Albert M. Rand he decided this was the proper home for the experiment. It was a perfect couple and it was an ideal situation. Both were educated and cultured. They were both from good middle class Yankee families of Maine and Vermont. They needed funds to keep their grown daughter at teachers college, or normal school as it was then called. They would take two children, three if they were from the same family. The legal papers were drawn. Angus Bent wrote the letter himself and delivered it by hand to the county welfare office. It was done.

On a pretty November Saturday the three girls were collected from their play, told to clean up carefully and change into their good clothes. Their few belongings were folded into paper sacks. They waited restlessly in the living room of the country home, jumping about and teasing each other from boredom until early afternoon when Mrs. Rand and her daughter arrived. They rode in sedate wondering silence to their next home.

In the back seat next to them was a box. So successful had three months of discipline been that not one of the girls moved to investigate the box as it was being bumped and rattled by the scratching of some mysterious thing inside. They sat far back in the seats, their hands folded, legs swinging out in front of them, looking from the car window as it passed long stretches of the Connecticut River, pine woods, white wooden churches.

Whatever they were asked they answered in monosyllable, gazing from the window as they spoke.

The car stopped in the driveway of their new home. "It's a small tall house," one of the girls whispered. Another giggled behind her hand. "It's a witch's oven with eyes for windows," and they all giggled shyly.

They were told that this was their home, to bring their packages into the house. With a childish sullenness they left the car. The youngest girl surreptitiously pushed the mysterious box to the ground. The lid flew off and when they saw the land turtle that had been imprisoned inside all three howled with delight, begging for ownership, pulling the helpless shell from one hand to another.

The baffled mother and daughter stood watching. The seemingly manageable three girls had become a wild jumble of whines and yells, quite oblivious to the women who had driven them to their new home.

From his study window upstairs Reverend Rand looked out at the noise. Indians, he said to himself, would have been quieter. He watched, smiling as the girls pulled at each other.

The oldest girl had possession of the treasure and began to run along the side of the house. When the pursuing two nearly caught up to her she tossed the turtle as far as she could over a high fence into a garden next door. After tears, but before bloodshed, the Rand's daughter summoned some knowledge of child behavior she had absorbed in her teaching and brought the matter to a close. She clapped her hands and shouted for quiet above the cries. "It's time for supper," she admonished them sternly. Follow her into the house this minute or there would be no supper. They would be put to bed without supper if they didn't obey immediately!

Discipline, stern and at times unreasonable, outwardly changed the three children into model daughters for a Methodist minister's household. Much as in the tedious training of a spoiled puppy, the commands, punishments and rewards were frequent and consistent. They were quickly made aware of their table manners, their voices, their language. They learned to curtsey and address grownups properly. They were inculcated with the rules of deportment toward each other and the world. Private property was sacred, cleanliness Godly, obedience the badge of a good girl.

Like sponges the resilient girls soaked in all that was expected of them. Their unruliness, their spontaneity, was covered and partially suffocated in the extreme changes demanded of their behavior. They reacted according to individual temperaments, yet the common effect was a blanketing of self-consciousness which none had felt before. They must now review their thoughts and actions in the sphere of proprieties they had not heard of three months before.

They were either good or bad according to new limits of behavior. Good girls sat properly with their backs straight, ankles crossed, hands folded on their laps. Good girls came directly home from school, changed their clothes, did not leave the yard without permission. They must wait for recognition before speaking to a grown up. They must stand in the presence of older people until told to be seated. They must obey without obstinance the rules they were given.

And there were rules for everything they did. A big chart on the kitchen door was a competitive reminder that one child might be a better girl than the others; might be rewarded with something as special as a cherry sundae or a Sunday dinner at a friend's home.

They were presented with material goods, which opened to them a world they had seen only in a Sears catalog but had never envied. The radio, the telephone, the special Sunday dinnerware, the pretty ruffled underwear. All these things they accepted as part of their lives once the novelty and surprise of each wore away.

In their former impoverished home their consciousness had been directed toward the constancy of God-given comforts and gifts, for there were few others their mother could give them. They were taught by her to relish the sunny days, the new mown hay, the magic of rain which left marvelous puddles they could squash through for hours if they desired, with no disturbing call to dinner or lunch. With that former freedom they had envied no other child. In that other life, a good child was one who could cut kindling with a child-sized hatchet, or start the fire in the pot-bellied kitchen stove when it was needed. Each had her own special berrying can with a favorite colored string as a handle, and could carry two cans if they were quick at the picking and didn't eat all as they picked. They could stay the day in the woods and never fear punishment, for they knew by the sun when they must be back from their jaunts.

If their parents' hearts had ached when they was forced to receive food and help from the welfare agents, none of their hurt was shown to the children. The shiny silver can wrappings that Angus Bent brought were delights for them. They gave no heed to the food or the help that came from him. They questioned no motives of the givers, but took the paper wrappings off as soon as the corned beef cans were in the house. Their father showed them how to draw on the back of the wrappings; their mother showed them how to make cut out animals, ducks, dogs, horses and fishes that stood like small silver figures along the window sill until the paper curled from the heat of the sun.

The shoes that had been brought to them by the welfare agent they received more in annoyance than humiliation because walking barefoot over clover fields and rain softened paths was a far greater treat, more envied by shoe clad playmates than the possession of new shoes. Using the plenties of nature their mother had shielded her children from the knowledge of their material unplenty. If there was name calling or verbal insults, the lesson was always the same: "A word is a bird...once it is said it flies out and cannot be brought back, so be careful what words you call out."

In this foster home the material needs and wants of ordinary children in a typical American home came tumbling upon them as though released from a Pandora's box of plenty. Envies and desires for what other children had became more common as they became aware of those things others had. The seemingly harmless corruption of naïve minds was accomplished with good will and good intention by persons who had lived only in the properly laid out life of comfort, worldly goods and acceptable duties to the Godless, the poor and the needy.

Now, like all other children, they must guard carefully their new shoes or coats against the wet snow, the wonderful mud. They must have permission to sail leaves and sticks in the swollen streams along the roadside. Access to the woodshed and attic was forbidden. Magic childhood resources they had known were withheld, were taboo.

Properly trained, they fell into the competitive and then popular striving for the great norm. Yet along with all that, they were given advantages that would mark and help them throughout their lives.

Reverend Rand exercised a more temperate discipline over them, and he saw to it that their church schooling was augmented with small sessions in his study. There they might be allowed to spend an hour or more in some disciplinary occasion. He put them to searching the bible for passages he would use in the next week's sermon. He let them work out their punishment by rearranging the myriad books that lined every wall of his study. They must dust carefully and line up the books a half inch from the shelf edge. They must remember the names of the books so they could find them easily should he call out for a reference. They must spend some time reading the bible where they could learn the moral lesson of the punishment being inflicted.

There was little open affection shown in the household. There was the formality of properly raised people who rarely showed anger openly. At first the tamed, even conversations were curious to the girls who might sense occasion for anger. Then it was understood and became the rule for their own behavior. Their needs were tended to. They were well fed, well nursed, dressed warmly and properly. They soon forgot the feel of their mother's arms. They forgot there was a time when they could run to her with their hurts and disappointments. In time they learned to nurse their hurts in the privacy of their own thoughts, sharing rebuffs with no one, holding on to whatever friend they found for small secrets. As months went by they were becoming good and proper young ladies.

THE CURSE

"Though He slay me, yet will I trust Him." Where was her God, her Savior? Why had he done this to her? He had slayed her, emptied and killed her from the inside. Yet she must trust the Lord and love Him.

To trust Him, turn to Him, to love Him in the midst of her anguish? That was the test this love demanded. Love can be cruel when it asks beyond reason. Love Him, when He had turned His eyes from her? Trust Him when she prayed each night for help and none came? When would He find her, when would He hear her wailing heart? So many times He had come to her in the past to help her, to save her. She no longer asked for herself. There were her children now for whom she must pray. She must pray and pray that He would help them. Now, more than any time before, she needed His help, but where was He?

Why wouldn't He come to her as He had before? Where was He hidden? She must find her children. Why couldn't He help now? Had He no pity now for her when her heart was shattered six fold? Had He given to her the gift of her children's lives, then allowed that they be taken from her?

Danya's troubled mind dissipated her old trust in Him into a place where she viewed her encounters with Him as nothing more than strange and coincidental dreams. She came to think she must, after all, do everything for herself. Perhaps there would be no help, only wishing. Alone she must find where they had sent her children. Alone she must find a way to bring them back to their home.

Angus Bent would not tell her. When she went to his office to ask he said she would be told when the welfare agency decided it was time. Then she could visit them. Not before. It would disturb the children if she knew their whereabouts and bothered them, he told her. They should have a chance to adjust to their new lives before she visited them and disturbed them.

She stared at him in disbelief. What was he saying to her? That she, their mother, would disturb her own children? Was he telling her they could not come home to their own home. Did someone else own her children?

"I am not crazy, my fine Bulldog," she nearly screamed at him. "I am proved not crazy and maybe now you should have your turn in the asylum. Do you think I will not get my children back before you destroy me? Oh, no, you will not keep them hidden. I will walk on every street, in every town. I will knock on every door. I will say, 'Did Ugly Bulldog Bent bring my children here?' Everyone will know your name and your crime, you ugly kidnapper."

He stood up from his desk. He tried to interrupt her. "Now, Mrs. Vorodinov, just a minute…now Mrs. Vorodinov, you had better calm yourself." The blood mounted in his face. He hoped there were no others near his office to see or hear this. Her voice had become loud enough to be heard through the corridor, he was sure. He became angry. He hated listening to her accented speech, hated to face her, didn't want to look at her, her eyes. Yes, those eyes…he could not look at her.

"That's enough!" He pounded his desk. "I remind you that you are on probation. If you expect any help you will have to adjust yourself. You must apply in an orderly way for visiting privileges and the welfare department will grant them to you when you demonstrate that you can behave normally, when you show that you are a fit mother." He sat down.

"It will be to your advantage to behave in a more rational manner, Mrs. Vorodinov." His anger went behind a more controlled voice. "Remember, you are on probation. You can be re-entered to the hospital if you insist on creating scenes like this, if you continue to act in such an irrational manner."

She would not be subdued. "Never! You will never put me again in that place!" She glowered at him, then lowered her voice. Although quavering with emotion, she spat the words out. They struck deep into his heart, in a place where old fears bubbled, ready to boil out into his dreams.

"I know things about you, you ugly Bulldog, that can make you such trouble you will have not time to chase me to the asylum. I see in your eyes and your white hands such ugly things that you try to hide from the world. When I watch you, I know what you are. You are afraid people will learn about you. So you turn red, you blush, you are embarrassed. But I will not tell these things I know now, oh no, not when you can call me crazy and give me back to the asylum. No, you can suffer and wonder when people will find you out. Yes, I will report you. This time I will wait until I can prove it. You can sit in your office and in your house and worry about when I will show my proof. You can go crazy in your dreams trying to shut me away from what I know. But I will win against you. That is my promise. That is my curse on you!" She repeated slowly, "Remember, that is my curse on you."

She paused, looked coldly into his eyes, then measured her last words.

"You cannot free yourself from the wrongs you made against me, nor from my hate, not in this world. When you made me your enemy you brought me so close to you as your own skin. Not one day that you live will you be free from the evil deeds you have done. They will chase you into your grave. Every time you see me you will remember what you are. That will be my curse even as you are dying."

He said nothing but waited for her to be finished and gone. With damp hands he shuffled a few papers as he looked down onto his desk to avoid her eyes.

She paused. He dared not look up. At this moment he dared not look into her eyes. She waited a few more seconds. With a triumphant toss of her head she leaded toward him,
"Hah, you ugly Bulldog, you have heard me, I know. You are afraid, you cannot meet my eyes. You are caught in my curse." Her words came from her mouth like a song.

She walked from his office, eyes afire, not looking at any who were in the outer office. She was filled with tightened hatred and new determination that she could conquer this evil man.

She walked slowly toward home, a small round woman to whose face and form suffering had added extra years. Her narrow shoulders were dragged low from the burdens she had carried. Her back, though still strong, had the tired curve of a much older person. The arms were lean and slightly muscled like a young man's, worked by the chores she had given them. She had been vain of her small hands and feet and perhaps the constant walking and working had kept them younger than leisure would have, yet now they seemed as tired as her body. There was no grace left now that child bearing and grief had stolen so much from her form.

Hers was a face that showed every terror, every ache, every hurt and disappointment endured. The lines were etched deep into once beautiful skin, making creases from the deep dark eyes that were often glazed over with tears. The creases surrounded the mouth that was thinning and beginning to harden the set of the once delicate chin.

But there was no hint of helplessness in that face now. Her determinations had struggled with the last soft contours and won. The fulfillment and love she had experienced as a young woman and through her children were not overt but had shown in her deeds or hidden in her thoughts. It seemed from her physical appearance that grief had always been her companion, that now it must fortify her, sustain the hatred and give her the strength to do what was necessary to get her children back.

That no one could help her, would help her, strengthened her forces until she could dispel some of her frustration and confusion and reach out for a plan that would at least give her the satisfaction of bringing some action into the standstill and void.

So she wrote letters. One to the governor, another to Mrs. Roosevelt whom she had heard once on the radio. The neighbor's daughter typed the letters for her, taking the dictation and translating the poignant requests into standard English.

'Dear Governor: I am writing in my tears to beg for your help. I am made sad beyond my strength because my six children have been kidnapped from me by the welfare agent in this town, Angus Bent. He put me in an asylum so he could hide my children from me and my husband. The doctors let me out right away because I am not crazy but the welfare will not tell me where my children have been taken. They will not let me see them or bring them back to their own house. Can you make an order before my heart breaks so I can see my children again please. I am a European woman and cannot write such good English, but my heart is like every American mother's heart.'

To the President's wife she wrote:

'Dear Mrs. Roosevelt: I know you are a good mother and you are proud of your children because I heard you say this on the radio. I am a mother of six children but I will never see them again if nobody helps me. When I hear President Roosevelt speak on the radio he said he would help the poor people. But when he gave the welfare jobs he was not careful who he chose. The welfare agent Angus Bent kidnapped my children from me and put me in an asylum. The doctors were satisfied that I am not crazy and they let me come home right away. The welfare agents are all dishonest because they will not give back my children. They will not even tell me where they are so I can see if they are alive and healthy. What would you do if someone stole your children from your house when the baby was only eight months old? I beg you from mother to mother to help me find my children before my heart is broken in pieces.'

Danya walked the two miles to the post office rather than mail the letter where the rural deliveryman would take note of them. Not completely forgotten was her experience with the postman's dishonesty in Russia years ago. She wouldn't take a chance on this one. These letters were too important. She would put the stamps on and mail them herself. Only then could she be sure they were on their way.

When she asked how much the stamps cost for Washington D.C. the plump, curiosity-worn postmaster did not hide his surprise. He spoke from behind his cage loudly enough for the others in the post office to hear.

"Who do you know in Washington, Mrs. Vorodinov, the president?"

"No, not the president but his wife. Everyone knows her, so you shouldn't be so surprised."

The two men standing behind her chuckled. One of them, a small wiry old man, was the town veterinarian who came every year to the Vorodinov farm to give the cows their tuberculosis tests. Two times he had arrived the day after her babies were born, the third and fourth girls which Danya had had a year apart. He had looked in on them and had made his little joke to her. "Each child looks more like the doctor who delivered the last one," he'd said.

She was in no mood to be amused by the joke this time when he repeated it to his friends there in the post office.

"You know, it's a funny thing, Mrs. Vorodinov's children look more like the doctor who delivers them than they do like the husband."

Red faced and angry, Danya turned from the window to face him.

"And it's a funny thing, Doc Latham, since you come every year to check my cows the heifers look more like you than like Tuttle's bull who should service them."

The men roared with laughter, though Doc Latham's enjoyment was hardly as great as the others. He could see that he had hurt and angered Danya for she stood there unsmiling and flushed, and he saw too that she was near tears.

"That's a good joke on me," he said, " but I hope you can take a joke, too Mrs. Vorodinov."

"To make jokes on my children doesn't make me laugh anymore. When I was a mother with my children in my arms you could say anything to me. Now when they are taken from me it is like poison arrows in my heart to hear your fun."

She turned back toward the postmaster. He had taken the letters and stamps and stood there watching, still smiling. Danya looked at him trying to collect herself.

"Where are my letters, Cantini? I put two letters here in front of you with money for stamps."

"Don't worry, Mrs. Vorodinov, they are already stamped and all set to go on their way. Here's your change."

He gave her the money and as she counted it he winked at the two men waiting behind her.

"What kind of trick do you play on me? I saw you winking just now. Do you lie when you tell me my letters are mailed? Where are they? Do you keep them or do you mail them?"

"Please, Mrs. Vorodinov," Postmaster Cantini protested, on the edge of anger, "You know we follow the government's rules. It's not a nice thing to suspect me of sloppy housekeeping."

"I don't care about your housekeeping. Just show me where you put my letters so I can be sure you mail them. I know other people, like Ugly Bent, who work for the government, but it doesn't make him honest, so I cannot trust you just because you work for the government."

Cantini shrugged in mild disgust. He looked through a nearby box and quickly found the two stamped letters.

"See, look here, both letters are stamped, ready to go. Watch, I'll put them in the proper sacks, there, that's it. Almost on their way. No one can take anything out of these sacks. Aren't you satisfied?"

"No, I'm not satisfied until an answer comes. Then I will know the letters were delivered honestly.

"Oh, for God's sake..."

"Yes, for God's sake, Cantini. Don't think you wear a halo because you work for the government. I am learning to watch more carefully when a man sings in a loud voice how honest and good he is, and I don't see any wings on you yet either to make you an angel."

Doc Latham interceded. "But you see horns, huh, Mrs. Vorodinov?"

"Not yet, but if I come some day and see his horns growing I will know what kind of postmaster he is."

To their laughter this time she smiled, then left the post office heartened a bit by her own joke. It pleased her to be clever in her words. She practiced in her mind so she could make a good job of it. Some day she would be able to have the right words to use against Bent. Then she would get him. In that she knew God was helping her, she could tell. She could use the language now and she knew she was making better uses of her talking all the time.

In that she thanked God. But doesn't He know she needs more help now, right now? She must have His help to find her children. In her aching heart prayed as she walked home. Perhaps she would have quick answers to her letters. The president's wife should have a big heart for another mother. Oh, she would like to see Bulldog's face when he finds out the president's wife will help her.

***

Danya watched eagerly each day for the postman's arrival. Mikolai wanted to know for what she was so anxious. She said it didn't concern him; it was something she needed that she waited for. She had decided he should know nothing about the letter. She would do everything herself because she could not rely on him. It was none of his business now. No matter what she decided to do he would know of it later, when there was no way he could discourage her or try to stop her.

Some days it seemed that the world was at a standstill because everything was exactly as the day before. When the children were there, each day was new, and a hundred unexpected things could happen. Now she and her husband were like two old people whose days repeated the past days. The waiting and hoping were the only things that took up their time after the work of the farm was finished. Like old people, she thought, as she sat watching Mikolai work in the yard. They had taken their children and they had made old people of them, the parents.

At times she experienced feeling of deep resentment against the governor and Mrs. Roosevelt for the delay in answering her pleas for help. The promises were easy to make with words. That she knew from other times. The truth is learned when you hold out your heart for help and find that the leaders have nothing to put into a begging heart or empty palms. Yes, she remembered it all from the other days. She had seen it happen after the great revolution and the big promises that went round and round in the people's mouths. More words, more promises, that was all, and not one good thing had come of those promises. She wanted to believe it was different here, in this country. It had to be. It must be. She prayed that it must be.

She seethed with anger each time Mikolai came home from work on the WPA. Why didn't he ask about the children? Didn't he care if they came back to their home? Why shouldn't he, too, be making some effort on his own? He asked nothing, as if their children no longer existed. It was clear to her that if she left it to him they would live in this house the rest of their lives without getting the children back. He would go easily into old age with no effort to find the children and bring them back from the ugly kidnappers.

Only once she had asked him if Bent might have said where he was taking the children. Had her absence been so long that he had maybe forgotten? He had shaken his head and turned from her. Yes, he should be ashamed for believing old Bent in the beginning. He should have taken the stick to the old Bulldog Bent and beaten the man for what he had stolen from his own lands: his wife and his children. For that he should have taken the biggest stick he could find.

It was becoming more difficult for her to believe in her praying. Too many times she couldn't reach out. Too many times there seemed to be no one listening. She deeply longed for some sign or word to her heart that He was near, that He would help her as He had before.

It was as though her hatred for Bent had obliterated the paths on which in former times had come her help. When at night she made her choice between praying for help and cursing her enemy she found the curse on her lips before the decision was in her mind. Yet it gave her satisfaction. It was the most real thing she felt these days.

When she saw Bent's face she knew at least those curses were having results. When she went to down town to do her food shopping she watched to see when he came out of his bank office. She walked toward him. He could never pass her in the street without turning his eyes away, and he would flush with the color of deep embarrassment as he tried to avoid her. Ah, yes, she had him now. He was cursed to remember his sin against her.

THE SEARCH

Then the first answer to her letters came. It was from the governor's office. He was sorry about her plight and he was referring the letter to her local welfare agent.

She rushed to the neighbor's to have the girl read it more carefully and explain all the words. She railed in anger. "What kind of answer is this, to send my complaint to the crook who makes the trouble? I must write another letter to explain."

The second answer informed her that the case was being given immediate attention.

The third letter told her that her case was being handled correctly according to the welfare laws.

Frustrated, she wrote in reply, "If the welfare laws are made to separate mothers from their children, to keep families broken, then it is not better than the laws of my old country where they made the same crimes. I will walk into your office one day and ask you to say to my face that you are honest men working in the government. I will send your letter to the President of the United States so he can see what kind of people are working for him."

The first letter from Mrs. Roosevelt expressed sadness for her and a promise that a letter would go immediately to her state welfare office asking them to investigate.

Despite the correspondence the weeks were passing and Danya still had no word or clue to her children's whereabouts. None of her neighbors or townspeople whom she asked could advise her how or where to look. They said that Mr. Bent must know the rules. Maybe she should just wait until he told her it was time to visit her children. She shouldn't trouble herself, they advised, but wait until she had permission.

She was disgusted and heartsick. She would make her own search if no one could help her. She remembered from the day they had taken her to the asylum that the children also were taken in cars. Perhaps she should start in that city where they had put her. She would go to Middletown and ask for the welfare department. She would ask them if they had news of her children.

The fare to the city was thirty-five cents. The bus ran every three hours, the only public transportation service along the Connecticut River towns. While she waited for the bus there at the center of town with six others, her impatience had its way. No, she thought, she must save every penny she could. She decided that she would start walking. She could try to get a ride by hitchhiking. It had not been so difficult that other time, coming home from the hospital. If she couldn't hitch a ride she would signal the bus when it caught up to her.

Every penny saved was more important to her since the welfare had taken away her children. She would show them that she and Mikolai could care for their own family with their own hands and their own money. To hell with their shoes and their cans of meat. They gave those things to help, so they said, but finally she could see it was only to own her and her children, to make a claim against her because she could not give them all things other families had, and because she would not fall into the lies that the Bulldog forced on her.

She saved every penny she could. She found ways to make money. She made little dresses for some of the neighbors' children. She kept the fifty-cent pieces she charged in a special cloth pouch near her sewing machine. She carried three of these coins with her now. If she could get a ride by hitching she could put the money right back into her treasury when she got home.

She was a curious sight plodding along the highway, stopping to hold out her thumb asking for a ride whenever she heard a car coming along. From some she extracted amused stares as they drove past. She was wearing an out-moded cloche hat that covered so much of her face that the eyes, even squinting, looked enormous and strange. It had been so cold when she left the house that she put on her winter coat, a beige caracal cloth with a now tatty fur collar. It was one of the special things she had bought for herself during the good times. It had been worn sparingly at first, had hung some years without wearing while she was carrying her children, yet now the shape inside made the coat look much more worn and older than it actually was. It pulled across the hips and stomach and dipped down in front because of her hunched shoulders. The long rust colored hairs of the fox collar blew up around her face so that to observers she looked very much like a great furry animal thumbing for a ride.

A car did stop. The driver was a middle-aged man whom Danya had never seen. The woman she recognized as a lady she had seen in the Stanton A&P. Two children were in the back seat.

"Are you in trouble, do you need a lift?" The man asked in a clipped New England accent.

"I go to Middletown, can you take me so far?"

The woman looked at her husband. She nodded. The children moved closer to each other away from the beige apparition that climbed into the back seat beside them.

She sat on the edge of the seat, holding on to the strap beside the window. Most of the way they rode in silence. The children were restless but quiet. When his curiosity overcame their manners, the boy asked if she was a lady or an animal.

The mother turned around from the front seat and scolded him for his question.

Danya interrupted her. "Never mind. It is no big trouble when a child sees what grown people cannot see anymore. I wouldn't be upset because I don't look like other people. Now when I talk he knows I am no animal."

"But you do talk funny, too, even if you are a lady."

"Because, young man, I am from another country. But my children talk just like you and I can learn, too, to talk your way."

The mother asked, "Oh, have you children?"

"Yes, but they have been taken from me and I don't know how to find them."

"Oh?" The mother turned around again.

"Yes, all of them, my six children. The welfare agents kidnapped them right out of my house. They took me to the asylum and when I came out they wouldn't tell me where my children were hidden. But I will not wait for their permission, the crooks. I am going now to the county welfare office to start my search, to look and find my children."

The man looked sideways at his wife. He raised his eyebrows, questioning.

"My, you've had some problems."

"Don't worry that I am crazy, please. I see questions in your faces when you look to each other. I am not crazy because the doctors let me out after one hearing. The man who put me in the asylum is crazy and he will pay."

There was silence for several minutes. As always when she told her story, Danya's voice became higher and raspy. Her cheeks were flushed. She cleared her throat.

"Please, when we come to the city can you show me where the welfare department is? First I will ask if they have my children somewhere. If they are not such crooks as old Bent they will help me."

"Bent? Is that Angus Bent from Stanton?"

"Yes it is him, the bulldog. If you know him you should watch out for him. He is a crook. I can tell you about him; I can tell you plenty."

The man ahemmed, pressing his lips together in the tight non-commital way of New Englanders. The wife looked at him again, smiling slightly.

"I guess you do know him, by your looks, I think so?" Danya asked the question eagerly.

"Well, yes, I guess I do." The man spoke slowly. "But I think in fairness to you and to him, personal matters of the sort you mention should be something between you two."

"Maybe so, but in this crime he made against me there was no fairness. I will tell anyone who will listen or who might be able to help me find my children, so they will know what the Bulldog has done against me. I will tell my story to the welfare agents and they will listen, too, and maybe they can help me."

"I'm certain the county welfare office will get whatever information you need. If you and Mr. Bent have had misunderstandings I'm sure they will try to straighten things out for you both …We'll let you out right here…it's that building across the street. All the county offices are there and they will tell you where you ought to go once you're in the main building." He turned to open the door for her and continued. "I sincerely hope you have some success. It's a pretty easy thing to misunderstand another person's intentions, but I'm sure this will come out all right for you. Good luck to you."

Danya said thanks, smiled at the children and walked into the big sand colored building across the street.

***

"Whatever do you make of that, Jordan?" asked the wife when Danya was beyond sight.

"Really can't say. She's rather a strange woman, isn't she? Haven't seen her at the bank, but I assume she's from Stanton."

"Oh yes, I've seen her at the grocery store a few times. But don't you think it's a bit unpleasant for the bank to have someone like that loosely accusing a vice president of the bank of being dishonest? Had you heard anything like it before, about Angus, I mean?"

"No, nothing has ever been said that's come back to me. Of course we've been here only six weeks. I'm sure we don't know all the local gossip yet."

"I'm sure we don't!" She smiled pleasantly. "But, Jordan, you'll be the last one to know if one of your employees is a thief."

He chuckled. "I don't think she called him a thief, exactly, just a crook. I venture to guess that as welfare agent for the town Angus has hurt some feelings, and this woman is one of the people who's been hurt. Or how do we know, perhaps one of them who's been helped by him. If she does tell this story about him I have a feeling no one would believe it, so it can't be anything for the bank to worry about."

"But you see that she tells it to perfect strangers. It's the kind of accusation that could be very bad for the bank, don't you think, Jordan, particularly at these times when people are so suspicious of banks anyway?"

"You have a point, Arliss. Mmmm. Yes, you do have a point, though it's difficult to be suspicious of Angus Bent. He certainly knows the banking business as well as the building and loan business. His family is one of the old timers around here, and from what I see at church, everyone is pretty friendly and extremely respectful towards him. Locally this kind of gossip couldn't mean much. It couldn't do much harm. But you are right, that if she talks freely of it there might be some bad publicity for us."

"Shouldn't you talk to Angus and find out what's behind the matter? She was very worked up, you noticed, when she began to tell us her problems."

"I hate to interfere with small town crisis, if that's what it is. I could say something to Angus, I suppose, without starting a rumpus, just out of curiosity."

"I wish you would, Jordan. Yes, I think you should. At least you would be informed. It's probably a small matter. Rather pathetic, though, if there's any truth to it at all."

"Well, I venture to guess that it's another welfare case where the family couldn't support the children. Six, you remember she said. We had so many of those cases in Boston, too. Can't remember though that we took the children from the parents unless there was no father...or because of illness. Perhaps that's it, perhaps there's no father. Did she say anything about the father? I couldn't recall. Did she mention her husband?"

"No, I don't recall that she did. I think not, though. The father may be dead, or may have deserted the family as some of them do these days. It wouldn't harm to ask Angus, would it, Jordan?"

MENDACITY

In the reshuffling of the banking business after the great crash of 1929 the Stanton Savings and Loan Company merged with the Building and Loan Society. Angus Bent's astute business knowledge and his various civic and church activities had earned him a reputation within the county banking circles unequaled to any man in the area. The new bank directors were so impressed with his management of the Society that they prevailed upon him to accept an offer of vice-presidency in the reorganized bank. His knowledge was invaluable to the new directors who knew little of the local area, having dealt mostly with city banks in Middleton and Hartford.

Bent kept his insurance business but came each morning to his desk at the bank to attend to whatever matters concerned the Society and his part time association as a vice president.

The syndicate that had bought the bank moved one of their Boston men into the Stanton bank as president. He was Jordan Haig, a quiet, middle-aged man whose family bank had gone under and whose wife was related to a member of the syndicate.

Haig spent a year with the syndicate's Boston bank, then was transferred to the rural town of Stanton. With his wife and two young children he settled into a large comfortable house at the edge of the town lake.

Arliss Haig was a beautiful woman. She had been born at the right time to suit her nature. She was a joyous, pert light person, a flirt. She had a near perfect young woman's figure and moved with the grace and self-assurance of a well-bred Bostonian. She was kind and almost unchangeable in her ability to make life and problems lighter for the people who brought those problems to her.

Serious, stuffy Jordan Haig met her at a serious, stuffy old people's party where she had shocked the assembly with her flapperish ways. He was eighteen years her senior. He had spent weeks torturing himself with indecision, then finally called on her for a dinner date. They married eight months later.

Now a woman of thirty-five, Arliss still projected the shining aura of a joyous person. The two children had the quiet serious mien of their father and it was left to Arliss to furnish the sunshine so badly needed during the hardship days of the Great Depression of the 1930's. What might have been considered a certain demotion for Jordan, being sent from Boston's banking world to a small town bank, Arliss treated as a call to adventure. She loved her Boston life style, Jordan knew that. But she insisted that she would be far happier in a small country place, especially with two children. Her secret wish, she convinced him, was to have an apple orchard and twenty sheep. She had always dreamed about it, she had no idea why, and if they could find a place to live where she could have those things she would be convinced that dreams do come true.

Jordan knew that without her stability he would not have recovered, at his age, from the shattering experience of the bank failure. In this incredibly dull small town she remained as gay and thoughtful of him and the children as if she were still in the center of the other world she'd known all her life.

It was quite against Jordan's nature to interfere in matters that had nothing to do with his business or his immediate family. But to please Arliss, who would not forget the incident, he promised to clear the subject of Danya's accusations with Angus Bent as soon as possible.

Soon after he arrived at the bank one morning Bent was called into Jordan's office. Finding a way to broach the subject was awkward for Jordan. He asked some routine questions about the building and loan business at the moment, listened attentively, nodded and pulled his lips together in thoughtful reaction.

"It looks a bit as though we're near the end of this awful time then, Angus?"

"From what I read and hear in the federal reports I would say so. It would show up early in the banking business, too, I should think. So far there seems to be no perceptible big change. Of course, a small town like this wouldn't be the first to reflect change, so I don't think we can gauge anything by these figures I've discussed with you. What we should have is a good federal report, right up to date. If we could get it rewritten and published in the area press it might make some difference to the morale, if nothing else."

"Seems like a good idea. It's been going on for a longer time than expected, hasn't it? By now people are probably frozen into the idea of gloom. It takes more than a good newspaper article to make any changes in their outlook, but you have a point that it might give a lift to the morale. You're pretty close to the people, aren't you Angus, through the welfare administration?"

"Yes, indeed. It's been my main concern since the depression came on. So many of the people here mortgaged by the Society were unable to pay their due notes so we changed our entire procedure to help them out. I'm proud to say I made some close friends through those early experiences. Luckily we had enough funds to tide us over the worst problems. Still, a good number of the local folks are just meeting their dates by the last penny and that does get them down as it persists year after year. I'm often concerned that in discouragement they will drop the mortgage and the bank will be left with a lot of local real estate. Some of it, too, of questionable value for any sort of resale. A great many old houses that haven't been kept up."

"I think you have a lot to be proud of. It's well known how much the Society's patience is appreciated. You're no doubt responsible for holding together a number of families who otherwise would have had to break up and sort themselves out with relatives. We had similar problems in Boston, but of course in a city there's a blow up, so to speak, of any situation. It's nice to know you've prevented anything like that here. Good for the bank, too, you know, to have your reputation, to have you connected with the bank."

"Why, that's really kind of you. I really appreciate it. There are times when I wonder if we're making any headway with the welfare, or whether this thing will just keep on the way it is. That's why I'd like to make an effort with this news item. I'd like to see these people take hold of more hope. I think that's what they're searching for, some hope, some path out of their miseries."

"I'm for it, anytime you can put the article together. Let me have a look at it so I can add anything if necessary. Oh, when you mention searching I recall an experience we had some days ago. My wife and I helped out a woman who had missed the bus. We took her all the way to Middletown. Picked her up in Cullham, I think it was, along the highway. Strange sort, with bright brown eyes, some foreign accent. A small woman, near fifty or so I'd say, maybe more. She said she was making a search for her children who had been taken from her…"

"Did she…Oh, I'm sorry, didn't mean to interrupt." Bent was caught off guard.

"No, go ahead. I just mention it as a curiosity. Arliss was upset by it. The woman was pretty emotional and seemed disturbed when we let her out at the county welfare offices. I have no idea who she was."

"She didn't give you her name?"

"No, didn't even say where she was from, which town. Just told us the welfare had taken her children from her and she was going to try to get them back to their home."

"It sounds like one of the rare cases the welfare department has when they're forced to break up the family for various reasons. It's always hard on the parents." He had regained his composure and spoke off handedly.

"Mmmm...doesn't happen very often, I take it?"

"Hardly at all. We do everything we can to keep a family together."

"Have you ever found it necessary in your welfare work?"

Bent knew he had to be careful. "Yes, only once. It was a dreadfully hard decision for me to make. I consulted with the state health officers and other authorities before I came to any decisions. Very hard thing to do, you know, to break up a family."

Jordan observed Bent carefully. "Of course it is, but when it's warranted that's understandable. We had incidents in Boston where the father deserted or died, and we were forced in some cases like that to split up a family. Was your case similar?"

"Not exactly. No, not at all. For more tragic. Far more."

"In what way?"

"Nothing wrong with the father in this case. Able bodied, willing to take any work we could find for him through the WPA. The problem was the mother. We tried for two years to let it ride, but it got to be a threat against the good of the children. And you know we try to put children first in these considerations."

"What was the trouble?"

"The mother was unfit."

"In what way"?

Bent hesitated, took a breath, shook his head in feigned sadness. "Well, at first we treated it as gossip. You know how a small town is about unsavory things. But when the stories began to circulate among the school children we thought we should make some investigation if possible. Very sticky situation, very trying."

"Were the stories true?"

"Unfortunately, yes. We talked to two men involved and they were willing to sign statements if necessary. Rather than bring it to public attention we decided to take the children from the mother before they were damaged by the kind of life she was leading."

"Wasn't that difficult without formally accusing her?"

"It would have been necessary to bring it all out, but she was also exceedingly unstable. There were rumors that the last two children belonged to men other than the husband, and we had the two men who would swear to that. We were prepared to do it all quietly, to discuss it with her and get a court order to remove the children. She was so unreasonable, however, that we never got anywhere that way, trying to spare the children any hurt or knowledge of the troubles."

"You did accuse her, then?"

"Yes, I tried to convince her that the life she was carrying on would injure her children. That it would be best to give them as wards of the state to protect their future."

Bent signed. Again shook his head sadly. He hoped what he said would satisfy Jordan.

"What was her reaction, Angus?"

"Naturally, as anyone of that sort would be, she was outraged. She turned on me with foul language and accusations, really a terrible scene there at her house. The children were nowhere about to witness it, thank goodness. Oh, I think the youngest was in her arms. She called me names, accused me of dishonesty in the welfare administration, things of that sort. I had never had any experience with insanity, or maybe I should say nervous breakdown, but it seemed to me that the woman even then was seriously unstable."

"Did you talk to the husband?"

"Only after talking with the health authorities and her doctor. Her doctor agreed that since the last child she had been in a precarious mental state. She had made wild accusations in public against me and others, neighbors who helped care for the children at times. It was a very, very disturbing choice for me to make. It truly bothered me, hurt me, but I then went to the husband, talked it over as best I could since he is partially deaf. He signed a committal paper and we entered her into the state asylum for examination."

"Is she still there?"

"No, she was given a hearing and released on probation to our health office. Her mental condition wasn't that serious, a minor nervous breakdown. But she wasn't in any condition to raise her children. She seems to be adjusting."

"And the children?"

"They were placed in foster homes. I felt so badly about separating the six that I carefully chose the best homes I could for them. The finest American homes from which we had applications for foster children."

"What was her reaction to that?"

"At this time we still do not feel it's wise to tell her where the children are placed. Naturally she is disturbed about that. My heart truly weeps for her, but for the sake of the children they should be given some time to adjust to their new lives before the mother is allowed to visit them."

"Isn't that harsh?"

"It's standard in such serious cases. I've kept the moral issue out of the reports so it won't harm the children in the future. The least I could do for the poor children, you see...you know, that could have been the woman you spoke about...yes, I didn't think of it when you described her, but it certainly could have been Mrs. Vorodinov, although you say you picked her up in Cullham?"

"We did give her a ride from there, but Arliss said she had seen her in the grocery store, here in Stanton."

"Was she a bit odd looking, around the eyes, dark eyes, set deep, very large, set in a small face?" Bent felt relieved, sure that he had hidden the fact the he knew from the beginning of the conversation who the woman was.

"Yes, that's what Arliss remembered about her, the eyes."

"It may have been she...truly a pity, a pity. I hope she will soon straighten out so we can get her together with her children. It bothers me often, but her progress is slow."

"How is that?"

"She continues these stories and accusations against public officials, against the doctor, against her husband, even against me. The state board has asked me to wait until she comes back to complete normalcy, so to speak, before we take a chance with the children seeing her this way. I'm certainly sorry, awfully sorry about it all."

Haig felt he had heard enough of the situation to satisfy his curiosity and Arliss's concern. Almost abruptly he brought the conversation to a close.

"She's in good hands, I'd say, with your interest, Angus. Let me know of any other similar cases, not so much for my curiosity, but because I think it's best for the bank to know these kinds of things, should it reflect in any way on our staff. Thanks for your time."

Angus Bent walked from the bank with a sad face and posture, purposely held to reflect what he wanted Jordan Haig to believe. He was convinced that Haig believed him. He also knew that the man would not check the story and would probably never discuss it again. What he had told him was for the most part true and verifiable. He often had wondered about the morality of women like that who had so many children. The foreigners had a completely different concept of morality and it was within reason that a farmwoman like that would dally with other farmers. Heavens knows that there were plenty of stories about the hired hands around the town. If they couldn't behave with the young girls, how much easier for them to get on with a breeding woman like that.

He wasn't about to worry, though. While he was talking to Haig he had surprised himself with the words that came from his mouth. Perhaps it was all true, after all. It seemed very believable while he was telling it, and from Haig's reaction, he too, must have believed it.

***

There was a revolting difference in Angus Bent's dream that night. The witch hovered over him weaving back and forth, smiling and crying at the same time. Soft moaning sounds came through her teasing smile. Under the tears the eyes shone with near violence. Nothing went together. Nothing made sense. She kept bending close to his body without touching him. He could see her and feel her nearness even though he was looking down at her from the ceiling. He knew he was suspended there high above her, yet he could still feel the nearness of her body against his on the bed.

Her flesh against his felt warm, at first perfumed, then came the smell of cooking and dirty children. Each time she moved against him she would weep and smile and move away again. He felt the weight of her body against him. When she moved away he saw the fullness of her belly, which she rubbed against him. Three times, four times she moved away before she took over his body.

In his sweat, in his sleep, Bent was sickened. He couldn't wake up. She possessed him. Her flesh and the flesh of the child she carried within her body had overtaken his own. He groaned under the horrible sensation. His stomach seemed to swell under immense pressure from underneath. His entire body rolled from side to side trying to cast out the awful weight. Then an outside force took both his arms and shook him forcefully.

"Angus, Angus, wake up, dear. Angus, wake up!"

"Oh…oh…" he moaned…"Oh Bertha, Oh, dreadful, dreadful…what a dreadful dream."

"Gracious, Angus, it must have been. You moaned terribly, not once but three or four times. I thought I'd better waken you. Was it such a ghastly dream?"

He shook his head in a dazed manner.

"God yes, Bertha, worst dream I've ever had. Awful...awful."

"I'm so sorry, dear. Would you like a drink of water or milk?"

"No thank you. It must have been the fresh ham at dinner. Lord, what a dream!"

"What was it dear?"

Angus caught his breath. Now was the time. Now he ought to tell Bertha and have it done with. If he shared the old tale of the witch it would lose its potency. He shouldn't keep it all bottled up inside, he knew that. He let out his breath slowly. He was sitting up in bed and had his hands pressed flat against his stomach. Good God, no! He could never tell her. What was he thinking? He looked down at his stomach. No different, the same as when he'd gone to bed. Nothing showed. He gave a quick relieved sigh.

"What is it, Angus? Don't you want to tell me?"

"Oh, Bertha, it's one of those dreams you can't remember a thing about once you wake up. You know, you remember only the feeling it gave you and none of the facts of the dream. Honestly, I couldn't recall a fact of the dream, not actual things. Just that my stomach ached terribly and I'm sure that's because of the ham."

"That makes me feel terrible. I know you don't care much for fresh ham. I don't know why I bought it really, Angus. Forgive me, dear. You really should say something, remind me. You're such a thoughtful husband. It wouldn't be unkind if you reminded me once in a while of your dislikes."

She put her hand to his cheek. "You've always been so careful of my feelings, Angus. You should consider your own as well. I think I could easily switch my plans if you told me you didn't like what I was making for dinner. Let's not forget, it would make me feel better than to have you pained this way. I had no idea you might be allergic to the ham."

"It's all right now. Let's get back to sleep. I'm so sorry I wakened you with my noise. Forgive me."

In the darkness of the room Angus lay with open aching eyes, trying to stand fast against sleep. It never seemed possible that the dream could become worse than it had been all these past years. He had become accustomed to the sameness of the dream. He shuddered now under the impact of this latest nightmare. He still felt disgusted and sickened from it. Damn that woman. If it weren't for the coincidental sameness of those eyes he wouldn't be haunted by these odd doings. It was those eyes...something in those eyes...

Plainly she was going to be a thorn in his flesh. He wasn't sure that she had said anything more to the Haigs than what he'd been told. If she had, he would now understand why she had carried on so when they gave her the ride. The best thing to do was to get her out of the way again. The sight of her was getting to his nerves. Whenever she walked into the town past his house she would stand there, across the street from his house, just staring silently, even when he wasn't home. Bertha mentioned it several times. How could he explain anything to Bertha? He mulled over alternate methods of putting her away again. Before he came to any conclusions he had fallen into sleep. He woke in the morning still shaken, but relieved that the witch hadn't visited him again.

THE VISIT

What Bent didn't yet know was that Danya was able to trace the two youngest children through the county welfare office. She had lied to the clerk at the reception desk and had extracted the information from her.

"My welfare agent, Mr. Bent, told me to come here," she told the girl. "He said you would give me the papers so I could visit my children." She rummaged in her shopping bag as though she was searching for some papers, then apologized to the girl and asked her plaintively if she couldn't give her the information without the paper Mr. Bent had issued.

"It's quite irregular. I'm not even sure we have the authority, but without some kind of written order I don't think I can do it." The girl was young, about twenty, and obviously unsure of her duties. She kept looking about to see if anyone could help her.

"I came all the way from Stanton, and I cannot go back for the paper. If you will give me the address I will bring the paper some other time. Mr. Bent said you would help me. He made a copy of the paper, too, and he said it would be all right. He will mail the paper to you."

The girl looked at her watch. It was lunchtime and she was impatient to get away. She asked Danya for her name, went to the files in another room and brought a manila folder back to the desk.

"The file isn't complete, Mrs. Vorodinov. It is marked for more information." She looked inside the folder, pursed her lips as she read the forms. She wasn't aware of Danya's over eager hand reaching out to take the papers. She was standing behind her desk, across from Danya. She sat down, kept the folder open and took a piece of paper from a note pad.

"I can give you this address. Both the children are at this home."

"Both? Only two? Do you mean not all my children are together? Where are the others?"

"As I said, the file is not completed for some reason. It doesn't have any more information than these forms on the boy and girl...let's see, age eleven months and two and a half years. If there are other children, the forms still must be in the hands of your local welfare agent. I'm sure...no, I'm not sure I'm supposed to give this information out. It seems incomplete."

When she hesitated, Danya became wary that the girl might really change her mind.

"It is not important for the others. Mr. Bent said I could visit the two youngest first. If you give me the address I will ask him when I can make application for the visit rights to the others."

Perhaps she said it too quickly, too eagerly. The clerk had some misgivings, but it was lunchtime and she had some shopping to get out of the way. She printed the name and address on a slip of paper and handed it to Danya.

"Thank you, my girl, thank you." She stuffed the paper into her purse and turned to leave. She walked quickly away from the welfare building to a side street where she stopped to read the address. 'Mr. and Mrs. Albert Hills.' They had her children!

They lived in the town of Cullham. She knew she'd passed through that town to get to the city. She must now take the bus back to Cullham. No matter now about the cost of the bus. She must go right away. She murmured the name, Hills, Hills, Hills. I will find them today. I will find them. I will find my children!

***

She stood still as she waited for the bus, as if frozen, oblivious to the wind and growing cold. She stood next to the waiting bench, staring toward the direction from which the bus would come. Then she saw it. When it stopped she asked if it stopped in Cullham. Yes. She sat right behind the driver, sat there looking eagerly out of the window, hardly blinking. She reminded the driver at each stop that she must get out in Cullham. Would he tell her when? Where in Cullham lady? There were five stops. Here, this address. Oh yes, it's the main highway. We stop real close, lady. Will you tell me? Yes lady, don't worry, I'll let you know.

When she climbed down from the bus steps she turned back to the driver, "Which house?"

"Well how should I know, lady. Back that way a little maybe, not much. Look on the mailboxes for the name or just go up to a door and knock, ask somebody. It's a small town, somebody will know."

Three houses away. She read the name on the mailbox. Albert Hills. In that house, so close now were her two children whom she had not seen since that summer day when they were stolen from her.

The house looked still and empty. It was a small white frame house trimmed with bright red sashings and red shutters. The lawn was smooth and undisturbed by any trees or bushes. There were some small evergreen shrubs at each side of the doorway. The house looked new, clean, empty, and moreover, it housed people who had taken her children to raise. She felt jealousy, even hatred. It housed her enemies from whom she must somehow rescue her children.

She was filled with excitement mixed with apprehension and some fear as well as some embarrassment when she realized she didn't know how she would be received. Suppose they would not let her in?...They must!

She rang the bell. It made hollow tinkling sounds behind the door. No one came. She rang it again. How very simple this had been after all. Here she would find her children. A third time she rang the bell.

Light steps on a wooden floor, coming closer to the door. It opened. Danya peered meekly at the youngish woman who stood there with a questioning look.

"Mr. Bent told me I could come to see my children." She burst out with the introduction in a tone of voice that sounded like an accusation. The woman was taken aback.

"Oh indeed? Are you Mrs. Vorodinov?"

"Yes, I am. I came to visit my children. I have the permission papers from the county welfare, here." She showed the slip with the address. It was marked at the top with the welfare department stamp.

"I see. Well, Mrs. Vorodinov, Mr. Bent didn't notify me as he said he would, but if you have permission from the county office, please come in."

They stood awkwardly for a moment, then Mrs. Hills asked Danya to come into the living room and sit down. Danya looked around the room where her children lived. Nowhere was there evidence of toys. In her house you could always tell there were children. In this house there was nothing that showed children lived here. It was a house too neat for children.

"I'm afraid you've come at a very bad time, Mrs. Vorodinov. The children are taking their naps, you see, and they won't be awake for another hour or more."

"Isn't it possible to wake them up to see their mother?"

"No, that can't be done. They need their nap time, and I don't let anything disturb them."

"My children never took such long naps. The could just lay down for a few minutes on the floor and they were rested the same as if they took a long nap."

"I'm afraid our methods of child raising differ a great deal in this country. It would be upsetting for the children to be awakened in the middle of a nap to see a stranger..."

Danya rose in anger. "A stranger? But I am no stranger. I am the mother! Why should they be upset to see me?"

Mrs. Hills was uncomfortable. "It will surprise them naturally. The boy is a little high strung and is very difficult when he misses his nap."

"What do you mean he is high strung?" Danya was struck to the quick by the superiority of the woman and the way she judged her children. Did she not know her own child, her son?

"He's very sensitive. He hasn't learned to obey too well and we're trying to discipline him before he becomes a problem. He cries a lot over small matters. I've found that he needs more rest than my own child. That helps his behavior."

"But he is too young to have behavior. He cries because he likes to have more attention, maybe. You should give him something to do with his hands, then he will not cry. He took his nap in my arms while I peeled potatoes or sewed. He is not used to going away from people for a nap. That is why he cries, I know." Her voice faltered.

Mrs. Hills cleared her throat when Danya stopped talking. She was a pale, sandy-haired woman in her late 20's. She had been napping when the bell rang and she still wore the annoyance of being disturbed, especially by such confrontation.

"I think it's probably best if we don't discuss these things. Naturally your ideas would differ from mine. However, I have taken my studies in Child Development and the methods we are concerned with seem to give the child greater security and discipline than old fashioned methods of child raising." She said it in a tired, quiet and final tone.

An hour passed with considerable strain for both women. Mrs. Hills took up some knitting. She made a weak attempt at conversation, of the weather, the bus ride, and answered Danya's questions about the children as briefly as she politely could.

Danya sat on the edge of the over-stuffed wing chair. She had not taken off her coat, and had become sleepy from the warmth. Finally she pushed the coat back. She felt dry mouthed and nervous from the waiting. She disliked Mrs. Hills more each minute that she had to sit there waiting. If she was a good mother she ought to have the same feelings and know that she, Danya, was suffering. What kind of woman was this to force her to wait to see her own children? Was she without a heart? Would she teach this kind of meanness to her children? Would she show them the same cold ways, the same lack of love, only behavior and discipline, without any kindness?

The broken whine of a waking child interrupted Danya's thoughts. The sounds stabbed at her heart. She caught her breath, stood up quickly from her chair, her face flushed and her eyes bright with expectation. She faced Mrs. Hills like a beggar.

"Please, I want to go to my child, please."

"No, I'm sorry, it might startle her. I'll bring her in before she awakens the others." Mrs. Hills seemed unaware of Danya's anxiety. That, and the jealously she felt weakened Danya's knees as she stood waiting,

She moved quickly toward the child when Mrs. Hills brought her into the living room. She blinked with surprise. The baby had changed so much. She couldn't know for sure that it was her child. Would a baby change so much in all those months? She didn't remember it from her other children.

The girl was dressed in a pink tight-bodiced dress with tiny puffed sleeves that popped out like starched wings over her little arms. Her head was a mass of dark yellow curls. Danya didn't remember that her child's hair was so curly or so thick...but of course she was only eight months old when she last saw her. But yes, they were the same eyes. But there was fear in those eyes now when the mother reached for her child. Fear, from her own baby!

"Come, my baby, come to your mother." The child made a quick little sound as though she would cry. Danya took her from Mrs. Hills who watched with a little smile. Danya sat down and hugged the child to her bosom. She rocked back and forth on the edge of the big wing chair, tears streaming down her face. Mrs. Hills stood for a moment watching, unsure of what she should do.

Another whimper from the bedroom called Mrs. Hills away. She went to get the other two children up from their naps, Danya's son and her own little girl.

Danya rocked with the child, then bounced her on her knees. She remembered that it was a laughing baby. Now she opened her big eyes and stared at her, still afraid. She smiled a bit as the bumpities Danya sang to her: "Bumpity, bumpity, my fat hen, bumpity, bumpity jump again."

The child didn't remember her. She could see that when Mrs. Hills came back into the room. The baby reached out to Mrs. Hills, away from its mother. Danya hugged her closer. Her stomach curled with hurt and jealousy. But her son, there he was. Her only son. He must know his mother.

But he did not.

He clung shyly to Mrs. Hills' hand when she put him down on the floor. He looked with trepidation at Danya, reacting timidly to the overtures she made. He looked confused at his small sister held in the stranger's arms.

"Come to me, my son, don't you remember your mother? Come to your mother, my son." She rose from the chair with the baby in one arm, reaching toward the boy with her free arm.

He at first hesitated and kept his hold on Mrs. Hills' hand. She told him to go to his mother, to behave nicely. He dropped her hand and allowed Danya to pick up his rigid little body. He frowned a little at his sister who now was distracted and playing with the fox collar on Danya's coat. His curiosity overcame his fear. He paid little attention to what Danya was trying to say to him because he was attracted by the collar and tried to wiggle closer to the coat, nearly falling from her. She moved onto the edge of the chair so the two children could have room to sit there on her coat, pulling at the fur collar.

Mrs. Hills began to scold the children for harming the coat. Danya interrupted her.

"It is only a coat. If they want to play with the collar it can make no harm. Let them play."

"You might try to understand that these small things can give a child very bad habits. The boy is old enough to respect property."

"It is his mother's property."

"It makes no difference. Habits are formed from just such indulgences, often with great harm to a child's future."

Danya looked straight at Mrs. Hills, tears in her eyes.

"What difference does it make if my children play with my coat? I would gladly give it to them if they were in my house, in their own home. Isn't it better to let them play than to make them nervous with so much behavior rules?"

What might have been a scene was prevented by the appearance of Mrs. Hills' daughter, a pretty little girl who bounced into the room with little jumps, then settled into a proper walk when she saw the visitor. She was like a prim blue hen in her starched dress, Danya thought.

She walked quickly to the younger children still playing with the fox collar. She dissuaded them from their criticized play and with some physical effort pulled them to the box in the corner of the room where she rationed out toys to each of them. In a few minutes the absorbed children had cut the two women out of their presence.

Danya sat watching them at play. She wiped her nose and dried the persistent tears. Mrs. Hills was a bit uncomposed but she made no other effort to converse or to bridge the now awkward silence. She kept to her knitting, would stop a moment when Danya talked to the children, but she said no word.

At five o'clock Mrs. Hills put down her work. She politely told Danya that the lawful visiting time was two hours and the time was over. From the look on Danya's face Mrs. Hills thought there might be a scene. The afternoon had unsettled her badly. She was not a person to cope with emotional people, and she didn't know what to expect nor how to handle this woman.

Danya thought it over and then reacted like an obedient child. She got up from the floor where she was talking to the children. She put on the furry collared coat under their interested gaze. She bent down to hug and kiss them. The collar hung down before her and they giggled and pulled at the fur nearly tugging her to the floor.

When she said goodbye at the door to Mrs. Hills she looked like a subdued, sad, round-shouldered old woman. The fierce determination behind her entrance had wilted. She was beginning to realize that the longer her children were kept from her the less they would ever belong to her again. It was an unexpected blow, not to be recognized by her own two children. She thought the boy remembered her when she was playing with them on the floor, when she was talking to them. She sighed. She was not really sure of that, if she was being very truthful to herself. If she could not see them often they might grow far away from her. Visiting was not enough. She must get them back before that woman worked her destroying rules into their lives.

She walked despondently along the road. When she was out of sight of the house she held out her thumb to ask for a ride from passing cars. Twenty minutes later she was picked up by strangers who took her within three miles of the Stanton road. She walked the last miles with troubled thoughts. In one good way she had been able to find her children, a blessing even if it was only the two youngest. She ached to think that her own babies did not recognize their mother, that they would turn to another woman looking for safety from her. She should thank God that she found them. But even so, in a bad way she still did not know where the other four girls had been taken. There had to be a way she could get all the children back to their home. She must do it soon, before other people changed them. She could see how easily a child can forget a mother. Maybe the older ones would be the same. She would not wait for them to be turned against her.

OBSESSION

Each afternoon at the precise time that they should waken from their naps Danya visited her two youngest children. Because the bus arrived early or when she would get a lift from a passing car, she would stand in the cold, out of sight, waiting until it was time. She carried a small bedroom alarm clock in her shopping bag so she would never be there too early. She did not want to sit alone with Mrs. Hills. The tick of the clock was sometimes the only sound she heard in those long minutes of waiting, waiting, each minute growing longer until she reached to look at the clock and saw that it was time.

After the sixth visit Mrs. Hills went to her desk and wrote a letter complaining to Angus Bent of the Stanton Welfare Department.

'...Is there something that can be done about limiting the number of visits a mother makes to her children in their foster home? Since Mrs. Vorodinov was given permission to visit she has been here every afternoon for nearly a week. I think it is beginning to upset the children. She reminds them so often that she is their mother that the boy is reacting quite strangely afterwards. I am not sure what the proper action is, therefore I am writing to you hoping that you can do something and clear up the problem if it is in the power of your office.'

Bent opened and read the letter at his desk in the bank. A wave of fury passed over him. The incredible gall of that woman! That she would visit the children without proper permission from his office. And how in the world did she find them? He had issued no information nor any permission to her. Then he relaxed.

There was an answer. Yes, he could take care of the problem.

He would have little trouble having her recommitted to the hospital now that she had broken her probation. She had gone against the rules of the court. His anger flowed away. This was working out for him better than he could have hoped. Without his having to do anything against her she had made it possible for him to get her out of the way. Now the way was given.

He was becoming obsessed with a desire for revenge against her. He was equating her with his dreams. That awful dream kept beating at his memory. He couldn't shake it off. He now totally identified the witch of his dreams with Mrs. Vorodinov, one and the same. The same eyes, the tears, the staring. If she went away, if she was put away, out of his sight, the dream might stop coming back to him. It had to be that way. He didn't understand it but he was sure that if he never saw her again he would never be tormented with dream either.

Angus Bent's life was full of concealing habits and mannerisms that belied any clue to the mortal fears that were overtaking his pre-sleeping hours. Since he began to believe that the dream witch and Danya Vorodinov were somehow one and the same he had spent hours in preoccupied distress, floundering in inadequate knowledge for an explanation. What little he knew of psychiatry in those days was utterly useless. The thought of turning his life over to a psychiatrist was out of the question anyway, in fact had hardly entered his thoughts. The self-righteous and religious New Englanders put such a stigma on the psychiatric professionals of the day that it would have hurt Bent more to visit one of them than to endure the torture of his dreams. They were doctors who dealt with people like Mrs. Vorodinov and other uneducated and disturbed people. He knew he was not one of those.

The beginnings of a sickness throbbed through his body, constantly reminding him of the abominations he had endured each night. Above the veiled fears he was a dignified, earnest man. Underneath he was covered with a growing urge to destroy the person he believed was responsible for his discomforts.

His immense good standing in the community was a source of pride to him. He had earned the gratitude and admiration of the town folk and of his business peers by unrelenting attention to every detail of his profession, including the peddling of good will and understanding that buoyed many households struck by the depression.

In fact, socially he was a standoffish man, not given to close friendships or casual mingling with others beyond what was necessary in business. In a way this was not unusual in a society of standoffish taciturn men. The tall white-haired man with the aquiline nose and hanging jowls was seen in business settings. He was appreciated more than liked because he was the backbone that holds together any small town, part of the stable, dignified heritage that stood fast in front of the onslaught into New England by foreigners, factories and modern times. He was part of the charisma that pulled the less fortunate from their own lands, that set the example, the upright God-fearing example for so many of the new citizens to follow. His virtues, especially his honesty, were accepted without question. And he knew it.

And yet…the more maniacal his obsession became the more he consciously strode with a covering veil. His overriding fear was that he would somehow break under the strain of those night visitations and either confide in Bertha or in some way show his distress in his work, that he would give himself away. The sooner he rid himself of what he believed was the source of his anguish the better for his health and, he had long ago convinced himself, the better for the woman's children.

He visited Dr. Cobb. With feigned reluctance he discussed with the Doctor the problem that Danya had presented by breaking her probationary order to keep away from the children until visiting rights were granted. He sought to convince Dr. Cobb that she was not sufficiently improved to get along without further treatment in the asylum. With deep misgivings, he said, he was asking Dr. Cobb to sign for her re-admittance. Successful with that, he broached, disguised as an after thought, a subject that had been milling about in his mind since the horrible dream.

"In view of Mrs. Vorodinov's instability, do you think the state should do something about additional children?"

Dr. Cobb looked up from the paper he was signing. He scowled slightly and asked out of the corner of his mouth, "You mean prevent them, Bent?"

"Yes," hesitating and thoughtful was Bent, "I think it would be a serious mistake to allow that kind of woman to breed more children. She is fairly old, as well as demented, and there is no way we can foretell that any children she has in the future would be normal."

Dr. Cobb pursed his lips in distaste. "It's not something I like to recommend. Age takes care of those things better than we doctors should, or at least nature is a better and natural judge. It's pretty difficult in this state, you know, so it's better to leave all that to heaven."

"Of course, Doctor, when there's danger of harm to the mother or future children it has been done."

"I know of no cases since I've practiced here or in the hospital."

"I believe it's been recommended a few times for patients in the state hospital."

"That so? Didn't know about it."

There was silence. But Bent had come too far to be cut off now. He would press the matter. His next words betrayed an over-keen concern.

"I sincerely believe we should have this woman sterilized so that there is no possibility of more children. Besides the possible mental irregularities of other children, there is also a question of just whose children she is breeding."

Cobb put down his pen, pushed himself back from the desk so he was balancing on the back legs of his desk chair. He snorted then with a biting guffaw he slung a teasing southern style retort.

"Land sakes, Bent, y'all have something against woman or sumpin? She been lifting up her skirts to you, has she, scared you a mite?"

Bent put on his most serious kindly mien. The agitations inside him were invisible on the surface. The ashen face had received and rejected a momentary flush. He held his palms out to Cobb in an expressive gesture of kindly pleading.

'Look, Dr. Cobb, this is a pretty serious situation. We have reports from two men to the effect that she gives her favors easily, even at her age. I haven't entered this information on our reports because it could harm the children in the future, but there's a possibility that the last two children aren't Mr. Vorodinov's. It's just this kind of thing we should try to prevent, both for the children and the expense they would be to the state."

Now Dr. Cobb was annoyed. "For Christ's sake, Bent, I delivered every one of those kids. They all jumped out with the same shapes, the same heads, the same legs and chin as their father. Hell, what man is going to chase an old woman with four, five kids hanging on her skirts? A woman like that can't get away from her family to service two other men."

With intense control Ben kept his calm. "Sadly enough, Doctor, it could be true. But it isn't necessary to pursue that. I don't want to damage the family with anything of that sort on the records. My main concern is to spare the state any more expense and to spare the woman any future anguish with recurring incidents as well as possible disease. I believe this request is justified within the law. Since you are her doctor I have discussed it with you before I make a formal request at the state hospital. If you cannot within your own conscience sign the order it will be taken up at the hospital when she is admitted."

"Damn right I won't sign the order!" Cobb was indignant and angry. "My job is keeping people alive and bringing new lives in to fill up the holes when the old folks go. I'm no judge of a woman's virtue, and I'm no judge of the old baby factory. She can have a half dozen more if she wants to. She's tough enough and so is her man. When it's time for the babies to stop coming the order is coming from somewhere besides this pen!" He threw the pen down on the desk with another burst of anger.

"Hold on, Dr. Cobb. I'm not asking you to do anything against your principles. I told you that. I just wanted to discuss it with you, that's all. I'll take your views to the hospital when I meet with the doctors there. This is a very difficult problem for me to run judgment on, I can tell you. When I accepted the job of welfare administrator I didn't expect to run into something like this. My interest was purely and solely to help the folks caught in the crisis."

He waxed to near eloquence with the following, "You, as a dealer in human lives, have stated an invaluable opinion that has brought me a change of view. I'm going to do all I can to see that Mrs. Vorodinov has the best care possible. Now that I can see the implications of this thing more clearly, I submit my original feelings to your worthy advice on the matter." He shook his head slightly as if warding off a cobweb. Nothing in his face betrayed him.

Dr. Cobb shrugged. "That's fine, Bent, just fine."

"Thank you for you time, Doctor. I rely on your judgment in these things. Good bye."

Tremors of misgiving ran through Angus Bent as he sat in his office later, thinking over the visit. Had he made a mistake bringing up the subject? He probably should have felt out the doctor's views before he so bluntly asked him to sign the order. However, he recalled that there had actually been a case in the state hospital some months ago where a chronically disturbed woman had been sterilized. With this second admittance he would note on Mrs. Vorodinov's records a recommendation for sterilization. He was certain it could be done at the decision of two competent doctors, whether it was her own physician or two of the mental hospital doctors. He would note that her mental problems were due to childbearing. He'd see what the hospital doctors would say, then he would know how to write his report.

Satisfied that he had a workable plan Bent contacted the state police. He asked them to detain Danya Vorodinov at the home of the Albert Hills in Cullham. He gave them the date and time that they should take her into custody. He included a copy of the order that Dr. Cobb had signed.

***

On a snow threatening Friday afternoon two state policemen with a female state welfare worker knocked on the Hills' door. Mrs. Hills had been informed. She asked them to wait until she could take the children to their bedrooms.

This time Danya offered little of the resistance she had showed at the original abduction. In her heart she had felt that Bent would somehow hear of her visits and perhaps try to stop her. She also believed that her letters to the governor and Mrs. Roosevelt would produce results in the near future and bring him to heel.

"Don't touch me you son of a bitches," she hissed in a low voice, wanting to spare the children who might hear. "I know who you are, and I know why you are here. Don't put your hands on me, I can walk."

The social worker spoke softly. "Please, Mrs. Vorodinov, come with the men as quietly as possible. Please consider the children before you make any disturbance." She was an attractive woman who had been a schoolteacher until that fall. This was her first experience with any other than routine visits to families on welfare relief. She was obviously nervous, having been told of the great commotion that had ensued at the other occasion of this woman's detention. With an effort toward kindness she took Danya's arm.

"I said keep your hands away from me, you vipers. Do not think I am a fallen down old woman that I cannot walk by myself from this house?"

Mrs. Hills had stayed with the children in the bedroom. Danya made a move to say goodbye to them but the social worker's emphatic voice warned her against it.

"As their mother you ought to understand how they can be harmed by a scene they do not understand. Please come with us quietly and spare the children."

Danya obeyed. It wasn't until she was in the car and it moved in the direction away from Stanton that she realized she was being taken again to the asylum.

"Where do you think to take me, back to the asylum?"

"Please, Mrs. Vorodinov, we have orders to do so. You were on probation as you must have understood. You haven't been able to conduct yourself reasonably and the welfare office and your doctor decided you would need more time to rest and recover."

"Why you stinking liar, that is not true. My doctor knows I am not crazy. So do the doctors in the asylum. Ah, but this time I will go quietly. This time I will explain more carefully why Bulldog Bent chases me from my children. Don't worry, social worker, I won't make trouble for you. You won't be able to report anything about me to the hospital. I know the tricks this time."

She sat resolutely on the edge of the car seat. She looked out the window noting the passing landscape with some pleasure, quite sure that within the same day she would be returning that way again. They would have to drive her home. She made a mental note to stop by the big apple farm to buy some cider for Mikolai and some of the Mackintosh apples for herself from the roadside stand. She would make them stop. She was audacious enough to tell the driver his cigarette smoke was making her sick to her stomach. She snorted her thanks to his hasty response as he quenched the cigarette in the ashtray. She noticed him look in the rear view mirror trying to catch the social worker's eye. "Hmph," she snorted, "if you welfare people would help your own sicknesses you wouldn't have time to run after me."

She walked ahead of the officers into the patient reception room of the hospital as though it were a familiar place. She stood obediently while the social worker gave the papers over to the nurse at the desk. "Now, she said with impatient disgust, "I would like to talk to the doctors so I can go home."

"No, I'm sorry, Mrs. Vorodinov, they are off duty for the day." The nurse looked at the clock behind her. "The go off at six, just half an hour ago. We can only call them for emergencies, not routine examinations."

"I don't need an examination. They examined me before and they know I am not crazy. I do not belong here. I want only to talk to them."

"Fine, I understand. However, you will have to wait until the morning. I can admit you now but your examination is not scheduled until ten o'clock tomorrow morning."

Danya's cockiness was deflated by this, yet she was so confident that everything would work to her favor that she submitted. She was not aware that the admittance papers included a medical form, signed by her welfare agent and her husband, ordering the simple sterilization operation. The order read, 'As soon as possible after confinement.'

As an afterthought and to insure against the possible demand for it, Bent had forged Mikolai's signature on the paper. He had only to go to the welfare file to find some of the receipts Vorodinov had signed that previous summer when he had accepted the welfare deliveries.

The ease with which it was done surprised Angus Bent. Four days after Danya's admittance a copy of the hospital record was forwarded to his welfare office. The doctors had concurred. He had not been called into the conference. The husband's signature was sufficient. The operation was performed. The patient's records were thus brought up to date for her local welfare administrator.

Bent tore the papers into small bits. An acute sense of relief flowed over him, even as his conscience tried to struggle with the mendacious act he had committed. The next day, after a dreamless night, after a deep and quiet sleep, he rationalized the good sense of his actions.

Whatever fears had troubled him were dispelled. Most likely his conversation with Dr. Cobb would be forgotten in the man's mental meanderings with alcohol. There would be no records in this office and he would make no reply to the state welfare office nor send any reports on the operation. And because the state voting consensus was strongly opposed to any liberalization of the law, the state hospital records on such things were generally relegated to confidential file status from where they rarely emerged.

Bent knew too that it was several months before a re-admitted patient was given a hearing. Enough time for the children to fit into their environments without any interference from their mother. Mrs. Vorodinov would be out of the way for considerable time. Enough time for his experiment with the children to have some chance to prove out.

He prayed also that it would be enough time for the dreams to be forgotten. He was sure that if he didn't see the woman for three or four months, and he hoped it would be even longer, that his mind would lose its susceptibility to her damned annoying stares, her strange eyes. He prayed that she would lose her hold on him, whatever it was. By the time she was released from the hospital he was sure he would be able to ignore her completely even if he was forced to face her on the street or through his welfare work. Or so he thought as he prayed.

THE CHILDREN FOUND

A student nurse, Kay Rizzoti, assigned to do the filing, noticed the impressive letterhead of Mrs. Roosevelt's writing paper in the Vorodinov file. Out of curiosity she read the letter through. It was dated a month back of the date on the second admittance form for Mrs. Vorodinov. The first paper the girl filed was the medical order, marked for the confidential file. Seen together these told a partial story that piqued the nurse's interest. When she was assigned to the ward, she made a point of befriending the dark eyed sick woman whose data she had read.

Danya was making a slow recovery from the operation, which under normal circumstances should have been a minor inconsequential event. But she had been so distraught that she suffered from severe depression and was still under mild sedation. She was not told the true nature of her operation, only that she had some female complications and had been given some corrective minor surgery. The problem, it was explained to her, was due to her child bearing and her age. She believed them, as they hoped she would.

The kindness and willing ear offered by the young nurse felt to Danya like gentle drops of rain after dry arid days. Kay Rizzoti was the first person from whom Danya received more than mild tolerance when she tried to tell her story. The girl was appalled by what seemed to her complete disregard of the woman's rights to be heard. She said nothing of the medical order, but she did confide to Danya that there was a letter on file from Mrs. Roosevelt asking the hospital authorities to cooperate with the county welfare department in the investigation of her case. Nurse Rizzoti offered to write any further letters Danya might wish to send if there were no immediate results from the letter on file.

This heartened Danya considerably. It also heightened her impatience. She asked the nurse to write new letters to the governor and the president's wife. Danya also wrote a short letter to Mikolai telling him that she had been abducted by the state police for visiting her children. She told him where they were and asked him to visit them whenever he could. Miss Rizzoti folded the letters into her uniform pocket and promised that they would be mailed.

It was six weeks before matters came together and Danya was scheduled for another hearing. Christmas holidays had intervened. Her nurse friend, having finished her eight weeks training at the asylum was back on duty at the medical hospital. Danya was beside herself with despair as Christmas came and she found herself still confined.

The governor's office had been instrumental in bringing about the hearing sooner than it had been scheduled. Copies of her letters to his office were in the hospital file as well as two letters from Mrs. Roosevelt's desk. There was also a copy of Kay Rizzoti's letter to the governor's office asking them to please look into the case that she could not follow any longer.

As the time before, the reviewing doctors found no reason to detain Danya. The one difference this time was the presence of a juvenile welfare officer. He said nothing during the hearing. Afterwards he spoke with Danya and told her that because of the Governor's intervention they had reviewed the visiting status of the parents. He gave her the addresses of the homes in which her children were living, along with official introductory letters of permission for visiting rights. She could visit the children once a month. She should make the arrangements in advance so that the families wouldn't be disturbed or inconvenienced by unexpected visits. He warned her that visiting privileges could be withheld if a parent made any attempts to deviate from the visiting rules.

She sullenly took her departure from the asylum and walked the remembered road to the center of the city where she waited for a few moments, than decided she could make her way faster by hitching a ride instead of waiting for the bus. She walked some blocks away from the bus stop station and stopped, hoping to catch a ride before long since the cold was beginning to close in on her.

Because she was still within the city limits one of the local policemen cautioned her that she must not beg for a ride within the city limits. He told her to walk on or wait for the bus at the designated bus stop.

She trudged farther along the road. In a small amusement she thought of that time long, long ago when she had been caught in the cold and snow, then saved by the wolves. And the blonde blue-eyed young man...oh, so long ago.

She waited only ten minutes before she was picked up by two women. They were going to the town past Stanton and dropped her off in the center of the village, three miles from her home.

She could rouse little anger this time against Mikolai. That was past. She had made her way these past months alone. She had made her decisions that other time. She could tell he was embarrassed, either because of his lack in helping her or perhaps because he believed she was crazy. She said nothing about it to him. She now knew he would not understand. Had he seen the children? No, he could not leave the house and the animals. He was waiting for her to come home. How did she know she would come home? He had talked to Mr. Bent one day. About her?

Yes. What had he said? That she would be home before summer, that she needed further rest. All right, if he must believe an ugly bulldog instead of his wife, she would make her own way. She did not need his help.

***

The next afternoon, a biting winter day, Danya stood outside the Reverend Rand's home holding in her hands the authorized visiting note that would permit her to see the four older girls whom she had not seen since July. The fourth girl had arrived just before Christmas to join the three others, though Danya wasn't aware of this and presumed they had all been together during these months.

No one answered the doorbell. She waited first on the front porch, then on the back porch stairs. Two hours passed before she heard a car come into the driveway.

She instantly disliked the two women who came out of the car. Mrs. Rand was a heavy set motherly woman with a full face built around a thin beaked nose. Her daughter Julia was taller by two inches but had all the marks that would develop her into the same looks as she aged. Each had the straight-backed posture of the New Englander. They were surprised to see Danya. She had not bothered to call because she could find no telephone and she was certain that for the first visit they would forgive her.

A vague presentiment had troubled Danya. She was coming to visit her children in a strange house, and in all probability the children would react to her as to a stranger. She could not forget the shock made by the younger children's reactions. Although these girls were older and would certainly remember who she was, they might, like the two younger ones, turn from her.

She had quickly conjured up a picture of these two women turning her children against her. She could tell by the way they looked at her, very disapprovingly, as though she were a bad child. She showed them the slip of paper and explained that she was making this first visit without previous notice but that she knew in the future she must tell them when she was coming to visit again.

The schoolteacher daughter was well informed. She understood and reminded Danya that visiting rights were permitted once a month. The time should be agreed upon. She was not to take them off their home premises. She could spend three hours with them at each visit.

This house, like the Hills' house, showed no evidence that four growing girl children inhabited the place. No toy or book or paper was in sight. Danya had never imagined that a house could have children and keep all the evidence so hidden. She was sure from what she saw while she waited that her daughters were being suffocated with Yankee upbringing...that they were being taught to chase the dirt and spend their time keeping things in place instead of playing freely like children are supposed to do. Behavior, behavior. That was what they were so concerned with, not their happiness or their nerves, she thought.

The girls came home from school at three-thirty, on the dot. They would never know how their reactions crushed their mother's feeble hopes that they had not changed so much. Each was an exemplar of good manners. They curtsied and reached to shake her hand. What hurt her most was not that they resisted but that they accepted her demonstrative hugs with cool, polite smiles as though she were not their mother but a stranger.

Could children be changed to feel so alien to a mother in such a short time? Even at their ages, was it possible, they could treat her like a stranger? They remembered she was their mother. They could not have forgotten that. Could they so easily be turned against her? Where had their feelings gone? Where was the joy, the hunger for her arms, the free little birds she had raised?

If Angus Bent could have viewed the scene he would have been pleased that his prognostications were correct. It had taken much less time than he had proposed to remold the Vorodinov children, at least outwardly, into the proper well raised Americanized children of his planned child communities.

The girls excused themselves because they must change from their school clothes into house clothes. When they returned, they politely sat in the living room with their mother. Each girl sat primly on the edge of the big sofa with her ankles crossed. They smiled, waiting as they had been taught, for this grown up to speak to them first.

It is difficult to imagine a greater social awkwardness and cruelty than what developed there for Danya. It was something this mother could never believe would happen between her and the children to whom she had given life. Not yet in pre-teens, the girls ostracized their mother by simple behavioral proprieties of which she was not even aware.

"How is the school in your new place, my daughters?"

"Thank you, ma'am, I like it very much. Especially my teacher Miss Thompson." Answered the oldest.

The next girl, "I don't like school but I like my teacher, too. Her name is funny, that's why."

"What is her funny name?"

The girl giggled. "Clegg, Clegg, ate a rotten egg!"

The other girls were embarrassed by this. The oldest blushed self-consciously for the bad manners. She gasped and scowled her disapproval. "You're not supposed to say things like that, Mrs. Rand said so."

There was another awkward wait.

"What do you learn in school?"

"Mmmm...arithmetic, reading, spelling, geography...and sometimes we have music."

"How come I don't have music?" asked the youngest.

"Because it starts in third grade, silly. Don't raise your voice, we have company and you know Mrs. Rand said not to raise your voice."

"Well, you shouldn't boss me, either. Mrs. Rand said so."

"I'm not bossing, so! I'm just reminding you, and that's not bossing, Mrs. Rand said so."

Mrs. Rand said so, Mrs. Rand, Mrs. Rand...no longer what their mother told them but what Mrs. Rand said to them. They were completely out of her hands, Danya saw it. Perhaps even more so than the two youngest. Oh, my daughters, her heart wailed, my lost daughters! Can you make me a stranger in six months when I carried you and fed you from my own body for a longer time that that?

She asked to see their toys.

"We can't take more than one out at a time, but if you come to the back parlor I will show you everything on my toy shelf."

"I will show you mine, too." Piped in the second girl.

"I will look at them all, my daughters."

At five thirty Mrs. Rand told the girls to wash up for supper. Then they must say goodbye to their mother until her next visit. When they were out of the room Mrs. Rand discussed with Danya the next visiting time. They agreed on a Sunday afternoon one month hence so that she could spend the full allotted time with the girls.

"Of course you may bring Mr. Vorodinov, you realize. The visits are open to two parents."

"My husband is too shy among people, so he will not come. I will visit my children by myself."

"As you wish, Mrs. Vorodinov. I'm sure the children will enjoy your next visit…Children, hurry down so you can say goodbye to your mother."

They did. Primly, stiffly, with no evidence that they yearned to go with her or to have her stay longer.

That made Danya dislike the Rand women even more. They must have worked hard to separate the children's feelings from her so thoroughly.

The only solution, the only way to change their feelings was to get the children back to their own home as quickly as she could. Every ounce of her strength she would use to that end. She would continue writing to the governor and the president's wife. Because of their letters, she was now convinced, she had been given the visiting privileges. That wasn't enough. She walked away from the Rand home embittered and disappointed. No, it wasn't enough. She was not going to let strange people keep her children. She wanted them back in their own home, and she wanted it done before more damage was done to them.

She sent several more letters, written by the neighbor's daughter. She made her visits as permitted, but they rankled her increasingly as she observed the continuing changes in the children. She became more and more a stranger to their necessities and affections. She was a visitor only, tolerated dutifully when at times they would rather be outdoors playing or reading.

The miracles she expected from the letters never occurred. There were routine answers from the governor's office and only one more reply from Mrs. Roosevelt, which did no more than assure her that her problems were understood. After all this understanding she wanted some help, some action from all these people who spent their time writing letters and promising help. She was getting fed up with the waiting. Every day was a threat. Now it was April. Easter was coming. The children were not yet home. No other resources for help came to her mind, as hard as she thought and tried to pray. To hell with ugly Bent. Let him wonder what she was doing on her own. She would not go to him for anything.

***

Two events changed the pace of her waiting.

Mrs. Hills had a recurrence of the tuberculosis that she'd had in her teens, and the two youngest Vorodinov children were put into the care of a Cullham minister's family, the Reverend McDermit Dyson and his wife. Danya received the notice on official county welfare stationery with a reminder that the visiting privileges would continue as before.

The other serious change came with Mikolai's WPA job. That same week he came home with disturbing news. He told Danya that all the WPA workers would be taken off the road jobs for two months later in the summer. Instead they would go each day to Middletown where they would make visits to every house giving out papers and voting information.

Because the president had given them their jobs, they were told, they would continue working for him in this way because it was necessary to reach all the voters and get the right people elected to the congress. If the wrong people got into office they would all lose their government jobs. The third selectman of Stanton who was in charge of the local WPA explained it to them. He had the paper from the state and it had all the information, which he carefully repeated so each man would understand it. He ended his talk to the men with the admonition that if any man refused to do the assigned job he would be taken off the WPA payroll forever. They must support the president or lose their jobs, which he had made for them.

Danya listened with growing incredulity. First she accused Mikolai of not listening carefully and not understanding everything. But he said two of the other men had repeated it for him and it was clearly as he had told Danya, just as he'd said. Danya's questioning irked him.

"It is a crazy business!" she spat out. "What do they think to do, use farmers and ditch diggers to walk on the city streets like crazy politicians? The president promised work, not sneaky tricks like this. I will write to him about the wrong things that are happening here. I think stinking Bent may be in back of this big idea. I will report it all to the president."

Despite her husband's pleas to be reasonable and not blame everything on Mr. Bent, Danya pursued this line of reasoning. She went that evening to the neighbor's to have a letter written.

'Dear President Roosevelt: A big mistake is happening in our town with the WPA. You should know about it before people are in trouble. Today they told my husband he would not work more on the roads. Instead he should go to the city and walk to every house with papers telling people who they should vote for. If he does not go he will lose his job.'

'I know you are against mixing farmers with the politicians because I heard you on the radio and I listen to you every time. That is why I am writing to you, so you can stop the town WPA people from doing this. Also the town selectman Mr. Bent who is somehow mixed in the bad things, and the other one who gives the orders and the jobs you made.'

'My husband also said they will take two dollars a week from his pay to pay for the papers and the workers' travel. We are poor people who need every penny because we are trying to finish our house so the welfare will give our children back to us. Also my husband is a farmer and he is too shy to go among people. He wants only to work like a man, not to be chased into the city streets to say dishonest things to people he does not know. He does not know anything about politics and voting.'

'Please make an investigation before my husband loses his job. I will not let him take one step to help the politicians. I know you understand the troubles of common people and will help us.'

'Sincerely, Danya Vorodinov.'

Of course Danya did not know that the president not only understood the troubles of the common people but he knew also how to use their problems to his own end. The vast army in the network of WPA districts were now to pay off for the jobs that had been doled out to them. The wild spending rabbit in Washington had in his hands the unprecedented power of billions in federal money. Anyone who accepted a part of this money should be grateful enough to work for the man who cared enough about their poverty and troubles to redeem them.

The threat in 1938 of a deepening economic crisis united the millions of federal, state and town employees toward one goal. That was to keep in office the men who had been responsible for their jobs, or to see that the local candidates supported by their president were elected. The appalling tragedy was that there was sufficient money at the end of the pole to make these efforts worthwhile.

The disconsolate victims of the depression were already convinced that the presidential magician had every answer to any ill. He could only work his magic, they were told, when he had full support of his constituents. This was happening not just in small hamlets like Stanton. It was happening across the United

States. Danya's letter could no more stop or correct the threat to her husband than the entire opposing political party could have.

The weeks passed without an answer, which she sincerely expected. Three days before the new working orders were to go into effect, she decided she must talk to Selectman Bent about Mikolai's job.

"I'm sorry, very sorry, Mrs. Vorodinov, that there is nothing our office can do about this. The orders for the WPA administration come from the state and they get their orders directly from the federal agency in Washington. We can change nothing. We can make no exceptions for any man."

"But is it not dishonest to give a man one job and then force him to do other work? I am not so sure the orders came from the federal government. Maybe they came from you. I think you crooks in this state make up the business yourself. You always have some tricky way to make a promise so people will trust you."

She hesitated. She saw Bent's angry face flush and was spurred on by that satisfaction. She jabbed her finger toward him.

"And then what do you do? After your promises? You become bloodsuckers! You lay in the mud like bloodsuckers waiting for us to take your help! Then you climb on us with your mud and your sticky hungry hands. First you try to suck our honesty, then you suck out our children, then you suck out the jobs you gave us. Bloodsuckers! I see you all now in the same sheepskin!"

"Mrs. Vor…"

"I will not listen to a bloodsucker! I would not believe one word that comes from your mouth. Your letters, and your committees and your meetings and hearings to talk things over. And your money to hold us in the mud with you. Not one word is honest that comes from your mouth. Not one penny do you give for honest help. In everything you do for us there is an evil reason in your ugly mind. And you will be found out, like any bloodsucker. When you are full and made too fat from what you have sucked from us you will be hanging on so hard that your black actions will come over you like a snake and eat you up!'

"That is enough…"

She stood fast. "I did not finish, it is not enough. If you walk from this room I will follow behind you and I will talk to your back so everyone can hear. So I will tell you every word in my mind. I know you have taken money from the welfare. I know you steal somehow from the bank. I know you keep too many secrets under your pale skin. And I know by the power of God you will suffer for all these sins. You will not force my husband to take dishonest work, not for one hour. Every help you give us is to bring back to yourself some dishonest money!"

"Now Mrs. Vorodinov, you know perfectly well you need the relief money, and the welfare goods as well." In his anger Bent spat out the words rudely.

"No!" Danya raised her head triumphantly. "No, we do not need any more help from you and your twisted welfare. With my ten fingers and my husband's two hands we will make our living and bring back our children! You have no power over us anymore, you ugly bulldog!"

She strode from his office with her chin held high, leaving him motionless in his chair. He was in a state of disgust with himself. As she passed by his office window she was singing wildly, a Russian lullaby remolded by her emotions. He gritted his teeth. God, she is a troublesome hairshirt. Why didn't I get her out of here without a messy conversation like this…her damn voice yelling out those things. He got up to close the window away from her sounds.

A mad woman, that's what she was. Screaming out at people and singing on the streets like a mad woman. For God's sake, when would they see that at the state hospital and keep her there out of everyone's way?

He was galled that he had not stood up to her. Galled that she could dare to speak to him that way in his own office without any resistance from him. But it showed one thing about her. She'd willingly take help from the government but she and her husband would certainly bite the hands that feed them when their worthless loyalty is asked for. He sat for a time scowling, remembering her words. He absent mindedly picked up his pencil and doodled on the desk blotter...oval lines that shaped into eyes, one, two three of them...he looked at what he'd drawn and threw his pencil down. He shook to awaken himself.

He must get her out of the way. It was bad enough that she carried on about the welfare. There were no records of that, and no one would believe her now anyway, after her time in the asylum. The bank business was another story. Of course no one would listen to that either. By the incoherent accusations she had been making against him and the welfare she had sealed off any chance that people would listen to her. The town was accustomed now to her ravings, or so he thought. No, he was sure of it.

But yet...you never could be sure when a person like that might do something that would get attention. For instance, supposing she wrote to the bank commission. He had seen copies of the letters she had written to the governor's office and he knew she had received answers. Furthermore, the state welfare agency had ignored his recommendations and had allowed the visiting privileges sooner than he had wished. There was always that danger again, that she would get it into her head to write about the bank thing, and that again her letters would be read and bring about some action. This time it could be a drastic threat to him.

How in Moses had she learned anything? Oh hell, what was he asking himself? Of course she knew nothing. She was making a stab at something, anything, that's all. And that's what anyone else would say, too. That she was off her rails, just throwing accusations at him trying to relieve herself of her resentment, trying to get at him for the imagined damage he had done to her children. Well, everyone could see the children would be better off anywhere but in their own home with a mother like that.

He worked it over in his mind, rationalizing and at the same time hoping he was right. No amount of her shouting would get results. He had to be positive of that. She could talk for weeks to everyone she saw and not one person would be credulous enough to give her accusations any value.

But the damn letter writing. That he couldn't dismiss as harmless. That could be damaging. It could start a so-called routing audit, one of the little weapons of the new governmental agencies. That might be pretty embarrassing for him...no, more than embarrassing. He had made no provisions yet for something like that.

He tapped his pencil on the desk, nervous staccato taps. If there were some way he could duplicate records, or lose them...at least the incriminating records. Or conceal the figures somehow, the way he had with the building and loan books. It must have been a foolproof method because nothing had been found when the bank audited the books of the Society when it was merged. He'd go over the old books and check it again. He was sure he could do something. He had better do something, quickly, before any suspicions were leveled at him.

He began to sweat from the apprehension of being found out. He swallowed several times like a man who had been running and needed saliva. He felt he'd been running against a wind. He was now afraid. He dropped his pencil and looked down at the doodling on his desk blotter. He stared at the unmistakable form

BELIEVE

When Danya was informed that the two youngest children were now in the home of a minister in Cullham she was relieved that they were away from Mrs. Hills. She felt sorry for the woman who was suffering from recurrent tuberculosis, and had to give up her own daughter to another family. But perhaps, she thought, it would give her some chance to think more like a mother and understand how Danya felt giving up her children.

The Hills had no nearby relatives and had appealed to their minister, the Reverend McDermit Dyson, to take their daughter and the Vorodinov children for the short time Mrs. Hills hoped to be in treatments. Reverend Dyson managed the transfer of legal custody in a visit to the county welfare office, sparing Mrs. Hills the bother.

On the scheduled visiting day Danya found herself knocking at the parsonage door one Saturday soon after her confrontation with Angus Bent. She was prepared to dislike the Dysons as she did the other two families who had her children.

Mrs. Dyson answered the door. She wore a slightly harassed air which Danya observed later was her everyday countenance. She was tall and thin, thoroughly grayed, and wore the age-making rimless glasses like a woman unconcerned with her appearance. Her years as a minister's wife, mixing in church socials and constant parish visits, had encouraged her talkative nature. She had learned that anyone who knocked on the parsonage door was coming with a problem of some sort. She was an outgoing woman, friendly though harried which showed in her voice as she greeted any parishioner, and it did a great deal to allay the reticence or ponderous mien of the visitor.

Because of her other experiences Danya was on the defensive before the woman spoke. She immediately felt the difference in Norma Dyson's pleased surprise and her warm invitation to enter.

Sally Hills, the little blue hen, saw her from where the three children were playing.

"It's the fur lady," she told the other two. By then Mrs. Dyson had called them all to come see who the visitor was.

Danya began to feel ashamed of her harbored resentments toward these new people. Mrs. Dyson fluttered over the children as though this were a special occasion. The children sensed it and for this Danya's heart went out with thanks to her.

"Now Mrs. Vorodinov, I'll call McDermit. He's in his study working but I know he's anxious to meet you, so I'll give his door a tap." Her voice trailed off, ending with a nervous laugh. "He's like a smoking steam engine if he's bothered when he's writing his sermon, but I know he won't mind this once."

Danya heard the great voice booming in greeting before the man reached the bottom of the stairs. "Well, now," he said in a burry voice, "where's the fine mother who loaned us her sunshine?"

Children have an uncanny way of sponging in the human attitudes of folks around them. They sensed from the Dyson's welcome that now the fur lady was someone special. The fact that she was absorbed in conversation with Reverend Dyson instead of hovering over them further intrigued their interest. It wasn't long before they, instead of their mother, made the overtures for attention.

"Ah, now," he said to them when the children interrupted their conversation, "can you not hear we are solving the problems of the garden pests? Now, my lad," he addressed the boy, "didn't I tell you this morning we must find a way to get rid of the garden pests before they ruin the lettuce? Well, now, listen carefully while your mother tells us her secret method."

After listening the boy whispered something to Mr. Dyson. He stood back timidly, waiting for the man's answer.

"Saints preserve us, laddie," answered Mr. Dyson in a surprised loud voice. He held his arms up toward the sky in an exaggerated gesture of supplication. "Now, Lord, can this good woman bring us some rain, too, he wants to know...don't know lad, don't know, but there's no harm asking the Lord if your mother can help bring some rain."

The boy wanted to show his mother the garden he had planted and tended. Reverend Dyson, Danya and her young son walked to the garden behind the house where the boy proudly showed his small tomato plants, the row of lettuce, the beets, and a lone watermelon vine struggling along with two undersized melons. The boy pointed to these sadly. "But don't worry," he told her affirmatively, "if you can get us a parcel of rain they'll get much bigger."

With what magic McDermit Dyson turned her two children to her, Danya could not analyze but she could feel it had happened and she wanted to give her thanks aloud.

Mr. Dyson walked with Danya down garden rows, at times expanding on the bug problem, pointing out here a special lettuce he was trying, there a new kind of squash. As he went along he ordered the small boy to water certain of the plants. As Danya watched he dutifully ran to fill his watering can from the wooden rain barrel at the edge of the garden tool shed.

By the time they returned to the house Danya knew her two children were in the hands of a man of God, a good man and his wife. He appeared at once part of the earthly world around him and in part of another spiritual world that shone out through his speech and small wisdoms. This tall man with the fair sun-marked skin of the Scots, the whitened hair that receded beyond a high forehead became, in the secret precincts of Danya's heart, the man sent by God to deliver her children. Within the time of that first visit the great hope began to take hold of her. She had waited and again God had sent someone to help her.

In the library she talked with him for two hours, telling her plight to the compassionate listener. Her hateful invectives against Angus Bent abated under the presence of a more commanding emotion. She was so filled with hope, so convinced from this short visit that the end of her grievous misfortune was tied to this man; that there were moments as she spoke that Bent's evil name seemed a profanity too coarse to be spoken before him.

She finished her story. Her cheeks were flushed with the deep emotions she had stirred within herself. In supplication she spoke after a short silence. "Reverend Dyson, can you help me get my children back? I feel like God is pushing me to ask you."

He leaned back in his old Morris chair, removed his glasses and rubbed his cheek with the palm of a tanned, freckled hand. He had very pale blue eyes. Without the glasses they showed to Danya a soft mystical light, a promise of help, kindness, all that she had sought for so long from someone, anyone. She drew in her breath. She must not make him embarrassed. She must stay quiet and listen. He would understand her, she was sure of it, even if she could not say the right words. He must know he had the power to help her.

"Well, now, it's a hard-hearted tale you've told me. And I must help you in whatever way I can. I believe sunshine comes to the place where it is loved the most. And I tell you we love the children like our own, as new as they are to us. But we would give them back to their own home and parents just as happily as could be because that's where they give the most light." He clapped his hands together quietly. "Now, do not worry if we can't solve the problem in a few days. I know it's a very anxious thing for you, but you must be a little more patient with me until I find a way to help."

"But if you talk to the welfare, perhaps they will listen to you?"

"Yes, it's very possible we should talk to them first. You must pray that the Lord helps us."

"I am always praying, every morning and every night I pray. But always my enemy Bent comes between me and God, and he makes me such troubles that my heart goes away from my prayers. I would pray harder if I could see only a little sign of real help."

"You must not look for the sign instead of praying. You do not need a sign, just pray and believe. Do not be troubled in your prayers with Mr. Bent. But now, I'll help you in that so you won't be alone. I'll pray for you and with God's help we'll find a way."

"Oh yes, I believe so, and I hope soon, soon." She was tearfully grateful. When she said goodbye she shook his hand lightly, then in a brief surge of emotion she bent her head and touched her lips to that strong thick hand as though it would be her guide out of a long unbearable wilderness.

BACKSTORY

McDermit Dyson brought into Danya's life the kindness, concern and unlimited hope that was a natural element of his being.

There are men who are given extraordinary spiritual insight. To some it is a commodity that is sold, priced according to the demands of the times. For others it is an esoteric burden that prevents a normal life. For still others it is a gift, returned in greater measure each time some part of it is given. The Reverend McDermit Dyson was born with that gift.

He lived his first fifteen years in the misted green hills of Balloch, Scotland. When he was eight years old he was allowed to spend the summer with his grandfather. The old widower packed up a tent, some pots and pans and with young McDermit hiked to a secluded knoll on the edge of the Loch Lomand where they lived for eight weeks, like God meant a Scotsman to live, he told the boy.

Grandfather Dyson had taken a sharp turn away from the rigid and logical Presbyterianism of his family. "God's too big to stay in one church," he proclaimed to his shocked minister. "I'm going to turn over all the rocks and the gravestones, too, maybe, to find out what He's saying to our brothers out there that he can't say inside these walls for fear of being criticized. Oh, do not worry," burred the witty Scot, leaning down to whisper, "I'm leaving my purse to the church just in case this is his only house after all."

That summer he knew the boy McDermit needed words put to the thoughts that must be swirling inside his young head. The child was tall for his age, built with the sturdy bones of the Dysons. He was born to know tenderness and compassion, the grandfather told the boy's parents. None in his family could remember the likes of it. From the time his eyes could look straight at you, his grandfather would tell, you knew he had a part of his Maker within him, just waiting for the right words to speak out. He was like no other child he'd seen.

They set out that summer day after promising McDermit's parents that he wouldn't put crazy notions in the child's head but just teach him proper prayers and hymns.

They were sitting outside the tent in the coolness of the summer evening watching the sun set.

"McDermit, my boy, we're looking at God out here. See him there, in the waves of the Loch, there in the trees, in this little whistle I'm making from the willow? Lean close to your Grandpa. Try to listen to what He's telling you."

"All I hears is a whistle."

"You must listen with a bigger heart, then. It's no whistle if your heart's big enough to take in the words. You must listen harder and you must look harder all about you. You'll see Him, and you'll hear what He wants you to hear. You must bend very close and you must concentrate like a man. Listen again."

"It's only music."

"Only music? Oh no, my lad. It's the voice of God telling us things he forgot to tell Reverend Gordon. I'll tell you what He's saying to you. Now listen with your heart wide open until you can hear the words yourself."

The boy leaned forward eagerly, captivated and thrilled that his fiery grandfather was going to let him into the secrets that were playing havoc with his soul...or that's what his mother said anyway.

"Hear those long high sounds? He's telling you to look up there for Him there in the sky, above everything, behind every cloud... there, behind those streaks of orange coming from the sunset. Then in these notes, listen carefully now...hear how they move like the waves of the Loch? Hear the deep voice calling up to you until it reaches the white caps of the waves? Then He wants you to follow Him over the grass. See Him there, calling out. Listen hard, He's moving fast across that meadow...you can see Him move...look, see where He went!"

"But what did He say?"

"Oh, you did not listen so well, my lad."

"But I saw Him, Grandpa, truly I did."

"Then I'll tell you what He said, but the next time you must hear it yourself. When He talks from the sky He says make your heart bigger, open up your little heart so you'll have room for Him. Then when He speaks to you from the Loch He says fill up your heart, lad, fill it with love, all the love you can think of. Fill it up as many times as the waves touch the shores. And you know, lad, when He's telling you all that He whispers a secret, and that's this sound...." He blew soft sounds through the little flute.

"What is it?"

"Listen, He's telling you your heart is so big you can never fill it up. You can love your Mum and your Pa, your old Grandpa and your sisters and your brother and everyone you know by name, but all that won't fill up your heart. You can even love people whose names you don't know. You see them on the street and you can put love in your heart for them and it still won't make your heart heavy. Then you can love people you don't even see. You don't know their names and you don't know what they look like, but God's telling you that your heart will hold love for them, too."

He played a few more moments on the willow flute. He put his hand on the boy's shoulder. "Can you imagine that, lad, now have you ever imagined that? You can fit the whole world into your heart and it won't ever get filled. You think about all those good people in the world, people you'll never see, and you put love into your heart for them, too, and they'll know about it because God will see to it and they'll be happier and better for it."

"What does He say to me from the meadow, when He runs away from me across the grasses?"

Grandfather Dyson lowered his eyes and slowly nodded his head. "Oh, lad, did you not hear a word He said? He was not running away from you. Did you not hear Him tell you to follow behind Him? Bring your heart filled with love, He's telling you. Bring your loving heart and follow Me, He's saying. He'll find more people for you to love, that's what He's saying to you."

"I think the wind was making too much noise and I couldn't hear him, Grandpa."

"Ah no, lad. That's Him in the wind, too. You'll soon get the hang of it when you concentrate like a man. When you hear Him through the wind He's telling you not to be slow about it. Move on with Him, like the wind. Don't be slow and stingy about filling your heart, move along fast, like the wind, bit and bravely, like the wind over the Loch and the meadows. You'll hear Him when you listen with your heart."

The child sat in thought for a while.

"Grandpa, is it true?"

"Now that, laddie, is the most interesting thing about listening to God. If you believe you can hear Him, it's true. You can hear Him like you're hearing me now. And if you don't believe it...well, you never hear a thing He's trying to tell you. He can walk along side of you. He can call your name. He can tell you great things that He wants you to do, and if you don't believe He's there, why then you can't hear a word He's saying. You miss it all."

"If you don't hear Him what happens to your heart? How can you fill up your heart?"

"Ah, it's sad, very sad. If you never hear Him your heart stays small as this stone. Feel it...that's how hard a man's heart can be if he doesn't put any love into it, if he doesn't listen to God. Small and hard like that stone you're holding now, that's how your heart stays. It never gets any bigger. It gets heavier and heavier every day of a man's life but it's really empty all the time. That's how mysterious love is. The more people you can hold in your heart the lighter it weighs. And if you have not love at all in your heart, no love for anyone, why then your heart gets so heavy you can hardly walk around with the weight of it."

"Then do you have to lay in bed and die like Grandma?"

"Well, now, most people die the same way, in bed like Grandma died. It's a comfortable place, get them rested for the trip to heaven. Grandma had a big heart. She just lay down to rest for her trip. No sir, when you have a heart like that little stone no amount of resting or lying down on your bed can help. It just feels heavy and terrible all the time. Then after you die you carry the same heavy heart all over the place"

"Grandpa! You mean...in hell?"

"Don't know, laddie, don't know. That's something God doesn't tell. That's the devil's business."

"You mean you can hear the...the devil talking, too? Does he tell you things? Can you really hear him as well?"

"Well, now you can't hear him when you're thinking about God, not when your heart is filling itself with love. That's why it's very important to think about love. Keeps the devil from bothering with you. Why, when you're thinking about God and love the devil won't have a thing to do with you."

"Did you ever hear the devil?"

"Well, I must tell you the truth. When I was a lad, about your age, long before my hair turned white like this, I began to wonder about the devil. Pretty soon instead of thinking about God I was taking up my time thinking about the devil, just like you are now, wondering about him and thinking about him." He signed.

"Did the devil talk to you, Grandpa?"

"Ah, it was a terrible truth I found out. I'll remember it to the end of my days. Now listen carefully so you won't make the same mistake. When you think about the devil, even if you just think about hating him, or if you take any of your time thinking how afraid you are of him, then you can't hear a word God is trying to say to you. You must leave the way open for God all the time. You see, He might have something very big, very important to tell you. And if you have the devil on your mind, if you're thinking and wondering about the devil, why then God can't get into your heart at all."

"But did he talk to you, Grandpa?"

"Yes sir, lad, he did. And I'll tell you how bad it was. I was about your age, and I was sitting in the garden thinking very hard about the devil. What a bad fellow he is, I said to myself. How ugly he must be. I wonder what the fellow looks like. I wonder if he's really red and carries that long tail behind him, that's what I was thinking and wondering. Ah, how I wished I could see him for just a minute so I could be sure he was real. Because as you know, laddie, Reverend Gordon says we must be on the lookout for the devil. And I wasn't one to be wasting my time looking out for him if he wasn't real or if I didn't even know what he looked like. So, while I was sitting there wondering and thinking very hard about the devil, I heard a bonnie voice calling to me from behind a tree."

"The devil?"

"Wait now, I'll tell you the full story. T'was a handsome laddie standing there, calling to me. Oh, he was a fine looking thing, he was. Com'on, Mac, he said to me with his bonnie smile, let's have some fun today. Well, now, what shall we do? I asked him. Let's go into the forest to hunt, he said. So I went with him even though I knew I wasn't allowed. Now he was a good talker, and as we were walking we talked about the devil. We walked deep into the woods, thinking about the devil all the time. We looked around from time to time for the animals, but there weren't any to be seen. Let's go deeper into the forest, he said, and I followed right behind."

"Well, then, it started to rain. It rained like the very devil was throwing water down on us. Night came on and we couldn't find our way out of the woods. We sat there under a tree…scared and trembling I was, and the bonnie lad just talking on about the devil. He told more stories about the devil's works and I trembled like the leaves of the trees in the wind. But I listened to every word. We stayed in the forest all night and the next day, and into the next night. Every time we tried to find our way back home we just got deeper into the forest."

"In the middle of the night we came to a river. It was running deep from the rains and moving along fast as a racehorse. Come on, let's go across, said the lad to me. Now I didn't want to, but by then I was believing he knew an awful lot, so I said to myself, I'd better go with him. Oh, the river was moving along fast. Moreover I wasn't such a good swimmer then. We were in very deep and I couldn't see anything, so I just kept swimming like a tadpole. But then I got very frightened. Suddenly I realized I was all alone, and I couldn't keep on swimming so well. So I started to say my prayers real fast, loud as I could, calling out to God. Help me, God, please help me, that's what I said. And do you know, laddie, right then I felt something near me, right at my hand. I took hold of it very quickly, I can tell you."

"What was it, Grandpa?"

"Why it was a poor little scrub tree floating past me. I held on real hard and I said thank you God, thank you. Then the swift water carried the little tree right to the edge of the river, with me hanging on tight. I got hold of the grass and pulled myself out. Now I sat there until morning, thinking how lucky I was that I had called on God to help me. I said thank you over and over again. I had a good long nap, though I tell you my stomach was empty as I can ever remember. When I woke up there was my Pa standing above me and a few other men with him. They looked all over the forest for two days, he told me, and they knew they'd find me. So you see, I was very lucky to call on God in time."

"But what happened to the bonnie laddie?"

"Ah, that's the great sad part of this story. They found the poor laddie miles away, caught on the roots of a tree half fallen into the river. Drowned he was."

"But why didn't God help him?"

"Now this is the thing you must remember. That maybe was a bonnie good laddie, but he was so interested in the devil, and he knew so much about the devil, and he talked so much about the devil that he forgot to ask God for help. Now maybe a little scrub tree came past him too, but maybe he wasn't thinking about God or calling out to him. He was so full of information and thoughts about the devil he didn't have any room for God. So he couldn't hear God say 'take hold of that scrub tree, laddie, take hold of that tree.'"

"But you heard him Grandpa!"

"Yes sir, plain as I can hear you talking to me now."

Grandfather Dyson had seen correctly the child McDermit's gift. He ministered to it, encouraged the boy's sensitive, gentle nature that often perplexed the rigid rule-following parents.

After that summer, after those weeks of tending and pruning the boy's thoughts, Grandfather Dyson tried to caution the parents that their child must be allowed a greater freedom of thinking than was the family tendency.

"He's not one to go stiffly by the rules, not of the house he's brought up in nor his church, and you'll be a bit of a devil's helper if you try to keep him from his right free path," he admonished the mother.

"Why, it's heathen to let a child go freely on his way, without abiding by the rules of his mother's church and the home his father gives him." She vented her anger at the old man's interference. "Now Grandfather, you've got to stop putting notions into his head about things he's too young to understand. You've mixed him all up with your stories and he's just a bother in church school, asking, asking all the time. Questions he shouldn't even have in his head."

"That so? Shouldn't wonder, shouldn't wonder at all. I tell you now, Maud, if the boy has a question and can say it right out in words, then he should have an answer. And if he can't get the answer from the likes of those school marms who spend their free time reading the bible, he'll find it some other way."

"Now, Grandfather, you mustn't make it difficult for the church school. He confuses the teacher and rattles up the entire class of children with his questions, so they tell me. He must stay on the proper subject and give the proper sensible answers to the questions that are asked of him."

"There's not just one proper, sensible answer, no sir, not for a boy like that. He sees a bigger world than they want to bother with at the church school. Now you'll be smart and a better worker of the Lord's if you let him alone, Maud. He mustn't be hindered in his curiosity, not by any human being. He's to be used as a tool of the Lord's. He understands that already, young as he is. He's gathering all his strength now; he's filling himself with the purest, most joyous love you can imagine. Perhaps we can't even imagine how his heart and his mind are working. That's how different he is from all our family. You've seen him and you've tried to stop him. But you cannot do that. Let him take in those strange people that come through the town. He's the only human being whose heart has time for a kind word or thought. Now would you turn them away from a chance to see some of God's goodness?"

"Grandfather! You know they could harm him, or they could be carrying a disease. Now why must you encourage him to spend his time talking to people like that?"

"Because they need him, Maud. And he's learning his way. Why last week he got two of them to come along to church and mind you, they stayed through the whole rambling sermon. Even said some prayers. I noticed them, and I said, good job, lad. Yes sir, I told him, good job lad."

"It's wrong of you to encourage him to do things like that. You know it created a bit stir, those ragged men walking into the church."

"But the Lord doesn't see their rags, Maud. You know that. He just said to them, welcome, come right in. And then he probably bent down to young Mac and whispered, 'that's fine, lad, that's fine. Now go find more of them and bring them to me.'"

"You're ruining the boy, Grandfather, no matter what you try to say. You're putting those grand ideas into his head, that he can speak to the Lord like a common man, as though he can carry on that way when he says his prayers. Yes, I've heard him, right out he says those words. Like the Lord was an ordinary man, just a common man. It's heathen, that's what it is."

"Well no, I wouldn't worry so Maud. But there's no idea of mine that the boy didn't have in his head before I spoke it. He's just got a closer way of talking to God. Nothing heathen about that. Just more personal for him, that's all. He just knows Him better. No harm will come to him. Let him be."

The exasperated mother turned from her father-in-law, vowing she would handle the boy her own way. Yet when she scolded McDermit or tried to restrain him, her efforts were quelled by her son's sweet acceptance of the chiding, and his consequent ignoring of her words. She turned her energies and controls to the other children, leaving McDermit to what she called the scheme of the devil.

When McDermit was fifteen, his family moved to America. There he finished his schooling and against his family's wishes chose the ministry as a career above school teaching.

He was first assigned as third minister in a New Haven Congregational church. His yearning for missionary work pushed him to ask for an assignment in China. Before he left he married Norma Leeds, the daughter of the head minister. They spent twenty-five years in China and Tibet.

In those years of converting the Asians to Christianity McDermit was given a greater insight into the spiritual world of which he preached. In their language, their customs, their own religions, he saw vividly the thread that united them all to the God he knew and understood. No unconverted man was ever a heathen in his eyes, but more often a teacher of ideas and nuances of the mystical Eastern religions that fulfilled the wonderings that McDermit often had.

With his gift of understanding and empathy he gave kindness and concern, unlimited hope to those who were in need. He took from them what they were unaware they were giving to him: a fuller, lighter heart.

The three Dyson children were born in China during McDermit's missions. When they were school age the family returned to the United States. McDermit asked for a small church somewhere in Connecticut. He wanted to put together his writings and lectures for other missionary groups and felt that a small town would give him that opportunity. He was given the ministry of a small Congregational church in the town of Cullham.

And in that town Danya Vorodinov had found the path to his door.

HOME

Danya's appeals to McDermit Dyson had called up the man's determination to help the distraught woman.

Angus Bent had built a formidable record against Danya Vorodinov. In the Reverend's earliest attempts to wrest from the welfare agency a hastened ending to the family's case he was confronted with serious facts contrived to support the grave charge that the mother was unfit to raise her children. Also that the father, out of work, shiftless and unwilling even to keep his job with the WPA was not equipped to support his family. The final summary in the case pointed out that the family had refused to accept any further help from the welfare, making it impossible to consider returning the children to their destitute home.

Dyson's visit to Angus Bent in his office was somewhat enlightening. The man he met could hardly be described by the adjectives with which Danya had drawn him. He impressed Reverend Dyson as a quiet, learned man, well practiced in the proprieties of discussing serious issues with a minister. He appeared to be grieved and concerned that the case could not be closed with the return of the children. He made issue of the unseemly living conditions the children had been rescued from. There was no running water, just a hand pump in the kitchen, no indoor toilet facilities, no electricity and no central heating. The house, he told Dyson, was unfinished, a monstrosity of twelve rooms, only five of which were usable. None of the upstairs rooms were finished; the beams of the attic were still exposed and there was danger of all kinds for small children in a situation like that. Then, in a philosophical-like confidential tone he added,

"It's a pity these foreign people could come to our country and attempt to build these grand houses without enough money or good taste to enhance the town. If there were some way they could be forced to turn their savings over to a committee, people with knowledge of building and economics, the results of their spending would less often end in the manner of the Vorodinov fortunes."

He continued in a sincere manner. "You see, Reverend, if the money that Mr. Vorodinov earned before the depression had been more wisely allocated there would not have been this hulk of a house, nor the terrible shortage of money that forced us to break up the poor family. We've had a lot of bad experiences with these foreigners, a lot of trouble with them when they try to get too much too fast. I'm glad to say for the most part we're able, in this town, to keep most of them above water. The Vorodinov woman is an exceptional case. She has, from the beginning, resisted any effort we made to help her. I think, since you have read the hospital records, you understand what I mean."

"Well, now, Brother Bent," replied the great voice, "it could be said you've rescued six helpless beings from a life of grave discomforts, couldn't it?"

"I believe, as an American, I should do all I can to help these children acclimate themselves to the American way of life. In their original home environment they were developing in a direction more foreign than American. That was because of the foreign parents, naturally, and the unusual living habits. I think you'll agree that in their present homes the children are being given far greater advantages, and they are also being shaped into better Christians and better citizens for the future of America."

"Of course it's kind of you to loan the children's sunshine to old folks like us and the Rand family. But as Christian men, shouldn't we find a way to give those children back to the poor deprived mother who bore them? Maybe they've had enough Americanizing to help them over the hump, now it's been more than two years, hasn't it? Maybe it's time for Christian men to work together to see that they get back to the home that needs them, where they're wanted so much."

"In view of the facts, as much as it would please me, I think it isn't possible. Not at this time. I would cooperate to the fullest extent, believe me, if I thought it was in the children's interest." Bent reeked of sincerity.

There was a polite impasse. Bent's description of those 'unseemly living conditions' had seemed trivial to Dyson who had spent so many happy years as missionary in a culture with such conditions. He contemplated the man opposite him. The only change in Bent's emotional calm had come when he spoke of the foreigners building their houses. Otherwise nothing of a personal reaction had risen from the man's conversation that would fortify the charges Mrs. Vorodinov had made about him.

He smiled warmly at Bent. "Well, now, we're dealing with a sorrowing mother here. I'm sure you know that, and I'm sure you want to help her much as you can."

"Of course, Reverend, naturally, we all do. Believe me, I've tried to convince both Mr. and Mrs. Vorodinov that the only way they will be allowed to have the children back is to make a decent home for them. Because of Mr. Vorodinov's refusal to work they are unable to go ahead and finish the house. It is, I believe, a sad state when the parents won't do all they can to comply with our regulations."

"It's a complicated thing, very complicated, Mr. Bent. But the good Lord always finds a way for the troubled." He hesitated a moment, then reflected, "You know, if you and I had had this fine modern plumbing and these fine heated houses when we were small boys, what do you think our lives would be like now?"

He got up to leave. "Yes sir, I think as Christian men we should think more about the mother and not so much about the plumbing…what do you think, Brother Bent? Let's work together to see if we can change a few of those rulings, shall we?"

Bent was not easily taken off guard. He shook hands politely, even warmly. "I'll do all I can to help, Reverend Dyson. Naturally, I'm bound by certain rulings that come down from the federal and state government. If there is ever a way that I can be instrumental in helping the underprivileged I am willing to do so."

"Fine, Brother Bent, fine. Now you're a good man, and a Christian man, too, so we'll work together when we can."

"Yes, just let me know if there is anything this office can do." As he closed the door behind Dyson, Angus Bent heaved a deep breath and swallowed nervously. Had he fooled the old Scot?

***

Reverend Dyson was determined to move forward to find help for Danya. He talked to a retired attorney who was a member of his church. He asked him if he would draw whatever papers were necessary so that Mrs. Vorodinov could petition the state authorities for the return of her children.

The long complicated process of petitioning for a hearing, being heard, petitioning the welfare court, being heard, petitioning probate court, being heard, then the final hearing for custody of the children took more than a year. Dyson prevailed upon the attorney to stand by the case until it was cleared. Otherwise, without funds, Mrs. Vorodinov would be unable to seek any other legal help.

There were long and fretful months of waiting when it seemed that everything gained might be lost somewhere in the jumble of legal papers and other processing of the over busy courts. In her lowest moments Danya was reminded by her nearly sunken heart that the man who was working for her would never let the matter drop until it was finished in her favor.

Whenever she visited the children she was seized with the panic that they were growing away from her faster than the Reverend Dyson was able to work in the courts for her. She saw the younger children more often, sometimes two or three times a month. But there was no way she could bridge the time she missed with them. They were not her children now, even though the Dysons tried to encourage ways that would bind them to their mother.

She tried once to make an unannounced visit to the Rands to see the older girls. It was a cold day and she had spent the morning with the small children at the Dyson's. She was about to take the bus home when a longing for the other children swept over her. She had time to take the bus farther on, to visit them at the Rands. It would be all right. She was too empty, too low to go home just now. The Rands shouldn't mind. She had never bothered them, had always stuck to the visiting schedule. She had kept to her visiting days and stayed the allotted length of time. They would surely not mind this once. She would explain it was near Christmas and she wanted to talk to them about Christmas presents. That's what she would say. Just a short visit. Just to talk about Christmas.

Mrs. Rand answered the doorbell. She was surprised. "Why Mrs. Vorodinov, this isn't your visiting day. Is something wrong?" She stood at the door, not asking Danya to come in.

"Nothing is wrong, but I would like to talk to my girls to ask what they want for Christmas presents. That is why I am here." Danya smiled nervously, puzzled by the raised chin of the plump unsmiling woman.

"I'm so sorry, it's quite against the rules. I'm sure you understand about the visiting privileges. It seemed quite clear all this time."

"But I will not stay long, only to talk a few minutes to my daughters, to say hello and to say goodbye. And only to ask what they would like for presents."

"I'm really unable to permit it. It's absolutely forbidden; we were told that when we took the children. Visiting times are strictly enforced. It's for the good of the children, you understand. They cannot be constantly torn between two kinds of homes."

Danya could hear the girls inside the house. She peered past Mrs. Rand. Why didn't she let her in? It was so cold there, and Mrs. Rand had no coat or sweater over her dress. Danya could see that her face and hands were cold. She should ask her to come in, for kindness sake.

"Couldn't I come in from the winter for only a few minutes? I hear my girls. I will not disturb them if I say hello." She couldn't keep the creeping anger from her question.

Mrs. Rand pursed her mouth. "Absolutely not. Not in this manner, without letting us know you are coming. It is impossible, not allowed. You mustn't expect us to ignore the rules any time you have a few questions to ask the girls. I'm sure you will be able to remember the questions when you come for your regular visit." She nodded. "I must say good day. Please keep to the pre-arranged schedule unless you discuss it with us by letter or telephone." She hastily closed the door.

Danya was stunned. She stared at the closed door. Should she have expected such treatment? Was she so bad to be treated like a beggar at her children's door? She shook from the cold, from the anger and the hurt. No! She would ask again. The fat unfeeling woman would not keep her out. She rang the bell again, then rang it several times more. There were no sounds in the house. She pounded on the door. "Couldn't I come in for some minutes? Couldn't I come in to see my children? I beg you, in God's name I beg you, let me into this house. Let me talk to my own children!"

She waited. There were steps along the hallway. Mrs. Rand's voice spoke to someone. Then Reverend Rand opened the door. Danya had rarely seen him on her visits. She was startled. He was a nervous man. He held the door open part way, cleared his throat.

"This is unfortunate, Mrs. Vorodinov. Mrs. Rand didn't mean to cause any problem for you, but we were carefully instructed on the visiting rules and if we don't abide by them the girls are apt to be taken from us. So won't you understand and forgive us? I'm certain you will be welcomed as usual when you make your regular visit." He sniffed nervously and cleared him throat again.

"No, I wouldn't understand. I am crying out to you in the name of God to have some feeling for me, to let me say a few words to my children, and you can only explain rules to me. Are you a churchman or a devil's voice? I heard my girls and now there is no sound inside the house. What do you do to my children, chase them into the attic to hide from their own mother? Where are they? Why can't you let me see them?"

"It would create a commotion, Mrs. Vorodinov. The girls are dressing for the Christmas concert at Yale and they would be held up if they are allowed to have a visit. It's very important that we get there on time. It's a performance of the Messiah and the doors are closed after the performance commences. It would be a tragedy if the girls missed it."

Danya wanted to spit on him. "A tragedy? But is not my empty day a bigger tragedy for my own girls? Devils run this house!" She made the sign of the cross.

Mr. Rand stood ill at ease but did not give way to the persistent woman before him. Danya saw that he was ashamed and she began to feel sorry for him. He must be like some of the priests, using the words of the bible and speaking every week to the people and only safe in his words when he didn't have to come in person among people. He was a fool, a man hiding in words. A man with no strength to make the world follow Christ's ways.

What she would like to say to him, this unfeeling person, this smart and talking man who spends his days shut up in the big dark study room with all the bookshelves. The girls had shown it to her one day. Books on every wall, dark red and brown with shining gold edges, books all over, walls made of books. And big bibles and little bibles, some old and some new black covered bibles. But he didn't understand how she was suffering before him. She was real life, and he only knew words from his books and the bibles.

"You are not the same good minister as Mr. Dyson. You are not human, but paper. Words and pages and paper. I will find a way to take my girls from you before you make them into paper words too. You will see!"

"Now, now, please try to be fair Mrs. Vorodinov. I'm certain this is a terrible misunderstanding on your part. We seem to be exaggerating the seriousness of this. Mrs. Rand says your regular visiting time is next week. Why don't you forget this unpleasant event and come visit the girls then? We never schedule anything on your visiting days. But you see, we're anxious that the girls see as much of these fine events as possible and the Yale choir is doing an especially good job this year. We have tickets for all their performances and the girls are thrilled to go…"

"To heck with your performances! Always you people make a subject away from the one I am talking about. Let them go the performance. I will not forgive you. And in their later lives they will not forgive you either. There is always another choir to hear, but if they do not have the permission to speak with their own mother you are stealing from them something you cannot give back with a performance!" She glared at him, then stepped back from the doorway. She did feel sorry for him and knew he was embarrassed.

He cleared his throat. "You have great love and need for your children, we know that, and believe me, we understand it. I certainly do, and I'm sure Mrs. Rand does as well. But we are given the task of raising four strangers and we've found that we must stand fast with our discipline or we can't manage them at all." A half smiled flickered across his face. "They have your temperament."

She would not soften. "I go. I will not forget this."

She walked down the steps to the edge of the lawn and turned to look back at the house. The girls were in the front bedroom, the one with the bay window. They stared solemnly at their mother. Should she turn back and try again to go into the house? They had been there as she talked with Mr. Rand, had probably heard her, and had made no effort to come down to see her. How they had been turned against her, with no pity or hunger for their own mother. She waved to them. They stared back. Did they not see her? She waved again. One of the girls held up her hand and waved. Danya saw Mrs. Rand at the window behind the girls. They all waved, then they turned away.

She walked down the road, down the hill to the bus stop. She cried like a disappointed child, mingling her feeling of injury and loathing with the cold that whipped at her legs and face, wiping the tears with stiffened hands. She would talk to Mr. Dyson and tell him. He must hurry with his help. The girls were not hers even to her own eyes. They were growing farther from their own lives every month. They must come back soon or they would be destroyed. Her family would never belong together if they grew up on such ideas as she had heard this day. Oh, she would pray, and pray and pray. She must get them back to her own house, fast, soon, before all the damage was done by the rules and the quiet unfeeling voices. She would tell Mr. Dyson. He would understand her worry and he would move faster with his help.

***

The reverend Dyson listened and understood, but even he could do nothing about the sluggish legal operations. He bade her to keep patience and trust; things would evolve in God's time and to her good.

Some solace that came during the waiting was that Mikolai worked again.

Some of the factories that had been shut down since the beginning of the depression were reopening. Everyone was talking about a war in Europe and the possibility that the United States might also fight. Mikolai read in his paper that Roosevelt was elected again to lead the nation through the perilous times.

Danya turned to him with disgust. Reminding him that the man made only speeches and gave jobs to hungry bloodsuckers.

"Now he makes speeches and gives more bloodsucking jobs to people like Bulldog Bent. Now the crook is head of the drafting board, the stinking snake, where he can send more lives to war."

The upturn in business provided a job for Mikolai as gardener at the large manufacturing plant in the next town which began making parts for the war gliders that were promised to England in a lend lease arrangement. He tried to explain this to Danya. Her response was a shrug.

***

Slowly Mikolai and Danya progressed with the house now that there was some money to buy materials. They both worked late into the night hammering wallboards or painting the raw wooden floors. At one time Danya had wanted fine woods and goods that would make the house special. Now she wanted only to finish the insides of the house as fast and cheaply as possible. It made no difference if the wood was so fine, she told Mikolai. She would go to the housebreakings, as she called them, to buy old doors or windows, light fixtures, whatever they could use from the houses that were being torn down to make place for new factories. If she couldn't find what they needed there she would buy the cheapest stuff in the lumber store. The house must be finished!

She remembered that at one of the hearings Mr. Dyson had testified that from his knowledge the condition of the house had little to do with the worth of a man. He gave a long speech about the living conditions in China and Tibet and he reminded the old judge that their own childhoods had not been blessed by the modern so-called necessities on which they were forcing the Vorodinovs to spend hours and money to provide for their children.

The judge concurred. He said the ruling was open to interpretation and allowed that he would make the conditions more lenient. By then Danya had forged ahead so vehemently that she would not have stopped for any change in the ruling.

She wanted the house finished. She wanted each child to come home into her own room and have all the things she had had in the foster home. And she and Mikolai could do it, with their own hands, she told Reverend Dyson after that hearing.

Although he was called to be present at the hearing Angus Bent was forced to decline a few times because of ill health and demands of his work and duties with the area draft board. He did, however, keep in close touch with the case through copies of the hearing proceedings that were forwarded to him. He was still the local welfare administrator.

When Bent felt there was impending success for Mrs. Vorodinov he prepared a statement for the judge outlining the serious moral considerations that he had omitted earlier. When the time lapse between the hearings lengthened, he decided it was best not to raise that rattle in case of repercussions should he be forced to show proof in court.

He was not displeased that at least three years of his experiment had passed, and perhaps a few more if the courts went about it as slowly as this. His concern was to stay out of the line of fire. It wouldn't do to risk a public confrontation with that woman now.

The final hearing took place in the probate court. The judge's decision was to let the children come home, but not all at the same time. He wanted to be fair to the children and to her, too, he told the unbelieving mother. The oldest girl would come home immediately, the next one at the end of the school year, and if there were no problems in their adjustment and if they could continue to support the family, the other four children would be released to their parents' custody at the end of the summer in time to start the next school year in their own home.

Danya cried tears of relief, stinging tears that could not allay her frustration. This black robed man was giving her only enough breath to keep her from dying. She needed to breathe freely and fully; she needed enough breath to live like a human mother, not like a caged animal waiting for food or sunlight to be thrown at her. She spoke.

"I have waited long enough, judge. Why can't you let me have all my children at this time? If as you say I am a fit mother in your eyes, why can't you give all my children to me now, at the same time?"

"This is a very unusual case, Mrs. Vorodinov. I am going above the recommendations of the welfare agency because I am convinced you should have your family in their own home. I do so on the strength of Reverend Dyson's testimonies on your behalf and on his assurance that there are no problems in the way of adjustment of the children to their original home. But because this court is charged first of all with the care of the juvenile, we must make sure we are doing the correct thing, the best thing for the children." His voice was calm as he continued.

"You realize the ruling is irrevocable. That is, once the children are in your custody, the courts have no power whatsoever to interfere with their upbringing. Because Mr. Dyson and your lawyer insisted on that, and I approved it, we must be absolutely certain that the children can be given the care and attention they should have. If the court put all the children in your hands at the same time, we would have to insist on probationary measures in the case that it didn't work out. You would remain under the jurisdiction of the welfare agency in your town. Your attorney pleaded strongly in private for this irrevocable ruling."

In her tears and her confusion Danya bent to listen to Reverend Dyson. He explained that it would be far better to wait a few more months than to have the constant pressure of local welfare restrictions and visits. She did understand, and although moved to a state of near collapse she quieted herself before she walked from the courtroom.

There in the hall waiting were Mrs. Rand and her daughter along with the four girls sitting quietly on the stiff wooden benches. The court secretary asked Mrs. Rand to talk with the judge. He informed her of the court decision and told her that the oldest girl could accompany the mother home at that time. He gave her the schedule for the others.

None of the children were old enough to really comprehend what the court procedures and the hushed conferences had been about. When the oldest girl went with her mother and Reverend Dyson who drove them home, the sisters waved a casual, if slightly jealous goodbye. Days later Mrs. Rand explained that their oldest sister was now living with her parents. That satisfied them and their life went along as usual.

For Danya, this single chicken on the roost was hardly enough to occupy her stored up energies. At first she submerged the girl with overcare. She soon saw the harm she might be inflicting and allowed the girl to fend more for herself. There were neighboring children with whom she spent most of her time. Aside from eating and sleeping she was rarely in the house unless it was to hide off in a corner with the books she brought home from the library.

The girl would stay up late into the night with her books, then cry and complain the next night that she had nothing to read. Danya walked to the library one Friday afternoon to ask if her daughter could take out more than the three books allowed. No, it was against the rules. Then couldn't she make out a card and let her daughter take three more books on her mother's name? Yes, that can be done.

When Danya told her daughter what she had done for her, that she could now have six books, not just three at one time, the girl wanted to walk right then to the library. Her mother went with her. Danya stood at the librarian's desk watching the girl walk through the stacks looking, searching for the books she wanted. She saw her go through the magazines on the reading table, completely absorbed. She left her there and walked back home, longing to be able to do more than that small thing for her child.

In a few months as the summer ended Danya could see that her daughter was happy with her neighborhood friends and anxious to go to school.

***

The second girl came home in late May, much later than Danya had expected. She was rebellious and harder to handle than the older girl, and she made no attempt to conceal her self-pity that she had been taken from the Rand's just as they were readying for the summer trip to Maine. She too settled into a routine of playing with the neighborhood children, returning home exhausted, ready for food and sleep.

Neither girl was dependent on their mother for the affection and attention she longed to give them. They were independent, secretive creatures, made so by events and by their disciplined care. They zealously took to the changes necessitated by their new lives. There were no traumas or commotions after the first few week of adjusting, yet they never dropped the impersonal façade that Danya had expected would fall away when they became used to their own home again.

They acknowledged their father with respectful nods but were no longer interested in walking to the fields with him, or going to the barn to jump in the hay when he called. Because of his deafness there was difficulty in communicating with him. He would sit there at the kitchen table, reading his paper, watching them as they read or talked with each other.

As Danya noticed this she could look out at the six maple trees, now in full leaf, that he had planted when each child was born. She could sense the sadness of loss for him. He must feel the separation of their dependence as she did. But she reasoned, she and Mikolai would do their job. They would keep them healthy and guard them against the evils and harms that might come their way.

STANTON 1940

The four youngest children came back to their home at the beginning of September. First, in the morning the Rands delivered the two girls, seven and eight years old. They ambled into the strange house, not fully aware that this would be their home until they were grown. They waved goodbye properly and sweetly to the woman who had raised and disciplined them for four years. They brought with them boxes of toys and bags of clothes, starched, ironed and folded neatly for whomever might look.

"Which is my room? You mean a whole room for me?...I don't need two bureaus...Where is a place for my toys?...I don't want them mixed up with the others because I don't like someone else's paints mixed with mine...Well, your paper dolls are all shaggy, Mrs. Rand said so..."

"Is the whole house ours? I said I wanted that room. Well, I need a bunch of bigger windows because I'm older..."

In the midst of their day's scrapping the Dysons arrived with the two youngest.

"Hello, my son and my baby."

I'm not a baby, I'm four now."

To these two who had no recollections at all of this early place of their lives the occasion was strange and unsettling. Two other homes had they known, and now a third, stranger than the others because it was filled with other people, big kids like the ones who go to school. And different things they had never seen, smells they didn't like.

The boy sniffed several times. The strange smell seemed very bad to him, but he knew somehow he shouldn't say anything. It wasn't polite. He walked toward a bucket on the kitchen floor and saw it was soapy water that Danya was using to wash the wooden floor when they arrived and surprised her. She hadn't had time to empty it, and the bucket stood there with the mop and rag hanging from it.

Danya noticed her son sniffing and explained it was her home made cheese that he smelled, not the washing water, and wouldn't he like to taste a piece of the new cheese she had made for them? He blushed and said no thank you. The smell was too unfamiliar and unappealing. He knew he had hurt her feelings and his young sensitive heart was experiencing sad little vibrations.

Neither could the boy understand why he should be kissed so much. He didn't like such goings on. Both of the young children were lost, out of place in their neat starched clothes, held by this odd smelling woman who didn't even talk right. They knew her well from the times she had visited them at the Dyson's, but they didn't think they'd go to live with this mother. They thought she came for visits, just to bring candy, to play with them and talk to Mr. Dyson. He had explained it to them. They just didn't understand it all.

"Have you got candy?"

"I want some ice cream, I don't like candy, only chocolate."

"We don't have a refrigerator for ice cream."

"I don't want milk, I want ice cream."

"A cow? Do you have a real cow?"

"Is that where ice cream is made, in the cow?"

"Let's see, let's see."

"Me first."

"No, I'm a boy. I don't hold hands like girls. You hold her hand because you're her baby. I can walk by myself."

Mikolai was in the barn. He had been standing watching out of the window of the wood bin. He had gone to the barn early in the morning when he knew the children were supposed to come to their home that day. He puttered about his workbench, straightening nails or sorting tools, separating jumbled hardware. He couldn't see the house from the workbench so he walked every ten or fifteen minutes to the window, peering out to see if they had arrived.

When he saw them coming toward the barn he busied himself stacking kindling. No one knows what he felt when they came upon him working there. He seem absorbed in his work and looked up only when Danya came close to him and touched his arm. These two youngest children had no memory of their father. The boy was two years old, the girl a baby of eight months when they were taken from their parents. They really didn't know they had a father like other children because they thought that Mr. Dyson was their father, sort of, only different from other fathers.

This man they met was gruff, too, like Mr. Dyson on Sunday morning before church. But he was nice to them. He opened the door to the cow stalls and he made the cow stop eating so they could look at her face. She looked back at them with bovine calm, chewing her cud with a hint of disgust at being disturbed. Later they could come back and watch him do the milking their mother told them. He was their father and he would let them come to the barn later.

"For ice cream?" The boy's brown eyes opened wide with eagerness.

"Can we have ice cream? Right from the cow?"

They asked their father, but somehow he didn't understand or hear what they wanted, and their mother explained they must talk very loud to their father and slowly because he was deaf.

"Like Jiggs and Maggie? I know what deaf is, like in Jiggs and Maggie," hissed the boy to his sister.

The mother didn't understand this. "What, what do you mean?"

The boy blushed with embarrassment. Then he demonstrated by putting his hand to his ear as if holding on to an imaginary horn.

"Speak louder, please!" he yelled.

The father heard and understood; he had read the Sunday funnies week after week that featured Jiggs and Maggie. He laughed as the boy cast his eyes down, then looked up again to see flash of pleasure from his father's blue eyes.

After Danya showed them the barn and the chickens, the apple trees and the raspberry patch, she took them back to the house.

To a maelstrom.

The hulking, nearly finished house was again filled with the sounds for which it was built. The two older girls had came from their play and found every private corner of their rooms usurped by two nearly-forgotten sisters from yesterday.

No mother's pleas for peace could be heard over the ravings and accusations the four girls exchanged. Dolls were thrown through doorways they shouldn't have entered; paper clippings and scrapbooks were flung against walls. Pillows exchanged without permission were pounded over innocent heads. Clothes were strewn, furniture moved, diaries searched, bobby pins mixed, hairbrushes hidden, and through it all, pinned to the wall with their fixed beautiful smiles, movie stars looked on quite unconcerned.

When the noise was drenched with tears from all four, the mother, red-faced from frustration and hurt, cried out to them.

"For pity sakes my daughters, what kind of gift is this? In your own house I have made room for every one of you. Each room waits while you run all to the same corner like chickens chased by a fox. Is this the only room with sunshine? No, look, every room has windows. Every room has a bed and a place for clothes. There is plenty of space; every room is the same size in the dark. Why do you make me wild with such noises? Every room is a gift, each for each. What does it matter so long as the same roof covers all my daughters? Have I taken back such wild animals to raise? Would you break my heart with your fighting before my family is one day old?"

There were pouts, sniffles, sulks, smiles, each according to her way. With some strain and talent Danya was able finally to settle each girl into a separate room, which pleased them for reasons they forgot soon afterwards. She would have kept the boy and youngest girl downstairs in the room next to her and Mikolai, but the commotion had intrigued their curiosity and of course, if there was something so special about an upstairs room, shouldn't they each have one as well as the big kids?

The young, with no inborn talent for tact lack the instinct for the sentiment of an occasion when it overrides or threatens their personal world. While a mother's heart can overlook many things when it is filled again with the blessings of the lost returned to her, a child is, in a way, more steady and will not let go of the tacit rules by which it has ordered the habits of its days.

So often the things prayed for do come true, but not always, Danya was learning, in the smoothest way. During the grief-laden times she had imagined a wonderful day when her bunch would be home in their own house. Looking into the future she could not have taken into account the depth of the changes being wrought on her children by hands and mentalities different from what she knew.

These were not the same children who had been torn from her a few years ago. They had been remolded and marked by a life to which she was alien. Their speech, their disciplines, the foods they liked, the places they'd seen, even their church…it was all a world sophisticated and beyond her knowledge to comprehend it.

She had harassing pangs of jealousy of the women who had been able to do this to her children, particularly to the older ones who should have remembered their old ways. Every time she spoke to them or asked them if they wanted something to eat, or tried to be their mother, it seemed that they turned away from her with vague polite little smiles she had never seen on her children before.

Her eagerness to please them, to find the magic bond that belonged there between a mother and the children she had borne, met sometimes with hostility as though she was interfering with a ritual she shouldn't have disturbed. Her suggestions for things to do were at times met with scorn, amusement or disinterest. They needed so little from her.

During the first weeks she was confronted with unexplained whining and tantrums that she wouldn't have believed her own flesh and blood could produce. She could not realize that these children had departed from a pleasant and comfortable upbringing where their lives were well-ordered, disciplined and scheduled. She could not grasp the obvious; she could not see into what confusion their return to this life of freedom cast upon them. The disorder, the freedom to come or go, the myriad things they could do without asking or telling.

As far as Danya was concerned the one thing that mattered was that they were all back in her house where they belonged. They were home. Everyone would settle down when the summer was really over and they went back to school. Everything would be all right when they were in school again and had things to take up in their minds and their hands.

This was not the last desperate holding on when a mother senses bonds between her and her grown children are loosened and ready to fall. This was the despair of a mother victimized by a trick of time. While she could not see, four mysterious years were added to her children's lives. They were handed back to an unchanged home and unchanged mother, and somehow she must continue raising them with ignorance of those four years. It was like a game, cruel and trying, where you bumped your head against the wall again and again, unable to find the clue to the puzzle.

She realized well now that by herself she must bring together this family to grow from the roots she had tended while the branches slept. She alone would have to do it. She believed she could do it. Yet those first chaotic days when the house was filled again, she walked down the stairs from the noise in anguish that was thickened by disappointment that her children could not feel and return the great joy she kept inside.

If Mikolai watched the children grow, Danya grew them. She took them in hand in a curious way of undiscipline and giving in, resisting and listening, hearing and not hearing, whatever suited her instincts in this unforeseen problem. These unruly weeds of unlabeled genre she tended, fed and watered like precious temperamental plants. She gave them the attention and anticipation a gardener gives mysterious new shoots, hoping that nurtured, they will prove to be the forgotten, latent seeds sown in an earlier season.

The oldest four maintained the independence that diminished necessity of an anxious mother's constant presence. At times their conversations left their mother bewildered. They spoke in little formal polite ways to each other, reminding her of the proper way the welfare and court people spoke, with no feeling. They could say words, any words to you, and they would show no feelings or care what you felt. Only politeness, that was what they liked to have in their voices. At least when they were not arguing.

"You talk falsely to each other," she tried to warn them. "If you raise your eyes that way and speak so coldly you cannot show your true feelings to another person."

"No, that's not true," one would tell her. "It is good manners, speaking carefully, being tactful when you speak. One shouldn't be sarcastic or boisterous," the child said, parroting Mrs. Rand.

Danya didn't know those words, tactful, sarcastic, boisterous. Could these children already be smarter than their mother? By whose teaching? Well, not in her language, she knew, but in their own language she saw they had steamed beyond her. She would have to learn more to understand them, that she could see.

When they brought their school and library books home she would look through them late at night after the girls were in bed. She would finish her sewing and try to read some of the books or at times she would sit quietly looking out the window, seeming to dream. She actually was listening intently to their conversations.

Because she saw that it annoyed them when she constantly asked the meaning of their words she decided she must listen harder and find the way to use the words herself.

Jivey and drooley she learned and used. Perplexing, annoying, utterly obnoxious, infantile, cozy, crackpot, archaic, corked off, famished, humdinger. It made her head swirl. Of course she made some big mistakes when she use the words. The oldest girl had said to the boy, "My dear, you are utterly obnoxious." The next time he played with his little chemistry set Danya told him he must work harder so he would be utterly obnoxious.

She never minded that they had such fun at her expense as she took over their language. It became their great competition and fun to see which girl could find the newest words for their mother's misuse. They made silly jingles from her mistakes. They would show her word jokes in the Sunday paper they brought home from the neighbor's. Gradually she developed a piquant sense of word humor. With it came a sharpening of her mind and under it, a growing desire to be able to say to Bent, in his own language, all the hateful things she thought of him. To that end she thrived on the humor and competition of this learning.

REVENGE

The victory she had won by the return of her children in no way cancelled the hatred she felt for the man who had conspired to take them from her. In those times when she wasn't absorbed with plans for her children, the quietness of her mind was soon filled with desire for revenge against Angus Bent. Some nights she couldn't fall into sleep because plots for executing the revenge writhed about her head. Clever confrontations in public so everyone would see his guilt...that is what he must suffer. That would be hardest for him because he wanted the world to believe he was a good and kind man. She would show them all his true person.

Also some physical suffering. If God is just he must give him a heavy cross to match hers, she reasoned. His heart should be attacked. If he had children...but he did not, so he could not suffer that way. But he should feel it in every bone of his body, some kind of suffering. Then he would know how she had been tortured.

She flung bitter invectives at him. She upbraided him in public. She exposed him to the townspeople and to the public everywhere. But all that was only in the privacy and ineffectual regions of her thoughts.

She knew she must not give him any reason to bother her any more. The probate judge had warned her that she must not harass Mr. Bent or it could become a serious matter of slander. Once the children were home she should realize the case was closed, the judge had told her. The court handed down their decision. They had found no guilt anywhere. The children had been cared for by the welfare department and it was for their good, in Mr. Bent's judgment. They had been placed in foster home care until their parents could provide for them. There was no crime, and she must not disturb the court with unfounded accusations.

She comprehended. She did not agree. She was even more determined to do things her own way, to find her own way to punish him, to get her revenge. Bent knew he was guilty of an ugly crime against her. His black deeds were spread on his carpet for him to look at every day.

Every time she passed his house she vowed she would remind him. She would walk slowly past the house and curse him in silence as she walked. He would see her and remember. She would look on him with her hate when she was in the bank to pay her mortgage and he would feel her curse rise out from her broken heart. Not one day would he be able to turn from those past deeds, she vowed it.

From the intensity of her dislike, her enemy's faults multiplied. Because he was vice-president of the local bank, she suspected he would steal from her small account from which she paid the mortgage. She wanted to warn the new bank president. No, he might not listen to her yet because she didn't have any proof. Let him work for a while longer there in the bank. Soon everyone would see the dishonesty on the man's face, and he would be found out. He would be caught. What pleasure it would give her.

But she had to force herself to withhold from warning others about him. She knew she must create a just and secure home for her children. She had been admonished so by the judge. She must give them time to belong to her again, and she dared not upset people who might try to make more trouble for her if they took the side of the ugly Bent. She continued her mental attacks on him regularly, her unspoken cursings, taking deep satisfaction when she saw his face flush when she stared at him in the bank or on the street.

***

When she heard that Bent had been hospitalized with an unknown illness she wanted to tell Mikolai that her curses were working. Of course he wouldn't believe her. Even in the old country he had said the mystics were just liars. Danya always believed otherwise and now she had proof…she thought.

Then a plan came into her head. She would visit him in the hospital. Yes, she could do that. She laughed to herself. I could take him flowers, sure, skunk cabbage from the back swamp!
I will go as his friend she decided, and they will let me in to just say hello. And she did.

She told Mikolai she had to do some fabric shopping in Middletown. She took the bus and walked from the bus stop to the hospital where he'd been admitted, as she'd been told by a teller at the Stanton bank.

She was easily granted a visitor's pass when she explained that he was an old friend who had helped her family when they were in need. The nurse in charge said how nice of her to make the trip. Danya smiled quite sweetly. The nurse took her to room and spoke quickly to Mr. Bent, "You have a visitor who would like to say hello."

If the nurse had waited a minute she would have seen the astonishment and fear on Bent's face when Danya walked into the room. She closed the door and stood beside his bed.

"I am here my Bulldog, where you are helpless against me, to lay on you my curse face to face. In your sick body every ugly deed of your thinking and doing will grind against your bones until you shrink into nothing. Even in your sleep you will not escape my curse. I see you cannot look into my face because you know your shame, but I am looking at you and I can see your evil! You will remember what I am saying to you because your ears are open and the fear goes into your brain even if you cannot see my eyes." She laughed. "And remember this, my children will bring flowers to my grave, and you…the dogs will come and piss on yours."

He gathered himself enough to ring the bell for the nurse but Danya was already out of the room when she came. Bent was in distress but dared not say why. He was sedated against his will; he did not want to sleep. It was the fear of the dream. And the dream came, off and on, again and again tormenting him.

Danya walked lightly back to the bus stop. When she came home Mikolai was surprised that she had not bought anything. She usually came from shopping with bundles of fabric when she went to Middletown. She said there was nothing there she wanted, and went on with her sewing. She sang as she sewed, satisfied with her effort against Bent.

Her hatred often carried her into a world far remote from the one she lived for her children. In their concern she never bound herself with negations that might sap her strength. Her overwhelming desire was to give them the gift of separating themselves from the trap that dislike and jealousy made for the young.

She did not reason that there were discrepancies in her two philosophies. She felt justified in her hate. It was a matter apart from the raising of her children. The one world grew darkly, nurtured by inflamed distorted reasoning. She committed herself to the Rabbi's lesson, an eye for an eye. Bent must pay. She welcomed with avenging strength the idea of each new method, no matter how uncomfortable that would bring Bent his due. Now at the hospital as he lay helpless she had delivered the words that he would never forget.

***

The world of her children grew wider. There she could speak clearly and convincingly to her growing brood. She taught them that they must search out the goodness in all people. She told them of how she had seen it abused in her youth. She taught them trust in the Lord, in nature, in themselves. This was reality and a far gentler world, separated as day and night from the other.

In her ability to give to her children she had been blessed. She had a superb understanding of curiosity, that instrument by which a child fills its mind. The seemingly useless sights and information, take up the space that boredom would lay claim to and stand sentry to admit the thousand small joys of life begging at the door.

In neither language could she have said to her young, 'Don't bother me now.' Every question had an answer. Every 'c'mere Mom" moved her from her chair and or any less pleasing task. Potatoes might lay half peeled, turning brown on the kitchen table while she showed a child for the fourth time how to take eggs from under the hen, or walked to the swamp with another to tempt a bullfrog with a bright red cloth tied a special careful way to a pole and string. Or while she taught them how a sapling should sing in the air to call the cows, or showed them where the first buds broke through the trees.

She could sense curious eyes watching the patterns of light made by the sewing machine wheel as it turned. She would obligingly treadle faster before the child finished his request. She would use a cracked cup for tea when all the glasses were lined up on the table as instruments in a comb and water band. She would give up the only comb she had when one child wondered if the curved comb she wore made a different sound from the other straight combs. Then she would spend precious pennies on combs of every size so they could learn all they might from this winsome noise.

There was no punishment for the son who had quietly taken apart the shuttle and wheel of her sewing machine while she napped. Let the sewing wait. Somewhere in the cellar was an old machine, rusted from unuse. That would be his, and his own tools from the barn. And his own room to work in, his own can of oil and drawers for nails and screws and bolts and needles that she could reuse if he would file them carefully, this way, with his own file.

"And listen, hear by the sound that the machine needs more oil…and look, see where the dust from the cloth hides and makes the machine go too slow…or maybe the leather belt is too old and stretched and then you make it tighter with your own pliers…like this…then when everything is running quietly and the machine sews, give it to one of the girls and I will find you another, at the auction, or from a neighbor's barn…maybe two old ones, or three. You can take the parts from one to the other…see…they all work the same…"

"And a clock? Here is an old one. Don't worry my son, I'll find you more. We'll ask the neighbors. Keep all the parts till you can make your own."

With her understanding was the tenderness of a mother's care for her child's world where secrets and fantasies confided ought never be revealed to another for fear of deadly ridicule or laughter.

"You won't tell I can't tie my shoes?… You won't tell you had to sew the collar for me?…You won't tell I'm afraid of that bogey man in the trees?…Do you think I'll be taller when I grow up?…Do you think my eyebrows will ever get dark so I can be a movie star?…I've got to go in the woods because Tarzan told me to come back on a rainy day to pick berries…When I close my eyes I see typewriters and they talk to each other with secret sounds, but only I know what they are saying…At night after I say my prayers I fall asleep and disappear into the milky way…The holes came in my shoes because I turn into a princess at night, but the other girls can't know or they will be jealous…The wet tar barked and jumped right at me, and I was walking far away, too…"

These things were wrapped in quiet unseen laughter and stored up in her heart until they could be returned as amusing memories to the children grown past the age of harming.

1941

The days hurried along. Danya heard that Angus Bent was back at work at the bank. No one could tell her what his illness was, but she knew that he was captured by her curse. She would wait to see the outcome.

The children were in school and as Danya had expected, their nervous energies were gathered into some direction. They were all top of their classes. She signed the report cards with silent pleasure. They had their friends. The interactions at home at most times ran more smoothly.

People in those days were caught up in the welcome tempo of a reviving, though apprehensive, economy. Each week the possibility of accumulating some of the good things of life increased. People began to talk about travel and vacations. Here and there a new car appeared in a garage, long unused save for storage of now worthless items that no one in depression America dared throw away. Young marrieds talked about moving into their own house or apartment, away from parents or other family with whom they had been obliged to live. Children began the winter season in new jackets and trousers instead of patched hand-me-down clothes. There was talk about how much money neighbors were making. The opening of a new factory sent men miles away from their homes to take jobs at pay that astounded them. A factory nearby was converted to making glider parts and Stanton men could walk to work.

Underneath it all, there were murmurings of war.

And then, that winter, the war came.

It was a Monday morning. The children from the neighborhood were walking the mile to the bus stop in the freshly fallen snow. The boys lagged behind so they could torment the girls with snowballs and perhaps arrive too late to catch the school bus that came for them at the bottom of the hill. Suddenly the boys became very excited at some news told by one of the group. They all ran up to the others who were walking ahead.

Someone bumped into one of the Vorodinov girls. Her blue lunchbox flew open and the contents spilled out. She handed her books to a sister and chased an apple that rolled down the hill toward a small stream, making a zig-zagged path in the snow. When she came back up from the ravine the children were all talking in animated excited voices. "What is it, what is it," she begged to be told.

One of the older boys annoyingly repeated the news. Their entire country was now at war, didn't they hear it on the radio yesterday? No, they had no radio. Well, it was true, it was on the radio Sunday, and the president talked on the radio, too. And they were at war, with Japs. Boy, let me at those guys!

The older boys were very excited. The girls were confused and disgusted with the boys' antics. The young Vorodinov boy, nearly seven, turned away from the others and began to walk back toward home.

"Come back, where are you going? You'll be late for the bus," yelled a sister.

"I'm going home to tell Mema."

"Come on, silly, she'll find out later from the neighbors."

"No, I've got to tell her right away."

"Why, it makes no difference, she can find out later."

"Yes, it does make a difference. I've got to tell her so she can do something about it right away."

He pulled away from his sister's grasp and walked as fast as young legs could, up the hill, back to the house. He was afraid and crying when he reached home.

"Mema, Mema," he called as he came into the yard. He slipped on the stone steps that Mikolai had just swept clean of snow. He righted himself and banged on the door with both hands. He pulled the door open at the same time that his mother opened it from inside.

"What is the matter, my son, why are you crying?"

"We're in a big war, the boys said so. Our whole country is in a war," he blurted between gasps and sniffles.

"It couldn't be, my son, they only make jokes to tease you."

"No sir, they heard it on the radio yesterday. It's true, it's true, Mema, the President said so on the radio."

"What did he say?"

"He said the whole country is at war, with Japs. You've got to do something, Mema."

"Oh, my son, what can I do for such a thing?"

"Something, you can do something."

"But don't cry for such a thing. You shouldn't cry when you hear about war. Don't cry. When you cry you can't think. There, now it is easier to think. Wipe your eyes. We must think…Ah yes, we should go to the Noviky's to ask what they heard on the radio. But you will be late for school, my son."

"I don't want to go because the war is all over, the big boys said so."

"I don't think so yet. Anyhow you are too late for the bus. Come with me to Noviky's house. But dry all your tears first because they will freeze on your face in this cold."

She hurried into her boots and heavy coat. She looked into her child's trusting face and wondered with a sinking heart whether she could withstand this kind of threat without showing her fear to the children. She took her son's hand and hurried through the snow to Noviky's house.

"Mema, what are you going to do?"

"First find out if it is true. It's no use to make a big plan and use energy before you know for what you do the planning."

Steve Noviky had stayed home from work to listen to the news. He explained all that he could to Danya. They listened to the various commentators until Danya was satisfied that she understood. She told Noviky she would send one of the girls that evening for more news; she must walk with her son to school because he missed the bus. She wouldn't have time later to come back to hear more.

"It is not the kind of war to be afraid of," she tried to explain to her son. "The people who started the war are very far away and they cannot come to our country. In other places, far, far away there will be war, but not here. I will show you on a map. We should not be afraid."

Her words told him that. In her memory were the same words from her younger years in Russia. Then, too, the war was far away and Mikolai had gone far away, and the war came closer and closer. She couldn't believe anything for sure that the President was telling them on the radio. If you believed him all the way, you were disappointed in his lies later. She remembered that from before.

But somehow she must hide her doubts from the children. It was much easier, she recalled, when she was a girl and believed the war would never come near them. She had been brave and strong then. Children should be given strength so they could have good believing years before any evils touched them or were shown to them. She would protect them somehow from fear.

"The war is far away, my son. Nothing will change here, so you must go back to school and at night you must say prayers for people who are fighting the war far away."

***

Her life seemed always threatened by new confusions. She had her family together now, but often they dealt unintentional blows to her efforts to unite them into a close family. It confused her to be so helpless in front of their myriad requests and demands for solutions. She felt at times that she was holding strings to puppets that would not always obey her directions. The strings wound around her and pulled at her, loosened as she caught them; each puppet did as it pleased. It made her head ache.

She had talked of it to Reverend Dyson when he came to visit. He reminded her that she had them under her wings now, but she mustn't expect them to go backward and be babies again. They would always belong to her. They had come through her and to her, but she could not own them as they grew. God knew they were her children. She should keep that always in her mind.

So it was true, there was a war. I see, I see, she told herself. You can't trust the stinking politicians in anything. One day the President says there will never be a war, and now comes the news that war is here.

THE WAR

As it progressed, this war brought none of the hardships Danya expected it should. Contrarily, as she witnessed with amazement, all around her it brought plenty. Sometimes people lost sons or husbands, but they celebrated their sorrows over full dinner tables or in warmly heated churches. Then they hung little flags with a gold star on the front window. Folks were proud of telling how many gold stars there were in each town.

What confounded and puzzled her, too, was the zealous fountain of patriotism that spewed forth from her children. The war, this war for freedom, as they called it, captivated their minds and produced incredible vigor in young bodies that used to tire at the sound of boiling dishwater.

"God Bless America," they would sing as they walked home from school. She could hear their voices across the pond long before they came up the hill to the house. They spent hours prowling streets and knocking on doors for tin foil from gum wrappers, for the war effort, they explained. Everyone patriotic should save the foil from gum wrappers, they told her.

The older girls had to have permission to join the Junior Red Cross so they could roll bandages. They walked all over the hill seeking the best points for spotting aircraft, using a Jack Armstrong telescope they received in the mail. They made small flannel nightgowns for English war orphans. They made blackout curtains for the house. They walked late at night with the area civil defense warden. They wrote essays on why they loved their country. They begged for a second-hand piano and they learned to play the military songs and patriotic songs that Irving Berlin wrote. They believed in the land of the free and the home of the brave.

"The land of the free and the home of the brave." She, Danya, knew the song now. She would hum it as she sewed, her voice cracking on the high notes.

Before long she became as susceptible as the children to the intoxicating clamor that was directed toward whipping up great bursts of pride for this powerful, righteous country that was protecting the vanquished and fighting for a free world.

As the war years stretched on, the pride and patriotism stayed with her. It really was a great country, she knew that now. No hardships touched their land. She would listen to the stories of enemy submarines and ships that supposedly came dangerously close to the coast, preparing to invade. But she knew well inside that her family was safe now. Nothing would happen. Despite her disillusionment with the once heroic President and the men whose political promises had come to naught, she was proud to say she lived in a country whose power and promise had no equal.

***

"If God is for us who can be against us?" she quoted to Reverend Dyson during one of his Sunday afternoon visits. They had been talking about the war. "I am sure God is on our side, and I am sure we will win," she said with the confident finality stolen from her children.

"Ah, me. We cannot think we can force God to take a side. He cannot because He is the father of all mankind," reasoned the reverend. "It is true that when men go to war against each other each side prays to God for victory and each side sends their young men and their accomplished generals out to fight in the name of God. But it's the same God they are both talking to. They're calling on Him to choose them as the victors. It's a very sad thing for Him to watch His children fighting."

"But He is always on the side of good and justice!"

"Yet good and justice do not always win, if you'll just think a minute about the wars that have been lost by the good and the just. Now I'm not going to say that God changes sides when he pleases, just to suit a big army or a powerful king. No sir, it's more like a father watching two sons going at a big fight with each other. How can a father choose between his sons? The best he can do is stop the fight as soon as possible and patch up the boys' wounds."

Danya listened. "Except in a war, one country has to lose, and our country is the country of freedom and justice. We cannot lose, or the whole world will suffer."

"Well now, it's a hard thing to say, for sure. God isn't so concerned with countries and things like that. He is more concerned with each person's heart. He wouldn't be much of the kind of God we believe in if He came on the side of one country and let all the good and loving people in the other country fall by the wayside, would He?...No sir, He looks into every heart and He tries to reach every heart that will listen. That's where the power is, in the hearts of the people, not in some man made thing called a country...Now you can find evil men in good-acting countries, and good men in evil-acting countries. But God has found His way to all those good people. And He is trying to find His way to all those unkind, unhappy, evil-acting people as well. No matter which country wins the war, there will be those powerful good people and powerful bad people. God will have to patch them all up and try to teach them to get along, just like the father must try to get his sons back to liking and understanding each other…Oh my, how they hate to wear those patches on their wounds after the fight, those boys."

"But Mr. Dyson, is it possible we can lose this war?" Danya wanted more assurance, especially from this man whom she admired. She did not want doubts.

"Well now, it seems we have enough men and guns to win the war, as it's going now. It's after that we should be thinking about. We must forget the works of the devil and take up our time to fill our hearts with love for the human race and the thoughts of God. That way we won't be worrying about other wars."

"But just the same, I believe in my country. I think even with bulldogs like Bent we have more good hearts here than in other countries."

"But we cannot use our hearts for good if we hold hate in them. You must teach the children to pray for their enemies to hear the voice of God. We must all keep our ears open to Him. It's very important, very important," he finished, rolling the words with his thick Scottish burr.

"I will tell them, but I also remind them to believe in their country's hearts the most, and in the goodness of their own country, even if man made such a place without a plan from God."

In his conversations with Danya, Reverend Dyson tried to bring into her thinking the lessons his grandfather had taught him in his youth. He never gave up hope that she would some day understand those teachings and free herself from the obsession with Angus Bent.

***

For Angus Bent the war was at first a disconcerting diversion. As soon as the federal agencies went into full swing with the war effort, other projects such as the welfare programs and the WPA lost their place at center of people's lives as well as the full attention of the bureaucracy.

He had been hospitalized again with the unknown illness, then diagnosed with the possibility of a cancerous stomach growth which, according to ongoing tests, was not life threatening. He had returned to his desk at the bank and took up the last strings of the welfare programs he was heading.

But Bent's reports and requests to the federal government agencies went unanswered. The county home for children was closed for lack of funding. He mused sourly that just as he was able to show that his proposed welfare project had been successful the federal government shut off their interest. He talked it over with his wife who agreed with him that it was a shame that the war had taken so much money away from the poor whom he was trying to help.

However, soon enough there were other opportunities for a man of his background that took some pain out of the setback in the welfare project which had become a handy part of his income. All those extras, of course, unknown to his wife.

The Office of Price Administration needed a local administrator. Someone must take charge of the rationing program in the area. He was, because of his previous government services, considered and approved for the job. As a member of the American Legion he was also kept busy giving speeches to local school classes and to clubs and church groups on the meaning of patriotism, what it means to be an American, the evils of totalitarian governments and why they must all march on Memorial Day.

As much as was possible he stayed out of Danya's path. If he saw her on the street or coming into the bank he would make every effort to disappear before they came face to face.

The frequency of the dream varied with the frequency of their meetings, although some nights for no reason he could remember, the witch would make her unwelcome visit. It was now so entrenched in his thoughts that he became less resistant to her claims. The sooner she took over his body the sooner he would get a normal night's sleep. The deepest torment now was his woe-filled hours before sleep would come. The anxiety gripped him so strongly he often lived out the half dreams many times before his aching body would let go of the day.

He began to toy again with the idea of visiting a psychiatrist. There were some acceptable opinions now about the profession. He might drive to Hartford or New Haven where no one would know him and talk to a psychiatrist. That would mean he must discuss it with Bertha, though. It would hurt her too much, he decided. And what would she think of him? He would perhaps find other ways to get the Vorodinov woman out of the way, to get the witch out of his dreams.

Bent kept careful records of the Vorodinov children's progress in school. He asked for semi-annual reports from each teacher, explaining that it was necessitated by requests from the state welfare office. They were good students, each at the head of their class. He was sure that his wise choices of foster homes was responsible for not only their high grades, but for their ability as class leaders and their exceptional adaptability to any of the changing teaching techniques.

He outlined his views carefully, should the time come when he must make a presentation for the state welfare program, which he thought must surely resume its important role when the war was over. He wanted to show that his plan had worked out exactly as prognosticated. He had taken ordinary, backward foreign children and had changed the course of their lives for the better by submitting them to the best available in a typical American home.

One of the Vorodinov girls was given the American Legion prize for good citizenship. Bent was head of the Legion at the time and was to present the award of ten dollars at the Memorial Day celebration held at the town hall. He had not considered the effect of Danya's presence since, as he remembered, she had never appeared at any of the school or civic functions in which her children took part.

That warm May day when he walked into the crowded town hall he was startled to see her standing at the inner doorway. He confined himself to a nod, though he felt the blood pulsing through his face when he was forced by the crowd to stand there under her gaze for several minutes.

He became so rattled by it that he couldn't shake off the nervous sweating that had started in his hands and now seemed to creep into the bones of his face. His throat began to ache. He was horrified to hear a squeaking voice come out of his throat when he turned to speak with a man beside him. He had no voice! A squeak! He cleared his throat a few times. It was no better. He whispered apologies to the secretary of the Legion and asked him if he would in his stead deliver the speech and give the presentation. "Caught a small cold with this early change of weather," he tried to explain.

He heard no word the man said in reply. He was unaware of most of the program as he sat through it, slumped in a chair on the stage. Later when the event was over and the people were assembling on the town green for their marching positions in the parade, his wife came up to him, quite concerned.

"You look unwell, Angus. Shouldn't you come along in the car with me? Why did Bob Horton deliver the address? ...Are you all right?"

"Bertha, I'm afraid I'm not...I'd better go along with you. Don't understand how I could get a cold like this at such a time. Terrible sore throat...just awful, so bad I couldn't give the presentation." He spoke it all in a raspy small voice. He begged apology from the parade marshal and went home with Bertha.

Bertha wanted to call the doctor when they got home. She was certain he had a temperature, from the looks of his flushed face and sweating.

He begged her to wait a day. He took two aspirin and slept long into the warm afternoon. He awoke with a relief close to joy. He had expected a visit, had been prepared to go through the agonizing experience during that sleep, simply because he had seen Danya and couldn't shake it out of his mind. But he had slept without disturbance. He was refreshed, filled with exultation out of proportion to reason. So small a reprieve was beginning to expand its effects on Angus Bent's troubled mind.

The night was not so benevolent. He dreamed many times the same dream without waking in between the anguishing event as the witch took over his body. It was like a movie reel showing over and over again the same scene until the awareness of its repetition was as bad as going through it. Stop, stop! Enough, enough! He tried to cry out to someone, to something. But he had to watch it all again and again. Oh God, he could not waken himself.

CELEBRATION

The torpid pulse of wartime living was to be challenged by the post war crisis and dilemmas that reached into most every home. Whatever life was like before the war, and however pressing and disturbing the problems of families were, it would seem like a slow innocent epoch when later it was remembered and compared to the events that followed the end of World War II.

The V.E. Day celebration rocked the town of Stanton as nothing ever had before or would in the future, except perhaps the visit by a Hollywood company who would choose the town as the setting for a movie. All other events celebrated by the town's inhabitants were renowned for their dignity. There never was any possibility at Memorial Day parades that beer bottles would be thrown through store windows, nor did Christmas cheer extend beyond the firesides to a great bonfire such as the one built in the heat of the May victory night for hastily erected Tojo, still to be vanquished. Even the naughty pranks of Halloween had been confined to winding toilet paper around street poles and carrying outhouses to the lawns of unhappy neighbors. There was, this extraordinary night, no limit to what the serious-minded had to endure. Everything came under the tolerance of good clean fun, sanctioned by the importance of the day and event. The European war was over! Next, Japan!

It was one of the rare times that the town let its hair down. In scenes similar to those repeated all over the United States, teetotalers took their first swig of 'that stuff.' Right proper church going men stole kisses from other men's wives, in plain sight of neighbors or behind parked cars, as though they were thirty or forty years younger. Yankee schoolteachers whose decorum was distilled to perfection in their slow deliberate speech suddenly found voice that could whoop up a regiment of Indians. "Veni, Vidi, Vici" yelled the now jovialized Latin marm, throwing her empty beer bottle into the roaring bonfire.

"Swing it, gal, swing it," rang out one of her ex-pupils, for the first time unabashed by the woman's stature as he'd known her in the classroom.

The minister, leery that some participating in the orgy might emerge with good memories, declined the invitation to join the singing at the bonfire. But in his car, honking the horn at full decibel, he led a dozen other cars in a motorized circle round-and-round the great fire overheating the center of the town green. His wife leaned from the car window wildly ringing an old cowbell someone had handed to her.

Now and then, lost children would be mulling through the unconcerned crowds, or a husband would be looking for a lost wife who might have made a clandestine appointment under the umbrella of war-end's propriety.

For the greatest number it was an innocent blast. The next day, late in the afternoon, they would take up the staid, patterned duties of small town life. Their dignity and inhibitions would be returned to them and although they might talk for hours of the previous night's happenings, they would lapse into the careful habits of creatures who are constantly aware that the neighbor's eyesight is superlative and that those who haven't seen, can still talk a blue streak.

Angus and Bertha Bent had been part of that jovial crowd around the fire. They went into the town late because Angus had books to put in order. There were records from the Building and Loan Society that had to be looked over, some so old they could be destroyed, and others that he wanted to peruse carefully for reasons known only to himself.

He'd told Bertha they would leave for town as soon as he burned some of the old papers that had accumulated. "With the entire town celebrating, I don't think the fire chief will notice a little smoke at these unlawful hours," he told her, smiling.

He walked through the back yard down the hilly path to the incinerator. Bertha often complained that it was far from the house, but he had wanted it there near the brook that ran behind their property because he would have nothing obscure the beauty of his lawn and gardens. She understood, and because he knew it was an inconvenience to her, he generally carried the trash and papers and tended the burning.

He stood before the incinerator waiting for the flames to subside. Something moved against the twilit house on the hill across the brook. It attracted his attention because the generally busy back yards were now quiet, emptied in preference to the downtown celebration. It was the only movement along the entire strip of green, well-treed lawns.

It was two people, shadowed by the dusk, but he could say for sure that it was a man and a woman moving hurriedly around the corner of the house. That was the Hyland's house, empty for the past three years since Grant Hyland had been killed in the war.

Could be prowlers, Bent thought. A good night for them with the population packed into the center of town. He'd best mention it tomorrow to young Rizzoti at the bank. The bank had the mortgage on the house and one of the tellers, Art Rizzoti, was handling the care of the house. The boy had the key and all the information for any prospective buyer. Bent knew he had shown it a few times earlier in the spring. Might have been Rizzoti he saw in the shadows. Looked about his height. Well, he'd mention it to be safe, he said to himself as he poked out the last of the burning papers and returned to the house.

Bertha and Angus drove within sight of the bonfire that lit up the village green making weird elongated shadows from the people animated by its light. They decided to park the car and walk the short distance rather than risk not finding a place closer to the bonfire.

Latecomers to any sort of din-making event experience an uncomfortable detachment that makes them want to apologize for their obvious unenjoyment. Angus forced his smiles on to the young celebrants who accosted them at the edge of the green.

"Take a swig, Mr. Bent, let yourself go," one of the schoolboys yelled from a noise-husked throat. "Hell, the war's over! Come on, join the victorious. You too, Mrs. Bent. Here, take a gulp or two." Another boy handed a bottle to Bertha.

Angus held one hand up with a calming gesture. He managed to beam a slow understanding paternal smile to the boys. "It's surely a day for celebrating, boys, a wonderful day. But I've never touched spirits, and I don't think you should waste the liquor you have on an old couple like us. Drink it up, boys, celebrate and have a good time. It's a wonderful day, wonderful."

The boys agreeably moved on from the Bents into the shadows made by the tall elm trees, ranting their songs as they passed the other people along the sidewalk.

Angus and Bertha threaded their way along the edge of the dewing green, greeting the people who spoke from hoarse unrecognizable voices. Sometimes Bent had to look twice to see who the speaker was, so changed by alcohol were the voicings.

In the distance he saw Art Rizzoti. He remembered he must tell him something. He took Bertha's arm and they slowly made their way toward the tall young man standing close to the towering flames.

Rizzoti wasn't alone. Next to him, close to him, was a small pretty woman. It gave Angus a start, the way she was looking up at the fellow. He pressed Bertha's arm with a motion to stop. Puzzled, she looked up at her husband, then shifted her eyes to follow his.

"Angus, that's Arliss Haig. See her there next to the Rizzoti boy. Let's keep going and go over to talk to them. I thought I saw Jordan pass us a bit ago. He's probably there too."

Whatever he thought he'd noticed between Arliss and the young man had disappeared by the time they made their greetings, but Angus had the peculiar feeling he had noticed something he ought to forget. Jordan was some yards away. He noticed them and came over to speak.

The two men had not been together socially except at church functions. Angus had never seen his superior under any alcoholic haze, and now it had loosened Haig's tongue and emotions so that his behavior was almost equal to Arliss' normally gay and spirited actions.

"Angus, if you don't touch a drop of liquor tonight, you'll surely go to heaven," laughed Haig to Bent's refusal of his offered drink. He took a sip, then chuckled, lowered his voice like a stage actor and in an aside told the Bents of the minister's antics.

"Before the cock crows our minister will have to deny this night, Angus. Not only is he a confounded lousy driver on the highway, but look at the tracks he's made on the village green. Look behind you. You should have seen him, driving at the head of them, twelve or fifteen cars. They drove round twenty or thirty times. I guess he couldn't straighten out the wheel! He won't believe it in the morning, Angus, so you'll have to tell him to confess to this scarred sod, or some innocent sinner will have to take the blame...For God's sake, Angus, don't look so long faced! Bertha, convince him this is a victory torch, not a funeral pyre!" Haig waved his arm toward the bonfire.

She laughed quietly. "Jordan, Angus just doesn't have an expressive face. Now don't try to get any spirits down him, it won't change him a bit. Every one of his ancestors had the same face, whether it was before their weddings, during their childhood or before their death. Why, even Harold Bent who was accused as a witch had the same expression in the old family portrait. And that drinking uncle carried the same expression on his happiest, drinkingest days. I remember him clearly."

"Now, Bertha, that's hardly fair or true. He never let womenfolk see him when he was drinking," her husband intervened, chuckling with the others.

"That's what you think, Angus Bent, but you don't remember him at our wedding. He nearly drove me wild trying to trick me into drinking whisky he had poured into a teacup. Why, from the smell of him I'd say he was right pixolated!"

They all laughed. There was a lull in which the Rizzoti boy excused himself to join a group of couples strolling past. Angus thought he detected a lingering to the handshake he gave Arliss, but...well, what a damn silly thing to dream up. But standing there together they appeared much the same as the outline of the two persons he had seen moving behind the Hyland's house earlier.

People kept milling around the fire, the whole town, it looked to Bent. They sweated in the heat of the night as they threw anything burnable into the blaze to keep it going. They joked with the fire chief who kept walking around as though his presence alone could keep the flames under control.

"Cantini," someone yelled out to the fire chief, "I thought you pledged to force the townspeople to keep their burning limited to two hours in the morning. You're fired!"

There was joy, conviviality, joking, roistering, all in good spirit in the name of victory.

A few days later after the ashes of the bonfire were cleared away by the fire department and after the minister's victory highway had been leveled and re-sodded by the Tarroni Brothers construction company, the town was good as old.

There was anxiety for the men left fighting in the Pacific war area but everyone was sure it would be over soon. In a last burst of patriotism folks participated in various civil obligations that soon would be shelved. Housewives with small families used their last sugar coupons carelessly. Other large families who always had more coupons than they could use gladly purchased extra sugar for friends or teenage girls who now were going to learn how to bake cakes like mother used to make before the war.

They were all hungry for the end of it all. The end of the war, the rationing, the return of their men, bright lights, travel, new clothes...all the promised things they could remember from before the war. Now they wanted it all faster, more of it and no questions asked. They had sacrificed for the war effort and by gosh, now they were going to live!

Every newspaper was read with hunger. As summer moved along the news became startling. The concentration camps, the atomic bomb, the hydrogen bomb, the Japanese surrender.

The victorious troops were coming home. Some brought foreign wives with them. Wartime infidelities were discovered by returning husbands. The tears, the divorces. The housing shortages. The frenetic building, building from any piece of wood or metal a man could lay his hands on. The hump-backed homes springing up like gray mushrooms in the woods when the government released the surplus Quonset huts to civilians. There was money, greed, happiness, misery, safety, loneliness. Everything shoveled into the post war bin at the same time.

But all that, mulled Angus Bent, was no excuse for the actions of Arliss Haig and Arthur Rizzoti, a man at least fifteen years younger than she, and employed by her husband.

STALKING

Angus Bent had seen them, several times, and now he was certain. They used the Hyland house across from his for their trysts. He had seen Rizzoti's car, a Studebaker, parked across the street from the Hyland house when he decided to go past on his way to church. Farther on he saw the Haig's car. True, he'd seen it there at other times when Jordan dropped the children off for Sunday school and took a walk along the river while he waited for them. This particular Sunday he knew Jordan was home ill, laid up with a bad cold. So it must be Arliss who had the car.

Arliss was not at church. Bent saw their two teenage children in the junior choir loft. Perhaps the boy was driving the car now, though Jordan had said not until he was eighteen. Angus remembered the conversation.

He had said nothing of his suspicions to Bertha. That Sunday he lingered in the church vestibule. He saw Arliss drive into the small parking lot. She looked into the car mirror, straightened her hair, swung lightly out of the car. She walked slowly toward the church door, stopping to greet each person she passed. She was pretty, really very pretty, thought Bent. Like sunshine. But you certainly can't tell a book by its cover, no sir, not these days. Arliss greeted the minister, talked with him a few minutes until her children came up to her.

"Mom, I'm famished, let's go," said the boy. She shook hands with the minister, turned and noticed the Bents, gave them a bright greeting and left with the children.

Haig was out of the office on Monday. Angus watched Rizzoti as he worked. He was that smart aleck Italian kind, good looking, sweet in the face when he talked to the old ladies, thought Bent sizing him up. He remembered giving him some athletic prize years ago...Oh yes, that was when the Legion was sponsoring the town baseball team. Nice enough as a kid, but this kind of behavior was something else. Damn foreign Catholics, Bent cursed silently. I'll bet he goes to confession and never thinks a thing about it the next day.

Arliss came into the bank before noon. Jordan wanted some of his papers, she told his secretary. She chatted with Rizzoti while she waited. Bent could see her clearly from his desk. He wanted to get closer to the two of them, to see if he could detect anything from what they were saying, or from the way they looked at each other. He fumbled over some papers he had wanted to sort out, but instead, lest he miss her, he picked up his briefcase and made a hurried exit, stopping only to shake hands with Arliss.

He hadn't heard any of their conversation. But he was now certain. Her warm hands and pink cheeks, not subtle at all. A man couldn't mistake something like that.

A few days later she returned with the papers. Bent noticed that Rizzoti left soon after Arliss did. It was before noon. Bent drove past the Hyland house. Rizzoti's car was parked in another spot, but still an obvious distance from the Hyland place.

He'd speak to Haig the day he came back to the office. This was a disgrace and a scandal. It should be nipped in the blooming before it got around and became common gossip. It would never do to have a thing like that connected with the bank.

But how does a dignified, upright man suggest to another dignified upright man that his wife is being unfaithful? Not in innuendos over cocktails. Not through a slanted joke, nor in meaningful stories of other infidelities. In fact, not at all, Bent realized. He couldn't say anything at all. There was no occasion, and moreover, no proof. Just his intuition and perhaps a few coincidences. Damn, I know it's so, he told himself, but it's no concern of mine, I suppose, unless...

Stupid of them though to use the Hyland house as they obviously were doing, especially now with the cold weather. From the kitchen window at the back of his house Bent discovered which room they were using. All the windows were clear except one that was lightly clouded, probably from the breath of humans inside, he decided.

He mentioned the house to Jordan Haig one day. "What's the latest on the Hyland house? It's been empty nearly two years now. No one interested in the place?"

"On the contrary, it's getting a good look over," answered Haig. "Arthur has shown it a couple of times. And we've given Arliss a key because some distant relative of hers wanted to see it when she was here a few weeks ago. It's an awfully big house for what young folks can afford right now. It also has a hard mortgage to take over. Arliss likes the house, says it has a lot of possibilities. I think she wouldn't mind being closer to town with the children so busy in school activities. She spends so much of her time driving them into town now, you know. But we're so attached to our place on the lake it would be difficult to change. You know the house pretty well, don't you Angus, it being right across the pond from you?"

"Yes, spent a number of hours there with the Hylands, before the war; before young Hyland went off. I don't think the wife changed it a bit in those few years she was alone with the children. Pretty house, sitting just across the brook from our house, or across the meadow I should say."

"Yes. Arliss mentioned your backyard which she can see from the house. She says you should have the garden club's prize for what you have done there. She thinks the little hill going down to the brook is so pretty with the willow trees and the maples. The way you've laid them out, you know. She's very impressed. She said it was like a secluded little forest waiting for some gnome to pop out. Even mentioned how smart of you to have your incinerator down there near the water. She was very complimentary to your gardening."

"That so? Why, that's most kind of her. You'll have to thank her for me. That yard is my great pride." Bent's thoughts drifted…"Yes, it pleases me that she mentioned it, Jordan. I've spent hours of my life making something beautiful of that big yard and the hill. Some of those willows were planted the week Bertha and I came back from our honeymoon. And some of the flowers, I must admit, are among the most difficult to grow in these parts…You know, I think digging in that earth has brought me some of the happiest hours of my life. I can't explain it, seems a bit foolish, I suppose."

"Hardly foolish, Angus, pretty natural thing, I'd say. We feel the same way about rummaging around our acres, the apple trees, watching the sheep. I never thought a piece of real estate could turn me into a farmer, but when those seeds go into the earth Arliss and I watch like hungry birds for the first evidence that they're going to make it into the world. I wish I had more time to garden. I feel the way you do about it. I suppose that's why I really don't want to give up the place for a house closer to town. She's at heart as bad an earthworm as I am. You get rooted to a place where even the inconveniences we accept are part of the good life we have there."

"Yes, that's certainly understandable, from my own experiences. Well, Jordan, didn't mean to take up so much of your time. I was curious about the Hyland house, that's what we started out on, wasn't it?"

"It's no matter, Angus, enjoyed our conversation. While you're here, I should tell you about Art Rizzoti."

Bent nearly gulped aloud. "Arthur?"

"Yes, I should have your approval for this, but it's a formality, actually. His recommendations are in order and I want to discuss it with you before it's announced so you'll not be surprised."

"You remember that when Art was hired I felt he might in the future become an important man in the bank, a special man on our staff? He had finished only his business schooling just before he came to us. No other experience at that time. He wants to get a college degree now since he's eligible for some government help; some years in the navy or merchant marine early in the war which qualifies him. He's exceptional with numbers, has a natural personality for a business like banking. I'd like to tie him to the bank after he finishes his studies. To do it, I want to advance part of his expenses so he can go to school full time. I'm underwriting him myself, but with that understanding. He's perfectly willing to commit to that. It will mean just over a year away from the bank. The formality, of course, would be to give him a leave of absence. If you have no objections it can be announced at the next board meeting."

Bent rubbed his chin in thought. "Isn't that unusual, committing him to a job he could have kept without further schooling?"

"At close range thinking, yes. But there's something special about the boy, that's obvious to nearly anyone who meets him. He won't return expecting to stay at the teller's window, of course. This is a small bank, Angus, but it is a fairly well-heeled one now and we're in an area that could forge ahead in the near future on an impressive scale. He's particularly interested in real estate and mortgage. I think that's where we'll need a strong man. We never could convince you to come in totally, which I understand and appreciate, knowing your ties in your own insurance business. You realize that without you these few hours a day we're pretty short in that department?"

"That's so, as you say. Frankly, I haven't been that impressed with the young man...Oh heavens yes, with his looks and his manner. He's certainly a handsome rascal." Bent spoke in a condescending tone. "I'm sure all the old ladies like him. But I'd have to take your opinion, Jordan, since I've worked very little with him. If you're impressed and willing to go along with him, why there's no reason at all for me to balk."

"Thanks, Angus. Just a formality, but I like to keep you informed and get your ideas."

***

Keep me informed! Bent thought to himself that night. I should keep him informed. Perhaps, he reasoned, Jordan knew about Arliss and Rizzoti after all. He might have cooked this up, or at least encouraged the boy to go to school to put a stop to the affair...to get him out of town. But that was ridiculous. What sort of man would float another man's education just to get him out of his wife's way? Thank goodness, there would be no more to that bunch of shenanigans.

Bent hated those shabby affairs. You heard a lot of rumors, both during the war and now with all the new folks in town. And of course not all of the gossip could be true, but just the same, it didn't reflect well on the bank of the community to have someone like Arliss Haig caught up in a scandal...and with a foreign kid, too. Jordan was prudent, Bent admitted to himself. He wasn't a fool, and he wasn't a man to jeopardize his home and business at the whim of some foreigner.

Angus learned later that the possible scandal was in no way shut off.

Rizzoti moved to Hartford where he was enrolled in stepped up courses given by the University extension. Arliss Haig continued her pastime of frequently shopping in that city. It was not more than thirty-five miles away and the only good stores in the area were there.

It wasn't unusual on a Saturday to see a half dozen or more Stanton matrons poking their way through the large department store. It was, as its ads quoted, the center of Connecticut living. Angus at times drove Bertha to Hartford when she wanted to shop for furniture or fabrics for their home.

A few months after Rizzoti left the bank, and when Angus had relegated the almost scandal to the realm of past curiosities, he was shocked to see Arliss and Rizzoti together on the street in Hartford.

He dropped Bertha off in front of the G. Fox department store and drove about looking for a parking space, cursing the bustle and crowds that were turning the city traffic into a miserable inconvenience. He saw Arliss and Art crossing the street, a small side street on which he had been forced to turn because of some new one-way signs. He was three cars back from the stop light but he could not mistake the two people he saw walking hand in hand on the crosswalk. He stared at them until they were out of sight, so engrossed that he wasn't aware the light had changed to green until the car behind him hooted an angry reminder.

Now, where would they be going? He was certain the college buildings were across town. He wondered where Rizzoti lived. He could ask Jordan. He'd better take down the name of this street, just in case. Maybe follow them if he could park quickly. Why that black-haired no-good! Taking money from Jordan and taking his wife in the bargain.

He couldn't track the two. When he found Bertha in the store he was going to tell her he had seen Arliss, yet something cautioned him that it might sound like female gossip. He'd let it ride, though he was drenched with curiosity and anxious to find out more if he could.

That week he spoke to Jordan about the traffic and the crowds in Hartford. "It's changing so fast I wouldn't believe it if someone told me, but I've seen it. There's a lot of new building on the north side of town, just past the city parking lot. I suppose you know the area?"

"I know where you mean, Angus. Seems I read something about it, or perhaps it was Art who wrote about it. He keeps in touch once a week, though I haven't seen him since he took off. He seems to think there's a bit of overbuilding for the situation at the moment, and that there isn't enough population right now to swallow up the new apartments, or use all the new office buildings. He a pretty observant boy."

"You should take a look at the city, Jordan, or do you have to drive Arliss up there as I do Bertha? You might take a look at the area while she's shopping."

Jordan laughed pleasantly. "No, Arliss does her own driving. She says I poke along as though I'm driving the old A. She'd much rather go up there with the children and spare me the agony of waiting while she shops. But I may drive up some Saturday, just to see the way things are changing. I'll drop a note to Arthur and ask him if he has time to poke around with me." His eyes crinkled with good humor. "It never hurts a banker's morale to see a boom in the making, does it Angus?"

***

Bent never saw Arliss and Rizzoti together again while Arthur was still studying. A few times he drove to Hartford, moving slowly in the area where he had seen the two, curious and eager to catch them together. Disappointed, yet somewhat relieved he would park the car and walk around a few blocks, feeling some guilt in his actions.

After a few times the curiosity, unsatisfied, became an obsession. His mind was occupied now with an annoyance far outweighing the familiar dreams that kept occurring. He shook them off like cobwebs so he could think more clearly of this brewing scandal.

He was like a bloodhound on the scent of something exciting. He couldn't say why it struck him that way, but he was determined to find out for sure, to have some proof, somehow. Not one hour of the day passed without some minutes in which he would crisscross the possible ways he might seek more information, anything that would lead to proof.

Bent welcomed Arthur's return to the bank with a sense of satisfaction that his victim…or he shouldn't call him that, he told himself…no, not is victim, but instead he, Bent, was the boy's nemesis. He was justified, he believed, because he knew he would be able to watch them now and bring the young man's affair to a halt.

The Hyland house had been sold. Where would they go now? He knew by the way they talked to each other in the bank that he was not imagining the affair. Arliss came in once a week to take the car so she could do the grocery shopping. She would walk into the bank with her husband, take money from her account and speak to whoever stopped next to her. And each time, there was Arthur Rizzoti, next to her. He would be wandering around as unconcerned as a schoolboy so he could be out in front of the tellers windows when she came in. Bent couldn't understand how everyone else missed such an obvious impropriety.

He found them, though it took him more than a month of driving around each day past the empty houses or secluded places that he guessed they might choose to meet.

The contemptuous, galling foreigner! Angus said it aloud. In Jordan's home. He couldn't be mistaken, for both cars were there, one parked in the drive, the other along the road. Arliss had the car that day, and he had seen Arthur leave the bank an hour before lunch with his briefcase with some bank folders tucked under his arm. Here, now, he had his proof. And in the woman's house, in her husband's house!

Bent hadn't expected that much nerve from either of them. He had driven out past the Haig home just to see if she might be there. He hadn't expected to find either car, but now, to find them both, well, good heavens, there was no doubt left in his mind now...not at all. He must tell Jordan. It was his duty to tell Jordan. He drove farther along past the house, turned around and drove back past the house without turning his eyes toward the drive.

THE EMBEZZLER

The great divide between resolution and action is separated by the ebb and flow of determination, conviction, conscience and that terrible grainy abrasive thing called doubt.

Before a logical man makes unfounded accusations he must, in keeping with his character, consider the reactions from any logical standpoint he is able to imagine. As carefully as in a game of chess he must suppose certain moves or questions, and until he is able, to his satisfaction, to cover these supposings, logic instructs him to hold his move.

The risk that a logical man takes is that he will be pre-empted by the illogical, the unexpected.

Had Angus Bent's conviction been keen enough that next morning he would have spoken to Jordan with the same emotional disgust he felt the day before.

He hadn't slept well. He wakened a half hour later than usual and arrived at the bank fifteen minutes after the opening. The doors to the offices were ajar. Jordan, at the end of the hall, was alone. He was sitting back in his chair smoking and reading some bank papers. That made it easier. Bent headed for Jordan's office. To get there he had to pass Rizzoti's open door, which he would have done quickly had it not been for the voice he heard.

What was Danya Vorodinov doing in Arthur Rizzoti's office? Bent still had a hard time making out her words because of the accent. Good heavens, he thought, she's been in this country long enough…but he heard distinctly, 'my building and loan is crooked'…and he picked out the words, 'please, if you can help me.' At that minute Rizzoti saw him, as Danya did when Art called out a greeting.

Bent flushed and nodded back. He was embarrassed because he wasn't sure whether he had stopped to listen or just heard the words as he'd come closer toward the door.

Out flowed the determination, now not strong enough to carry him past his own closed office door. He sat at his desk, his absorption with some papers hiding the waffled thoughts that cross-hatched his mind.

For what purpose was she there? She rarely came into the bank this early. Usually she came for the simple deposit or withdrawal or payment. What was she discussing with Rizzoti now? Their voices were hushed, as though they feared he might hear. He heard the click of Rizzoti's door which meant it truly was something he shouldn't hear, …something that concerned him?

Jordan called to Angus. Did he have a minute before he got into his work? He got up. It could be done now, but he thought this so feebly that it moved him not at all.

They talked for a few minutes about some reports Jordan was reading on government loans. He wanted Angus to read them and pass them on to Arthur. Was there anything important he wanted to take up with him? He was leaving the day after tomorrow for Boston. A bank convention that he'd mentioned to Angus before. He would be gone about five days.

Angus was emptied. He should have spoken then, but he found himself back at his own desk before any words could come. He strained to hear more clearly any of the words that came from Rizzoti's office. At times he could hear Danya's voice grow louder and higher, but he couldn't divine any of the words, and he couldn't tell if she spoke in anger or excitement.

He left his office earlier than usual and went home to his insurance office. His head was throbbing and his throat ached as if he had been talking for hours. He had heard Danya leave. She had been in Rizzoti's office an hour and a half. He was sure, when he said goodbye to Arthur later that there was a difference in the tone of his reply.

Jordan went to the convention. Arthur took an extra hour at noon times. Angus knew where he spent that time.

***

The day after Jordan returned from the convention he called Angus into his office and asked him to close the door behind him. Bent's stomach fluttered with uncertainty. Jordan's face was set more sternly than usual, and that quality he had of being distant was now more obvious. It was something important, and he suspected that perhaps the man had discovered by himself the deviations of his wife.

"Sit down, Angus. I have a serious matter to discuss with you. It is to go no farther than this room and I want you to know that my mind will be open to anything that you wish to say. I don't want to put you on the defensive. I want to place this matter before you and try to understand it better."

Angus saw that the man was upset. Jordan took a deep troubled breath. He pulled a folder from his desk drawer and opened it. Without looking at the papers he spoke again.

"I'm afraid, and I apologize for it, but I will have to be blunt. We have asked for a special audit of the bank's books and the old Savings and Loan books. There are some discrepancies that point to a serious shortage. Since you are the person concerned I want to talk with you about it before we do anything." He paused, noting Bent's startled reaction.

"Believe me, Angus, it is damn difficult to put a man on the spot like this. That's why I assure you that I am open to anything you have to say in explanation."

They looked at each other. Except for the change in color Bent's face was now an inexpressive mask. His reactions were more apparent in the trembling hands that suddenly seemed not to know their owner's wishes. He cleared his throat.

"That's a pretty shocking situation, Jordan. I'm not sure there is anything I can say..." He hesitated. "I...I...You'll have to explain just what those shortages stem from, and...well, as you see, there's nothing I can say unless you let me know exactly what the books show. I'm dumbfounded, but I'm willing to clear anything up if I can. You'll have to give me a clearer idea of what's been misunderstood."

"I would like to think it's bad bookkeeping, especially the old Savings and Loan books. But after the audit we know it's not. The pattern is too logical, too obvious to be a sloppy bookkeeping matter." Jordan was almost apologetic.

Bent countered. "I was under the impression that the Building and Loan books were audited by the bank before the company changed hands."

"They had a routine audit, yes. It was after Mrs. Vorodinov talked with Arthur that we had the special audit made."

Bent could barely control his incredulity. "You had the audit made at that woman's request? I don't understand that."

"She didn't request it. She came to the bank a week or so ago to apply for a re-mortgaging of their house so she could buy a piece of land from the Hyland's old farm. Originally, as you may remember, you made the mortgage as the Savings and Loan company."

"Of course, we made most of the mortgages at that time."

"At first it was a routine application. She wanted to talk with Arthur because she knew someone in his family, one of his sisters, I believe. She was a nurse Mrs. Vorodinov knew some time ago. There wasn't anything unusual, Arthur said, until she insisted that the house was valued higher than we had it listed. She has a sack full of papers with her, dating all the way back to her husband's purchase of the property before the first world war. When she insisted she was correct Arthur agreed to look over her records. When he did, he found that her receipts and the books were not reconcilable."

A short laugh of relief exploded from the worried man across the desk. "Good God, Jordan, so that's where this all came from. I'm glad you've told me this before doing anything." He loosened his taught body and leaned in a confidential manner toward Jordan's desk.

"You remember of course, the problems I had with Mrs. Vorodinov, years ago, before the war?"

"Yes, I do, Angus. I recalled all that when Arthur first brought the case to my attention."

"Then doesn't it seem obvious to you that she has spent all these years harboring this hate against me, and that she has somehow found some papers, perhaps even forged them, who knows, that will stir up trouble for me?"

Jordan shook his head. With studied patience he answered, "I thought of that at first, that she had made some mistake. Arthur thought not. I told him to go ahead with the special audit. Both of us expected the result would show some small mistakes, that something obvious had been overlooked. But from the pattern shown by her receipts against the books, other discrepancies were traced in other accounts."

"My God, Jordan, are you saying that I'm under suspicion of something because of that woman's crazy accusations?"

"Perhaps it was strange, even silly at first. Yes, it started with that. I would rather it had not gone any farther, Angus. After all, that was an age ago. But the clever, logical pattern of the bookkeeping so impressed Arthur that he wanted an extended audit of the old books before we took over the Society."

"And?"

"The same pattern was there. I don't know how to hedge this blow, Angus, but there is no one else to whom it points. I'm afraid we will have to make a formal accusation."

Jordan lit another cigarette. He wasn't much younger than Angus. At that moment, though, his thin handsome face showed a generation of worry less than the other heavy-jowled face staring at him.

"Well, Jordan, I suppose I will have to tell you some distasteful things." The words exploded from Angus' mouth before he had really decided to say them. His voice became hard, calm, sure.

Jordan blinked slightly, took a deep puff on his cigarette and waited to hear.

"It has probably not occurred to you that Arthur Rizzoti has any reason to dislike me, or to put me into a position of this sort." Bent now spoke slowly.

"No, Angus, it has not." Jordan scowled, annoyed and waiting.

"This accusation leaves me no alternative but to tell you something I would rather carry with me to the grave. By whatever means the boy was able to fiddle with the books to put me in the wrong, I do not know. He is probably, in that, a lot more clever than you and I. In his private life he has made a misadventure and a botch that I am now forced to expose." He let the words rest for effect then continued.

"Jordan, it grieves me and hurts me to be the one to say this. With any doubt of it I would hesitate to mention it, even in this situation. I would not try to save my skin on an ill-founded suspicion. However, what I will tell you is true beyond any doubt."

Jordan was plainly puzzled and still annoyed.

Calmly Bent continued.

"Arthur Rizzoti has concocted this preposterous bunch of figures against me for one hideous reason. He wants to make trouble for me before I can expose his dishonest, adulterous deeds to you...Jordan, for nearly three years, Arthur Rizzoti has been conducting a brazen affair with your wife."

It was said. It was said just the way Bent had wanted to say it. In the righteous, calm tones of a man not given to gossip, not given to harming others. Bent could hear the echo of the last words. Somehow they didn't sound quite as convincing as they should have...or was it Jordan's reaction?

Jordan's first reflex reaction was to laugh at the ridiculous nature of Bent's information.

"Angus, do you insinuate...?"

"No, I do not insinuate. I accuse, and I accuse with proof upon proof. I can name times and places where your wife and your young banker have been together. The Hyland house and the

Hartford apartment. Yes…there, while he was enlarging his career with the help of your money. And even in your own home, Jordan. In your own home!"

Jordan sat back in his chair. He folded his arms across his chest. The impact of this kind of news served to convince him that Bent was indeed deeply involved in a serious mishandling of the old books. Not one part of the accusation at that moment did Jordan believe. His face must have shown the strain of his tolerance.

"Believe me, Jordan, if you want any corroboration of what I have told you, just ask Arthur or your wife. They could not deny a bit that I've said. You can ask neighbors. You can ask your children whether their mother stays for the church service when she drops them off for Sunday school or whether she runs off to her lover. Everything I've told you can be proven. If I am the first one who has mentioned it I doubt that I am the only one who knows about it."

"That's a grievous charge, Angus. I do question your bringing up something like this in the face of the banking investigation. As I told you, I would listen to anything you had to say. I consider this out of that privilege. I'm sorry. I have no alternative but to turn the books and papers over to the directors of the company."

He got up to dismiss Angus. "I think it would be best if you left your desk today. Take only your personal things. You needn't say anything to the others. There's nothing for you to do but wait to hear from us."

He reached out to shake Angus's hand. "I'm truly sorry."

DEATH

The next morning Jordan Haig was dead.

The townspeople awakened to a day much like the day before. The sun shone though damp spring green leaves making them glisten like tinseled trimmings. Early risers noted with the same pleasure as they had yesterday the warming sun.

Factory whistles blew at 7:25. Put out the cigarettes. The whistles blew again at 7:30. Time to start work. Clocks not in accord were changed to synchronize. Mothers hurried children with their dressing and eating. The children trudged to school wearied from the waiting for spring recess, coming soon and worth counting the days for.

Arthur Rizzoti entered the bank at fifteen minutes before the hour. At exactly 9 o'clock he unlocked the door to the public. None of the people who came into the bank that early morning noticed anything unusual. At 11 o'clock Arthur was going to call the Haig home to ask if Jordan would be in that morning. He decided it wasn't necessary since Jordan had said he was taking some papers home to work on. There was nothing urgent for which he must be bothered.

No one knew until the incident was reported on the noon radio news programs. Before the children were home from school that afternoon the majority of the town inhabitants knew about Jordan Haig's death.

Angus Bent had stayed late in bed. He pleaded fatigue and the beginning of a sore throat. His bedside radio was turned down low so he would know when the news program came on.
He never missed the noon news programs. He generally heard it on the car radio on his way home for lunch.

Bertha was calling up the stairs to ask if he wanted a tray lunch when he heard the story. He called to her, "Hold on, wait a minute, there's something on the radio."

He sat back against the double pillows, stunned. He stared blankly at the papers spread out on his bed. His eyes didn't blink. They seemed to stare from a dead man's immobile face. A pain in his chest forced him to take a breath. He had been holding his breath unknowingly. How…how…good God, how, he wondered.

The implications were enormous. When Bent fathomed what it meant to his own situation he experienced near convulsive shortness of breath. He was like a man who had been running madly before a pursuing unknown something. Now he could stop.

He breathed in short staccato sniffs. The breathing came quick and hurting to his chest. Now he had stopped and found no pursuer. The relief overwhelmed him. The bitterness and fear engendered by yesterday's conversation with Jordan were ebbing. The strain and worry with which he had spent the morning was alleviated. By what act this had been accomplished he would have to wait to learn. It would not do to call the Haig's home. Bertha insisted he call when he told her what he'd heard on the radio, but he'd convinced her that it was best he did not.

As calmly as he could, praying that none of his relief showed to her, he said, "No, I think it would be kinder to wait until we are notified, or at least until we know more about what happened. The bulletin said only that he was found dead at his home. I would have qualms about calling with so little information. I would hate to bother poor Arliss in the midst of what she must be going through. We'll know the details soon enough. I had no idea he was ill."

"Then why don't you call the bank, Angus? Surely they will know more?"

"Let's not join the frantic and curious, Bertha. I'll keep the radio tuned in the news station. I'm sure there will be details at one o'clock. There's another news program then."

"Oh Angus," her voice was a partial wail, "it's such an awful sadness. He's got those two growing children and Arliss is so young. I don't think anyone had any idea he was unwell, did you?"

"No, I thought he looked fine yesterday, just fine, normal as could be. Never had any idea he wasn't well."

"He wasn't so very old, was he Angus? He seemed quite young to me."

"I suppose not yet sixty, I'm not sure. Arliss is a lot younger, of course."

"Yes, I know. I think she's in her early forties, forty-two or so, maybe younger. I can't ever remember them saying how old they were, can you? Nobody's business, really."

He pulled the papers together from where he had strewn them on the bed. "I'm speechless, Bertha, I really am. I can't tell you how this shocks me."

"Of course, dear, it is a shocking event. It's so unexpected, such a terrible way to learn about a friend's death, from a newscast. I do wish we could speak to Arliss. The poor girl."

"No, as I said, I think we shouldn't right now, really not. At the moment nothing we could say would be remembered, nor is it kind to add to the questions she has already been asked, I'm sure."

"Oh, I agree, Angus, I do agree. I'd just like to be able to help her. But perhaps we'll know more when the next news is on at one."

***

Jordan Haig's son had found him, the detailed newscast said. He had come home at midnight after a school dance. The light in his father's downstair's study was on. He could see it from the driveway. As he'd walked past the garage he thought he heard the car motor running. He tried to unfasten the garage door, then realized it was caught from the inside. He was going to call his father but decided he could more quickly go around through the sheep barn and get into the garage through the door that connected the two buildings.

In the dark garage he opened the car door to turn off the engine. The instant the car door opened wide enough for the car light to come on his father's body fell toward him. He shook his father, calling out to him. He turned off the car engine. He shook his father again. The boy started to cough. Then he understood what had happened. He moved quickly to the garage door, flung the double doors open and ran across the wide lawn toward the house. He started calling to his mother as soon as he came through the door, yelling more loudly as he ran up the stairs to her bedroom at the back of the house.

The coroner marked the death certificate as suicide. When questioned about her husband's health, Arliss said she knew of nothing wrong with her husband. Nothing, to her knowledge, had happened that would provoke this act. She asked to be left alone. She was in a state of shock and could not be reached again.

Both Angus and Bertha were struck dumb, hardly believing what they had heard on the radio. "I just can't understand it, I really can't. I'd never believe Jordan was capable of that, never!" Angus shook his head sadly.

"What in the world do you suppose is behind it, Angus, for heaven's sake? Could he have kept a serious illness from Arliss? And from the bank directors?"

"I don't know, Bertha. I have no idea at all. I just can't believe it." He sighed.

Actually Angus had to endure the agony of uncertainty rather than present a suspicious appearance by his anxiety. He could not know, of course, what had happened between Arliss and Jordan. He had no idea what had happened to the accusing papers from which Jordan had taken his information about the bookkeeping shortages. Nor did he know what his official standing was with the bank, since it was only some twenty-six hours earlier that Jordan had given his dismissal. Who else knew, and what was he to do now?

***

The bank directors and the Boston syndicate were hastily advised of the suicide, first by the bank secretary and then by Arliss. It was decided that a new audit of the books should be ordered immediately. When a bank president commits suicide for no apparent reason the banking community goes through great shuddering apprehensions until certain questions are cleared.

The folder and the papers were found in Jordan's top desk drawer. The employees were questioned about the audit. Angus Bent knew nothing. He had been called the next afternoon.

Arthur Rizzoti chokingly admitted that he had pushed for the audit against Mr. Haig's wishes. Mr. Haig had tried several times to dissuade him, but he felt he must trace what looked like a long term of discrepancies. No, as far as he knew, Mr. Haig had not discussed the findings with anyone after the accountant had given him the report. Yes, the day before he died.

No one wanted to believe it. The papers carried the obituary one day, the story of the suicide the next day, and a week later the crisply understated news item of the bank shortages. At the end of the item the public was reminded that last week Jordan Haig, president of the bank, had committed suicide for no known reason. He had left no notes and his wife and doctor said he was in good health. His desk had been in order. The auditor's report of the shortages was in the top drawer of his desk at the bank.

All sort of disjointed facts of the death and the bank shortage made the rounds of every home. The few facts of the story were thoroughly chewed and digested in enlarged quantities, as in most private tragedies. The people retraced a thousand insignificant events of the man's life in the new light of his suicide: His expensive suits, his new cars each year, the prize sheep he raised, the expensive furniture, his wife's clothes, their expensive vacation trips. All these things assumed a different importance measured against the amount of money that had disappeared from the bank.

Danya refused to believe that such a nice-faced man would do such a thing. She told Mikolai that somehow the ugly bulldog Bent was behind it, but she couldn't prove it yet. She would talk again with the Rizzoti boy when she went to make her mortgage payment. He was a bright boy and he always listened to her. She would tell him more about Bent.

Mikolai snorted. Anything that happened she blamed on Mr. Bent. Even a hurricane is somehow his fault. He hoped she could pay for the land she had just bought. Let her worry about that and not about Mr. Bent.

"Don't worry about money, my husband. I make plenty now sewing chair covers for people, and you make plenty on your job. We need the land more than we need the money, so don't drive me crazy with crabbiness."

Well, he thought, it was a pretty good piece of land even if he hadn't seen it before she bought it. It added some good hay and pasture acres, which meant they could have another cow. Before it was too warm he would walk the land and measure the boundaries. She was always calling Bent a liar, but she never measured the land she bought from other people who might be ready to cheat her. Only Bent she worried about, and now she blamed him for the banker's trouble making.

Danya wanted to say something to Mrs. Haig but she never saw her and she didn't want to go to her house without an invitation. She told one of the girls to write a letter instead.

"Dear Mrs. Haig, I am in sorrow because your husband is dead. I appreciated him very much for the times he gave me the rides to Middletown and for his help in the bank. Without his explanation I could never own the new land I am buying with a new mortgage. You are a young woman still and you should not live your years in sadness. God found you a good husband who was Mr. Haig and he will bless you again. You should carry good memories in your heart and you will have a good life."

She signed her name carefully so Mrs. Haig would have no trouble reading it.

***

Angus Bent stayed on as Vice President of the bank. No word of his and Jordan's interview was known. Arthur Rizzoti was given greater responsibility in the real estate and mortgaging department. A new bank president was appointed from the local directors.

Angus and young Rizzoti were polite to each other. Nothing of the Haig situation was ever discussed. Neither knew what the other might have learned, and neither was willing to risk the breakdown of the status quo.

Arliss never came to the bank. Angus never knew whether she and Arthur saw each other again. Angus saw her once at the funeral and once after a church service. She looked straight at him, clear-eyed, unsmiling, unwilling to give him a trace of her knowledge. Thin, impersonal greetings were exchanged.

At the end of the school year Arliss moved with the two children to her family's home in Boston. They drove with her father away from the shocked, perplexed, gossiping town. The pretty farm and the great house were put on the market, underpriced for quick transfer.

For endless hours Bent mulled over the event. He had held his accusations as long as he possibly could. He reasoned to himself that had he told Jordan sooner the same thing would have happened, just as it did when he obviously learned the truth from Arliss. Of course, if he had told Jordan sooner there would never have been the audit. Whatever Rizzoti knew about it, however he might think that Angus was involved, would remain hidden for a long time, a good long time. To risk exposing Bent as an embezzler would bring up the what-for of Jordan's suicide, and that would not be smart for a young smart banker to do. Angus Bent felt he would be safe for a good long time.

TIME MOVES ON

Outwardly the town changed very little in the next eight years. The Haig incident was submerged by the nowness of other private tragedies that sped in half-truths over telephone wires until they were made common property by the retelling. Conjecture generally substituted for unavailable information. While they might gossip about someone else, the inhabitants of that small town knew by instinct they should divulge nothing of their own private affairs. However, what was seen by one was told to all.

A child returning to the town after an absence of a dozen years would experience through now matured eyes, the nostalgia of looking again at its childhood. The physical panorama of the neat sleepy town was bypassed by the personal events that marked the changing times.

The Westham house had not been undignified by age. The house gleams white; the yard is changed only by the substitute of evergreens for the flower gardens at the front since Miss Carrie's stroke kept her from the gardening. And one day a passing neighbor saw the ambulance drive up the winding way to remove the senile woman to a rest home where someone could tend to her. They'd found the once prudish woman cowering, naked, in the garage beside the house, laughing like a child. She was singing, "Come and find me, come and find me," and of course that story was a good one for the shocked proper people.

The Noviky house is guarded by full-grown trees set out as shade makers years ago. The three sons have gone their ways to other towns and homes of their own. The youngest daughter came to visit one afternoon and stumbled over her mother's cold lifeless body, distorted by a drunken fall down the stairs.

Kate Donahue sits glumly staring over the fields from her attic apartment to which she has been relegated by her family. This is the house she built for her fatherless son with scrimping and sweating through endless days after the money disappeared which had been given to her by the bastard child's father's family. For years she sent letters begging her son to return to his home. Forgive me; you will understand some day; I was so young; you are all I have; nobody knows; I should not have told you; I am getting old; there is a house here and the land; the field and the pond that is yours, my son, my only child. He did return after the war, claimed his house and married a hard-working Polish girl younger than he. His mother still works through long tiring days and at night must endure the accusations of a drunken raving son who suffers unsilently the cross of his birth.

The Bennet's red house is silent except when the Craille family comes from New York for the summer months. For three years after Mr. Bennet died, no one lived there. The daughter was a victim of the war killed in a strange place with a forgotten name when she flew as a press photographer over the Hump. That's all the townspeople could remember of her except those terrible pictures Bill Gaston found when he was cleaning up the place after Mr. Bennet's death.

Doctor Cobb's Cape Cod house was sold to two families who had come from Nazi labor camps to Stanton a few years earlier in the DP rescue program. Dr. Cobb's life was hurried to an end by his own hand, reaching too often for the bottle, the story went. His practice had diminished as his health gave way. He was found one morning by his housekeeper, asleep forever at his office desk, gun in his hand. A woman who everyone supposed was his wife flew up from Georgia to arrange for the burial. No one knew how they had traced her. They guessed the police chief must have gotten a good look at the Doctor's papers and found her name.

The Munsons, their fortune divided many times by divorces and minor scandals, left the big house to a favorite grandson who lives with a too-blonde girl he found somewhere in England during the war. She does all the gardening, and she even rides around the lawn on a new fangled lawnmower, and there she is, in a half naked state where all the men can see her from the factory across the street. Nobody can understand why she doesn't wait until later in the day or on weekends to mow the big lawn.

Old Senator Grant Hefford's big fieldstone mansion is now a rest and rehab institution. It was bought by two Hartford doctors when the estate was settled. The Senator had suffered too long with the knowledge of a brain tumor and took his own life before the affliction could. He hadn't made a will, so it took some time to settle the complicated estate when all those long forgotten relatives turned up to make claims to part of Hefford's estate.

Danya Vorodinov had heard talk about the Hefford land when she was in the bank one day. She talked to Rizzoti about mortgaging her house again to buy some of the land. She had looked longingly at a certain portion of that land during her walks to town, and now there was a chance for her to have that special ground.

She had learned how she could get any piece of soil she set her heart on. She had discovered how wide the world of mortgaging can be. That square great nest of stucco, wallboard, paint and shingles that she and Mikolai had nailed and plastered together with the sweat of their labor was no longer just a home for their family. It had accrued into something that she learned was called collateral. Once she had scrimped every penny to pay off the mortgage on that house. She wanted no one but her family to have any claims on the home and the land. When she had first learned from Rizzoti that she could mortgage the house again to buy a piece of the Hyland farm she at first considered it a ridiculous and foolish action.

"What for," she had asked him, "why should my husband and I work like four people to pay off our mortgage and then go in a debt again?"

When he explained she was thrilled and incredulous as a child. "You mean I have a treasure chest?"

He laughed. "Not exactly, but decent collateral, should you want to make another real estate purchase."

"Land?"

"Or buildings."

"Houses?"

"Yes, any structure properly and fairly assessed."

"Well, I don't need more than one house. But I have a big growing family, so someday they will surely need more land. I think they should build their own houses, though. They have too many ideas against my house, so I could never satisfy them in choosing a house. But yes, the land they could not change, so there can be no ideas or suggestions from them. I think each one should have some land."

"I think the piece you like from the Hyland estate is a good beginning," he told her.

"Yes," she replied absent mindedly, settling into a half dream. I always wondered who belonged to that land on the hill behind

Old Bent. I always thought it belonged to Senator Hefford from his early days before he was a big senator. I used to look on it with jealous eyes. And other places, too…mmmmm. But now, from my sweat and my husband's sweat I find enough gold drops to buy my wish."

"Real estate isn't exactly gold, but it's pretty good and sound collateral."

After that she always asked to talk to Rizzoti when she went to the bank. He was a gentle person, she told Mikolai one day. He would be a good son-in-law for them, but she didn't know which girl would like him. Mikolai said maybe she should worry more about whether he would like any of the girls. It isn't the old country, he reminded her, where they could choose the marriage for their children. True, she said thoughtfully as she remembered their own choices, but you can never tell when two people will discover each other.

Another day when she returned the signed contract for the land to Rizzoti's office she hesitated at the door.

"Are you not going to marry some day, young man?"

He feigned a serious reply. "Only if I can find a nice girl, not before."

"You know I have three daughters not yet married?"

"Oh yes, I know all of them. They have all been into the bank at different times." He stood smiling, almost laughing.

"I think my fourth daughter would be a good wife to you. She is the tallest and you are very tall, too."

"Mmmm…I don't know." He nearly burst into laughter. "No, I don't think so. I think the youngest would be better for me."

"Roslyn?" No, no…I think she is too young for you. You would be smarter to stick with one of the others, one of the older girls."

"But I can't do that…I've already asked Roslyn."

"What? You mean for marriage? Are you making a joke?"

"No, didn't she tell you yet?"

"By heck, no, nothing, not one word. My girls keep big secrets from me sometimes. By heck." Danya frowned.

He pretended seriousness. "I thought you had much better eyes and had seen us together."

"For some things my eyes are perfect, but I didn't suspect my youngest girl would want to marry so early. When I saw you on the street together or in the drugstore with my daughter I could only think you found her by accident, not on purpose." She mused under a mild disappointment that the secret had escaped her.

"Do you give your permission for me to marry your baby?"

"Baby? My children never were babies after their first years." She shook her finger in a warning. "You should notice that my girls don't run to their mother for permissions. Each makes up her own mind, for good or bad. So you don't need my permission but my warning, young man."

"Warning? Against what?" His voice was teasing.

"I only warn you to be a good and strong husband because my girls are able to find their own way against trouble. If you cannot be a strong husband and keep ugliness and trouble away from my daughter she will be able to make her own way, and then for you it will be an uncomfortable life."

"I'm pretty aware of your girls' independence, but I'm sure I can handle Roslyn."

"Yes, you maybe can. I hope so. You are a very smart man I think. But remember to stay smart and keep a strong hand on your door."

"I will do that…but now, are you sure you approve me for a son-in-law?"

"Yes, you shouldn't worry about that. If I dug under every stone I couldn't find a better son-in-law."

"And Mr. Vorodinov?"

"He will be glad, too, because he worries that the girls will never find a husband who like the farm and the land. I will tell him only that your business in the bank is buying land and he will like you. I will tell him that your father was a farmer and that you are a farmer in your heart."

"Then it is all right with you?"

She shrugged light heartedly. "Of course. I could not choose any better looking one." She smiled, prepared to leave, then hesitated. "Are you not Catholic?"

"Yes, why?"

"My daughters are not raised Catholic, you know. Sometimes I don't like the rules made from your church. And also I cannot forget that when I was having all my troubles trying to get my children back, the Catholic church people were no help to me. Not one priest or nun would listen to me when I asked for their help, even to write a letter…Are you close to your church?"

"Well, I go often, if that's close."

"But will you allow a favor to me?"

"If I can."

"I would like my daughter to be married by our special minister, Mr. Dyson. He is like a shepherd to my family through all our troubles, and even all our happiness. He always has brought us out of our big problems. Roslyn was raised three years in his house, you know, and it would be a blessing on the marriage because he loves her like another father."

"Of course, if she wants to be married by Mr. Dyson I have no objections. I know she won't become Catholic, we've discussed that, so it's no problem at all."

"But you must make the suggestion about Mr. Dyson to her. I am sure she will not ask you away from your church unless you say something first."

He was agreeable. "It makes little difference to me. I'll ask her if it wouldn't be a nice honor to Mr. Dyson if he married us. Is that all right?"

She answered in a gentle voice. "Yes, but the honor is to you, my son, because he is such a special man in his kindness and his soul. From him will come the blessing on your life. You will learn that. So, good, I am very happy to know such news. I will run home now to tell my husband. Oh yes, you must ask for a piece of land as a present."

"Oh…well…but I'd better ask Roslyn first, don't you think?"

"No you must look at the land and choose it. That is better. A man should choose the first earth he gives to his family. My husband came alone to this country and found a good farm and gave us a good place to raise up a family. A smart bird knows the best place to build his family's nest. Come some day and look with me at the land and choose the piece you want for your own life." She left his office satisfied with Rizzoti's news and her discussion with him.

***

Arthur announced the coming marriage to the bank staff before it was in the newspaper. Angus Bent was dismayed, though he managed to offer good wishes without betraying any unusual emotion.

Bent sat back in his office chair staring at the closed door. There had always been the every possible threat that Rizzoti might come forward with an exposure of his role in the bank shortages attributed to Jordan Haig. He had borne the agonizing discomfort of the threat since Jordan's death, suffering day and night alone inside his exterior calm.

At times he had read impending exposure in the young man's cooler than usual good morning greetings. He suffered agonies of curiosity whenever Rizzoti's office door closed behind unknown visitors who appeared in any way to be possible state banking officials.

He offered his resignation from the bank. The board, men who had known him for years, begged and persuaded him to stay on since his retirement was so few years in the future. Rizzoti had been adamant too, insisting that he stay. Why, he depended on him, he said, there were so many things he still could learn from him about the mortgage and loan business. It raised Bent's ire. Perhaps Rizzoti wanted an eye on his victim, wanted him exposed to the world while he was still connected with the bank, active in business, when it would hurt more, might ruin him, destroy his wife.

Another thing, this marriage to the Vorodinov girl. There was no imaginable way to anticipate how much he would tell of the bank affairs. Men sometimes told their wives all sort of confidential business matters. If it once got to the mother, one word or suspicion of anything…Bent dreaded the possibility that after these seemingly safe years that the woman might have another reason to nip at his heels.

He had become accustomed to her bank visits. He simply turned his back to the door and became engrossed with the books behind his desk. He tried to avoid her on the street, and generally he was successful. He was aware of her pattern of shopping and banking, and had rearranged his lunch hour to avoid any confrontation. It maddened him that he could be pushed into the position, that she could thus force him out of life-long habits.

And he dreamt. He ached constantly in the aftermath of the dream. It often was so garbled he couldn't tell for sure the next morning whether he had dreamed of the witch or some other terrible thing. His throat felt raw and overused some mornings and he knew then that he had been used by this other person, this other body, that he had sung his way through the stillness of the night without a living soul's knowledge, and too often without clear memory of it. Only the aching stomach, the stinging throat.

He preferred those times to the vivid nights, if he could say preferred. He began to keep careful accounts of the times he dreamed vividly, noting exactly what he had done and eaten the day before, hoping that he might find a logical pattern that could be held to account for the suffering. It brought him no knowledge, and whenever he took a small coil notebook from his briefcase to make notations it served only to amplify the occasions of his dreams. They were written and chronicled in the notebook that he carried with him for fear Bertha might accidentally read what he had written. If he left his briefcase in the car or at the office when he went to lunch he would first remove the notebook and tuck it into his jacket pocket. He guarded the notebook more keenly than he did any other confidential papers. He wore it against his chest where the sudden awareness of the written words would bring sweat to his hands or a pumping coloring sensation to the flesh of his face.

Very casually he once mentioned to Bertha a wish to move from the town to a place in the south, Florida perhaps. She had not taken it seriously, but had been amused.

"Why Angus, I suppose you're remembering my indignation over last year's awful winter storms. But truly, I wouldn't ever ask you to leave our home and this town that you've loved and worked for, given so much of your time to. I love our home and our gardens and trees as much as you do, and there is nothing on earth that could pull me away from it all. Don't give it a thought. And you must remember, if you hear me scolding the snow drifts next winter it's done with love of the place."

"I had supposed, though, Bertha, that as we're getting on in years it might be more comfortable in a warmer climate."

"We're always so cozy in our own home; it's no bother to me, honestly, Angus." She touched his arm. "You have always been so thoughtful of my comfort, dear. I know you're happy here, therefore there could be no greater comfort for me."

The idea of moving stayed within his thoughts for many days, but it came to nothing after he felt thwarted by his wife's inability to sense anything else behind the subject. He knew, agreeing with her reasoning, that he loved his home and grounds. If she had been anxious to move he wasn't certain he could actually have gone through with it. From his youth he had not in the slightest way considered any other place as a possible home. Yet underneath it all was that damn woman. He'd leave Stanton, leave everything to get away from her.

DANYA'S PEOPLES

Bent took as personal affronts the assaults made upon his town by the foreigners moving in after the war. It was, he reasoned, his home, his family's home, a haven from the world's ills. It should somehow have been spared the changes.

Years after the first droves of foreigners had been assimilated there were the current problems with the displaced people of post-war Europe. The town, with its small factories, made a clear beckoning to the unskilled and unsettled immigrants, the DPs. And Bent found this infiltration as disagreeable as the earlier one of the nineteen twenties.

When his church took part in a program to help settle some of the DPs he was astounded to learn that the minister had approached Mrs. Vorodinov for help as an interpreter. He tactfully tried to convince the minister that because she was of another religion it might be awkward for her to work in their church.

"That's a logical concern, Angus," The Reverend Baines answered. But she's a bit of a liberal religious type, especially surprising for her foreign background. And of course three of her daughter are members of our church, as you must know."

"That's so, yet it could present difficulties if our church contributes to these people's settlement and she spends her time proselytizing in the direction of the Catholic Church."

"I doubt that she will. In fact some of the DPs are probably Catholic. And I've talked at length with her before asking the committee's okay on her participation. I'm sure in matters of the church she has no converting ambitions. On education now, she's altogether different." He chuckled.

"Is that so? In what way?"

"Yes. She has said we should make them learn English right away, even make it a stipulation, a must-necessary she calls it, in our offer of help. She says the greatest problems for her and her husband came from not knowing the language. She wishes someone pushed them to learn our language right away. In some ways I could go along with that."

"You can't mean it! Why she has the worst foreign accent I've ever heard. How can she teach English. Isn't that a matter of the blind leading the blind? Naturally it's important, I agree. But our church isn't an institution that forces anything on to people we want to help, Bart. It's differences like this we ought to consider before Mrs. Vorodinov takes part in our church program."

"You're far-sighted and sensible, Angus, but I'm certain in this case there will be no problems. Besides, she's the only person in the area who can act as interpreter. We have a professor who speaks German but he has no knowledge of the dialect or any Slavic language. As you may know most of the DPs come from those areas. We've had no problems in our first interviews. She has an incredible knack for interpreting, kind of interesting to watch, the way she uses words, English words...or I should say American words. If she doesn't know their actual language she can find enough words from other dialects that they understand. Rather impressive. Mabel O'Hare from the high school will sit in and help, especially with the pronunciation. She'll take over the classes when they have enough basic knowledge of English and go on from there. It really pleases me that Mrs. Vorodinov will give our church that much of her time. In fact, she's on loan, so to speak, to a church in Hartford until they find someone locally who will be able to help with interpreting."

"If that's the case I'll give my approval, of course. I'm sure it will work out just fine, Bart."

"Yes, I'm…I'm sure it will work out."

But Angus damned her every time the Reverend Baines told him of her progress. He damned her when she began leading the DPs into the bank. She led them in as though they were children. They came, paychecks in hand, and she showed them how to open savings accounts, told them about house mortgages, acting like a public guide through some sort of financial museum. She spoke to them in loud foreign words as though they were deaf, then she would turn her quiet voice on when she talked to the teller, to give the information needed.

Next she began to act as real-estate agent for some of them. Whenever she saw an empty house in the town she would race to the bank to ask her son-in-law if it was for sale. Or if someone died she'd be in the bank before the papers carried the obituary.

Many of the houses the DPs could afford were the small tumbling down homes no longer sufficient for more affluent owners. Danya would haggle over the price until she could get it down to the amount she knew her DP could pay. The owners were generally happy to rid themselves of the burdensome property taxes on unoccupied houses left to them by parents or grandparents.

Danya tramped over farmlands and woodlands with the hardier DPs to show them any saleable plot she heard about. Some small farms had stood unoccupied since the war when owners had moved to the cities for defense jobs and had not come back to Stanton. They had long despaired of selling the unheated old-fashioned frame houses with the now overgrown gardens and pastures. Danya would have one of her daughters drive her to these places so she could show them to various DPs. She explained which things would grow, how electricity could be installed, what a good place the country acres were for children. She always warned them to keep money in the bank, backing up her warning with stories of the welfare threat she'd experienced, if they could not care properly for their children.

If a new family had insufficient funds she would buy the house and rent it at the low rates of her payments. Some of the older unkempt houses of the town, meager stone or frame squares built badly long ago were salvaged for her Peoples, as she called those she had taken under her wing. The citizens who carried great pride in their town's appearance often were dismayed to learn that one of those shabby houses would remain standing longer than they had supposed. They would have preferred the unused building be destroyed to keep the town neat and pretty.

A black couple, African-Americans, moving out of the Hartford area, heard about Danya's ability to find low priced rentals. They were middle aged, had no children, and needed just a small place with little property to care for. Danya had bought a small house on the river street that had been empty for several years. None of her DPs liked it. It was just yards off the road, had a very small yard, and probably less than an eighth of an acre around it.

It was what the couple needed. When they went with Danya to the town law office to make the rental agreement the town clerk said there was a problem with the house, and she wanted to talk to Danya later about it. She reminded Danya that she could not rent to black people. That was an agreement the town had had for years.

She was taken aback. "In my days in this country I never heard such a thing. Maybe I should talk to my own lawyer to see why there is such an agreement."

The town clerk smiled. "We try to keep the town all white. It's better in the schools, you know."

"These are older people. They won't bother the schools with children."

"I'm sorry, Mrs. Vorodinov, it's an agreement. They might bring relatives in, things like that."

Thinking it over Danya decided she didn't need a lawyer. Instead of renting, which the town clerk said was not possible, she would sell the house to them. Then see if they could find a law against that. And she did. They went to the bank, she talked it over with Rizzoti, made the papers out for the mortgage and deed. It was done.

It was inevitable that some of these foreign families would buy a home next to an unhappy neighbor. Angus Bent hadn't even considered the possibility. He assumed they would always buy the places in the hills or the farmlands. The old houses along his street had belonged to the same families for generations.

Marvin Crayton who lived next to the Bents died. When his spinster daughter decided to sell the house and move to Hartford to care for an invalid aunt she approached her neighbor for help and advice in handling the sale.

Angus obligingly promised he would help with the sale. He suggested that it be placed with a good real estate agency so everything would be handled properly and Miss Crayton would not be required to make any trips from Hartford to show the property or spend any time in the care of it.

He talked to Rizzoti, asking him which agency had the best luck handling the nice old homes in the area. The house was over one hundred fifty years old and quite possibly much of the furniture to be included was of that vintage as well.

Arthur recommended an agency in another town that specialized in selling old Connecticut homes, promoting them as weekend country places for the harried New York city dwellers.

Danya saw the For Sale sign on that house next to Bent's as she walked one day to do her marketing. She crossed the street so she could have a good look at the information on the sign. Angus saw her from his window. He was walking toward the door to leave. He'd best wait. He saw her stand there some minutes looking at the house. Still it didn't occur to him that she could possibly consider the costly house for any of her Peoples. He gritted his teeth in anger when he realized he was thinking in the terms she used for her DPs. The Reverend Baines had told him, enjoying it as a joke, and now Bent couldn't shake if from his mind. Her Peoples, those foreigners who again threatened the dignity of this town.

CAUGHT

Two of the DP families pooled their savings and bought the house next to Angus Bent. He learned of it from Rizzoti one morning just after Danya and the two couples had left the bank, after the deal was done. Cool, calm, arrogant Arthur Rizzoti who gave him the information from some papers he had on his desk. Angus sensed that the young man enjoyed giving him the news. He couldn't read anything on his face, but he seemed to feign an extra seriousness that fanned Bent's annoyance.

That he, Angus Bent, should have those foreigners…two families in one house…on the edge of his property was more than he could bear. The Craytons would all turn over in their graves, he was certain, when those people came to take possession of their home.

That day he told Bertha they must plant some hedges along the property line. Something that grew very fast; arborvitae might be best, planted close together. He would have none of their nosy faces peering into his yard. Imagine, two families occupying the house built for only one family. No telling what they would do there, what they would do to the house, let alone the yard and the gardens that Miss Crayton had kept so beautifully. Three children in one of the families, Rizzoti had told him. They would certainly change the calm of the street.

Before Angus Bent had time to adjust to his new neighbors his past became a greater concern than his present neighborhood worry.

In the process of clearing the title for the Crayton property, Rizzoti had come across some discrepancies that went back to the Building and Loan Society books and had been transferred on to the bank's ledger very cleverly. It had not been disclosed in the former audit that was presented to Haig in the past. The manipulation of the figures went back to the 1930's when the Craytons had borrowed money for a new roof, and the installation of a new furnace and central heating. The incoming payments and the credit to their account over several years could not be reconciled. Though the records showed a payoff on the account, payments continued to come in from the Craytons. Somehow the money disappeared from the ledger records. Miss Crayton had never questioned her trusted neighbor. The initialed entries pointed directly to Angus Bent. It was not the perfect crime.

This time Rizzoti was in a position to pursue the issue personally. Before he approached Bent he ordered an outside audit, then conferred with the bank's lawyer who brought in the state bank examiners. It was, they all agreed, too serious and too obvious to be ignored. Rizzoti also convinced them that they should visit again the old records that had convicted Jordan Haig as the embezzler of missing funds.

***

There was a brooding quality to the air the day that Angus Bent came into the bank and faced the evidence spread out on his desk. The bank lawyer presented the facts of the case they had against him which was concurred by the examiner. Arthur stood by but did not enter the conversation. He would have liked to say "Gotcha!" but did not.

Bent listened intently without interrupting, trying to gather some words that could put a question on their findings. But he knew that the evidence they had in front of him could not be disputed. He asked to sit down. They gave him a chair, not his desk chair. He tried to speak but his voice betrayed him with that strange high squeak that always came when he least expected it. Without acknowledging his guilt he pleaded with them that he was unwell, that he was not himself at the moment. Stoic, calm, burning inside.

These were gentlemen. They considered Bent the same. Yet there was no possible way for them to excuse this crime that had gone on for years and at one time had possibly been responsible for taking the life of another gentleman, Jordan Haig.

As well, the bank's reputation must be guarded. It was the only bank in the town, relied upon for years by old-timers and now getting fatter thanks to the growing population of newcomers.

In the discussions following the accusations, Angus Bent was convinced by the bank lawyer that confessing to the embezzlement would be the only way for him to avoid a scandalous trial and the possible public exposure of the earlier Haig incident. The sensible way to handle all this, both for Bent's sake and the reputation of the bank, was a confession. By law he would face a year's jail sentence. At most it would be a small news item; he would serve a year at the county jail in Cullham and that would be the price he must pay.

Stone-faced he listened. He thought he might faint at any moment. His throat ached; he could not speak. It did not take him very long to agree to the solution presented to him. But...should he bring up Rizzoti's affair...and surely that woman was behind all this...it was after all her Peoples' buying the house that opened up the books. His words would not come. He felt caught in a reality much worse than the haunting dream that disturbed his sleep and his daylight thoughts.

It was all done quietly. Bent was allowed to go home to discuss this outcome with Bertha and to spend the night at his home. She at first wouldn't believe that he could do such a thing, but when he told her there was no doubt and that if he hadn't confessed there would be a scandalous public trial which would harm her as well, she understood and tearfully left the room, left him to sit there in misery.

The next day the bank lawyer went with Angus to the county judge, the case was quietly presented, and the judge's verdict was one year in the county jail.

There went Angus Bent, head unbowed yet with shame flowing through his veins, burning under his skin. Bertha did not accompany him. She said she would visit whenever she could get a ride, since she did not drive. He had shamed her, he knew. He also knew she was bound to him and would be loyal and never betray him with blaming.

The county jail was a large handsome gray stone building on the main highway cutting through Cullham. From the window of his cell Bent could look out at the country home for children where he had placed the Vorodinov children those many years ago. He asked for another cell. Nothing available at this time. He passed his days without looking out of the window.

Of course when the little news item was printed in the local paper it was the talk of the little gatherings in the downtown near the grocery store. When Danya heard that Bent was in jail for embezzling from the bank she could not contain her satisfaction. To the three men standing there in front of the A&P from whom she'd heard the news, she spit out the whole story of that Bulldog Bent who was dishonest from the time he was born, had stolen her children to cover his sins and now finally was caught by his bulldog tail and would spend his health in a cold jail.

She decided she would visit him. His punishment was not yet complete. She took the bus to Cullham, stood there at the jail and looked across the street at the county home for children. Her hate was still warm.

When the warden told Angus Bent he had a visitor he believed it would be Bertha, and he gladly found his way to the visiting room, sat down to wait for her. Aghast, it was Danya Vorodinov. He tried to rise from his chair and could not. Fear held him.

"Hello again my Bulldog," she said with some glee. She did not sit down. "I see you are now caught in your sins and are having a good time in the jailhouse with other crooks. Did I not curse you and say you would pay a price some day? So again, take my curse for you have not finished paying for your sins against me. Do not think God is finished with you!"

He found his voice, called for the guard who came and escorted Danya out of the building. She smiled at the guard, "You have a big crook in your building. Watch him carefully or he will try to steal the stones of your jail from under your nose."

The bus came, she went home and told Mikolai she had visited the Bulldog and given him another curse to help him suffer. Mikolai shook his head. He hoped that would be the end of listening to stories about Angus Bent.

PROGRESS AND PAIN

While Angus Bent languished in his cell, trying to keep busy with newspapers or books that his wife brought to him on weekly visits, the town he'd left behind kept growing and changing.

State engineers were seen surveying areas for the new superhighway that was to replace the now crowded two-lane route to Hartford and Middletown. The first reports in the newspapers published rumors that the highway might cut the town in half. From the map published with the story, homeowners, including the Bents, feared their home was in the path of the highway.

The rumors, the not knowing, kept the town in dithers for months. Several proposed locations were published before the final decision was made. It would skirt the edge of town far from the center.

The State took half of the twenty acres Danya had bought from the Hyland estate. At first she was angered that her piece of land could be requisitioned from her. One of her daughters convinced her that it was far better to have a few dollars to buy more building or residential land than to own those wooded useless acres.

"Maybe you are right, my daughter, it is better to be able to buy more land. But sometimes I think you do not understand. It is our land. I say why should we be forced to give up land we have bought and own?"

"For progress, mother. Besides, you aren't forced...well, in a way forced, but they do pay you pretty much I think for such useless land."

"No land is useless. Have you not all walked in those woods with dreams and secrets? Even your father has spoken with pleasure of the trees in October. Always in the future one of you can own the land and clear it for a house or for pastures, or even for gardens. No matter what is on the land, the land itself is never useless. You cannot make more. You shouldn't forget that."

"But there is plenty of other woodland around here you can buy for us."

"I suppose, I suppose. But I think some day you will know how it feels to belong to a piece of land. It will hurt your heart to think you must leave it or give it up to strange people, or to the state so they can make big roads for more cars."

She was thoughtful and continued. "Now when you are young you cannot believe this. You want to run away to college, to other places, to travel to other countries. But that is because in the bottom of your feet you know the land here will wait for you. That is why you feel hungry and safe to travel, because you know you can come back to your own land again. One day when you are all older and tired of looking from your eyes, your hearts will see what I am telling you now. You will come back to your own land, to this land that your father and I have marked out for you. You will see from your heart all the good places of your younger years, and you will never want to let the land go away from you, to lose it."

As she explained all this to her daughter, Danya had a wistful recollection of her own childhood in a place so far away in a past that she could not recall enough to describe it when her children asked. She remembered some songs, but she remembered clearly the rescue of the wolves and the laughing blonde boy. The suffering had been put to rest.

When the construction company started blasting into the stone ledges and cutting into the thick oak trees in the woods to lay out the highway, Danya stood silently in her house feeling some sadness creep into her heart.

Late one afternoon she told Mikolai she had heard them blasting over the hill. She said he ought to walk there to see what they were doing to their property. She would go tomorrow to have a look, not now.

***

During the year that Angus Bent was away, the local politics run by established men gave way to the Italians who were the largest group of newcomers: the selectman, the postmaster, even the head of the town services and the school bus company.

With the coming of the four-lane highway the town of Stanton began its move into modern times. The town was prosperous; the school classes were filled with children of immigrant European backgrounds who mixed comfortably with those of the old families.

Bent was released from the country jail exactly after one year. He was thinner, almost gaunt. He had paid his price. Or so he hoped.

THE VOICE

Bertha had worried about her husband's health while he was incarcerated, but he had insisted that he was just fine, although unable to get used to the small space and the sounds of the night. She convinced him that he should have a thorough check at the New Haven hospital.

As they drove home from the examination the gray atmosphere contributed to the man's despair as much as the news the doctor gave him. There would be tests to confirm it, but the prognosis was a problem, possibly a cancer of the throat, the larynx.

He simply should have gone sooner, he thought to himself. It would have been all right. But he just couldn't believe it was something like that. The dreams, he thought it was the singing in the dreams. He never imagined it could be something as bad as this. But he should have suspected; he didn't understand why he hadn't suspected something worse. The dreams were warnings, just warnings that all wasn't well. He should have talked to someone, Bertha, or a doctor…should have described his aching throat before this.

Since Jordan Haig's death years ago the dream had plagued Bent's sleep endlessly, deserting him to mornings that were as irksome as the nights. He couldn't remember in the morning whether the witch had worn the face of Danya Vorodinov, of

Arthur Rizzoti, of Haig or his wife Arliss. It was always the same full woman's body, and the same singing voice, but the face changed…or was it other dreams?

So warped and frightening had the specter become that in fear, lest he actually would sing out in his sleep, he took to a room of his own, explaining to his wife that she kept him awake by her restlessness and occasional dreams.

Perhaps if she had been surprised or questioned him, he might have then have told her about his dreams. No…he wouldn't have. It was too sinister, too strange a thing for a man to explain to his wife. She had asked nothing. He had explained no more.

As often with couples grown old and comfortable together the request for a separate bedroom stirred no emotions beyond a desire that the other should be pleased. Had they been younger she might have pressed for a stronger reason, and he might have told her. Theirs was not a relationship of passion and never had been. They were close because she accepted her marriage to this man who furnished a secure and respectable life. There could be no children from a union like this, Bertha realized early in the marriage. She accepted this as well.

As they drove home she wondered if she might have watched him more closely and would then have sooner suspected the stirrings of the malignancy he now faced. They would wait for the tests, hoping the outcome was not what they feared.

There were mornings when Bent's throat felt tortured with the songs he had sung in his dreams, times at breakfast when he could barely swallow, dared not speak, not sure of whose voice would come from his mouth. Odd he hadn't suspected something of the sort before. He'd been fairly diligent about his annual checkups he felt. Maybe he should have mentioned the dreams to the doctor long before. But then again, it wasn't something a grown man would need to discuss with anyone, let alone his doctor.

Twice at dinner one evening he endeavored to bring up the subject, thought better of it at the table and instead listened to his wife's concern over the storm windows and approaching early winter.

The frost had never come so early. The bleeding hearts were ruined, and the geraniums too, no doubt. Next year they should pull the pots in earlier, just in case. A shame about the hearts, too, isn't it? They've become so scarce around the area gardens. I daresay not a dozen gardens have them any longer. They don't fare well any more for some reason. They have such a pretty little flower...don't you think so?

He could hardly put together her sentences as she spoke.

After dinner he read, much later than usual, and as she said good night his wife asked if something had gone wrong that day. He seemed so far off. He couldn't answer.

The tests came back from the hospital. He told her. It was definite. The doctor thought the operation should be immediate. They could get a room in New Haven, he was sure. No, only the larynx. The cancer hadn't spread anywhere else so far as they could detect before the operation. It's been done successfully now many times...many times, the doctor said. Involves using a voice box contraption afterwards. Might make rather unpleasant sounds, not usually too noticeable.

Angus was downcast, Bertha could see, and tried to comfort him.

"Now, now, Angus, it can be hardly noticeable at all. Remember my friend Eva's brother? That wasn't such a long while ago and why, you would never notice a thing."

"That's true. Yes, I remember. Funny that I had forgotten it. You never noticed anything wrong. A strange voice, not objectionable though. That's all I remember…different from the one we were used to."

Bertha agreed. "Yes, just a bit strange at first. As though it were coming from someone else, that's all."

"What do you mean, from someone else?" He began to panic.

"Well, you remember, the vague little echo. Nothing too noticeable. You got used to it very quickly and never noticed it after the first time or two you heard him speak. Don't fret, Angus. If the doctor says it's isolated it's not as bad as it could be. We're lucky, very lucky that it's been detected early enough not to spread."

"Yes, but it's damn frightening, I tell you. A pity we hear so much about the disease. It rather takes hold of your mind, you know Bertha. Just seems to grip you, take over all your old thoughts, rubs them out so to speak."

"Of course. I understand. Why don't you move back into my room? I'll make up the other bed. You'll feel better near me than you would alone in your room thinking about it there by yourself."

He hesitated, uncertain how to reply.

"No, I shouldn't like to keep you up all night, dear. I'm restless and it will tire you too much."

"Why, Angus, one night's sleep lost is no worry to me."

"No, no…I'll read a while longer. It's best if you sleep well. I'll need you to be fit after my ordeal."

***

The operation was easy on Bent and successful. With grateful hearts he and Bertha were assured the cancer was isolated in the larynx and had not gone to any other parts of the body. They kept him in the hospital a week longer than expected only because he had some difficulties accustoming himself to the use of the voice box.

Despite three changes of mechanisms there was no way they could adjust the sound of the voice that came from the box when he spoke. It was of medium pitch, just high enough to be a woman's voice, with an echo surrounding it like a gentle wind. Even his flat Yankee accent couldn't cover the provocative, teasing cadence of the sounds.

The doctors were deeply sympathetic to Bent's reactions. It never is easy for a man to be dispossessed of any part of his physical being. This they understood and tried to show him from other cases. But as the days proceeded he seemed to fare rather worse than better, even, one of the nurses said, weeping after his efforts to speak to her. His own doctor who had known him for years began to sense other problems. When he suggested lightly that a few sessions with a psychiatrist might help his frame of mind, Bent protested so vehemently, urging his wife to stand by him, that the matter was dropped.

He was dismissed from the hospital with reservations by his doctor. He was told not to worry about his illness. The operation had been made early enough to arrest the cancer. He should get about and lead a normal life just as soon as he cared to.

It was the day he took the car out for the first time since his operation that Bertha discerned that her husband was afraid of something. She had convinced him one Saturday that he should get out and do the marketing. It would put him with people and because there would be a number of folks hurrying about they wouldn't stop him in a long conversation. That was a hardship for him even after the three months at home.

He was gone fifteen minutes, not long enough to market, when she heard the garage doors close.

He wouldn't explain the real reason. He said just that he hadn't felt like waiting at the store. The place was so crowded he'd decided he'd come back. He'd go another day.

"Dear me, Angus, you ought to have gone in, you know. It's been three months and you ought to get out and try to use your voice. Dr. Jones is so concerned about you, he must have told you that."

He broke in, the harshness of his outburst gentled by the light voice that came from him. "Bertha, please. You know I don't care to wait in the grocery store. It's nothing more than that."

"I'd be glad to go along with you if you would feel more at ease with me there."

"No, it isn't that at all." He was angry now and went on to explain further. "There were so many people waiting in line. All those women, you know, and their Saturday shopping. I just didn't want to wait there. There's so much talk and confusion."

"You could have spoken to some of them. You know them all, I'm sure, Angus, and I'm certain they would have been glad to see you out and about. Surely some of them are our friends. They know what you've been through."

"Yes, but she was there, standing at the door, just standing there staring at me."

"She? Whoever do you mean?"

"That Mrs. Vorodinov. Just standing there, staring at me."

"You mustn't mind that, Angus. She simply holds her grudges too long. It's to her detriment, not yours. She can't possibly matter to you, nor can she harm you."

"I can't anticipate what she'll say to me, that's the problem. And there were too many people around who might hear."

"How can what she says effect you? It can't matter at all what a woman like that says to you."

Now it was that she saw the real fear in his eyes as it spread into a quiver of his mouth.

"You don't understand!" the voice wailed. "She says strange things. Things that make no sense."

"Well, she is strange, Angus. You've said so often. But no one would listen to what she says. You know that too. "

"But I tell you, Bertha, people do listen!"

"What does it really mater? What can she say that would intimidate or hurt you? She's uneducated; you can barely understand what she's saying in her accent. What she says wouldn't make a bit of difference to anyone who heard it."

He couldn't be stopped. Words came faster, mixed by the little echoes from the voice box.

"You know what she does? She's done it before. She stands there staring at people, then she asks if they've been sick. 'I can see,' she'll say, 'you have not color in your soul now. You won't be here so long.' Oh yes, Bertha, everyone listens to what she says!"

"You're not making sense, Angus. What a dreadful and silly thing to listen to. She just isn't normal, that's all. She's always been strange, since she came to this town. Very different, we all know that."

"Except she has been right. George Colvane, for instance. You know how long it was after his accident? He'd been well for months. He saw her one day. Gave her a ride home from the town. He laughed about it the next day when we were talking after church. She had told him he had no color around him that he should get his business all together. And Monday he was dead. You remember that, don't you?"

"That's ridiculous. Such a thing is ridiculous, and downright sacrilege for you men to repeat after church."

"You say so, but after that there was Tuttle and his heart attack. She told him that day when he was up there helping during the haying. You recall his sister told us about it later? She'd told him his soul had no color. He died that week. Unexpectedly, too."

"Yes, yes. I do recall something. But it doesn't make sense to me. And it certainly shouldn't keep you out of the grocery store. You shouldn't let a woman like that intimidate you."

He kept on.

"And Angie? Didn't Steve say Angie had been told the same thing? And she broke her neck on the stairwell that next day. I tell you, Bertha, people listen, they do listen!" He barked out in a high wail, "She's a witch!"

His voice had strung out higher than she had heard it before. It bothered her that he was so greatly distressed over what she considered insignificant matters.

His pale cheeks had turned dull red with emotion. Sweat came along his eyebrows. His mouth quivered. Oh, she wished he could have his own voice back. That accounts for his upset, she knew. How very difficult for him to speak with that other voice. She tried to calm him.

"Angus, Angus dear, please, do calm down. She's no witch. All of those things are coincidental, that's all. In fact, knowing some of those people, they probably made up the tale after it happened just for the telling. You certainly didn't hear Steve tell the story before Angie died did you? Nor Tuttle either? No, of course not, you heard the tales afterwards. It's a bit foolish to give any credence to the truth of those tales."

He was resolute but now more controlled. "No, believe me, she is a witch. She puts some kind of curse on you or she reads the future. I don't know what it is, but she is a witch, I tell you!"

"You sound like a superstitious peasant, Angus. I'm sure the days of witches and their curses are history in some book of political expediency. You ought to be more sensible about this and not get such thoughts going around in your head. I'm so sorry you're upset. Perhaps it is too soon for you to go about. I'll make you some tea. Why don't you sit here and rest a while? Did you lock the garage or do you want me to do it for you? And Angus," she bent closer, touching his arm softly, "You are well and strong and whatever she might say to you wouldn't carry a bit of truth. It's completely insignificant."

Again he had a chance to tell his wife the entire story of his dreams, the voice, the eyes, and this last incident. It would have been so easy and much wiser to have told Bertha the truth long ago. Why, he wondered, could he not just tell her? Now, just tell her now. Why must he keep it inside himself and suffer with it alone?"

She was a witch. He was sure of it. Bertha didn't understand, didn't want to.

He had seen Danya standing there at the grocery store when he got out of the car but he was determined he'd make this effort to talk with people as Bertha and the doctor had pleaded he should. He could have walked past her without a glance. He could have gone along into another store except that she turned and saw him. She just stood there, waiting. That so familiar sure smile, lit by the strange dark eyes. He tried not to look at her, turning away. But she spoke.

"Aha, Bulldog, I should say hello right to your face today now that you come among people again."

He had wanted to get quickly through the door, but some women had stopped to talk. They must have heard. He tried to smile, nod and walk on. They were in his way. They didn't move.

She continued. "And to your face I tell you now, you will be punished for your ugliness and for your rotten heart. Your time in jail was not enough. Wait for the end. You will suffer and die like a dog for what you did to me and my family. Your time is short, I can see everything in your pale face."

It seemed to Bent that her broken, thickly accented voice had gotten so loud everyone in the store could hear her words. The two women stopped talking and turned toward him. Were they smiling? Or laughing? He knew they had heard. And the others near the door. He was certain everyone was looking at him now. They must all have heard her words, had seen him cringe.

In a kind of panic he had turned and walked quickly back to the car. He might have run, he couldn't remember for sure afterwards, thinking back. He had felt the heat of his face, the heat on his neck, across his back as she was speaking. He hadn't said a word, must turned and gone back to the car. Had he run like a fool? Is that what those people had seen?

No, Bertha was right. He was well. Other than the voice he felt perfectly all right. All the tests had been good. The doctors weren't worrying at all. He was cured, able to be out and about leading a normal life...Normal?

She hadn't said anything about the color missing, as she had in those other cases, just that he was pale, which is his normal complexion. Oh Lord, what a fool. He'd looked into the car mirror to see if the color was missing. He wouldn't let it get him. He would put it out of his mind, somehow. He must.

The dreams, though, they stayed. The hell. He couldn't control them. They hadn't stopped with the operation. He was so sure the dreams wouldn't recur after the operation. They were warnings, just warnings, weren't they? Why should they not leave him now? Now that he was well he ought not to have those same awful visits.

Still the dreams came. The witch came. She would toss her head, laughing. And come to take his body. Over and over again. It was so easy for her now. He never resisted. The anguish was always the same. He never resisted and still there was the anguish and the morning fear. It was always the same whether he gave in or tried to resist. She won.

He hated to go to bed at night because even if sleep came with it came the dream, again and again. He tried reading later into the night, chose books that should grip his mind; adventures, mysteries, anything. National Geographics with colored illustrations that might overtake the dream, or his illustrated books of the war. Nothing worked. Nothing could overtake the awful measured appearance of that dream.

The days slowed down, dragging toward the hours when he must sleep. He didn't want to be left alone during the day, and he cried inside with the fear of the coming nights. But he couldn't let Bertha bring a cot into his room as she wanted to do. He feared that even without his voice the secret might somehow be revealed to her while he slept and dreamed.

SPAIN

Early in December the Christmas cards came into the Bents' mailbox. A few friends from far off places, some distant relatives in Maine, a few business contacts who still acknowledged Angus despite his financial failings.

This year, a long note in the card from an English cousin of Bertha's. Ethel and her husband were living in the south of Spain. They had left England in August after Derek's retirement and had taken a lovely house near the sea. They were so sorry to hear of Angus' illness and prayed he was soon fully about. Why not, wrote Cousin Ethel, spend the winter with them in Spain? They had an extra room and the weather was a perfect delight, sometimes a bit too warm actually. It would be a good change for Angus as he recovers, and so lovely to see them both again after all these years. Do consider it seriously. They would be anxious for a reply saying yes.

With persistence from Bertha Angus agreed to take some of their savings and make the trip. Neither were good travelers, preferring weekend drives rather than long trips away from home. Bertha talked at length with the doctor and he, too, pushed the plan to Angus when he visited him for a check up. Everything was under control. Just some nervous strain that would benefit from new interests, a new place under the sun, just the thing, a trip like this. It couldn't be anything but good for

Angus, the doctor said. He suggested to Bertha that being among strangers might help Angus lose some of his reticence to speak, and for that reason as well he encouraged Bertha to persuade Angus to agree.

They flew to Spain after Christmas week midst threats of snowstorms and New England's whimsical winter weather. When the plane landed in Madrid they were both disappointed and surprised that the wind and cold had followed them. Yet the bright, teasing mid-day sun struck out against the clouds that looked as though they would bring snow. Surely there was no snow over here?

It was the next morning on the sleeping train that they awoke to the expected warm sunshine of the Costa del Sol. The sun coming through the train windows indeed was almost too warm, as cousin Ethel had written. They should have arrived at nine in the morning, but noticed that the train was already two hours late.

An English woman in the dining car noticed their concern over the time and assured them that one should never expect a Spanish train to arrive on schedule. "One should always have plenty of knitting and reading when traveling by train in Spain," she told them. There wasn't much to look at on this trip, why, of course most of it was overnight, but even now you could see there wasn't anything worth calling scenery. "That's why I take the night train. There is another, mid-morning or so, I can't remember. But this is so much nicer, since there's not much you'd miss."

She prattled on. "The towns are quaint, you might say, but you don't get a fair look at them going through by train. The area is all flatland, the Mancha they call it, something like that, can't be sure. It's in the guidebook. Much prettier when you get near the coast." She'd made the trip many times. "You can actually see the earth change color and you know you're getting close to the sea. Things just look better and you know you're getting near the end of the trip. You see there, the cactus? And the orange trees in full fruit? My, they are wonderful." Nothing ever tasted this good in London.

They arrived in Alicante three hours late, more worn down by the last hour's listening than by the long train ride. Ethel and Derek met them. The half hour drove along the Mediterranean highway brought them to Altera, the small fishing village where they had their home.

Before the tourists and sun seekers made the town their own it was for centuries a fishing village eking out a poor existence from the sea. Now the sun-weathered people shared the rebuilt streets with the fair-skinned Nordics and Germans who came bundled in heavy tweeds and fur coats to escape relentless gray winters. There were a good number of English, retired from service or jobs in Middle Eastern countries. They couldn't give up the winter sun to go back to the still smoggy UK.

What they had in common was that they were all strangers, homogeneous and unstrange to each other. By their clothes, their physical being, and their voices they stood apart from the native inhabitants. The gesturing Spaniards' song-voice and lisped words mingle with the almost secret sounds of English ladies discussing a new place for tea. Or the cool mannish sounds of Germans watching in amazement the bricklayers' progress with trowel and song, but no leveling rule. Here and there the Algerian French with their nasal sounds, lighter here, as though the sea and air have washed part of the words clear. And the infrequent American twang, a quaint surprise to those who can't believe that the sounds they hear on television westerns could really be in serious and daily use.

Here, when he spoke, Angus Bent's voice was noticed only as much as one would pay extra attention to another foreign sound the first times it is heard. Sensing this, it became easier for him to give a friendly smile and salutation to the casual friends of Ethel's and Derek's when they met on the street. He jokingly suggested to Bertha one day that they all take a Spanish language course so they could get about more easily in the market and shops. Derek's rejoinder, "For goodness sake, since so many of us have been here quite a while now I don't understand why more of the Spaniards aren't speaking English."

Within the week Bertha was convinced they had done the right and sensible thing. Angus chatted easily with Ethel and Derek. They hadn't seen Angus for so many years that they supposed his odd voice was an unfortunate part of his aging. Much of the time he seemed his old self, more so than Bertha could remember since before the operation. She felt easier and happy again.

The newness of everything pleased and stimulated Angus' curiosity. The four walked each day to the municipal Mercado where food and wares were sold in small stalls arranged in rows under a great roof. They had never seen such a colorful impact of fruits and vegetables. And goodness, all those sausages, and the flowers! Why, they had no idea there were so many they'd never seen or heard of.

Ethel and Bertha did the shopping and buying while the men followed behind. They stopped at the coffee stall, learned to drink the strong coffee with milk and sugar, exchanged pleasantries with their favorite poultry man or vegetable lady, dallied before the cheese stall discussing the merits of each new kind they tested. It was a leisurely stroll from the Mercado to the post office to pick up mail and stamps.

The formations of the hills piqued Angus' memory of the nearly forgotten geology course he'd had at college. He and Derek would walk along trying to recall the identity of various rocks and minerals. Their lives moved with a pleasant slow order, where the unfamiliar soon belonged to their daily habits and expectations.

The four strolled along the beach bulkheads before their late evening meals. Bertha couldn't believe they would ever come to such a state of affair when they would have dinner at nine in the evening. Sometimes if they walked after dinner they could see people in the sidewalk cafes having dinner at eleven or later. She was amazed.

After warm days the nights came cool and pleasant. There was always the gentle steady lapping of untroubled waves against the rock shores. Angus slept more easily after these walks, hardly able to recall the next morning whether or not his dream had come. He rested.

He felt an exuberance he hadn't known for years. His perspective changed for the good. He felt he had control of his mind again. A few times he considered telling Bertha about the dreams. They were no threat to him here, and in his refreshed humor he could make light of it. Then it would be told and done with. The depths of his fear had not been searched, however. Far below his good intention he found the same distress as before. He could not share the dread thing with her after all. Not even in this place where he was safe from those dreams, where he believed they had been shed.

The now routine days slipped into February. Both Bents were convinced that, as New Englanders, perhaps they had clung too long to the only place they had known. They could have sold Angus' business long before and traveled, and if they had known it could be so satisfying and attractive, they could happily have lived here in Altera.

Derek surprised them when he disagreed. His life had involved a series of moves, first of all because of the war, then later as a representative of an English firm with business on the Continent and in Africa.

"From my point of view this moving about so easily is behind the instability and the growing problems of our times," he ventured. His outspoken comments surprised even his wife. He continued.

"I rather envy you two, Angus. You who have lived your life in one home, in your own town, near old and dear friends. You know the language, the people of several generations. You can plan years ahead on such small secure things as new plants for the front yard. You've watched your own trees grow from saplings. You paint your house and clean up the garage knowing you'll be there years on to enjoy it all. Oh yes, even to do it all over again. You know your grocer, your doctor. You read the same familiar newspaper year after year. You pay to have your streets paved, the town hall repaired. It all belongs to you and becomes part of your bond to the human race."

No one interrupted.

"With Ethel and me the hardest decision was the first move. It was after the war...I actually mean our first freely chosen move; can't count the moves we made because of the war. You see, everyone by then was accustomed to an upset in their lives, after the war. Children had been sent all over the place to keep them out of bomb's way, as you must remember. Ours had gone to Canada. When I took the job I knew it meant moving. It was all rather exciting, for me at least. Ethel wanted to settle down with the children and keep house. Which we did, mind you, for about eighteen months...wasn't it, Ethel? I had started my own little roots there, too, though I didn't realize that when I planted them what it really meant to me. I'd wanted a greenhouse since I was a boy. The one I had was keen, built it myself. It was just what I'd dreamed about, and I'd spent hours searching out just the right seeds for new plants..." He hesitated, then went on.

"It was rather difficult, as I say, the first move down to London. Not far at all to an American, I suppose. To us it was. It meant pulling up roots that hardly held on to the earth. We found, sadly enough, that once the first move was behind us the next one hurt less. It felt a bit more exciting each time. A challenge, even with the two children, though they had a few problems being constantly thrown in with new friends, new schools, even new languages after a while. The next move was a game, and the next and the next. It's all very easy after a while. Moving becomes the essence of your life, and before you know what's happened to you, you've lived your life, are ready to retire and you can't find a place you call home. I confess it left me rather empty. Someone asked me one day, what place do you call home. I had to say: I have no home, I travel. I couldn't believe how deeply that answer would strike me…"

"Not that we haven't had a good life; interesting places and so many friends. But you can't take them with you each time you move. They become characters in a good book you'd like to read again if you have the time…which you never do, since there's always another book, so to speak…And it's the same with most of us foreigners living here now. Don't believe we're all running from snows or fogs or demanding children. It's more accurate to say we've just come to another of our stopping places. Probably the last for many of us, alas. I like to think when I water the plants each morning that someone, after I'm gone from here, will know that I've lived here and worked the soil. But there'll be people here after we're gone, just like us, taking a few minutes of the day to search for their own roots in the earth, probably never a thought about who went before them."

He was silent. He pushed his hand through his thick straight hair, disturbing the neat part. For moments no one else spoke until Ethel said, "I see now how strongly Derek feels about this. I think he only mentioned it when his retiring time came and we had to decide where we'd settle afterwards…but dear me, he's never gone on so before."

She smiled, somewhat embarrassed. She was a kind-faced, nondescript woman, save for the large blue eyes that always seemed to have more life in them than the woman showed outwardly. She smiled at her husband, then turned to Angus.

"After we got here the first thing I wanted of course was some furniture. Derek couldn't keep me out of the antique shops. They're lovely here, such nice things, though you can't know for sure if some are copies. I understand they sometimes take wood from the old buildings and copy old designs, calling them antique, which in a way they are. The Spanish artisans are quite good at copying antiques and they do look truly authentic. No matter. Well, Derek was so exasperated while I puttered about he said, 'for heaven's sake, you don't think you're going to plant roots by surrounding yourself with a lot of old junk, do you?' It was quite a joke for us when we looked at it that way, wasn't it Derek?"

"Yes, saved us a pound or two as well. You can't start a home plot at the end of your years, so you ought not to spend your last energies trying. Just enjoy the life that is left to you, that's the way I finally have to think."

"We mustn't go on like this, Derek. Angus and Bertha will be homesick for their own home, and we do want them to stay and be comfortable as long as they can. Oh dear, we have gotten a bit sentimental. Forgive us. But you see, it shows you how comfortable we feel with you both here. Or we wouldn't be so relaxed and so full of reminiscences…"

Bertha broke in. "No, no dear. It's not like that at all. We haven't thought about home at all. This has been a grand change for us, a wonderful change for Angus who has worked so hard all his life. We ought to have done it a long while ago. It's done a world of good for him and we do feel so at home with you both."

Angus agreed. Then slowly, trying to control his voice, he tried to find words for his thoughts. "There's a difference though, in America. It's true we ourselves have stayed in one place, one home. We have our wonderful home, which was my family's house, too, and I can trace my family back to Salem…to old

Massachusetts. I can see the house and the land they owned there that is still cared for by some distant relatives. I could buy the house and land, too, I suppose, if I wanted to be there. But since the war, it's the things happening around us that make us feel less grounded, threatened in the same way you describe, as though our land is being taken from us…"

Bertha wanted to stop him. He went on.

"All those unsettled people of Europe have rushed to our land and I think, rather than find security or plant their roots, as you say, they have threatened our heritage, our way of life. They come to our country and before they learn the language or the laws they buy a piece of land. I can't tell you how many of the big farms and estates have been butchered so these peoples…er…people can have their little piece of land. It's the DPs, you know, the displaced people from the war camps, the slave labor. Great many of them in our area. When you see your neighbor's place inhabited by such strangers a month after he's died it gives you quite a start. Certainly it gives you the feeling that you're in a temporary place, waiting for the next owner to arrive. You've tended something for most of your life, and tomorrow when you're gone, unknown people with odd names will take over the house, your gardens, plants, trees, everything. Even the beds we sleep and die in. In a year your days on earth aren't even remembered by the trees you've put into the earth with your bare hands."

"Yes, yes, I can understand that," Derek added, "but if you think of those who have been dispossessed of their lands without choice, lands that their own families have had for generations also, you can understand their hunger for a piece of land of their own. There's a good example of that here. Well, one good example, and probably many others similar to it if you asked about." Derek turned to his wife to see if he should go on. He did.

"A German chap, I know you've seen him about. Rather tall, nice-looking, has the black eye patch, eye missing from his chemistry school days. You recall seeing him? I spoke to him one day at the café while Ethel was having her hair done. I asked him what he was doing here. Too young I thought to be retired...and certainly not one of those old Nazi immigrants who hide out in their vincas and never come to town."

"The German answered, 'I have come to this place to begin my past.' I thought either he was talking in Zen riddles or had confused his English. But he meant exactly that. His grandfather in the first war and his father in the second war, lost their homes and lands in the settlement of the German boundaries. He himself had started a home and lost that too, when Germany was divided. For twenty years now he has tried to build a life or to find roots, from nothing. He's looked for twenty years for a way to begin a life he said, until it all ended a year ago with the collapse of his business and subsequently his marriage. Of course he sees these as losses, too. But the fact that he could find no place to plant his roots, to attach himself to something that had gone before, that's what haunts him most..."

"I asked him if he had misgivings about this living away from his country, about leaving his homeland...you know how the Germans are supposed to be about their fatherland. He said no, he had found no roots there. He could build no roots there in one generation, he said. He felt no more kinship to that land than to any other. The roots are not made in one generation and only when you can say this is the land of my father's father, and their fathers before them; that is what stabilized a man and roots him to his country. He believes he could find that here, the same beginnings in this ancient place as he could anywhere in his native country."

"And that, Angus, could be why those DPs you speak of in America buy the pieces of land and the old houses as quickly as they're emptied. The German chap explained it this way. Rather than buy just land, empty land, which is actually readily available, he's dickering for that piece with the ruined old farmhouse on the road to the mountains. He wants to preserve all that's left of the house. He wants to rebuild it and build around it. He wants to keep the old trees, the ancient and crumbling cactus, to put new life into the whole vinca. The roots are there, laid out by some one before him who may have felt the same way you feel about your place, Angus. And that's how this displaced German will find the beginnings of his past. Do you see?"

He could not stop. "And he believes, too that there, with the land under his feet, he will be able to bring together the fragments of his family and graft them back like a single tree to grow with the stability of the land. If he could do this that he dreams of, if he could take that ruined house and unused land, seed the earth, preserve its water, establish a home for living things, then he would find his past, his roots. Then, he said, the earth would give back its song."

"It would have been a blessing to us to have thought and felt these things when we were young and able to give the knowledge to our children. But we moderns are scattered now and it's too late. I think sometimes if we had stayed there in one place our life might have turned out so much better..."

"Derek!" his wife interrupted sharply but quietly, "Don't put the blame on that. Circumstances can't be changed. What's past is done..." She smiled. "Let's have tea now, shall we, and take a walk before dark. The wind is coming up this afternoon and I think the sea is so pretty with the breakers."

Derek pulled himself into a lighter mood and in an amused tone said, "She insists that these swollen little waves should be called breakers, though I'm positive they're not...nothing like what we've seen in the Atlantic or the North Sea. I suppose you've had some good ones there in America, too? There on the Long Island Sound, isn't that what you call it, near your place?"

AGONY

That night, for no apparent reason and without warning Angus came down with a cold. He stayed in bed the next day, insisting that the others go to market and the post office, that he was content to stay alone and read.

He complained that afternoon of stomach cramps from the Spanish paella they'd eaten the night before. He had never liked seafood and every time he ate it his stomach bothered him. For the days he nursed the cold he was also miserable with the upset stomach, retching after his small meals and running a slight fever. When Bertha wanted to call a doctor he insisted that it was all due to the cold. And when it had run its course his stomach did behave normally.

Days later he vomited blood, but it easily could have been the wine from the evening's meal, so he decided not to mention it. He had never touched spirits before and at his age he reasoned it was not wise to become a drinking man.

The pain began to waken him in the gray stillness of pre-morning, at first chafing and irksome, gradually sharpening until he could not excuse it away as inconsistent attacks from bad food. He had to tell his wife. He couldn't hide any longer the agony of what he assumed was happening.

Derek drove them immediately to Alicante to the hospital where they waited three hours for a doctor.

Bent was morose, frightened as a man would be who is convinced he might be counting the days to his end on earth. The awful sensation that he couldn't control his bowels, or that he might vomit in the waiting room was a cruel embarrassment to this proper and fastidious man.

He read the anxiety in his wife's eyes. He could say nothing to console her. What was unsaid between them was known and already accepted in their hearts. The moment of mortal separation confronted them. There were days left, weeks, maybe months before it would be done. They could never speak of it. Only comforting words could be spoken. No truths or fears. That was the manner of dying properly. Feelings must be spared. Grief understood, not voiced. Close the door, don't bother the neighbors. Suffer in silence. Suffer alone.

This once dignified white haired man sat like a stoic while excruciating pain explored the vitals of his body. At moments he fancied he would like to drop off into his dream and actually leave this body, to watch it from afar where he could feel none of the pain. Let the witch possess it now, let her have this dying decaying mound of flesh he had carried through seventy-two years of earthly existence. He willed the body to her in a strange silent curse as though he could, by doing such, pass over to her this hideous surprise. She would be left with nothing. Her victory over his flesh would be her undoing. She would rot with it in the earth long after he had floated away.

He closed his eyes while they waited for the doctor. Bertha touched his hand with hers and kept it there, cool and ageless, he thought, like a woman's hand should be remembered. But he wanted to scream out, 'Don't, don't touch me! Can't you see it is only putrid flesh that was once your husband. Take your hand away. Don't look any more. Don't touch my body. It is too ugly. Clean you hands!' The thoughts went round and round in his head, pounding at his skull, trying to come out into words. He said nothing aloud. He dared not.

The thought of his body going to waste repulsed him, choked his breathing. The antiseptic smells of the waiting room, which had been barely noticeable when they arrived, enveloped him with a stench of death and wet rotting dung. Memories from his days in the trenches of the First World War returned more real than they had been in the happening. Dead flesh. Swollen limbs. Dried blood. Vomit. Nobody cared. You walked right over those nobodies. You were still alive. You were still living…then. No body. If he could leave now and have no body. The dirty words he'd heard came back to him, ran through his thoughts. The perversities he'd seen. The depraved thoughts passed through his consciousness like a silent movie reel at breakneck speed. The sights and memories accused and sickened him, all in silence.

His wife's quiet voice rescued him from the tortuous depths. "The doctor is here, Angus. You can go in now. Derek and I will wait right here. Have the nurse call me if you need me or want me with you."

They stayed in the city three days waiting for the report on the tests. The doctor talked to both of them when they returned to his office.

His lilting Spanish voice speaking English gave to the situation an aura of a stage play where the actor playing such a serious part had been badly cast. He was young, not much above thirty years. His black eyes were quick and sharp, warmed now by the compassion a virile healthy man must feel when he speaks to an older man about dying.

The almost delicate hands that held the reports he read angered Bent. How can you know, he thought. How can you, still wrapped in the skin of your youth, read the words that will separate my soul from my body? He thought he cried the words aloud. He thought he heard his old voice saying the words aloud.

He turned his head slightly to see if Bertha had heard. She smiled faintly and sadly. He had imagined it. He must listen now to the doctor, pay attention. He sighed. Bertha sat so still, her hands folded over her purse. She looked at that moment so very old. She will be alone and grow older, he thought. She had seemed so much younger until these hours.

***

The tests affirmed that the cancer had spread beyond control. They could offer only vague hope through cobalt treatments, but it would be false of them, two doctors agreed, to advise it. The pain could be compounded by the treatments, and it would mean moving Mr. Bent to a Madrid hospital. The doctor felt this was unwise, untruthful and an expense he could not justify for them unless they insisted.

Angus wanted Bertha to speak for him. She must help him now. He felt alone, isolated already from these living persons only a few feet away from him.

"Do you mean there is nothing we can do? Isn't there an operation that can help my husband?"

"It is not advisable. It is too late. I must be honest."

"But there are drugs. I know in the United States there are new drugs. Do you think we should go home right away? Would it be better for him there, would there be more hope?"

"Yes, there are drugs." The doctor spoke slowly. Angus watched the man's dark eyes as they looked straight at Bertha. Soft, sweet eyes, like Rizzoti. Looking at women sweetly, so full of trust, like Rizzoti.

The doctor continued. "The drugs are effective, frankly, only for keeping the person comfortable. We can prescribe the same drugs here. We can care for Mr. Bent in the hospital here, and I strongly advise it. A trip now is too difficult and extremely uncomfortable for everyone. I understand that you would like to be in your home, but I advise against it, for both your good."

They spent a half hour talking with the doctor. The arrangements were made. Angus Bent entered the hospital that same evening.

He was weary. He though he would like to end his time at this moment. Now, so Bertha could be spared the waiting. He submitted to the sleeping pill but could not keep it down. The nurse gave him a hypodermic and he remembered the easy lapping of the Mediterranean Sea as he sank into darkness, thick turquoise, dull blue, black. Nothing.

***

Doubly dying he went to the depth of imagined hells. By day he was conscious of his body's deterioration. The groaning, swelling complaints that showed in the formations of the flesh. By night his soul was taunted with the dream. Constant, pitiless, changeless. The same surrender, again and again. And he watched from above, watched his grotesque body taken over by this strange dark-eyed phantom. And now as he watched, he could still feel the pain.

The increased dosage of drugs gave no relief from the pain nor the knowledge of it. He prayed he could die. He wrote to Bertha in an unrecognizable script that she must pray for his death. When he handed the paper to her he looked at his dying fingers and wept. The dehydrated skin hung so loosely from his hand and arms he could see the sharpness of the bones underneath. He was aware of it all, as if his eyes were watching another's body. Except that he could feel every bit of the pain. It was his body, not someone else's. He could not get rid of it. Here it was, waiting, unwanted by himself, unwanted even by the old grim reaper. But claimed and then discarded every night by the witch as she smiled and sang.

His gums shrank into lifeless skin that once had formed his cheeks. He could no longer use his false teeth, but in a last vanity he kept them at his bedside in case he had visitors, someone from home. In case he felt better tomorrow and could eat.

His glasses hung from the gray flesh of his nose. Eyes which could no longer focus looked through them. Why couldn't he die? Why should he stay longer to know this ghastly world? How long could he bear this pain?

He thought of love and hate, good and bad, God and the devil. But they were all mixed up somehow. He couldn't identify anything. Every thought was so warped by pain he couldn't call up the feelings he searched for. Love was ugly and hate felt good. Evil smiled at him and God's angels brought him more pain. The devil caressed his shoulders while his good wife watched laughing. Was she laughing? Bertha why do you laugh? No, she weeps. She is weeping. Rocking and weeping. She is leaving him. Again and again she goes, leaves him alone with the pain. One day he will surprise her. One day he will leave while she is still there.

The person of Angus Bent stayed to suffer until the body died. He was not blessed by unawareness or coma; he could not be released by drugs. His being clung to life as though willed to consciousness. He moaned, he screamed in the night begging the witch to take his body. He knew and he didn't know. Then, finally, in a scream of pain, he was gone. He died cruelly.

THE CEMETERY

In this land that Angus Bent had come to, the dead are buried the same day that death comes. Ethel and Derek made necessary arrangements, sparing the tired and exhausted widow the needless worry of petty decisions on trappings of the last rite which says in vain, to the world, 'Look, look, I have been here.'

There are no places for burial of non-Catholics in this land and Derek quickly realized would need to fib to the priest to have Angus buried in the town cemetery. "Yes, he was a Catholic, but he strayed, Padre."

Their last good memories had been there in the village by the sea. Bertha was sure he would have liked to stay longer. He wouldn't mind so much, not so very much she thought. It would be all right to have him buried there in Spain, in the sun.

The hilltop cemetery separates the cloistered white adobe town along the sea from a green-splotched valley that continues into shallow mountain ranges and blue skies beyond. Houses so new they haven't settled into the pale sand are perched on the rolling valley slopes, placed near pine trees which give shade in summer and whistling company to winter breezes.

Along stony beaches the new skyscrapers are incongruous modernities against the crumbling adobe buildings of the old town that they obliterate with their shadows.

To this ancient, sunny edge of Spain have come today's invaders, the retired folk of Europe and the rootless younger, artists and young families, who can follow climate or enterprise like a new breed of nomads. Racy sports cars must give way to man and burro who share the same newly paved road and who may, in fact, be neighbor to a sophisticated apartment house over the hill.

Since the days of the Armada the great forests are absent from areas of the land, giving the infrequent torrential rains centuries of freedom to steal the living soil and rush it to its final fate, the blue Mediterranean. The arroyos of the hills and sharp cliffs at sea edge, intriguing to an artist, look to a hungry man like the dried, white breasts left on a picked chicken after someone else's good meal.

There is a mystery to the land, enhanced by the sight of things growing in unexpected dry places. No elaborate irrigation system brings water to the fields and groves and the troughs made in the fields by man and burro look long dry. Yet ripened citrus hangs on dust covered trees. Brilliant pink geraniums grow wild beside the highway, their breath half-squelched by the dust thrown from passing cars. Almond trees spring forth with blossoms so profuse and early that a sane man must say it's not possible; they do not understand the laws by which they are fed.

Then the big rains come. The leaves are washed and roots of trees are laid bare. The rivers of sand hurry by. The earth rushes to the sea.

All the colors that once were hidden in dusty stones appear after the rain washing. Glistening streaks of quartz in grape-stained nuggets, deep golden freckled egg shapes veined with mica crystals, rust fragments smoothed against moss toned cones or amber crescents, rose and lavender so vibrant they ought to give up the perfume of flowers. The stones spend their last hours in vain resistance, blend and finally are gone into one final beige form, the sand. Into the sea. Here, in this vibrant land, Angus Bent could see no more.

***

Past the poverty and the beauty of this land the two black cars wind the long mile up the narrow dusty road to the cemetery. The paths were meant for beasts. Here the cars must curve and dip slowly to avoid the hazards at each corner.

The white walled cemetery stands larger than it looks from the town below, like a minor fortress from another era. The cars stop, the hearse in front of the open iron gate and the widow and others walking behind. There is some confusion until she realizes they must wait for the priest.

A burro loaded high with twigs shuffles head down toward the two cars. The half-sleeping rider, a browned and deeply wrinkled man, sees the shiny hearse and with a small gesture lifts his black beret to the widow.

The priest arrives in a small car that precedes the gray dust that puffs out from under the wheels. He is tall, tanned from the winter sun, dressed in a long black cossack which shines in the slanting light. He nods to the hearse driver and speaks in Spanish. They go through the gate. There is some chattering and in a minute three workmen come to join the driver as pallbearers.

Angus Bent is carried by strangers in a strange land to his final earthly resting place.

A few words are said in a language his widow does not understand. Then the casket is raised by four men to an oven-like brick chamber, the fourth and highest in a row of chambers like those found in underground crypts. The grunts and quick words of the Spanish workers as they try to push the casket into its place crackle the utter silence of that warm afternoon's ceremony.

As the widow is about to leave one of the workmen hands her a portion of flowers from the casket. She holds it for a second, wondering, then with a faint smile of thanks hands it back. The large wreath and all the flowers from atop the casket, the last living things that will accompany Angus Bent, are stuffed into the cubbyhole with the casket. It will be sealed off later by the impersonal mason's hands of this foreign grave tender.

The priest is anxious to be about his day and steps quickly along the concrete path, past the oven graves, past vibrant geraniums, around an olive tree trimmed to the shape of a cross, through the iron gate, into his car. He leans out to shake hands with Mrs. Bent, starts his machine and drives down the hill leaving gusts of gray dust.

As the Widow Bent is driven from the cemetery she turns to smile at the black haired young girl sitting against the cemetery wall. How alive and unsad the sounds, the wonderful strange wild singing sounds of these dark-skinned people, she says to Derek and Ethel.

The black-eyed girl watches the cars disappear down the sharp hill. She continues her song, smiling, and a gentle teasing wind takes the notes and carries them over the cemetery wall, through the olive cross and shimmering cypress tree to the newly buried soul beyond.

EMPTIED

One of the girls read the news in the local newspaper.

"Mom, Mr. Bent died."

Danya's heart began to churn. "Oh yes? What does it say?"

"Just that he died of cancer. Somewhere in Spain."

Danya was overtaken with emotion and it showed immediately on her face. Her heart was hammering against her chest. She expelled a full breath as though a weight had been taken from her. "Good, finally. I'm glad. I hope he died like a dog, the ugly animal!"

"Oh, Mom, you shouldn't be glad when someone dies. It's not nice."

"Nice? Not nice my daughter? Yes, it is nice. It is nice when a devil's workman leaves this earth. It would be nicer if he had gone years ago. But then he wouldn't have suffered so long. I am happy, I am glad as I can be, that my enemy is taken off this earth to hell!"

"Oh honestly, Mom, you shouldn't hold a grudge like that. Even if he once did something against you, or if he did bad things at all, you shouldn't be the one to judge him."

"Oh, I do not judge him. God made the judgment against him a long time ago when he gave him his face. All his ugly deeds and his ugly mind showed in his pale face. And I tell you, God judged him when he gave him his disease, when he lost his voice and had to speak like a woman. And in the final judgment I hope he died in pain. I hope his heart broke in pieces like he broke mine. I hope his tears burned his body. I hope he screamed in his pain so he could hear himself suffer. I hope his guts came into his mouth so he could taste the hate I have for him!"

Her passion filled the room where they sat at eventide. The other girls heard their mother and came in from another room.

"What's the matter Mom? Did something terrible happen?"

"No, something wonderful. Old Bulldog Bent died at last. I have lived to see my enemy go to hell."

"That's too bad."

"Too bad? Don't you understand my daughters? That evil man took my children from me. He kidnapped you all from your own house. He is your enemy, too." She opened her palms out to them for understanding.

"But Mom, that was a long time ago."

"But my broken heart could never measure the time. So long as he stayed on earth my heart would not heal."

"Well now you ought to be able to forgive him, or at least forget it, Mom."

"Never! If God wishes to forgive him, his soul will know of it. But as he lived he was my enemy. Now in death he is nothing to me. There is no one I must forgive. I will hate forever what he was, what he did. I will hate always his sin against me and my family. Now on earth he is nothing, not a grain of sand or a drop of water. Nothing. There is no one to forgive."

Exulted she turned from the girls. Her face was flushed, her eyes bright. She felt relieved of a burden she had carried for so many years. Yet as it left her it moved through her body with odd sensations of hot and cold, tightening and loosening its grip around her heart, in her throat.

Each time she had walked past his house she had silently cursed him. It had become her daily task, a ritual. Any time she saw him she repeated the same curse, glaring at him. She expanded her curse when she had visited him at the hospital and at the county jail. She knew he tried to avoid her many times on the street, turning his eyes and looking past her. She could always tell by his pallor, by the way he held his head away from the direction he was walking. He knew his enemy and was afraid.

The girls didn't understand. They would know more when they raised their own children. Then they would understand the depth of the crime Bent had committed against her family. They were still young, too young to walk with her feelings in their hearts. When they were older they would know what it is to lose their children. They would understand her then.

She would like to sit alone. The girls sensed it and made their goodbyes, going off to husbands or friends.

Now her mind was hers alone. She sat relishing the immense freedom from some mortal danger that she had allowed to inhabit her mind. Hers alone. Gone was the constant pressure of her living hatred. It seeped away like water through gravel, disappearing to where she did not care.

When once her thoughts were constantly interrupted by stabs of hate there was now clear passage. Each thought could take its full time, as much as it needed to be disposed of or digested and understood. Finally there would be time to savor all the subtleties of a single thought without that nagging presence of remembered hate. This relentless essence could no longer twist or change or harden the interiors of her private mind.

She realized now how often her thoughts had been severed in mid-making since those tragic days when her earthly enemy showed himself by his cruel deeds. All the exposed ends of unfinished thoughts had roamed about her mind, touching, twisting, changing the direction of her happier feelings. Now everything was clear to her.

She sat for hours. She was reluctant to move from her chair. She sat there in the kitchen with her hands folded in her lap. She was overwhelmed with the swift images that sprang around her. It was as if a great dark cloud had gone away. The wheel of life they talked about on the radio was turning faster and faster, no squeaking now, no muddy road, no heavy cloud sitting on her head.

Her mind was young again. Was this the feeling to be born again? She felt new energy, new awareness. Like a young woman. Like a girl. Was she ever a young girl? Was something taken away, she wondered, or was something given back to her? Was God giving her the youth she had lost? She looked at her creased face reflected in the window and smiled at the thought. But inside, inside she had become a young girl again. She could remember that much clearly, how it felt to be happy and young in your heart.

She had to acknowledge that there was now a great empty place in her heart, the way it feels when you are young and yearning for unknown worlds. She felt she must look now to find a way to fill the empty place. Her heart must be filled. She would be more careful. Such a destroyer as Bent would never reach her again.

Everything seemed good, after all those years of carrying her burden of hate. Now anything good could happen. Forgotten wishes and dreams danced around inside her senses. She would throw none of them away. She would put every dream to work. They would all become reality.

Something should happen. Her world had changed. Surely there was something to which she could put her new energies and her hopes. She had not thought ahead about how she would feel given this strange gift. All she knew was that she had hated that man. She had never supposed how it would feel to be emptied of that hate. It was a staggering loss, a fantastic revelation of her inner feelings. But yes, it was a gift that she could feel in every heartbeat.

She was as though unemployed. Hating Bent had been the major job she had given her battered heart so long ago. Suddenly by one minute of news she was freed from the battle. She must use her energy better now. She must find something bigger to do.

There was little more she could do now for her family. They were all grown, independent and capable of handling their own families and adventures. She had turned them that way so they would never need help from the Bents and the welfares, never need help even from her, not more than what a mother gives without the asking. She was satisfied with the way she had raised them. They had never shamed her. But it meant that now they would have no use for this great need that was bubbling out of her. Reverend Dyson had said they would come back to be her own children and now when they were grown she knew by their ways that he was right, they belonged to her. And to Mikolai.

She would not alienate them. She would find other ways to use her new life and energies.

The knowledge that there was no one like herself ran through her mind. This was what she had tried to teach the girls when they were younger. Don't expect people to understand you in everything, she had told them. Don't expect everyone to see through your eyes, to see the same revelation of heavenly things in the clouds or feel the same power given by another's presence. What you accomplish can be someone else's impossible task. Look for your own gifts from God and use them. Don't make your path from another person's light. Each one is different. Don't look to your neighbor or your sister in jealousy. You must make your life from your own heart and hands. Don't spend your time explaining why you do something or try to see yourself from other people's eyes. They have their own nervousness and troubles. You should not bind yourself with their opinions of you. What does it matter if someone says you dress funny or talk funny? If he dies the next day what difference did his opinion make?

If he dies the next day…but she no longer had to think about him. He was dead, gone. In her past she would never be rid of him or the hatred of him. But she would live her future life free of him. Now she understood keenly all those truths that she had given in words to her children.

Now she was responsible to no one but herself. Her children were raised to find the rest of their way without her, that she knew. Now she was in complete control of her mind and her hours. She could blame no other person for her thoughts and her feelings. She must lean on her own mentality and imagination. Her long battle with Bent was over and the paths ahead were open, waiting for her to take her own free steps.

She made some tea and sat there at the window as she slowly sipped the steaming amber liquid through a lump of sugar. She had to think everything through again. She wondered if he had suffered enough, if he had truly paid for his evil. She would like to know for sure. Perhaps she shouldn't question God's ways of sending justice. He surely knew how to measure out the sinner's price. Still, it would satisfy her if she could know, if she could be sure he had suffered enough.

Some years ago she had wanted to sue Bent for what he had done against her family. The girls thought they had persuaded her against it. So had her son. One of them had heard Bent was sick and tried to reason with her mother that it was unkind to add to a man's misery when he was weakened.

It would have given her an acute sense of revenge if she had been able to sue him then. Weakened? There was no reason to protect him. Because a man is weak should he expect to be free from justice or punishment for his deeds? If he was strong enough once to commit the crime, he should not hide behind weakness from his just punishment. Some men like to cry after their crimes and mistakes and say they are sorry, that they had a stomach ache. And in such weakness the world likes to take pity on them. But she would not let a man's weakness rule her. When the time comes for punishment it should be given. Remember my girls, she had told them, if you look for a person's weakness to excuse his crimes every bad seed will grow into a twisted vine until it is strong enough to choke you.

Yes, she had talked to a lawyer about suing Bent. He said too much time had passed and she couldn't sue any longer. She didn't tell the girls. She let them think they had talked her out of it. It made no matter now. It was all taken care of this final way.

She sighed, lost in her thoughts. Still, if she could know he had suffered it would be ended for certain, in every way. What did she remember from long ago? From the rabbi who had helped her so long ago when Mikolai was in the Tsar's army? Cruelty is the just dessert for one who has been cruel. Those were his words. And after the law is fulfilled the cruel are forgiven. The eye is taken for the eye. It was clear. If this was really so he had surely suffered his due.

A sadness came over her when she thought about Jesus and forgiveness, how He must have seen into her heart all those years of hating, even as she prayed. Many times she had tried to believe she must forgive Bent. Seventy times seven and more she must forgive him. She couldn't accept that part of His teachings. Bless those who wrong you. She could not; she would have choked on her blessing. They must have made a mistake interpreting parts of the bible, she decided. He couldn't mean a mother must bless the man who tears her children from her arms.

On the other hand Bent was an educated man. He went to his church every Sunday and he must have known all the words and the laws, too. Do unto others. He must have known he could not escape the punishment. He could not have expected his life to end easily. It was no more a matter for her. Nothing could be changed or taken back or remade.

She convinced herself that she had not gone against the words Jesus had given. When they didn't make sense to real life it meant the church writers interpreted wrong. They couldn't understand all feelings, she decided. Nor could they look ahead to all evils that men like Angus Bent could be capable of in the future after they wrote the bible words. She would just leave Bent in hell from now on. He was gone. She would give him no more of her strength and her mind. She was emptied of all that.

Her sentiments and ruminations following the news of his death had exhausted her. She must go to bed early so she could begin her new life tomorrow in good shape. Right now her head couldn't hold any more thinking.

She left a note on the kitchen table for Mikolai asking him to strain the milk because she must get up early in the morning. She was going to add the news about Bent but it wouldn't be so important to him. He never took him for an enemy and he wouldn't understand how she felt now. Even in those days he had not believed her when she told him how evil the man was. He would just turn to his newspaper and read. He had lost nothing. He felt nothing for his family's troubles and his wife's tortured years. His life was always the same, quiet and steady.

She put his dinner toward the back of the cook stove so it would be warm when he came in. She put the newspaper with Bent's obituary next to his Russian newspaper. If he should read it he would know. If not, she would never say anything. Probably one of the girls would tell him anyway.

The next morning the magic was still in her heart. She looked out at the spring hills. The land was washed and lightly perfumed with early blossoms. It looked freshly dressed like a young girl anxious to make her way toward life, waiting for every good thing, every joy.

Danya dressed and put on her barn boots. She would milk the cows this morning because Mikolai had done all the work last night. It was their understanding. Later she would go to the DP neighbors to teach them some English lessons. If she were a little late they wouldn't mind.

When she walked under the grape arbor to the barn she realized she had not even thought of Bent until that minute. For the first time an all these years she had awakened without cursing him. She breathed in deeply and signed. No need any more. He was gone.

She leaned down to pet the cat who jumped in surprise. Danya didn't like cats close to people. They were only good for catching mice and ought to do their job in the barn and keep away from humans. None in her house. That was one of the few rules she had for her children. No dogs and no cats in the house. But this morning the cat looked very pretty and friendly to her. In an unfamiliar voice she made clucking, friendly overtures to the cat, which startled the animal even more. They were the sounds she used for calling the chickens to feed, and the confused cat bobbed its head around to see what might be happening.

She greeted the cows with softly breathed good mornings. Will you give up plenty of milk today, my fine cow, for it is spring and it is time for your finest butter, my Daisy. From habit she put a scarf over her silvered hair, tying it at the back of her neck, the same way the milkmaids did in the old country.

She poured the first milk into a dish and called to the cat who was watching timidly at the doorway to the cow's stall. "Come animal, taste the fine milk my friendly cow has made for you during the night. Come nice kitty, drink your milk…come you small jack ass, come here for your breakfast!"

The cat hesitated, unsure. Then she stuck her pink nose proudly to the side, gave a secret cat signal and walked cautiously to the milk dish, her six silly kittens stretching their necks in and out and walking obediently behind her.

IN THE WOODS

The six maple trees stood straight and thick leafed, allowing the western sun to glint against the outer foliage without finding its way through the meshed branches. Every leaf had been touched by exquisite tones of red and gold, some even fringed with brown, but despite the persistent late autumn winds they clung to the branches loath to give up their kinship with the life giving stems.

More than fifty years ago he had planted the first one, then the others as each child arrived. He had watched them grow, had watched years longer than he ever dreamed he would remain on this earth. Each fall it was a surprise to him that he was still there to see them turn color again, drop their leaves and sleep. In the spring when the first green knobs warted the limbs the surprise was compounded, running through him like a pleasant recurring wash.

He could foretell each storm, each heat wave, even the cold snaps by the behavior of those trees. The way the leaves turned in the wind, or the way the bark showed white with threat of approaching deep cold. This year he knew he would take his time readying the burlap bags in which he would gather the fallen leaves to be used for the cow's bedding. The leaves, the most beautiful in years, would stay maybe two or three more weeks. Already they blazed like a great fire reflecting the sun, but there was time, plenty of time before the next touch of frost or rain that would send the leaves to the ground.

He was an old man now, in his ninetieth year. The remarkably unlined contours of his square jawed face showed how seldom the depths of his feeling had marked his face in the long years of his life. In repose the face had an incomplete serenity, somewhat like the dreamlike face of a youth who had heard of life's travails and who waits patiently for the days when he must take part in those dramas.

He was that part of humanity which chooses to observe rather than participate in life. From the time of his arrival in the United States he had tried to cover himself in the safety of shut off feelings and uncommitted emotions, living on the perimeter of his family's tragedies and successes, escaping any direct involvement by surrendering himself to a passive acceptance of any upheavals. He knew, and his face verified the knowledge, that from each day comes the next; from each season the following one; from each seed a plant. In whatever way the day or season or plant was unlike the previous one or the expectations of them, he accepted it and observed.

The beautiful and the base things of a simple life were accepted with the same measure. They were taken for the value they had to him and his immediate circumstance, unquestioned for motive or future effects. The great disorders that seemed to rage in other people's lives came to him in watered down and simplified forms that were assimilated easily into the patterns of nature which he understood.

The sudden flashes of temper or the marvelous blue laughing lights in his still youngish eyes made occasional brief threats to his stable countenance. When gone they left the face with the same pleasant calm.

More discernible evidence of his years was in the shuffling walk and the stooped thick shoulders that curved toward a prolapsed paunch he had developed in the past few years as his activities gave way to his years. It would take extra hours now for him to do the farm chores. It made no difference; there was no need to move faster. If he finished the morning's work too soon he would find himself sitting at the kitchen window watching out for the mailman who still brought his Russian language newspaper each day and which he still read without glasses. Every day he could count on the newspaper's arrival. Some times there were letters and pictures from the children, living in different parts of the country or from far away places where they traveled. He never understood why they had left their own town and home where they were born and grown. They all should have gone to work here, married and raised their families here in their own place, in this village where they would inherit the acres he and Danya had bought and tended for them. There was no good that could come from running to strange places to live.

He would read any letter hastily, glance at the pictures and hand them to Danya with a grunt and a short comment. Later, when she was out of the house he would look with more care at these grandchildren his family had produced for them. Which one would come back to this place they had made for them? Why would they chase the life of the half dead, the city people and the factory people who spent their days shut away from the living earth? Why should they live and raise their children in places where people never learned to take their own food from the ground?

Had he worked this fertile land for naught? Would his farm, the house, the barn, be sold off when he and Danya were gone, like the Noviky farm next door, because the children no longer had use for the soil?

Now the farm and pastures were increased by twenty more acres, bought when old Noviky died. His boys lived in the town and went to work each day in the airplane factory. They had no need for the farmland. They had settled the estate by selling the land

and Danya had negotiated to buy it, sparing them the expense of real estate agents and time.

Mikolai had often walked every square foot of their properties. On days when his head noises bothered him most he would walk his land. Or when he knew the snows were coming. Then he must see the earth for the last time, uncovered. Supposing he should not live through the winter? He must walk over his land again, measure all the trees with his eyes, replace loose stones in the stone walls, savor the last overlooked apples, watch the squirrels and the birds that also readied themselves for a winter of unknown circumstances.

He would stop to rest under the pines that marked the end of his property. The needles lay thick on the ground, slippery under his shoes. He should remember to bring his walking stick next time. If he fell or was hurt it would be hours before Danya would think to look for him. Sometimes as he sat resting there he imagined he might die under these deep green trees, on the edge of the steep ravine, on his own land looking out over the rolling hills he had first seen seventy years ago.

Strange, he could no longer recall clearly his mother's farm. Once in a while he thought he could remember the look of that land, but then he realized he was thinking of some other place he had seen long ago in this country. Poor Vladimir. He should have given up the farm and tried to come to America. Oh yes, Danya said the government had taken the farm. It didn't matter. His own feet were not planted there, but here where he had found his own roots, in this free land. No one could take it from him. But supposing none of the children wanted it? What would happen to his house, his grape arbor, the trees? Who but his own children should have these pines, the generous spring with its icy crystal water, the smooth green pastures, the iris-filled swamp?

He must talk to Danya. She would make sure one of the children promised to come back to their home. The boy should keep the farm. She should tell their son to come back home to live. Why should he work in his engineering and grow old so far away, in the factory filled with people and noise? What did he want there with those tiny wires and crazy talking machines? They could never grow food or bring in sunshine. He was a farmer's son. Shouldn't he leave the crazy business of sending wires into the sky and come back to grow food instead? He should come back to the land. What was the use of walking on the moon when people on the earth were starving because they could not grow enough to feed themselves? He had read it in his paper, both stories the same day. His son should come to work the farm and help feed people. He could work on his inventions and keep the farm too. Danya would have to persuade their son to return.

***

The snow surprised him. He thought it would come much later. It was too early. It didn't feel cold enough for snow today. He couldn't believe he had made a mistake about the weather. The sky seemed too clear for snow, just a pale blue, not gray enough for a storm.

There was no wind. No tree or twig or fallen leaf moved in the silence from which came the first thin flakes.

How harmless and quiet the snow fell. His mind roamed to other snows. He smiled when he thought about Danya's story of the wolves, so long ago. He'd never seen a wolf here but there were foxes in these woods. He had seen them many times, skulking around these very trees. Once his son had hunted some but they got away. They never bothered anyone; why should they be hunted? But in the old country the snows were greater and lasted longer and the foxes took away the farm animal's food, stole from the farmers. Here there was food sufficient for woodland animals and farmers both.

He thought about the big snowstorms he'd known in his youth. How hard he had prayed as a boy that it would snow every Sunday so he wouldn't have to go to the church to hear the old priest. He didn't really mind hearing him, but he was such an awful looking man, so ugly. He hated to look at him. His mother had explained it was evil to wish for the snows to come. He must pray instead for a short winter like everyone else did.

He remembered the winter he had been sick in the house of strangers. He remembered the woman's name, Ada, and the picture of Christ she had sent with him. Other things he couldn't remember so clearly, only that he had been sick and it had snowed.

The snow fell faster. The flakes were growing larger and thicker, making a blurry white screen between him and the sky. He could look out from his protected place under the pines and see the snow collecting on the ground. Weeks later it should snow, not today. Usually he didn't make a mistake. In his old age he was more sure than ever before. He never made a mistake about the snow or the rain coming. Is it possible he could lose time? He tried to remember whether it was yesterday or this morning that he had stood at the barn door watching the trees move. He had told himself then that it wouldn't snow for a while. Perhaps he was getting too old to separate the days. He should keep a calendar in the barn. Or he should wear the wristwatch his son had given him last Christmas. It told the hours and the days. If he carried that watch he would always know the day; then he would never make a mistake.

Well, it didn't matter so much what day it snowed. But he didn't like to make mistakes at the end of his days when he was so sure he knew all the signs. He should keep better track of the time. He must have forgotten what day it was.

Now he remembered. The lawyer was coming this afternoon. Danya had bought more land from Hefford's son and the lawyer was bringing the papers today for them to sign. Mikolai was angry with her. She had said nothing to him but had made the contract with Hefford herself. Now she must wait until he, Mikolai, was ready to sign. He would make them wait a while.

She should tell him before she makes any business, not afterwards when he could not even disagree.

Why did they need more land anyhow when none of the children might want the farm? Danya said to divide among the grandchildren. She always had a reason for her crazy actions. Maybe the grandchildren would run all over the world like their parents. What then? Who was the land for? For the great grandchildren she said.

So she spent their dollars and bought land to leave to great grandchildren who were not yet born. Acres of earth. He wondered how far down you could dig into the earth. 'Did you ever dig to China in your own back yard?' He remembered that from a song the children sang when they were little, before he was so deaf. He smiled to remember the holes they had dug, wishing. He couldn't be sure whether China was under the earth or not, so he didn't stop them. He had given the two oldest girls bigger shovels for their digging. Later he transplanted some small fir trees into the holes. But now the trees were gone. One summer when all six children came home for vacations they wanted to make a badminton court in the back yard. He let them cut down the trees. They were too thick anyway and kept the sun away from the house in wintertime.

That was when he found out Danya had been spoiling his wine. He was so proud of his grapes and his arbors. And he was even more proud of his special wine. Anyone who tasted it said it was better than any made in the state. He made four great barrels each year, even when he gave bushels and bushels to the Dysons for grape jelly. But Danya was always crabbing and nagging him because she said he drank too much. He didn't think the wine was so strong, but year after year she got crabbier. Then one year the wine was not good. Was he getting too old, he wondered? Had he forgotten how to make the wine? Then the next year, even when he was so careful making it, the wine went bad again.

But that year when he cut the trees down for the badminton he discovered it wasn't his age but his own wife who was spoiling the wine. He needed more room in the cellar after he cut down the trees, to dry them out in the wood bins next to the furnace. When he was moving the wine barrels around to make room he discovered what she had done. He found the baking soda boxes behind one of the barrels. If she has been home he would have beaten her, even if it is against the law in this country. No woman should ruin a man's wine, and worse, make him think his mind is running away from his memory.

Well, he had to fool her in order to keep any good wine. He decided not to reveal his discovery. Let her work hard to creep down into the cellar late at night with her baking soda boxes. Let her spend her energy and worry how she could keep the wine from him.

He wouldn't let an old woman steal his wine from him. He put one of the barrels behind the barn that summer. Then in the winter he rolled it into the barn to the back of the narrow wood bin that was used now for storing old furniture. She would never catch on. He made that barrel at the same time he made the wine in the others, that next fall. He would carry the grapes when she wasn't home and she never suspected. The next year he had two barrels in the barn. Now when the nights were cold he had his good wine. He would sit and drink a glass and he knew she was watching, wondering how he could keep drinking such spoiled wine.

He sat there under the pines in a reverie as the snow kept falling. He pulled the corduroy collar of his denim barn coat closer to his neck. Danya should make him a heavier jacket this year, he thought. A wind, sharper now began to blow the giant snowflakes into his dry haven, reminding his that it must be hours since he had left the house. Should he go yet? He felt tired from his walk even after the long rest under the pines.

He took pleasure in watching the snow swirl over the bayberry bushes and marveled how these small bushes could hold so firmly to the ground as the wind shook their limbs. Sometimes a gust of wind would lay bare a rock that had been covered with snow. How light the snow felt before the flakes piled on top of themselves. They weighed nothing as they fell. You felt nothing when they touched your clothes. Only the wind was a bother.

It was getting dark. It must be later than he thought. He really should carry the watch. The cow must be milked on time or she would start bellowing. He knew it was his turn for the milking, and he didn't want Danya to run into the wet snow. He should not sit here in the woods watching the snow in wonder, like a child. He should get back to the barn to do the milking.

He sighed. They didn't really need the cow anymore. He and Danya could not use all the milk, the butter and the cheese they had. They sold some, but it was not enough to pay for the cost of keeping the cow fed. People didn't want thick cream anymore. But they couldn't get rid of the cow. No one kept cows, just the big milk farms. He remembered the old butcher who used to drive his truck up and down the hills trying to buy old animals. Now you couldn't give cows away for any money. Maybe if they kept the cows long enough the children would like to have them when they came to take the farm.

The white dancing flakes fought against the descending darkness. In a while he couldn't see them but could feel their dampness when they melted against his face. The first layer of pine needles was getting wet. He shuffled them aside, found a dry place for himself so he could lay down on the pines as he watched the snow fall.

From the darkness he heard voices. A woman's young voice calling to him. Children's voices in laughter, clear, then fading, clear, then far away. It was late but there was time. He covered a stone with dry needles, used it for a pillow as he lay there. He closed his eyes in the soft night that was enveloping his lands.

***

Not long after he was gone, his children found his old journal. Tucked into a bureau drawer under old shirts and faded silk ties the pages had not yellowed; the fine Cyrillic writing was clear. They had the writings translated into English. The last entry was written long ago when he was a young man waiting for his future wife:

THE SONG
Thoughts, feelings and moods
Are the source of inspiration,
A fit of my brave youth.
Like tidal waves in the sea,
Like an endless flame of a volcano,
Freedom of a whirlwind, of a storm.
Dreams of charm,
The power of the feeling of beauty,
The song expresses all my wishes,
An echo of an endless suffering,
An abyss of the spirit, the sea of tears,
The thirst for happiness, the kingdom of dreams
Lit with rays and full of magic.
The world of fantasy, of wonderful dreams,
Full of glitter and flowers
The song expresses the torture of waiting,
A wonder of a tender date.
Mirror-like surfaces of the seas
And the breath of the fields
And the twinkling of the stars
And the heart's secret wish...

After the journal was translated it was put back into the top drawer along with other old letters and photographs, newspaper clippings and postcards cleaned out from other drawers in the large marble-topped bureau.

Alone in the house, Danya brought the journal into the light of the kitchen window and read...

'And the heart's secret wish...'

And she remembered.

END

Epilogue

Two years before she died I visited my long-widowed mother in Arizona where she was living with one of my sisters. She knew me then and could smile when I told her she didn't look much older than ninety.

Two years later I visited her again. She had moved back home to the town in Connecticut where she had lived since 1923 when she came from Russia. She was now ninety-seven, a thin fragile person with no bodily evidence of her once capable strong self.

"Who are you?"

"I'm your second daughter Matilda."

"Oh, how many daughters do I have?"

"Five daughters and one son."

"Oh, I'm sorry, I don't remember."

Sad? Heartbreaking? Yes, at first it hurt to be a stranger to my own mother. Some part of me had disappeared with her faded memory. At age fifty-seven I was still a child with a worldly anchor, just so long as I had a mother.

After I'd felt sorry for myself, for all of us who no longer exist in a parent's mind, I realized how free she really was. I thought back to the years of toil and anguish, of hurts and misery she had endured. I could contemplate the blessing of her faded memory.

And yet she could still smile and I imagined just a tiny twinkle in her eyes when she said, "I don't remember."

Perhaps behind the smile was the young woman who had dreamed and planned and in whose fragmented memory was the knowledge that her dreams had come true. She believed in eternity, that she would live forever through her children.

So she does live forever, on these pages, through her children and onward after them.

Made in the USA
Middletown, DE
13 November 2014